P9-DCY-797

THE MAN IN THE TREE

ALSO BY SAGE WALKER

Whiteout

THE MAN IN THE TREE

Sage Walker

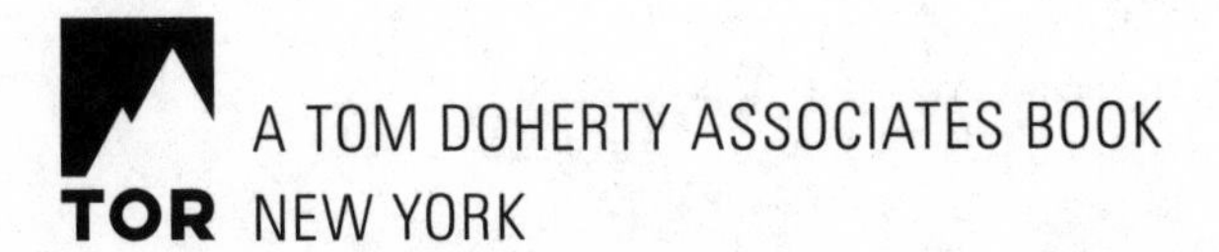

A TOM DOHERTY ASSOCIATES BOOK
NEW YORK

This is a work of fiction. All of the characters, organizations, and events portrayed in this novel are either products of the author's imagination or are used fictitiously.

THE MAN IN THE TREE

A Tor Book
Published by Tom Doherty Associates
175 Fifth Avenue
New York, NY 10010

www.tor-forge.com

The Library of Congress Cataloging-in-Publication Data is available upon request.

ISBN 978-0-7653-7992-4 (hardcover)
ISBN 978-1-4668-7109-0 (ebook)

Our books may be purchased in bulk for promotional, educational, or business use. Please contact your local bookseller or the Macmillan Corporate and Premium Sales Department at 1-800-221-7945, extension 5442, or by email at MacmillanSpecialMarkets@macmillan.com.

First Edition: September 2017

Printed in the United States of America

0 9 8 7 6 5 4 3 2 1

For Melinda M. Snodgrass, Kay McCauley, and Claire Eddy.

They persisted.

ACKNOWLEDGMENTS

Melinda M. Snodgrass, M. T. Reiten, Ian Tregillis, and Brett Shapiro offered invaluable comments on this novel, one rough draft section at a time. Eric Kelly did a superb beta read. Toby Messinger supervised IT. Geoff Landis (www.geoffreylandis.com) and Steve Howe (www.hbartech.com) graciously permitted me to misuse some concepts they work with in real life. Daniel Abraham listened to my ideas way back at the beginning of this, while a very young Scarlet sat on my feet and watched *Chicken Run.* A list of some of the links I mined for odd things is available at www.sagewalker.net.

Science fiction is recursive. It's a discussion, often a heated one. Poul Anderson, Fritz Leiber, Gene Wolfe, Michael Bishop, Chip Delany, Greg Bear, Stan Robinson, and Neal Stephenson, among others, have done their best to teach me about generation ships, in person and in print. I am deeply grateful to each and every one of them.

THE MAN IN THE TREE

1

Pleasure Centers

The sun in the hollow center of *Kybele* is supported by six Eiffel Towers.

In daylight, the clusters of petals near the top of the towers, closed, look like bulbous minarets. As they unfold, black shadows strike the fields and forests below. Kaleidoscopic patterns of ever-increasing darkness spread over the landscape until the edges of the petals almost touch each other and the day-bright interior of the asteroid is dimmed for night.

Kybele was Earth's first, perhaps Earth's *only*, seedship, and she existed because there was a chance, a statistically infinitesimal chance, that someday she or a daughter ship of hers might return, headed back toward Earth with hope and life. *Kybele*'s singular existence was possible because of asteroid mining, hope, and diverted resources from an Earth that said it couldn't afford her. The Mars colony, small and underground, was only viable because of money from asteroid mining. The time frame for terraforming Mars, a planet with no seas and no magnetic core, was centuries longer than *Kybele*'s voyage.

Earth's humans were in a battle for survival that constantly teetered near disaster. *Kybele* was a long-shot insurance policy of sorts. Some very good minds had run the numbers and found an intersection, a window, between dwindling resources and increasing technical ability where a seedship could be built. *Kybele* was that intersection.

Helt Borresen, Incident Analyst for the seedship, walked spinward from the base of Athens tower on a path he knew well. He sat down beside a creek and fitted his back against the trunk of an aspen. The creek talked a little of this and that.

This was a private place, one he liked. He came here for solitude, but last night and the night before he'd caught glimpses of an interesting woman, barely seen in the shadows, a woman who moved quickly and quietly, as if she were watching something but didn't want to be seen.

Downhill from the aspen, a marshy meadow flanked the creek. Tall grasses grew there, late summer yellow, some of them seeding for next year. Cattails marked soggy ground. Beyond the meadow, anti-spinward, the deep gash of Petra canyon was darker than the forest that grew to its rim. Beyond it, up the curved inner surface of *Kybele*'s hollow interior, the forest ended abruptly at the edge of croplands, squares of plowed black soil and yellow stubble, striped by shadows from the legs of the towers and going monochrome in the fading light. The warmth of an October day began to fade and a cool breeze came up to rustle the cattails. *Kybele*'s night was programmed to replicate the twenty-eight-day cycles of Earth's moon, and as Helt sat, half-dozing, the light dimmed toward quarter moonlight, dark enough to silver the grass and turn the shadows black.

A flicker of white brought his focus back to the meadow. White-tailed deer, a dozen or so, appeared in the tall grass, as quickly and quietly as if they had been popped into place by a special-effects team. Two yearling bucks, their antlers only brave stubs, were with the females, but none of the big guys. The herd was close enough that Helt heard grass tear as they munched their way toward the water. He had never been able to see a herd of deer, or elk, or reindeer, without counting them. Fourteen. The herd went downhill in the tall grass and vanished.

The show was over. He thought about getting up.

And then he didn't, for the pair of young bucks reappeared at the edge of the meadow. The woman he had seen here briefly last night stepped out of the pines on the far side of the clearing. She had a bottle tied to her belt and something small gripped in her right hand.

The deer came to her. She was on the far side of the deer from Helt, so he couldn't see what she did to the neck of one and then the other. Whatever it was, when she finished, she shoved at the neck of the deer she had just handled. It didn't move away. The little buck lowered his head to have the skin around the nubs of his antlers scratched. His buddy decided he needed some attention, too.

The woman groomed both of them for a little while. Then she laughed, low and soft, and clapped her hands. The deer bounced away. She unhooked a bottle from her belt, put things in it, and screwed down the lid. The motions caused the interlocked squares of her plaid shirt to tighten and loosen over her breasts in pleasant ways.

She turned and walked toward Helt's aspen. He supposed she saw him. He was visible enough against the white trunk of the tree, so he stood up.

She was a tall woman. The top of her head would have fit comfortably just under his chin. She had dark hair, tied back. The faux moonlight made it shine.

She stopped walking.

"Hi," Helt said.

She gave a little shrug. It looked liked resigned acceptance of his presence. "Hello," she said aloud. "I disturbed you."

"I enjoyed watching you. I'm only a little disturbed."

"About what?"

"About what you did to call them in."

"Oh." She reached in her shirt pocket and pulled out a little control box. She stepped closer to Helt, to show him. "They have electrodes in their pleasure centers, and the buzz they get gets stronger the closer they come to this. The guys you saw were numbers thirty-three and thirty-five. I pushed their buttons. They came running."

She was close enough that he could smell her hair, her skin. He didn't smell perfume, just clean healthy human, and whatever scent there is that tells a hindbrain a woman is nearby. She was maybe ten years younger than Helt and her eyebrows were dark wings above her large eyes. In the moonlight, he thought her eyes were gray.

Helt felt lonely. He was lonely. He had no one special right now, and hadn't for a couple of years. Well, four, actually.

"I'm disappointed."

"Why?"

"It's just tech. I wanted to think it was magic."

"It's sufficiently advanced to seem so. To a deer."

"Clarke's third law. Advanced technology looks like magic. Did you ever read any of his novels?" Helt asked.

"No. I came across that quote once and liked it."

The novels had been written in the twentieth century. The 2209 Helt lived in was very different from the future the old dreamer had imagined. Humanity had stayed at the edge of disaster, as ever, and survived some of its own failings—so far.

"I'm Elena," she said. "Biosystems."

"Helt. Systems Support." He wondered why he'd never met her. He wondered how long she'd been on board.

They started walking toward Athens tower.

"Thirty-three and thirty-five will be leaving the herd soon, out for a tour of enforced bachelorhood," Elena said. "The stags will see to that. I needed some blood from them. We monitor hormone levels, nutrition, muscle mass, many other things." She spoke standard Omaha English, but there was a touch of hesitation, of indrawn breath, before some of her words. "These yearling bucks have stayed with their moms a bit longer than we expected," Elena said. "If they're developing normally, their testosterone levels should be lower than they were a few weeks ago. Rutting season is almost over."

Helt didn't mind a discussion of testosterone levels at all. His were rising a little, and he decided to take her willingness to play biology teacher as a positive sign.

Beneath the support pillars of the towers, the ground was in permanent shadow. People walked there because it was easy. Nothing much grew underfoot. Helt thought of giant mushrooms, blind insects, cave-adapted species, spooky creatures made of old fantasy. Perhaps he would avoid mentioning them to the SysSu techs. They might manufacture some displays to jump out and go "Boo!" Just because they could.

"Are you worried that the deer won't be guy enough for their jobs?" Helt asked.

"That's what I'm checking. They have a lot of adapting to do," Elena said. "They seem to be thriving at half-g. They love to jump, but we've seen no broken legs yet, so they've sorted that out. They can't be really wild with this much human contact; there's taming, of sorts. They don't get shot at, so they don't flee us the way their cousins back home do. And there aren't any large predators to give their adrenals a workout."

No large predators, except for humans. When it came time to thin the herd, to harvest venison, would Biosystems establish a hunt? Would running the deer become a sport on *Kybele*, good for working off human frustrations and sharpening the survival skills of the herd? Surely Biosystems had thought of this, and had made a list of pros and cons. Helt would look to see what they were, later. "Do you think the fear of getting eaten would keep them healthier?" he asked.

"Perhaps. They are active without that, so far. They play. The males battle each other. But there's so much to think about. Maybe they're missing mosquito bites, or something," Elena said.

"You're teasing me," Helt said.

"Yes."

"Please tell me you won't put mosquitoes up here."

The woman named Elena looked up at him and smiled. He still couldn't tell exactly what color her eyes were. The lights near the elevator door made them look sort of hazel, maybe. Her plaid shirt was black and white and gray.

He hoped she liked men who were sort of sand-colored all over. He hoped she didn't mind a five o'clock shadow with a few white whiskers in it. He hoped she didn't mind that his hair looked like someone had cut it with a pair of office scissors, for that's what he had done four days ago when he'd noticed it was falling in his eyes.

Helt wished the walk had been longer. He liked Elena. Walking with a woman beside him felt good.

The elevator was large enough for twenty. There was no good reason for him to stand really close to her as it took them down from Center, so he didn't.

The doors began to slide open on Level One. "Could we keep talking?" Helt asked.

"I really have to get back to my lab before my blood gets hot," Elena said. She looked down at the thermos bottle clipped to her belt, tapped it, and walked away. She was going toward the train station that would take her back to Stonehenge, he supposed.

But he'd seen a little smile at the corner of her mouth.

His interface gave him her name; Elena, Biosystems, was Elena Maury, MD, PhD. He found a headshot that gave him a good look at her huge eyes, her high cheekbones. Her eyes, in the photo, looked more hazel than the gray he'd seen in moonlight and in the elevator lighting.

That was enough to know for now.

2

The Man in the Tree

It was Wednesday evening, and Helt Borresen wasn't up in Center for the sunset. He was beneath Center on Level One, eating supper in the Frontier Diner. The diner was a mundane place of stone-topped tables and bamboo chairs. The air held a reassuring hint of French fries and coffee, and because it served a 24/7 clientele, you could get breakfast at any hour. Helt liked breakfast for supper, so he was having a spinach omelet with a side Caprese salad.

If Elena followed a daily schedule, she would be back in Center about now. He could go up there. She might not be there. She might be looking at her deer and think he was pushy or weird, or, worse, if he went up there she might think Helt Borresen had come hunting for her.

Yeah, it was time and past time to look for a love that would last a lifetime. So he really was hunting and he might as well admit it.

He was afraid, and he might as well admit that, too. His mother had been injured when he was young, and the injury had left scars on her brain. He knew, intellectually, that it was nothing he had done, yet he was still afraid that anyone he loved would get hurt. It was an irrational fear and he knew it.

Admit it, sure. Change it? Not so easy.

Helt scooped up the last bite of the nutmeg-laced spinach with a piece of toast and looked up at the man approaching his table. Navigation coveralls, dark five o'clock stubble on his chin and his shaved head, a lot of muscle in neck and shoulders, and the brown eyes of a puppy who had just been yelled at and didn't understand why.

"Helt Borresen?"

"That's me. I'm Helt."

"Yves Copani. I went to your office but you weren't there. I apologize for coming after hours, but—" Copani pulled his interface out of a pocket and gripped it tightly.

"But you just got off work and there's something you want me to see," Helt said. "It's okay. I'm still working, actually." A moonlit walk wasn't going to happen tonight. Fine. Now he wouldn't have to worry that seeing Elena again so soon would make him seem like a pest. "Sit down. Send your file to IA Helt." Helt reached for the folded screen next to his coffee cup and popped it open. "Want some coffee?"

This evening's waitperson approached and filled Helt's cup. Copani waved him away. "No, no thank you."

What came to Helt's screen was the Curriculum Vitae of Yves Copani, welder, whose engineering doctorate had been earned in Milan. He was overeducated for the job of tunneling out nickel-iron from *Kybele*'s Level Three. That he was overeducated was no surprise; most contract workers held doctorates in something or other. Helt scanned the rest of the info as well.

"I want to stay here," Copani said. "I want to spend my life here.

A lot of dreamers on Earth below wanted to come here, live here, take the risk that their descendants, seven generations down the line, would reach a new planet and be able to live on it. Only a few of the rich, a few of the lucky, made it past the barrier of requirements and became outbound colonists.

A lot of realists on Earth below thought they were crazy to take the chance. Earth was a sad and damaged place, but parts of her still functioned, and that she could support human life was a given. No one knew if the new planet could do that.

"Is it still possible?" Yves asked.

"Barely. There's still some shuffle room on the passenger list for the last shuttle, but there isn't much. You've asked David II for a colonist slot, I'm guessing."

"I'm not sure he's looked at the request," Copani said.

David Luo II was the Engineering boss on *Kybele*, a busy, busy man.

"So you came to me."

"I hoped you could help," Copani said.

"I may not be able to. I'm the Incident Analyst. My job is to arbitrate conflicts between Navigation, Bioscience, and Systems Support if and when they come up. I do some intramural work in the divisions when I'm called in, but it's only advisory." Helt permitted his overdeveloped sense of fairness to come forward and ask questions. Why me and not him? Why don't I get sent off so he gets to stay? Not fun. Why not him and me both stay?

"Yves, it's true that in extraordinary circumstances I can make upgrades to colonist status, if there are no objections from the division chiefs. For me to sponsor you, I'd need to show you would be of extraordinary benefit to the ship. Are you extraordinary?"

"I don't know. I don't think so."

"You aren't grandiose, anyway. That's good, but humility isn't something I can sell to David II or his boss. Your CV says you have a job waiting in Cape Town for three times the amount of money you're making here."

Salaries on *Kybele* were high. Contract workers usually drew enough AUs, Access Units, *Kybele* currency, to meet expenses, and converted the rest to euros in Earth-based accounts. The AU was a sound currency. The conversion rate was, as of last week, something like 1 AU to 2.3 euros.

AUs, like any currency, were tokens for barter, their value based on energy expenditure, physical or mental, and traded for other energies or material things. For now, they could be converted back to euros for Earth-based transactions.

The lottery for colonist selection and funds from supporting nations had given *Kybele* a fat bank balance. She spent like a sailor on shore leave, but she also exported tech advances and media to Earth below and was making money from them.

"You're telling me you are willing to give that up, to stay here as a flunky welding steel rods to keep tunnels from collapsing, for the rest of your life. Why?"

"I'm in love," Copani said. "She's in Biosystems, a colonist. She doesn't want to leave."

Oh. "I see." Elena's name was a version of Helen, and a Helen in a time long past had launched a thousand ships and a war. Helt was screwing up his courage to go to war with himself, his old fears, his new ones, over the Helen he had met last night. Love, the possibility of love, counted, damn it.

"That's an honest reason to want to stay," Helt said. "In that case, why don't you order some dinner and we'll figure out a narrative I can use to bring you to David II's attention. That would be the place for you to start."

Helt signaled the waiter.

Back in his office, Helt promised himself he would only work one more hour and then go home.

Because linear information, lists, two-dimensional graphs got too visually busy too fast for him, Helt looked at the humans on *Kybele* as bubbles of information. He liked Venn diagrams, spherical ones. His programs rendered facts and factoids about a particular individual into colors, shapes, and varying degrees of opacity. In the past ten years, some of the bubbles had acquired accumulations of biography, work history, friendships, frictions. Over time, as events, likes, and dislikes pushed and pulled, aggregates formed. Attractive traits drew other bubbles closer. Givers and team players attracted other souls; takers and users were often, but not always, repelled.

Sometimes he displayed the ever-shifting groups as a coalescence of wrinkled balloons, sometimes as clusters of spiky morningstars, ferocious weapons. Over time, they had formed ameboid blobs that corresponded pretty well with the three working departments on *Kybele*, Navigation, Systems Support, Biosystems.

Take thirty thousand people and create a framework of habitats, interactions, and work that will let their descendants survive and reproduce for two hundred years, while keeping the skills needed to live on a new world. The population will live in isolation. No one gets to go outside and play. There will be no visitors.

It was a prison or a paradise, depending on your philosophy. The people in Helt's new world, his fellow passengers, were prisoners of nothing but their own hopes and dreams. They had chosen to live in this enclosure, a hollow asteroid on a one-way journey to a relatively nearby star. They knew the risks.

They knew the risks of staying on Earth as well. Wars were continuous, but entire civilizations sustained themselves on arable land at the poles. The population was down to three billion and might have stabilized there. It would be centuries before the planet's oceans, her basic life-cycle drivers, recovered from the acid the Anthropocene era had dumped in them. Maybe old Gaia could heal herself. Maybe not.

Odds were, this worldlet named *Kybele* would get where it was going. It would reach a new world, a full-sized one, a planet with liquid water and all the building blocks of life. That the new planet would sustain human life was not a given. Even so, a lot of people were willing to take the gamble.

Odds were, the only thing that could make Kybele herself uninhabitable were the people inside it.

The hollow rock that was *Kybele*, once thrown toward its new star, would get where it was going, but by design and necessity, its air and water and food supplies would fail without the constant input of skilled human hands and human minds. That reality, hopefully, imposed a social contract of mutual tolerance that would survive the stresses and conflicts humans make for themselves. Maybe. If everyone worked at it.

Helt was daydreaming himself into the what and how of scenarios he could not, on his own, control. The broad-spectrum lights on the west wall of his office had gone dark so the greenery could rest. A bot searched for leaves on the floor. Helt searched for a pear in yellowing leaves, but all of his were gone. He got out of his chair, walked out into the hall, stretched out his arms, remembered a plaid shirt worn by a beautiful woman, and went back to his desk.

A lot of people weren't entered in his State of *Kybele* construct. Only the ones who had been players in interdepartmental disagreements of one flavor or another interacted in Helt's spheres of data. The three divisions on *Kybele* handled their own internal affairs when they could, and those interactions didn't usually come to Helt's attention.

Yves Copani wasn't in there.

Only one more hour's work, Helt had told himself, but he really wanted to find an excuse to let Yves Copani stay on *Kybele.* He liked the man.

Yves Copani was trained as an architect, but he'd hired on as a welder. He loved his quarters in Petra, and music, and his buddies, and hard work, and his girl. Oh, he loved his girl. She worked in Stonehenge and her name was Susanna, not Elena. Yes, he checked, and felt a little embarrassed about it.

In short, Yves loved everything he saw or touched or ate, unless he hated it, and if he hated something he wanted to make it beautiful so he could love it. He wanted the stars, and he wanted to stay with his true love.

True loves seldom lasted, but Helt liked the simplicity of the man's outlook. He liked it, but he wouldn't let it change the multiple factors in his off-list protocol, the one designed to sort out who went back to Earth and who stayed aboard.

The protocol was used to sort through nets of relationships and interactions if the three division chiefs disagreed about who should go and who should stay, and no one was disagreeing about Yves Copani. He was just a contract worker who had never come to their attention or given them a problem. But Helt was sifting the files all the same.

Yves had worked some off-shift hours in the vineyards in Center. Helt wondered if that's how he'd met his true love, or if he worked there to please her. Yves's grandfather had worked for Ferrari, certainly not a sound reason to want to keep him aboard.

Helt was admiring a Ferrari in one corner of his screen when Severo Mares's face took over the other. The chief of Navigation Security Services, *Kybele*'s euphemism for cops, was in uniform, well past time to be off-shift.

"Why do you look so happy?" Severo asked.

"Because you reminded me it's time for me to go home three hours ago."

"It's about a man in a tree," Severo said.

"Tell me."

"At twenty forty-four we got a call from a couple who were out, uh, hiking. They saw something in a tree, and it scared them. We went up and found a man in a tree, and blood everywhere. We just got him down. He's dead."

Location coordinates flashed across the screen. The tree, and the EMTs who surrounded it, were half a kilometer spinward from the base of Athens tower, in wilderness. "We think he jumped. There are broken limbs on some of the trees around. He must have tried to glide down."

"What the hell? Did he hallucinate a hang glider or something?"

Hang gliding in *Kybele*'s half-g and strong Corolis force was fun, the survivors of the sport had said—before Navigation started giving stiff fines for trying it.

"Damned if I know," Severo said.

3

An Autopsy

"A dead man," Helt said. Oh, damn. He kept his voice calm, a reflex learned in years of practice at dealing with people under stress, but a sea change in his blood readied him for storm conditions, heavy weathers, struggles.

"What's his name?"

"Charles Ryan. Navigation," Severo said.

A quick glance at the records showed that Charles Ryan was a contract worker, a three-year man, not a colonist. A suicide?

"Do you know him?" Helt asked.

"I don't. You?"

"No." There were a lot of people in this world of thirty thousand souls whom Helt didn't know, and some he would probably never meet.

"I've blocked off the area where he came down and sealed his quarters. It's what a good chief of police does."

"We haven't had a suicide in years," Helt said.

"I know. I hate this sort of thing. I'm chief of a little police force that serves three little villages, and if there's funny business about this, there ain't no FBI here to call in. All I can do is follow protocols and pretend I know what I'm doing."

"Where's your boss?"

"He's at home. He'll come over to the station in a little while."

Wesley Doughan, the Navigation Executive, would finish his dinner first, Helt predicted. Because, in fact, it would take time for the rescuers, the three EMTs on call for night emergencies in the Athens area, to haul a body cross-country out of wilderness and get it downstairs.

"You're going to ask me why this is your problem," Severo said.

"It's my problem because if it's a suicide, Navigation will say it's a Biosystems problem. Biosystems will say the guy never reported being depressed, so it must be a homicide. If it's a homicide, my boss will say the safety protocols are in need of revision or it couldn't have happened, but Systems Support is working on something else until we reach the rings of Saturn, so the problem belongs to the Incident Analyst.

"That's me. I'm coming up there," Helt said.

"Here are the coordinates," Severo said.

Helt took the elevator to the base of Athens tower. When the door opened, he smelled a Rocky Mountain forest after a rain. The illusion was a pleasant one, built of forest loam, young Ponderosa, and the mineral scent of irregular outcrops of raw stone left by the world's builders. He crossed the roughened stone of the floor near the Athens tower elevator and traveled in a rapid half-g lope. The path that led to Severo followed a line of permanent shadow cast by Athens tower.

Three people had died so far in *Kybele*'s thirty-year history—four, if you counted the rumors of the ghost in the third level of Stonehenge. One suicide. Two construction accidents. There was another death, a woman with a cardiac defect that would have been fixable in childhood, but she had been poor then. The woman had worked hard, and her extended family had chipped in for a lottery ticket, and she'd been lucky enough to win a shuttle seat, a chance to get off-planet. Her prosthetics failed under the g stress of liftoff, so technically it wasn't a death on *Kybele*. At least her genome was here, some of her cells, frozen, awaiting a possible genetic reawakening in a distant future.

Helt zigged around a stand of young aspen whose leaves pattered in the night wind. Aspens in the wind always sounded like rain, but tonight's air was dry. He was far enough from Athens tower to see past the edge of the "moon," the shuttered sun. He looked for the lights of Stonehenge, high above him, a third of the way up the curve of the world. They were obscured by swirls of mist. His breathing dulled the sound of water from the little creek that ran on the right side of the path.

Helt wondered if he would have heard a scream, a crash, if he had been outside when the man jumped. He wondered if he could have talked him out of it.

Close now. Around the foot of a cliff, seen through interlaced pine branches, lights hung from branches and illuminated a square of white ropes. Chief Severo Mares sat on the ground nearby, his back against a pine tree.

"Not bad time for a geezer," Severo said.

I am forty-eight, Helt told himself, but I don't look like a Buddha, and you do. The air was thick with the vanilla scent of crushed Ponderosa needles.

"Thank you, my friend. What was my time?" Helt asked.

"Eight minutes from the tower."

"And yours?"

"I didn't time it," Severo said. "But I didn't run, anyway. Full stomach. Big dinner. Here's where he landed. Right here." Mares raised his arm toward a Ponderosa in the center of the rope square.

Helt crouched beside Severo and looked up. Bent and broken branches marked a slanted path through pine needles. Beyond, above, the trajectory intersected the balcony of the observation platform high on Athens tower.

Helt got up. "What else did you find?" He walked over to the ropes and stared down at scuffed-up pine needles, scattered twigs, and pinecones both crushed and not. He didn't see blood anywhere on the ground, or any clear footprints left by the rescue team. The ground was dry, rainfall kept within the near-desert limits specified by the climate people in Biosystems and fine-tuned by Navigation engineers.

Severo got to his feet with a groan that surely must have been exaggerated. "We had to cut him down." He pointed up to the white scar of a wrist-thick branch cut off near the trunk of the young tree. "And next, we go view his autopsy," Severo said. "But there ain't no question about what killed him. Speared by a pine tree."

On the way back to the elevator, Severo fell back a few steps. Helt glanced over his shoulder and saw him stop to vomit into a stand of scrub oak beside the path. Helt kept walking. Hadn't noticed a thing. Nope.

"You'll want to go to the NSS office and debrief the crew that came out here," Helt said. "What to say, what not to say, to the curious. To his friends. When I've finished at the hospital, would you wait for me? I'd like to look at the guy's quarters when you go over there."

"Sure," Severo said.

Helt went into the Athens clinic through the waiting room, which was empty. Its chairs had only a forest of potted plants to keep them company.

"Dr. Calloway is on duty," the screen at the empty desk told him. "Touch screen for assistance." Not much business was expected on a Wednesday night early in the fall semester, and the night tech would be busy in the back. The space allocated for the hospital in the rock of Athens would permit two hundred beds, but only twenty patient beds were outfitted as yet. Two surgical suites and a delivery room were stocked and in occasional use. Helt pushed through the double doors and walked into the corridor beyond them.

The door from radiology opened. Calloway and a night tech rolled a loaded gurney across the corridor and into the smaller OR, the day surgery room. The body was wrapped in a sheet, anonymous.

Calloway was a big guy with big hands, young, trained in general surgery and orthopedics. He took his turns as clinic doc in rotation with a couple of other MDs who had different sets of specialties. Helt had brought the occasional Support tech to see Calloway. The usual complaint was stomach pain; the usual cause was too much coffee and not enough sleep.

An autopsy table was up and ready for use, stainless steel mesh over a metal box fitted with hoses and drains. A wall display near the head of the table showed X-rays and numbers, information already gathered about Charles Ryan, usually known as "Cash," an engineer scheduled for departure on the final shuttle back to Earth.

Elena was in the OR, dressed in white cotton scrubs. Helt knew who it was even before she turned to pick up the transparent face mask that would guide her through the procedure. So this was her day job. Oh my God.

"Everybody know each other?" Calloway asked.

The tech, thin, tall, blond, and around twenty-five, if that, shook his head.

"Helt Borresen, SysSu honcho and the only Incident Analyst we have," Calloway said. "Martin Kumar, flunky, physician's assistant, and second-year medical student," Calloway said. Helt and Martin exchanged nods. "Dr. Elena Maury, Biosystems, tonight's visiting pathologist," Calloway said.

"We've met," Elena said. "Good evening, Helt Borresen." She smiled, a smile that told him yes, she had searched his full name since they talked, a smile that held a touch of sympathy.

Calloway and the tech positioned themselves at the ends of the gurney. Elena went to the left side of the gurney and reached for the sheet beneath the body. Helt was on the left side, and he moved closer.

"One," Calloway said. "I see you're already on the job, Helt. Lift part of that sheet there, okay?" Calloway pointed to the right side of the man's body, near the waist. "But don't start heaving until three."

"Two." The tech added his voice. "Three."

They slid the body from the gurney to the table. Martin rolled a stand covered with sharp stainless steel things close to the autopsy table and left the room. Elena pulled on a set of head-up display goggles.

Helt stood there in his civilian clothes, and although he had seen a corpse or two, he wasn't sure he wanted to be this close to slicing one up. Elena pulled the sheet away, exposing a naked male body, early forties, a man with the sort of symmetry in face and body that humans call beauty. A calm face, opened hands, as if asleep, but death is not sleep and doesn't look like it. The man had curly brown hair and a triangle of brown curls on his chest that thinned into a line arrowing down his belly to the pelvic thatch, the limp genitals. His only injury seemed to be a wound high on the left side of the chest, a curved flap of skin like a love bite with a little line of black clotted blood at its edges.

"Are you staying, Helt?" Elena asked.

Her nipples were taut against the OR's chill, faintly outlined beneath thin white fabric. Dark nipples.

"It's okay with me," Calloway said. "But no fainting."

"I've never seen a forensic post," Helt said. "I should watch." But he wasn't sure he could.

Elena looked at Calloway and frowned. "Forensic protocols?"

"That's what Severo asked for," Calloway said.

"It was a traumatic death, so I see the sense of it," Elena said. "Helt, you'll get the same overlays we'll be seeing through the goggles, along with a better view, from one of the monitors. If you concentrate on the procedure rather than what we're doing, it might help." Her hair was tied low at the back of her head in a shape that looked like a butterfly. Helt heard, again, those little hesitations of breath before she voiced some of the words.

"Yes. Good idea. Okay," Helt said.

He went out to the waiting room of the clinic, dimly lit and still deserted, and pulled the view of the autopsy room to one of its wall screens. Theater, he told himself. It's theater. Observe it through Elena Maury's eyes. He settled himself on a couch in the waiting room and watched Elena stuff the sheet under Cash's back and roll the body up to look for injuries, lesions.

"Not much external damage for falling out of the sky. The EMTs pulled a branch out of his chest at the scene," Calloway said.

"Is that what happened?" Elena asked.

"Came down from Athens tower. Corolis took him pretty far away. That's the theory. We pulled the trach tube here at the clinic, after I pronounced him, and the IVs. NSS took his clothes and stuff."

Elena nodded. "Did they bag his hands before they worked on him?"

"No," Calloway said. "The protocols say to do that with gunshots or attacks, but I imagine that didn't occur to them at the time."

"Let's swab his fingers anyway."

The two docs did that, and they cleaned the dead man's fingernails, too, putting the cotton swabs and toothpicks into bags that Martin marked and set aside. Elena's eyes, and the camera on her mask, looked closely at Cash Ryan's skin.

"There are no external injuries on examination of the right posterior thorax. The skin is intact," she said, speaking for the mike. Elena held the right shoulder out of the way while a camera rolled itself closer and recorded what she saw. She lifted the right knee and flexed it over the left, which rolled the hip into view. "No external injuries on the right flank, hip, or leg." The camera whirred and retreated after it had done its close-ups. Calloway repeated the process on the left side.

Elena looked up at the X-rays mounted on the wall screen. "There's a first rib fracture on the left," Elena said. She reviewed the films in rapid order. Helt watched them flash by, labeled, so he at least knew what he was supposed to be seeing, monochrome art of white bones and dark flesh. "And one in the right hand. Did I miss any?"

"One rib and a broken right fifth metacarpal is all I count," Calloway said.

Elena's eyes went back to a lateral view of the cervical spine, the graceful curve of stacked bones that supported the back of the skull. "He didn't even break his neck. Poor bastard," Elena said.

Calloway held a scalpel in position over the chest. Both of them stood very still, as if in reverence. The pause had the feeling of an old ritual, and it probably was, for the corpse, supine, waiting for the knife, looked like Michelangelo's *Pietà*.

Calloway's incision carved out a huge Y, beginning beneath the man's collarbones and continuing down to the pubis.

Helt closed his eyes and heard Severo Mares's voice coming more or less from the direction of the wall screen. He opened them again to look at Severo's face.

"It really is your problem, IA. Your nerds closed down the tower cameras for an hour this evening," Severo said.

"Shit."

"Yeah. Nineteen hundred to 2000. Here's the gap."

At 1900, the video showed views of Athens tower from below, views looking down from the empty observation tower to the wilderness that surrounded the elevator shaft, empty. A camera on the ceiling of the elevator cage looked down at an empty floor.

Gap.

At 2000, views of the Athens tower from below, views looking down from the empty observation tower to the wilderness that surrounded the elevator shaft, empty.

At 2026, the elevator's motion sensors woke up and looked down at Elena Maury, riding the Athens tower elevator down past Center to Level One.

Helt swallowed, hard. A woman he'd just made the first tentative steps toward knowing was entirely too much involved in a death he hadn't expected.

Helt stopped the video.

"Severo. This isn't right," Helt said.

He heard Severo draw in a breath that would have decreased the air pressure around him by several millibars.

"Yeah," Severo said. "The doc doing the autopsy is looking like the only person of interest we have right now. Should we stop her?"

There was no connection between the death and this woman, surely. Surely it was just a coincidence that put her in proximity to Ryan's suicide.

"I don't know." Helt brought up medical personnel on *Kybele* and looked for pathologists. "Severo, she may be our only person of interest but she's the only pathologist we have. And as far as we know, this *was* a suicide."

"Aiee," Severo said, a sound of dismay offered in a reflective tone of voice.

"Heh. I get the feeling anything we do is going to be wrong. But Calloway's right there, and everything's on camera."

There was a pause while Severo thought about that. "Yeah. I can't think of anything else we could do, except stop this before it got started. We didn't do that."

"No, we didn't," Helt said. "I could clear this with Mena," Helt said. He meant Mena Kanakaredes, the Biosystems exec.

"That would cover our asses," Severo said.

"Maybe. How does this sound? 'Sorry to bother you after hours, ma'am, but your pathologist was the first one down the tower elevator after a guy jumped off the platform, we think, except the cameras were shut down for an hour so we're not sure she was the first one down, but she should do the autopsy?' "

Mena Kanakaredes would think they were both nuts.

"When you put it that way . . ." Severo said.

"Yeah."

"Okay," Severo said. "We'll live with it."

"That we will," Helt said. "Let's see the rest of this." He released the pause button on the video clip.

Elena was carrying a stainless steel cage that held stacks of little cylinders. She looked at the buttons near the elevator door, and she didn't look worried or tense. She stepped out onto the platform near the Athens agora. The doors closed.

"You finished with your interviews?" Helt asked.

"Yeah. Doughan's over here at the station. Reviewing records on this guy Ryan. The dead man is Cash when people talk about him. Never went by Charles."

"Do you have his interface? Anything that has a privacy barrier on it? We can work around that," Helt said. SysSu would need to look at every record on the man, anything that might give a glimpse of his hopes, his dreams, his fears.

"We've been looking for it. He wasn't carrying an interface. Maybe there's something in his quarters."

Helt nodded, his eyes on the captures of empty views of elevator exits in Center before and after the SM hour. It wasn't that rare for Center to stay deserted for a night. Crops in the fields near Stonehenge, animals moving through wilderness, often weren't in a camera eye, and the paths in the shadows of the towers sometimes spent entire nights without a human to disturb them. Charles "Cash" Ryan had come and gone unseen, and the only human in the camera's view after his death was Elena Maury. That probably meant nothing, or maybe it didn't.

He split the waiting room screen into side-by-side views and scanned the records currently available at NSS. An ID mug shot of Cash Ryan, engineer, on ship for the past three years. His job had been placing and testing some of the stabilization engines outside, the ones that gave tiny and ongoing corrections to *Kybele*'s spin.

No family on ship. The notice of his death would go to his mother in—southwest Idaho, a retirement community. NSS would notify her before morning.

He closed Ryan's picture and looked for Elena Maury. Her status in Biosystems was very high, second in influence only to Mena Kanakaredes, the division chief. Elena Maury had impressive credentials in genetics and clinical medicine.

Helt looked for her in his interdepartmental dispute histories. She wasn't there. He looked for her in crowds and at concerts, and she came to those, sometimes, so she wasn't a complete hermit. Sometimes she came with a man, sometimes with one or more women. There were a couple of captures that showed her with Mena. He checked for repeats on the men and women he saw beside her from time to time. It looked like she wasn't in any sort of partner relationship.

Her name was listed in a few papers in genetics before she came to *Kybele*, but then the list got really, really long. A lot of stuff was happening up here and a lot of data was going back to Earth. Helt returned to Severo. "Which SysSu kids found the body?"

"Beauchene. Tay," Severo said.

"Thanks," Helt said. Jerry, Gerard—Jerry—Beauchene and Nadia Tay. He hadn't known they were a couple. They were young. Helt didn't know if either of them had ever seen a dead human before tonight. "How are you handling them?"

"I gave them coffee and then they went away. They still looked shook up some."

They might have gone to SysSu. The techs on duty during the outage hour might still be there. The names were Akua Mirin and Guiren Le. The recording of their session looked like routine maintenance stuff but it would need to be gone over with a fine-toothed comb.

Helt signaled Jerry Beauchene. He got audio. Jerry was listening to a man's voice, loud enough to hurt Helt's ears, reading, "*. . . red shadows from a pinoñ fire bloodied the vigas above us. . . .*"

"A bit much on the volume," Helt said.

"Hi, Helt." Jerry turned the recorded voice off.

"Is that Ryan?" Helt asked.

"Yeah. We're working up a bio. He did some slam poetry when he was a kid."

"Heh," Helt said. "Sure, we'll need a bio on Cash Ryan. You sure you want to do that tonight?"

"I'm not exactly sleepy," Jerry said. "Nadia and I came over here."

"Here where?"

"SysSu." Meaning Systems Support's offices, on the agora.

"Okay. Have you found this guy Ryan anywhere today? In the past few days?" Helt asked.

"Not yet," Jerry said.

"Jerry's scouting the public cameras," Nadia's voice said. "I'm searching his work history."

"I'm at the clinic. I'll meet you at SysSu as soon as I can," Helt said.

Helt didn't know if he could help them, help Jerry and Nadia, burn off some of tonight's stress hormones. If he could have thought of an excuse to send them on a five-mile run, he would have. Data mining was probably as good for them as any other stress reducer. A way to work off energy when you've walked up to a dead body while you had other things in mind.

And please let it be a suicide, nothing more than that, Helt thought. Please let it be just professionalism that's making Elena so calm about this. Let this stay simple, an event we can deal with quickly. SysSu has plenty of work to do before the last shuttle leaves and we fire up the big engines.

Helt looked up at the screen in the waiting room of the clinic. He fed it the view Elena's goggles showed her, the overlaid diagram that coached her and Calloway through a procedure they had seldom, if ever, performed. Helt shifted to a long view of the OR, and shifted it again, to stare at the ceiling lights when he saw Calloway at work with rib cutters. But fascination drove him back again.

They lifted the sternum out and Elena laid it aside, to be replaced later. She aspirated blood from the heart. The left hemithorax, so spacious with its lung collapsed down to the size of two fists, held clotted blood.

"There's less blood in the thorax than I expected," Elena said.

"Yeah. If we had as much blood in us as Special Effects people always think, we'd explode. This looks like plenty to make his heart stop," Calloway said.

Elena scooped out a clot and put it in a jar.

A jagged cut lay beneath that puncture wound on the shoulder, marking the slick pleural membrane of the apex of the chest. The subclavian artery was severed clean.

Wow, Helt thought. The names are on-screen before I see what the real things look like. Anatomy lesson. Elena's distancing technique works. At least it's working for now.

"Cold," Elena said when she slipped her hand into the opened chest.

"Don't know how long he was out there," Calloway said. He slipped a probe into the heart muscle. "Twenty-eight degrees Celsius."

"Climate programmed frosts at night last week in Center. I guess the ground is cold," Elena said.

Calloway pushed his finger through the broken skin above the collarbone and watched it emerge in the chest cavity. He moved the broken first rib back and forth with his finger.

"Yup," Calloway said. "He was speared by a pine tree. The rescue crew thinks he was trying to fly down, break his fall by skimming trees. Little branch stabbed his subclavian artery. He bled out into his chest. It must have taken a while."

"Spare me," Elena said.

They were working as a smooth team, coached by the program, Calloway doing the heavy muscle work while Elena's hands slipped into corners and crevices. Her translucent gloves darted and swooped, lifted instruments from a tray beside the table, used them and replaced them with calm and efficient motions. Her body as it leaned and stretched was calm, too.

Helt decided he was definitely a weird duck. Because watching Elena work at the business of exploring death, he wanted to talk to her, wanted to erase the trauma that had just fallen into her life, wanted, perhaps, to leave open the possibility that he would someday watch her work in peace and smile with pleasure. He wondered how and when she would learn that she was the first person on record to come off the Athens elevator after Cash Ryan died.

Helt switched to view her favorable waist-hip ratio through a different camera.

The blond kid, the night tech, came into the waiting room and sat down beside Helt, sharing the couch at a distance. He was all bones and angles, with hair and eyelashes so pale that "albino" could cross a person's mind.

"Hi," he said, immediately focusing on the wall screen. He wore his name tag, Martin Kumar, PA, MSII. "Wow, stunning views you've called up."

Martin's accent came from somewhere in the British Isles, but that was as close as Helt could call it. It was apparent the kid meant the autopsy views, not Elena's hips. "This is a better look than I had in the autopsy room," Martin said.

"Thank you," Helt said. "I jiggered the color a little. The overlay had too much contrast in the outlines, so I paled it some. More see-through."

Script appeared from somewhere and took over a corner of the screen.

"Here comes the first lab report," Martin said. "This is from the heart blood sample."

Normal chemistries, the screen told them, normal blood count. Blood alcohol 0.06%.

"So he had a buzz on, but he wasn't even legally drunk," Martin said. "He kept a good crit, too, so he was getting enough exercise."

"What happens if people don't exercise?"

Martin grinned. "Well, sir, the daily health maintenance pill has an erythropoietin booster in it, so everyday activity usually keeps bone marrow functional. But some people get anemic anyway. If there's no other cause than lack of exercise, we recommend that. If people don't get around to doing it, we offer some sessions in a centrifuge. It's a great motivator."

He leaned forward as something changed on-screen. "Oh, that's a good view of the liver! Nice and smooth. This person was no boozer."

They watched as Elena helped lift the brownish liver, the dark red spleen, into the camera's view. By the book, she showed the intact appendix to the camera, let it fall back into place, ran the slippery lengths of small intestine, palpated the large, examined the colon for lesions, took samples.

The work, once divided into small sections with defined tasks, went quickly. Don't think of the big picture, Helt reminded himself. Martin remained intent on the screen, very much like a dedicated fan at a football match.

On through the stomach, tied off and packaged, kidneys, sections of ureter. Elena rinsed things and suctioned juices, keeping Calloway's access clear. She needled other things and squirted the samples into tubes, and set them into the cold box.

"Helt?" Jerry Beauchene's voice, from the SysSu feed. "It seems Dr. Maury and Charles Ryan lived together once."

"You're kidding me," Helt said. He had heard the expression *my heart sank* and he knew it didn't really happen, but in his chest, something dark and heavy woke and stirred. Elena Maury was slicing up a man she'd made love to. He had never seen anything so cold.

"When they were students together at MIT."

"Thanks, Jerry," Helt said.

Martin, on the couch beside Helt, seemed not to have noticed Helt speaking, and Jerry hadn't sent his audio to the shared screen in the clinic. Helt was grateful for that. This wasn't news everyone needed to hear right now. And if he could get MSII Martin to move out of earshot, the young man could get back to his work. There was no reason for the night tech to babysit; Helt felt, well, not fine, but competent enough to look away if the dissection stuff got to him.

"Martin. Would you like to go back to the action?" Helt asked. "I'm fine here. Really, I'm fine."

Martin looked at Helt as if he'd forgotten anyone else was in the lobby. "Oh, sorry. I'm on duty if anyone shows up, and I came through because Elena sent me to turn on the cooling in the morgue storage box and start the bloodwork. And to . . . to check the lobby."

"To see if the IA was whimpering in a corner, perhaps? Thank you, Martin. I'm okay. Actually, I'm fascinated. And I'm grateful for Dr. Maury's concern."

"I'll go back, then. Calloway said to tell you there's coffee in the lounge. Down the hall, left."

Uh, no, Helt's stomach told him. "I think I'll pass," Helt said. "But thank you."

Martin smiled, unfolded himself from the couch, and went away.

On-screen, Elena and Calloway continued their teamwork, Elena so measured in what she did, so businesslike, Calloway looking for all the world like a construction guy carefully demolishing a house with an eye to repurposing everything in it.

The room's cameras hovered over them as they replaced the sternum and closed the long incision with big staples, turned the body over, and went to work lifting the scalp. That done, they sawed away the thick bone of the skull in a circle and lifted out the brain.

It wasn't gray, Helt saw. It was a sort of gray pink. And that was pretty much it, but Helt was surprised that they replaced the skull plate, pulled the scalp down neatly, rolled Cash Ryan's body supine, and folded his dead hands across his chest. As if for a family to see.

Elena shut off the gurgling drains. She and Calloway pulled a sheet over the gutted corpse and Martin helped them lift the body onto the gurney and roll it to the morgue. Helt shut down the screens and caught up with them as they slid the body into a waiting box in the wall.

"We're done," Calloway said.

"What did you find?" Helt asked. "I didn't watch all the time."

"The chest wound. You saw that. A fracture in the right hand. Cause of death is stab wound to the left thorax and subsequent exsanguination," Calloway said, "unless something shows up on the tissue slides or chemistries."

Elena looked tired and sad.

"Okay."

"I'm still on duty. Want some coffee?" Calloway asked.

"Martin has offered me some already. No. No thank you," Helt said.

He followed Elena out into the dim hallway. She turned to look at him full on. Her pupils were large in her large eyes, gray in this light, and Helt wanted to see her eyes in different lights, to see how the color changed. He was sure it would. She was beautiful, and she was a woman who could do an autopsy on someone who had been her lover. She was terrifying. Helt shivered and tried to stop the shiver with a deep breath.

"It's not easy," Elena said. "I would advise a stiff drink before bedtime."

He knew he would have to know who she was and what she was, and he knew it was hard, right now, even to stand this close to her. He kept his voice as neutral and friendly as he could manage to make it. "I would have one if you would join me," Helt told her. He wanted to run away. "But Navigation Security has my time for a few hours."

"Rain check, then."

"Of course."

Helt watched her walk down the dark corridor and wondered if her calm steps, her straight shoulders, her poise, were honesty or total lies.

4

A Lonely Man

Old habits ruled; Helt scouted the dark street because urban plus late hour still told him to act as if he were walking a city. No sense in it, really. No gangs, no traffic, no people at all. The area surrounding the Athens agora was not residential but devoted to biz, and only the yellow glow of sconces marked storefronts. If anyone was working tonight they were behind office doors.

Overtime pay was good on *Kybele.* Flexible schedules were the norm, though. Helt liked a 24/7 work environment, and he liked flexible as a concept.

Kybele had and would have a capitalist economy, because no other economic system channeled greed as well, and greed wasn't going away. Incomes were and would be taxed. *Kybele*'s survival would forever depend on a healthy, well-fed population who had somewhere to sleep at night, and the safety nets to ensure that happened were paid for with tax dollars. Public projects had to be funded, new constructions, pure research, had to continue. The balance between runaway wealth and social entitlements was and would be tricky, and subject to continual debate, which wasn't going away, either.

Helt was working flexible time right now, on his way to assess the status of two tech workers who had just seen the corpse of a man who had died a violent death. He didn't know Jerry's and Nadia's prior exposure to raw life, or to death, natural or otherwise. His knowledge of their lives did not include how and when they came to *Kybele* or why Archer Pelham, Systems Support exec, had picked them from the clamoring throng of the wishful.

He didn't even know which offices they used in SysSu. Helt's office was within easy reach of Archer Pelham. He'd nested there. When he sat down to work, his hands knew where to reach for what; his coffee cup was familiar to his lip, and his start-up delay was minimal. By and large the rest of the geek crew moved from one office to another, in migration patterns that might be worth study, someday. For now, Helt just enjoyed the seeming randomness of where people decided to claim territory while they worked.

Under his feet, *Kybele*'s bedrock, its original surface glass-slick, lasered out of solid asteroid, had been slightly roughened for traction. Chestnut and beech trees rustled their leaves in courtyards. Quarter-moon light came from above, from a sky that was a ceiling carved out of a slab of nickel iron. It separated Level One, where the cities (well, little towns at this time, so early in this new world's history) were, from the hollow Center of the world. The stars projected on the black rock sky of Athens, four stories overhead, were arrayed as they had been seen over the Acropolis in 400 BC on a clear night in October, a factoid Helt knew because he had heard opposing viewpoints voiced about contemporary versus historic skyscapes. Athens was a college town.

Severo Mares, in high contrast and black shadow beneath a sconce, leaned against the wall at the corner of the agora, arms folded, head down, braced as if to sleep there all night.

"Hey," Helt said, softly.

"Saw you." Severo stretched and yawned.

On the south side of the agora, lights marked the windows of Systems Support, and farther down the row, of Navigation's Level One office. The complex where the real police work got done, Navigation Security Services, with its vehicles and offices and its few lockup cells, was a block away from the center of Athens. The clinic was on the same street. Those facilities were close at hand, but placed out of sight of the calm facade of the University.

Severo and Helt paced side by side, not hurried, not slow, as if they were in charge of the night.

Helt stopped at the door of SysSu. "What's your boss up to? What's Doughan doing?"

"Don't know. He wants to go with me to the guy's quarters, but he said fifteen minutes."

"Severo. You're in charge of the investigation on this death. You'll be reporting to Doughan."

"Sure."

"I'll be feeding you everything SysSu or Biosystems comes up with that might be of help. I'll take the results of your work to the division chiefs. I'm the interdepartmental Incident Analyst, and that's my job. I don't want a turf battle with you. I don't want to step on your toes."

"But you're gonna breathe down my neck, or Doughan will."

"Not as much as the media hounds will," Helt said. "This *incident*, if we may call it that for the moment, is going to get a lot of scrutiny. Doughan and I won't be the only ones watching every move that's made about it. You're going to be seeing your face everywhere."

"I hate that," Severo said.

Helt hated that, too. He was aware, perhaps less than he should be, of how he looked in public. It was part of his job. But he liked to keep private things private.

"Come on in, Severo."

Helt, with Severo following, walked into SysSu and threaded his way through the lobby. Its wall plantings were dark; its tables and displays were dimmed for the evening. A screen here and there was live, one with international news from the world spinning below them, on mute. Another showed constantly changing readouts of internal temperatures of residences in Petra, of soils in wilderness areas and in the fields of Center. The next was an animation, completely inexplicable; Bach's Prelude in C Major, played softly on a xylophone by some horse-headed creature using all ten fingers and a tail? Helt turned his head toward it. The animation played a wrong note and stopped. Helt looked away. It played the phrase again, correctly. Probably it was just up for the night.

SysSu didn't have a receptionist and it didn't have a waiting room. It did have guest chairs in some of the offices, including Helt's.

"I want to come along with you, Severo, after I check—" Helt smelled fresh coffee. He aimed for the sound of clicking keyboards, at least two of them, and an open door three doors down a hallway.

"That you, Helt? Come in," Jerry said.

Jerry and Nadia sat across from each other at a narrow table, almost nose to nose, and neither of them looked up. Since cameras were on his mind, Helt noticed that in profile, intent on their work, they looked like Central Casting might have picked them to play young, bright technocrats. Jerry carried broad shoulders on an athlete's body, ripped so that the veins stood out on his forearms as he worked. Nadia's flawless skin looked like old ivory. Her delicate hands seemed to require a fan, one painted with multicolored, perfect flowers. Both of them had dark hair, Jerry's the brown-black of Europe, clubbed to stay out of his eyes, Nadia's the shining black waterfall of the East. Loose down her back, it seemed too heavy for her to carry.

Elena's hair was a different dark, with the red color of some exotic wood in it. He didn't want to think about that now.

Jerry and Nadia really were beautiful. Maybe that's why Archer had signed them on.

Three monitors on Jerry's side and four for Nadia. The artifacts on the table seemed female to Helt, although he could not have said why the sheaf of wheat tied with twine or the purple Koosh ball, a soft, spiky rubber anemone of sorts that became a new toy every ten years or so, made him think this was Nadia's place. He watched Severo scan the clutter and the coffee cups on the table and give a respectful glance at the scuffed and sadly deflated soccer ball resting on Jerry's side of the table. Two bedrolls occupied a corner of the office, standard equipment, marked with the SysSu logo, probably hauled to Center tonight and back to the office again.

"Hi, Severo. Helt," Jerry said.

Nadia leaned back in her rolling chair and pushed her hair away from her face with both hands to smile at them. "We're looking for every trace of him. We're looking everywhere. I've found some things in Earthside archives and we're pulling what we can from those."

"Cash Ryan doesn't have a very interesting bio," Jerry said. "He has left a sparse record. I can't call it laundered, but it's—it's stingy. School, work record, addresses, credit ratings; they're all dull. He's one of the engineers working grunt under David Luo II in Navigation."

"Did he ever come see us?" Severo asked.

"NSS? Not that I know of. I've found Cash Ryan in random captures on the trains, going back and forth to work. Street cameras show him going in and out of his quarters. He hasn't done anything to leave a record in NSS, so if he acts out, it isn't physical, Severo."

"And he's never been in the same camera view with Elena Maury, not since he's been on *Kybele*," Nadia said. "Caveat. We haven't covered all three years yet. Do you wonder if they were lovers, Helt? Because of the poetry?"

Ouch. "I wonder," Helt said. "But I know you'll tell me when you know." Oh, he did wonder. He was spending a lot of emotional energy on the past of a woman he didn't know, had met briefly, had thought, briefly, about getting to know better. This was a hell of a way to do that. This was biz, only biz, and he was an idiot.

"Wait a minute," Severo said. "Here's the deal, everybody. We have a missing hour to explain. It looks like the guy offed himself, but until we know that for sure, everyone who knew about that hour, including you two, are going to need to be cleared for that time. Jerry, Nadia, Helt, were you on camera anywhere? For that matter, was I?"

"Uh, maybe," Jerry said. "I'll look."

"What about you, Helt?"

"You found me here, in SysSu. There should be time and date stamps on what I was doing." Helt felt like squirming. He felt accused, and then he felt defensive. A lot of people were going to feel that way, very soon.

"I'll get them," Nadia said.

"Meanwhile, Helt, you clear me. I'd better talk to Sonia anyway; I haven't checked in to tell her how late I'm going to be." Severo opened his pocket interface and made the call. "I'll catch hell. . . . Hello, *mi corazón*. Yeah, I know it's late. This dead guy is gonna keep me gone for a few more hours. Will you talk to Helt, at SysSu?" Severo passed the interface over to Helt, who listened, and explained, and asked questions for the record. He passed the interface back to Severo, who walked into the hall to say goodnight to his lady.

"Your desk unit was active during that hour, here in SysSu," Nadia told Helt.

"To be paranoid about it, I could have set up a program for my desktop to talk to itself," Helt said.

Jerry nodded. "I tried that once with my mom when I wanted to clear a few night hours."

"Did it work?" Nadia asked.

"The program worked fine. But with Mom? Hah. She knew. Like I said, 'once.' "

"I'll talk to David II," Severo said when he came back into the room. "He'll know something about him. You guys alibied now? Safe to work with?"

"Yeah. We're on camera at the Frontier Diner for some of that hour," Jerry said. "Helt was here in his office." Jerry turned to face Helt and grabbed large handfuls of air. "How it is, is that I can't get a feel for this Cash Ryan. He's not . . . not in there, somehow."

"And now he won't be," Nadia whispered. The expression on her lovely face was concern, for Jerry, for his needs. She's a caregiver, a soother, Helt realized. And I came here to see if she needed something, to see if she, or Jerry, needed a father figure. Maybe that's not my job tonight.

"No," Jerry said. "I guess not."

Nadia looked up at Helt, at Severo. "We went back up to Center,"

Nadia said. "We jogged the path from the tower to where we found Cash Ryan. The ropes are still there. We sat for a while. It's quiet again. There's just moonlight, and the creek, and a little wind in the pines, as if nothing's happened there, ever.

"We want to work for a while, Helt. Severo. It seems like the right thing to do."

Help him. Help them. So much altruistic energy is called up by a violent death, or the unexpected injuries of fire, flood, riot, war. So, this pair of innocent bystanders had found their own way to try to understand a violent death, to repair the knowledge of how and why it happened, to put it into place in their lives. To do what they could.

Fire, flood, riot, war. Navigation had emergency plans for all of those. There were schemes for defending life support systems, succession trees for leadership, security barricades on power plants, on water sources, of course there were.

War, by all measures ever known, was a human necessity. If it weren't, the species would have figured out some other way to get that particular set of jollies long, long ago. That, in time, *Kybele*'s population would make up reasons for war was a fairly certain bet to Helt, and a certainty to Severo's boss, to Doughan. Doughan actually seemed to enjoy calling life support drills. Maybe it was the sirens.

Setting up parameters to keep a viable population, a viable knowledge base intact through a war, or to find a way around battle tropes, was a problem *Kybele* would face whenever she faced it. Theories abounded. They were only theories.

This was only a single death, nothing more. It wouldn't wreck the ship. Helt would not let it wreck the ship.

"Another thing," Nadia said. "There's not much interest in Cash Ryan's death, at least not in the Security Bulletin announcement of it. Hits from the EMTs and their families, and that's about it. So far."

At the sound of shuffling in the hall, Severo moved away from the doorway and turned to face it. SysSu's boss, Archer Pelham, arrived, dressed in a baby blue cardigan, sweatpants, and bedroom slippers. His pale gray eyes were icy, as always, and he looked ready to disapprove of what he saw, as always. He carried a dignity that overshadowed the spiky disarray of his white hair.

Archer pushed some clutter aside and sat on the table. The purple Koosh ball fell overboard. Nadia picked it up and gave it a squeeze.

"Tell me about the SM hour," Archer said.

Nadia turned her attention to one of the screens. "Guiren and Akua were on duty."

Their full names were on the screen, Guiren Le and Akua Mirin, quiet guys who gamed a lot. That meant nothing. The whole department gamed a lot, as far as Helt knew.

"They timed the elevator cameras to add some intermittent floor-level views with a heads-up if there's rapid movement on the floor. Not that the sonic barriers aren't supposed to keep animals out of the area round the elevators; they've worked so far. But Mena wanted the extra coverage, so if anything tries to scurry out of Center, it will set off an alarm. It was routine. No blips, but the techs took the cameras out of service for that hour."

"Where are they now?" Severo asked.

"Home in bed," Jerry said. "Their interfaces are live. Should we wake them?"

"No," Severo said.

"Who checked in to see when the SM would be happening?"

Nadia sent a list of names to the wall screen, black and white, scrolling slowly, like a list of movie credits.

"I could use a chair." Archer got off the table and went into the hall to find one.

Helt looked over Jerry's shoulder as the names went by. David II had looked at the list; several others in Navigation, the duty officer at NSS. But none of the execs, and not Helt.

The execs of the three divisions on *Kybele* got notifications of when and where things were going to be shut down. Helt was on the notification list as well. A lot of people were.

Systems Maintenance was irregularly scheduled. The SM outages were announced a day in advance, if possible, to give critical personnel a chance to ask for a reschedule if something was going on that shouldn't be interrupted. Like the timing of a blast in the ever-lengthening maze of tunnels on Level Three, for instance.

Information flows about the status and operation of the ship were not classified on *Kybele.* The system was designed for transparency. It was a deliberate decision to accept what's inevitable anyway, for all information leaks in time. No state secrets.

If Cash Ryan had seen the list, he could have decided to off himself in the dark. If someone had pushed him off Athens tower, there were a lot of someones who could have done the pushing.

Severo, who had focused on Archer since the old man appeared, muttered something to his interface and looked up at Helt. "Doughan says he's on his way over to Ryan's quarters."

Helt nodded. Some of his ducks were in a row in here, Archer on guard, all of them busy for a time.

"Let's go have a look."

Three blocks from the agora, a two-story complex of workers' dorms and transient quarters, aka guest suites, had been drilled out and finished in the early phases of the building of Athens. Cash had lived on the first floor in a unit an architect had designated as Basic Single.

Wesley Doughan, Navigation Exec for now and for the first burns that would take *Kybele* out of Earth orbit, walked the lonely street ahead of Severo and Helt. Doughan had the slightly toed-in gait of a Texas cowboy, which, in fact, he had once been. Severo and Helt caught up with him very near Cash's quarters. Doughan had the alert, aware gaze of an aging shuttle pilot, and he was that, too. "I went around the block and there's nobody out here," Doughan said. "No curiosity seekers. The techs are inside."

Ryan's unit didn't front on the street. It was in the back, beyond a courtyard. An olive tree sheltered a gurgling fountain in the center of the space. Cash's quarters were on the far side of the complex; walled at the back by solid rock.

Helt went in with Severo and Doughan. Every light in the place was on and set to noon daylight. Cameras on wheeled tripods stood in corners. A tech in coveralls with a Biosystems logo brought gloves for the newcomers. After Doughan put them on, he wrapped his arms around his chest and just stood there for a while, as if afraid to touch anything, even with gloves on.

"Was there a suicide note?" Severo asked one of the workers, a woman with an NSS logo on her coveralls.

"Not that we've found." She had the look of a sturdy Midwestern housewife, faded maple-colored hair, plenty of muscle, broad shoulders, and broad hips. Evans, her nametag read. "No sign of a scuffle, or anything like that, not that we could recognize."

Doughan turned to look at the window that faced the courtyard. Its drapes were closed and a set of shelves stood directly in front of it.

"Liked his privacy," Severo said. "Loner."

Socks and shirts littered the living room floor. A desk faced the blocked front window. A keyboard and a monitor were placed dead center on it. Sofa, chair, side tables, ottoman.

The techs had opened the lid of the ottoman, but there seemed to be nothing inside. They were turning up the sofa cushions to take samples of whatever might be under there. Doughan had still not touched anything, and Helt realized that he and Severo had followed suit.

"Look, Severo, you're the cop. I'll follow your lead," Doughan said.

"And I'll follow a protocol I just read," Severo Mares said. "Not like any of us do this every damned day, you know. Protocol says to video everything in here before it's moved. I gave that job to one of the guys and it's already done. But I want to see what's here, protocol or not."

Helt followed Severo and Doughan to the kitchen doorway. They didn't go in; it was a small space. The cabinets were open and showed a few pouches of precooked food. A gloved tech put juice and beer from the fridge into a cooler, to be hauled away and tested.

One at a time, Severo first, they peered into the bathroom. The cabinet over the sink held combs, razors, the usual grooming stuff, and some OTC medicines, none of them remarkable. The sink was coated with a layer of whiskers trapped in translucent soap scum. Its impressive thickness might be used to trace its age, a timing device, like tree rings.

Ryan's bedroom was that of a monk. Loner indeed. If loneliness had pheromones, Helt was sure he smelled them in the air. The blanket on the bed, which must have been the same one supplied to bachelor quarters when Cash moved in three years ago, was stretched tight and tucked in. It was an example of military order, with precise diagonal folds at the corners. There were no pictures, even projected behind the bedroom window, no personal artifacts at all in the room where Cash had slept. None.

"Somewhere he learned how to make up a bunk and hide clutter before inspection," Doughan said. "Then there's the mess everywhere else. Some clowns just never get it right."

Severo opened the bamboo closet doors. The closet light was on. A few shirts, a few pairs of slacks hung there. Modest stacks of shorts and socks and two pairs of well-worn boots looked lonely on the almost-empty shelves. Severo tapped the black rock of the closet wall. "Not likely to be a safe bored into that, or a secret passage, do you think? We'll check, anyway."

Helt followed Severo and Doughan back to the living room.

"We're almost finished here," Evans said. A little line of vials holding colored fluids had been added to Cash's desk. She swabbed the border of the monitor stand, stuck the swab in a vial, and screwed the cap tight. "We'll haul this over to SysSu when we're done."

"I'll carry it," Helt said. "I'm going back there."

"You'll need to sign off for it. Chain of evidence."

With the entire procedure on video. Okay. Backup is good. At least what Evans handed him was a tablet recorder and a stylus, not tree paper and a quill pen.

Helt told his inner self to behave. Rule of Law. However exasperating it is, it's what we have. When it works.

He accepted the canvas bag Evans gave him. It weighed about half a kilo.

Doughan left them at the train station and headed for bed. Severo went back to the NSS office for, he said, one more check.

"On what?" Helt asked.

"I'm gonna clear out everybody who should be asleep, and then I'll clear out, myself."

Helt carried the bag into SysSu offices. The lobby felt chilly. By contrast, Nadia's office held the warmth of intent concentration. Jerry, in heads-up display goggles, leaned back in his chair. His bare feet on the table kept him balanced so that the rollers on the chair's legs didn't roll him elsewhere. He worked a keyboard ball with his hands. Archer worked beside Nadia. The Koosh was in his lap. Helt pushed the deflated soccer ball out of the way and put the sack down on the table.

Archer tilted his head forward and looked at it from beneath the shelter of his bushy eyebrows. "We've been all through that thing and there isn't much in there. Just a cruiser and playback; that's all anyone has at home these days."

"No self-written eulogy? No good-byes?" Helt asked.

"If there were, we could call this a suicide and go to bed," Archer said. "Quite frankly, we don't need a murder now. It would foul up your Get Out Now list."

"You have that straight."

The population of *Kybele* was small now and partially dependent on imported food. Limits on the food supply were sort of true, and sort of a lie. The ecology of Center was set for semi-arid, and her food crops were small and varied, constantly rotated in and out of test beds in the gardens below Center on Level One. *Kybele* had plenty of water, an excess, and she could triple the food production right now, even with no additional cropland. In addition, she planned to vandalize one of the rings of Saturn, roll her way through enough water ice to make her, truly, a snowball in hell. But she planned to be a very water-rich snowball. Specs said that *Kybele*'s ecology could support a quarter million humans, once more of her four kilometers of solid shell were tunneled out into dwellings and farms. That would happen generations from now, if her residents wanted that much population density. For now, thirty thousand was the limit.

The last shuttle would lessen the population burden by a few souls and it would also hold some of the unwanted. Let's not talk too much about that, everyone didn't say to each other. But everyone on *Kybele* knew it.

The procedures for sending someone back to Earth were written, and defensible, and uncomfortable as hell.

Culling people who weren't going to work out here was a job that the execs and the psych staff did, and Helt was involved in it more than he liked in these last days before departure, this brief time when getting people back to Earth was easy and expected. Culling *Kybele*'s population had been an ongoing process, one that began in her earliest days. Shuttles had called at six-month intervals since the beginning of her history. The problem of what to do with outright psychotics and overt criminals, the ones whose liabilities were obvious and disturbing to the people who were building the ship, had been solved in a very simple way. The unwanted had been sent back to Earth on those shuttles, and sent with plenty of money for their ongoing care.

A lot of people had come and gone as contract workers who had never hoped to stay on the ship forever. Some of them had been invited to stay and were extremely happy about it. Others, people who knew they were on board only for three- or ten-year contracts, had been hauled off *Kybele* to one station or another over the years, fifty at a time, where they transferred to the regularly scheduled big transports that shuttled in and out of Earth's gravity well. The last of that group would fill thirty of the passenger slots on the last shuttle going to China Station. Most of them had jobs waiting in near space, or had plans for careers Earthside. A stint on *Kybele* had embellished their CVs quite nicely.

Filling the other twenty seats on the last shuttle was the IA's problem. Helt's GON list was subject to review by the executive trio, but it was his list to make.

In nine days, the list had to be final. This death was going to be changing some names, one way or another.

"This guy Ryan. He's a little too standard," Jerry said. "What we've found in that little box you're carrying is that while he was on *Kybele* he was Joe Average Engineer. He watched an average amount of heterosexual porn, did an average amount of sports ogling. Even the mix is standard: football, American football, tennis. He went to poetry archives sometimes. Seemed to be cyclic about it. Would hit on the sites for a week or two, and then not again for months."

"What average amount of porn?" Archer asked.

"Average amount for his demographic." Jerry's voice was the voice of someone who was multitracking. His attention was on something in his goggles, and his fingers kept tapping the keyboard ball.

"The physical object Helt has hauled in here exists, however." Archer frowned at the sack.

"And will need to be locked up somewhere. Chain of evidence," Helt said.

"Do we have a safe?" Archer asked.

No one knew.

"Does your desk have a locking drawer in it?" Nadia asked. "It's an executive desk, and it's so big. Let me find the schematic . . ."

"I'll go look," Archer said.

Helt picked up the bundle and followed him.

"Does Mena know about this?" Helt asked. Mena Kanakaredes, the Biosystems exec, worked hard and long but she said she didn't sleep well, or much. She would probably still be awake, even this late.

"I talked to her," Archer said. "She's coming over here in the morning."

A face-time meeting of the execs would be expected. Some sort of announcement would be expected.

The lower right-hand drawer of Archer's desk was large and it did, in fact, have a keyhole near the top. There was a key in the keyhole.

"Fancy that," Archer said.

The drawer was empty. Helt put the sack in it.

5

Night Work

Jerry and Nadia looked up as Archer and Helt reached the door to Nadia's office.

"Good night," Archer said. "I'm going to bed."

Helt watched him walk away, shuffling a little in his slippers, slightly stoop-shouldered from a lifetime's obsession with monitors and keyboards. Archer reminded his staff about sleep from time to time, but he would never have told anyone in SysSu to close down.

Odd work hours were the norm. SysSu was occupied most of the time, day and night. Helt and Archer pretty much kept to a nine-to-five day, but that was because Biosystems and Navigation followed a day-night business schedule and Earth seemed to expect some sort of standard times for communications. Helt sat down in the chair Archer had brought into Nadia's office. "What about we get this whole mess cleaned up in two hours?" he asked.

"Good plan," Jerry said.

Jerry was still working on Cash Ryan's activity over the past three years, dates, places, times, work résumés, paychecks, grocery bills. Ryan didn't spend much time in the bars. Video captures were slim, sightings at train stations and, in the past, the brief interface captures Jerry had wormed out of a coffeehouse in Cambridge, Massachusetts. "Is this all there is to him?"

"Yeah. So far," Jerry said.

"Let's bring in what NSS has," Helt said. "Wait. Let's bring in whoever's working the night shift at NSS. I want to try not to step on toes here." He brought up the station contact site and Severo looked up from his desk. "You said you were going to chase people out and go home," Helt said.

"I lied. I'm the chief and I'll go home when I want to. I don't want to, so I told Evans to take a nap. I'll wake her up when I feel sleepy."

"I take it you're still working Ryan's death. Wanna work screen with us, or would you like live company?"

"I'll come over there. If anyone needs Evans, they'll call us or buzz the door. If they don't, maybe she can sleep until morning." Severo lifted himself from his chair. "Be there in a minute."

"It's time to pull files and set up some algorithms," Helt said. He crossed his hands behind his head, leaned back, closed his eyes, and spoke to the ceiling. "Let's game it for suicide. I don't know what we need to nail that, but we need to find something definitive."

"Accident?" Nadia asked. "Isn't that a possibility?"

"Maybe," Helt said. "But I think the first thing we'll end up doing is ruling that out. I made the trip up Athens tower about a year ago, just to look around. You might take a look at the specs for the observation platform. It's designed to make accidents unlikely."

Nadia did, and she and Jerry perused them while Helt concentrated on the phosphenes behind his eyelids, clusters of tiny blue and green spheres moving from lower left to upper right across his visual cortex. Jerry and Nadia would be looking at the walls around the circular deck on the observation platform, and the ledge outside the walls. *Kybele*'s planners hadn't enclosed the space. Wind could come through it, and rain.

"Look at that," Jerry said. "Why haven't we been there, Nadia?"

"Because the last time we thought about it, it was summer and it was too hot up there," Nadia said. "So we went swimming instead."

"The guard walls are one point four meters high," Jerry said. "A child couldn't fall off by accident, but any full-sized determined idiot could climb over."

"There's a three-meter walk outside the wall before you get to the edge," Helt said. He kept his eyes closed.

"Another example of built-in risk factors?" Jerry asked.

"Done by design," Helt said. "The concept is that, over time, boredom will be a worse risk for us than some kinds of individual danger." You could climb a cliff and fall. You could drown in a lake. You could climb up the walls of Petra canyon and fall far enough to die. You turn off your interface and get lost in Center. You could hide in camera-free areas. You could fucking kill yourself.

But it would be difficult, very difficult, to damage air supplies, water supplies, or the power systems that made them happen. Redundancy, security, and limited access procedures were obtrusive and thorough when it came to safeguarding vital systems. Would the safeguards stay safe? For how long? Who watches the watchers?

Helt opened his eyes. "If I may paraphrase. The physical space and the regulations—the laws—of this group endeavor—this ship—hope to give people room to be themselves. The social conventions we follow are based on current beliefs about what's pleasant. There's no guarantee that they work."

"I observe that this suicide is making you depressed," Jerry said.

"You got that right," Helt said. The easy camaraderie between Jerry and Nadia was making him wish for a trek in Center with his imagined version of Elena Maury beside him. The woman who had attracted him so before he got scared of her. He wanted to be up there for the first snowfall this year, wanted to see Elena among the pines and the deer. He wanted to know if she loved some of the things he loved, ripples on still water, frost at the edges of lakes, wanted to find out if those things were as entrancing to her as they were to him. He wanted to learn what particular wonders were beautiful to her, to see if creature tracks in fresh snow delighted her, if ferns and grasses pushing through duff in the chill of spring made her catch her breath, as he did, every spring, in amazement at the resurrection of the world.

It wasn't going to happen. Even if Ryan's death were proved to be a suicide, tonight, the voyages of exploration he was imagining could never be as innocent as Jerry and Nadia's had been when they discovered each other. The axiom is that every suicide is a murder of more than one person. A murder makes the number go exponential. Cash Ryan had killed a part of whatever Helt and Elena might become.

Severo walked in. He carried a sack and it smelled good. Helt cleared a space on the worktable next to Jerry.

"Food," Severo said. He put the sack down on the table. Nadia got up and moved the sack to a stand in a corner of the room. It held a coffeepot, microwave, and fridge. The stand hadn't been there earlier in the evening. Jerry scooted a monitor and keyboard into the vacated space on the worktable.

"Food break?" Nadia asked.

"Not for me. I finished a sandwich just before you checked in," Severo said. "I'll just have a little coffee now, but you guys go ahead if you want." He located a mug and filled it. "So, what do we need to declare this a suicide?"

"Been watching us, have you?" Helt asked. "We need lab work that isn't done yet, and witnesses who saw something beforehand that looked like suicidal behavior," Helt said. Had Ryan been in therapy here? He checked psych records. No.

Helt ran an imaginary scenario where he wakened Jim Tulloch, *Kybele*'s chief psychiatrist, told him he wanted proof of suicide on a person who had no record of ever having seen a shrink, thought about the response he'd get, and thought better of it.

"We don't have those yet," Severo said. "We can't start questioning witnesses until we have some."

"I'd like to know about the lab work," Helt said. "Maybe Martin doesn't know to post the results to NSS."

"Martin?" Nadia asked.

"Martin Kumar. He's on duty tonight at the clinic."

Helt called him. Martin Kumar was awake and sitting in the lounge at the back of the clinic, a screen in front of him. Its blue light made his hair look blue and turned his white skin an ominous shade of gray. He rubbed his eyes and smiled. His eyelids were red, but it looked more like fatigue than tears.

"Hi. It's good to see someone else awake." Martin stretched in his chair.

"We are that," Helt said. "All four of us." He sent views from the monitors. "Nadia, Jerry, Severo, Helt."

"Hi, Nadia! Jerry, everyone, hi," Martin said.

"You've all met?" Helt asked.

"Don't know if he knows Severo," Jerry said. He got up and came back to his screen with a sandwich from the bag and a glass of something tan from the fridge.

"I haven't met—Chief Mares." Martin said. He brought up the lights in the clinic lounge and suddenly looked a lot healthier.

"Are any lab reports ready?" Helt asked.

"Just the automated stuff," Martin said.

Severo leaned forward and stared at Martin. He didn't look threatening. He just looked sort of puzzled, but it was a calculated puzzled. "Dr. Calloway and Dr. Maury did what is called a forensic autopsy," Severo said.

"They did." Martin's expression looked a little puzzled, too. "Everything was recorded, and every sample of tissue and blood is under locked protocols."

"And the body is locked up, too?" Severo asked.

"The morgue has limited access, always. Nothing had to be changed for that."

Severo nodded. "I'm figuring you just did a crash course on chain of evidence."

"I did. Sir."

"Yeah, I'm learning a lot tonight I didn't plan to worry about, too," Severo said. "Martin, I'm Severo Mares, Chief of Navigation Security Services."

"Oh." Martin blinked at Severo's broad, tired face. "Pleased to meet you, sir."

"Likewise," Severo said. "And you've just been deputized by NSS. Helt will send a release over to you so you can get us the medical information as it comes in. May take Helt five minutes to get it to you, but tell us what you have so far, okay?"

"I guess this patient's privacy issues are different than most," Martin said. "Sir, the last time I looked, everything we've run is in normal range."

"NSS will need it anyway," Helt said. "Any scrap of information Biosystems comes up with. Could you set up the lab work to go over there when it comes in?"

"Sure," Martin said. "Here comes the first batch, then."

Severo looked at the lists of acronyms, abbreviations, and numbers that appeared on the screens. "Can you interpret this for me, doctor?" Severo knew all the MDs on board, all four of them, and knew Martin wasn't one. Severo was teasing the kid.

Martin was still young enough to blush, and his fair skin made his blush impressive. "I'm a medical student, sir."

"Even better. You've studied this sort of thing more recently than that lazy Calloway and won't brush anything aside."

"He isn't lazy, really," Martin Kumar said with great earnestness. "He just likes to look relaxed to help people stay calm."

Helt found a release of medical information form and sent it to Severo, who signed it and forwarded it to the Athens clinic.

"He looks like he's half asleep when he plays poker, too. You'd better watch him," Severo said.

"I have," Martin said, deadpan. "Cash Ryan's blood chemistries are all within normal range except, of course, for the two starred results over on the far right. Abnormals are pulled out of the list to make them easier to see." Martin pointed them out. "His blood pH is very low, acidotic, which happens when there isn't oxygen, and then there's low oxygen saturation. But he wasn't breathing, sir. He was dead when the samples were taken.

That, and a little alcohol, is all we have as yet. The drug screens take a little time to cook, and the pathology slides—Dr. Maury will be doing those."

Uh-oh. Helt looked at Severo for guidance. Severo was looking at something infinitely far away, but Severo knew about the elevator capture, knew that Elena Maury was the next one on it after Cash Ryan's death.

"Where do those get done?" Helt asked. "There in the clinic?"

Martin shook his head. "No. Only frozen slides are done here, quick reads while a patient is in surgery. The rest are done in Dr. Maury's lab in Stonehenge."

"You'll take the samples to her?" Helt asked. The question of how many samples of human tissue were in that lab, accessible to Elena, was a biggie.

"I will," Martin said. "But not until the next tech comes on shift. You don't think she wants them tonight, do you?"

"I don't think so," Helt said.

She didn't work alone there. It might be okay.

"Sounds like a plan," Severo said. "Martin, have you been looking at lab results on suicides? I have."

"Yes. The indicators aren't specific; any sort of stress looks much the same as depression if you check blood chemistries. Suicide assessment is based on behaviors. We would need reports from people who knew him, or evidence of some sort that he was making end-of-life plans."

Severo sent a list to the screens.

Threats of harm to self.

Seeking pills or weapons.

Talking or writing about death, dying, or suicide.

"That's the list I found," Severo said. "We'll be looking for the first two things. But we haven't found his interface, and SysSu hasn't told me where he hid his personal data stash."

"I'm working on it," Nadia said.

Helt continued down the list.

Recent losses.

Feelings of hopelessness.

Cash Ryan was a contract worker scheduled to leave the ship forever.

Difficulties with relationships.

Elena Maury and Cash Ryan had lived together for a time, in their college years. Who walked away? Elena or Cash? Why? Were they still in contact? Helt didn't want to know, but knew he had to find out.

"We don't have much personal information about Cash Ryan," Severo said. "We don't have it yet. Martin, do you want to sit in while we see if we can find some of it?"

"I'd like that very much," Martin said.

Jerry's alertness increased, a subtle thing, a glance at Nadia's studiedly neutral face. Helt wasn't sure he saw it, for in a blink Jerry was back to his normal slouch. It could be that Jerry was on guard against any age-appropriate male who might make a claim on Nadia. Jealousy was old style, immature. Denying it was the norm, verbally.

"So here's the plan," Severo said. "We interview every contact we can find. That starts in the morning." He centered the current time on screen.

0134

"Make that, starts later this morning." Severo scrubbed the time away and brought up a list of names. "Here's the first tier of interviews. I'll be starting with Ryan's work crew. It's what we've got."

Helt didn't recognize any of the names.

"When Archer was here, we used the NSS protocols you've put up and added what we've found," Nadia said. "We've been searching for biographical data and ship contacts as well."

"Lemme see it," Severo said. He peered at the schemata. "So. You've managed the info to highlight information that might be critical, and you're running suicide versus probabilities of murder, side by side. You've come up with a system that lets us look and weigh the probabilities of either and switch focus to the better bet without breaking stride."

"I hope you don't mind," Nadia said. "It's just a candlestick chart but I modified it."

"I don't mind," Severo said. "We'll take the revisions. Send them over. That's what the morning shift can see when they come in."

Jerry leaned back in his chair and gave the chief an exaggerated look-over. "Wow," Jerry said. "You don't do turf battles?"

Severo thought about that and frowned. "Not when my turf is improved by the invaders," he said. He looked at Jerry as if he'd just become aware of him and then turned his full attention to Nadia. His visual inspection could have come across as offensive, but it didn't; Severo seemed to be evaluating new and valued coworkers and looked satisfied with what he found. "You two did most of this work, didn't you?"

"The set design is mostly Nadia's," Jerry said.

"If Archer fires you, come and see me," Severo said. He got out of his chair in that deliberate way he had. It looked slow, but it wasn't. It was just efficient. "I'm going to get some sleep. This time I mean it. Thanks, guys."

The office was quiet for a few moments after Severo left. Helt went looking in the vault records. Pathology slides were virtual and comparison algorithms to find matches for tissue of any sort were really good. In the process, Helt discovered that pig liver cells don't quite look like human, but the differences are subtle.

He glanced up at the live world around him. Nadia and Jerry had turned their focus totally back to their screens and Helt felt a twinge of the peculiar loneliness that can happen in a crowd of strangers. He scanned captured footage of Elena, beginning ten years back. The train station cameras at Stonehenge caught her face now and then; he added her profile and the width of her forehead to the protocols as he watched. He didn't know why he'd never talked to her, never run across her at Biosystems conferences about this or that.

Elena worked closely with Mena Kanakaredes. Mena was easy for the scanners to pick out of the travelers coming and going between Stonehenge and Petra. She was tiny and her height made her easy to spot, so he scrolled again to see if he could find Elena traveling beside Mena. While that set of stuff sorted itself out, he set parameters for brunette women plus dark-haired males, narrowed them for Elena's shoulder width and height and Cash Ryan's body build, and scrolled for a while, but the false positives were thick on the ground.

Helt's eyes were tired. He sampled the music Jerry was playing to himself while he worked, a synthetic marimba for the melody line, shifting harmonies by a chorus of shimmering woodwind equivalents, a bass throbbing at about 22 hertz, just above the lower limit of human hearing. The tags on it said it was *Kybele*-grown music, a pickup band named, at least this week, Infinite Regression.

"So that's our chief of police," Martin said.

"Did he charm you?" Jerry asked.

"He's a little clumsy at it," Martin said. "Calling me 'doctor' set off a bullshit alert."

"He saw it and compensated," Nadia said.

"I'd like to play poker with him." Martin yawned a wide yawn in his corner of Helt's screen.

"Good luck with that," Jerry said.

“You speak from personal experience, I take it,” Martin asked.

“I lost my shirt.” Jerry didn’t look up when he said it.

“Ah. Group, I’m going to try for some sleep,” Martin said. “I’ll check in if anything shows up here.”

“Thanks for that,” Helt said. Murmured good nights came from Jerry and Nadia. Martin vanished from the screens.

Nadia lifted her head and looked over her screen at Jerry. “Which shirt?” she asked.

“Blue silk,” Jerry said. “That raw silk they’re making that looks rough, not silky.”

“You didn’t lose it. You loaned it to me. I’m wearing it,” Nadia said.

Jerry blinked and looked abashed. “Oops,” he said.

“Oops?” Nadia asked.

“Helt?” Jerry asked.

“What?”

“I can’t think of a clever, fond rejoinder that would imply I noticed how lovely Nadia looks in blue silk.”

“Neither can I. I’m going to avoid confrontation and leave.” Nadia and Jerry had planned to camp out in Center tonight. He didn’t want to keep them from what they had planned to do before they slept. He imagined their kisses, the beauty of their intertwined bodies, the healing brought by the primitive comforts of sex and shared warmth. He was jealous. Helt pushed back from his desk. “What’s that stuff you were drinking?”

“It’s apples and pears, mostly,” Nadia said.

“It’s good,” Jerry said. “Nadia mixes it for me.”

“I’ll try it, then. Jerry, my only advice would be to hug her and say you’re sorry.” He poured himself a mug of the pale tan stuff and went down the hall toward the bunk room. The smoothie was good. It tasted like apple pie with honey and cream.

Helt took his work to bed with him, images and searches projected on the bottom of the bunk above him.

Eventually, he slept.

6

An Unexpected Death

Helt opened the door to the conference room.

"... shows the number of hits on the death announcement is at background level, no more than that," Archer Pelham's overly quiet voice said. "Good morning, Helt."

"Yes, it is. Morning, all."

The chiefs of the three working sections on *Kybele* were together in SysSu's largest meeting space. Archer Pelham, Support Services; Mena Kanakaredes, Biosystems; Wesley Doughan, Navigation. The videos would show Helt Borresen, SysSu Incident Analyst, yawning but freshly shaven. And he wasn't late. He was just last.

Helt zombied his way to the coffeepot and worked on increasing his caffeine titer while he stared out through the windows that looked down on the Athens agora. Chrysanthemums blazed gold in urns near shop doors. Students and shoppers moved, bright and alive, in and out of shadows, in and out of the buildings that fronted the agora. The University Library, across from SysSu, was designed to look impressive, and it did. This building, although more extensive, was deliberately less grand.

"He's a Navigation employee," Archer said. "Did you know him, Doughan?"

"Not to speak of," Wesley Doughan said. "I don't think he ever showed up at my desk in person. He was here on a three-year contract with engineering and scheduled to leave when it was over. We've been looking for his contacts, and we haven't found many. Severo talked to David II last night. David didn't see Ryan often, he says. Didn't see him yesterday."

"I thought Chief Mares would be here this morning," Archer said.

"Severo's out with Ryan's surface crew this morning. They said Cash worked morning shift and left it alive, but Severo's out there talking to them anyway," Doughan said.

Suited up, breathing canned air out on *Kybele*'s cold hide, with the starscape spinning by every seven minutes, with fat blue Earth so close, Severo would like that. But he wouldn't be back for hours; travel to one of the poles and out to a surface worksite took time.

That Cash Ryan had worked his shift yesterday meant it had taken him time to get back, too. It set a time frame that meant there were fewer hours to reconstruct.

Helt refilled his coffee cup and turned away from the bright morning sky outside, which was a view not of infinity but of artifice. Someday, after generations had passed—how many would it take—Two? Seven? Someday, the illusion might seem foolish, and students would paint slogans on the ceiling. Generations after that, there could be real skies again for people to walk under, and real seas with real tides. Helt wondered if sky would seem strange and unnatural to them then.

The trio in charge of *Kybele* looked too few, too human, too fallible, for the job of guiding the first, perhaps the only, fragile egg full of Earth-based life to a new world outside the human basket.

Mena, at least, had gravitas to fit her role. Her profile, that straight line of forehead and nose, came straight from a Greek statue. Her stern expression came from a slight case of myopia that she chose not to treat, but it was effective. Doughan flanked her on one side, Archer on the other, looking much less impressive.

Helt had worked with all of them for a decade. At this moment they were strangers, unknowable. A million secrets lay hidden in red blobs of pulsing wetware cased in bone, thousands of purposes, memories, agendas.

So that's what a live look at an autopsy could do. Add a night's work, with only three hours of sleep in the bunkroom here in SysSu. Helt needed his coffee this morning.

Helt sat down beside Archer and pulled a work screen closer. It showed the roped-off space in Center.

"This death is a headache," Wesley said. "It was a suicide or it was murder. A suicide would be no surprise and maybe even expected. Not everyone gets to stay at our party and some of the rejects aren't happy about that."

"In either case, it's a matter we can't treat lightly," Archer said.

"We won't," Doughan said. "If evidence doesn't appear to define this death as suicide, we have to treat Cash Ryan's death as a murder under investigation. Personally, I think he offed himself. But if—*if*, I say—it's a murder, the tower elevator SM outage came at an inconvenient time."

Archer's eyebrows lowered in a visual *hrrumph* you could almost hear.

"The . . . hiatus leaves us with questions to answer that are going to take a lot of time and man-hours. As of this morning, we have no views of Ryan getting himself up Athens tower, and we have only one person in proximity to the Athens elevator near the time Ryan died," Doughan said. "It's Elena Maury, Biosystems. She has a history with Cash Ryan, and she was on Athens tower last night."

Helt knew Elena's face now; he'd seen it in shadow near the Athens elevator in Center, in the flesh. He'd seen it on his screens in crowds near the stations, in captures taken in the clean neutral light of her lab. He knew her voice. He knew her the way fans know celebrities; he had sought glimpses of her on every public camera on *Kybele*. He looked up at Mena's face, live and real and near him, and saw signs of thunder. Mena could look calm to everyone else, but Helt knew better.

"You saw her there?" Mena asked. She had cut a flower from one of the urns below and tucked it in her hair. Her dull green work shirt looked ready for a red carpet. But Mena always looked ready for a red carpet, except for her hands, her thick strong fingers and unvarnished nails, the dirt-stained calluses on her palms. Mena was a hands-on farmer.

"Cameras show her in the Athens tower elevator just after the SM," Helt said.

The video came to the screens. Elena Maury carried a stainless steel rack, which Helt now recognized as a container full of Petri dishes, those little covered plates that he remembered from biology class. She looked at the elevator walls with the expression of a sphinx contemplating riddles, those amazing eyes so calm, so quiet.

Mena curled one hand around her coffee mug and rubbed the rim with her thumb.

"So, you show Elena on the Athens elevator. Huh. Find another suspect, Doughan."

"You work with her," Helt said.

Mena stared into her cup. "Her lab tests out the embryos of the initial breeding pairs for any species we want to introduce in Center. She's a genome wizard and has done some clinical medicine. I do botany, she does zoo, more or less. I run Bio for her so she can say I'm her boss. I run Bio for her so she won't have to. I don't waste that head of hers on committee meetings."

Helt felt a sudden rush of relief. Elena had someone in her corner.

Archer wasn't as protective of Helt's time in committee meetings, and both of them knew it. Archer tried to stay a stranger to long discussions, a sort of Anubis who gave final judgment on disputes, and only after Helt had held up the scales that balanced the soul of a matter and found that it weighed more than a feather.

"I didn't say she's charged and convicted, Mena," Doughan said. "I don't think riding an elevator is grounds for arresting her. And even if she's this morning's prime suspect, she's the on-board pathologist. Should we let her do the tissue work? Should we trust her results?"

"It's possible she could fudge the results on the micro stuff, right, Mena?" Helt asked.

"With great skill," Mena said.

"But the body fell or was pushed from Athens tower, the murder weapon was a branch of a pine tree, and we have the branch. The autopsy she did is well documented. Any odd results are going to look—well, odd," Helt said.

"Photos of the path slides will be reviewed by Mass General. We can't get their opinion on the actual fluid samples no matter who does the work. Reviews of the slides won't be back for weeks, but they will be reviewed," Mena said.

Mena was protecting one of her own. She was like that.

"There's timing," Archer said. "I would really like this matter settled before the last shuttle leaves."

"Because you don't want a murderer on board?" Doughan asked. "I know I don't."

"I don't," Archer said. "But I would imagine we have several murderers on board as it is. Our population is varied, and it contains family units. Most murders are kinship based, or so I've read, and I doubt that axiom will change."

Kin and lovers, and Cash and Elena had lived together once. The thought made Helt queasy. He told himself to put the image aside. He told himself the facts weren't in.

Ten thousand berths on *Kybele* were filled with lottery winners. The price had been steep, and that was a selection method of its own. Lottery winners had started coming up twenty years ago, and love and marriage came with them. The other twenty thousand, two-thirds of the *Kybele*'s population, were technocrats. *Kybele* was top-heavy on the IQ scale, skewed by highly skilled people who could do the work required to get a mini Earth habitat on its way and keep it running, but high IQs were not always associated with emotional stability.

Kybele's population also had a variable whose ramifications could not be determined or dismissed. Every adult on board had decided to leave Earth forever, to live and die in a generation ship so that, assuming their genome survived, in whole or in part, their descendants might someday colonize another world. All of them nuts, if you looked at it that way, and Helt sometimes did. He figured he was nuts, too.

The safety factors, all sorts and kinds of genetic material, were frozen in liquid nitrogen and stored deep and out, close to the big cold beyond *Kybele*'s skin. If you bought a lottery ticket, you bought storage for a tiny vial with a few of your cells in it and your name on it. Part of you got to make the trip and might live and breathe here someday. Part of you might walk on a new world. It was a lottery, but it was real.

"Our handling of an unexpected death sets precedents, as most matters do these days," Archer said. And then there's the matter of jurisdiction, as well."

"You'll hear no objections from me if we manage to hand the problem off to Earth," Doughan said.

Helt waited for Archer but Archer's stare at his screen said it was Helt's turn to talk.

"I'll state the obvious, for the record," Helt said. "Every human on *Kybele*, including lottery winner colonists, is, as a legal fiction, an employee of Biosystems, Systems Support, or Navigation. Once the ship is under way, everyone on board becomes a citizen, with the traditional rights and obligations inherent in that status. The debate that brought this system about was long and heated, but the employer-employee relationship seemed to be the most efficient way to get the ship built, stocked, and ready to travel."

Coworker reviews counted, peer evaluations counted; those safeguards were in place and guidelines were followed, but anyone on *Kybele* could be fired. Including Helt Borresen, for that matter. "Elena Maury has colonist status. Until the last transport goes back to Earth, she can be dismissed by her exec—that's you, Mena—for any stated or unstated reason."

Doughan didn't seem to like that statement. "It's been our tradition not to state our reasons. If somebody messes up here, we try to stay neutral so they get a fair chance at a life and a job when they go back down. We send facts, but no felony record if we can avoid it. But we've never sent a murder suspect down. Seems like we would want to give fair warning if we do."

"We knew we would be cops," Wesley Doughan had told Helt once. He'd been stretched out in a bamboo chair in Helt's quarters in Petra, his feet on the upholstered cushions of the stone banco that could double as a bed, staring at a moonlit view of the Pyrenees on the screen behind the interior window. "Shore Patrol. Whatever.

"Navigation will have jack all to do for decades at a stretch, other than wobble correction, simulated lander runs, and equipment maintenance. Industry is under our umbrella; that's a different thing. But the pilots and the outside crew can't sit around polishing boots forever, and somebody will have to keep this overeducated group of absentminded professors from throwing garbage in the streets."

"Yeah, well, garbage is our job," Helt said. "Systems Support. Maybe it should be Bio's job, but I can't get Mena to take it. The miners get physical now and then. That should be enough to keep you in shape. That's if Bio manages to breed any that can operate machinery. Want another beer?"

That had been years ago. In the bright morning, here in the conference room, Helt got up for the coffeepot.

"Send the problem away," Doughan said. "I take it that's the plan. I don't like it, but the fact is that a murder trial is not on my departure schedule," Doughan said. "Look, all Severo has had to deal with is the occasional fistfight, the occasional student prank. We have some jail cells at the Athens station, but we've never used them. A couple of people have had to be locked in their own quarters for the night to rethink their situations, and we check with their Division heads first if we need to do that. That's our working protocol."

"As far as experience in matters concerning criminal law," Archer said, "Ju Zheng from our legal staff has the job of judge in magistrate court, if one needs to be convened. She's only had a couple of cases to deal with so far."

Helt brought the coffeepot to the table and topped up the cups.

"Legal says the algorithms say that with this limited population, at this point in time, if there's a murder trial, the Division Execs are the judges. That's us." Doughan frowned as if the idea disgusted him.

Legal had a staff of five. One attorney did finance and estate planning and civil arbitration, two worked on *Kybele*-Earth matters. There were two paralegals. "That's assuming you're crossed off the suspect list," Helt said.

"Yeah," Doughan said. "Everyone here's on it, except Helt. He's cleared."

"I have some time and date stamps from work last night here in SysSu. There's no cross-check yet. I'm not completely off the hook," Helt said.

"So everyone here's a suspect," Doughan continued. "Until we aren't, it's probably a good idea for us to leave the cameras on in the offices."

"Spy on ourselves, yes," Archer said.

"Interfaces, too," Helt said.

"Sure," Doughan said. "Severo will be asking you for time and place verification during the SM hour, if he hasn't already."

"He hasn't, yet," Mena said. "But what connects Elena and this Ryan person? This engineer who was scheduled to be gone in three weeks?" Mena asked.

"It's possible Cash and Elena might have been an item in their college years," Doughan said. "SysSu found a video of them in a club; not much, but it could mean they knew each other in face time, at least."

They might have been roomies, just roomies and nothing more. For some reason, that had not occurred to Helt until now. He liked the concept a lot. Maybe a bit too much.

SysSu had worked on Ryan's history most of the night, but SysSu's exec, Archer, didn't take his cue and say how his division was researching this mess, and Helt wondered why. Archer was playing Old Man, and not just in Navy style. He seemed lost in his screen and looked half asleep, although Helt knew he wasn't.

"Nadia Tay and Gerard Beauchene are the SysSu ITs who found the body," Helt said. "They wanted to work on this, and they're good. They're searching archives. As of 0300 they had not found any contact between Maury and Ryan, anywhere, anywhen, since they were enrolled at MIT at the same time. One semester."

"Not even in a crowd shot? I mean here, on *Kybele*. In commuters coming and going?" Mena asked.

"Not even that," Helt said. "Or, not yet. In a population of thirty thousand—"

"Captured on video only when they show up on some public security camera somewhere," Doughan said. "Captured by position sensors only if their interfaces are live. I know, I know. I'm one of the ones who pushed to keep us as much privacy as we could handle."

The streets and the trains had security cameras. There were panic buttons in shops, but only as much video surveillance as a shopkeeper wanted to review on her own. There were smoke alarms in every dwelling, but cameras in bedrooms were a private affair. A scream in the night would get attention, though, if it sounded like a cry for help. Fine-tuning the system for people with nightmares or small children was still ongoing.

In the wilderness sector of Center, many of the introduced animals and birds had locators implanted under their skins and some wore cameras. Helt had met a couple of monitored deer with Elena, only two nights ago. There were cameras and smoke detectors out there, monitored in Stonehenge, but surveillance of the forested areas was minimal by design.

Doughan looked around the table, a commander evaluating his resources. "Archer, sorting this out is a problem for Navigation, but SysSu will have a lot of cross-departmental traffic to supervise for us."

"Which I plan to delegate to our Incident Analyst," Archer said.

The statement was no surprise. Helt had known this would happen even while Severo was making his report last night. That he had called it right was small comfort. An ugly death had happened in his *home*, damn it, and he had to fix the damage, and he knew he might fail.

"I see," Doughan said. "So it's all yours, Helt. Severo is in charge of the human investigations and he'll report to you. You take what Severo finds and bring it to the execs," Doughan said. "I wish you luck."

"Thank you," Helt said. He would need more than luck. He needed legalese in place that would let him cross-check everyone on the SM list, including the three people in this room. Damn. Unlike Doughan, he had never known he was going to be a cop.

The trio had a sort of shorthand, after working together for ten years. Archer stared briefly at each of them with his Anything else? Let's get on with it, shall we? Look.

Mena glanced up from her screen. "The statement's ready to go out, if you want to review it. That the trio is taking all necessary steps, et cetera. As you wrote it, Archer. Nice job."

Biosystems was the official voice for announcements of *Kybele*'s policies, and so it was Mena's pronouncements that would enter the news feeds. When the ship began its burn toward the rings of Saturn, that job would go to Doughan. After that, the plan was three-year rotations between the departments, adjusted for times when the ship would be in maneuvers. The ship's governance would always be headed by Navigation during those times.

"Nadia Tay wrote it, Mena. I'll tell her you like her style."

"Copied mine, did she?"

Archer gave Mena a wink.

The meeting was over. No need for discussing the timing of the next meeting; it would happen when needed. No need for social joshing; all of them were in one another's data streams several times a day as it was.

"Do you want some video with it?" Helt asked Mena, as the others got out of their chairs and headed elsewhere.

"Sure," Mena said.

The stone wall behind Mena was covered with a mildly green fabric, a choice subject to several discussions between the ship's architects and its workmen, a felt made from pulped grass and bacteria-grown glue. It was handy for green-screen work.

Mena stood, straightened her shoulders, and drew a deep breath. "I think just a sentence or two in voiceover will be enough. Text for the rest."

Helt captured her saying, ". . . unexpected death . . . last night after a fall from Athens tower . . ." and so forth. She had learned to look at a camera lens, but she didn't like it.

"An unexpected death," Helt repeated.

"A suicide, Helt. Tell me when I can say that and I'll stop being camera shy. That's a promise."

Because her face said she needed it, Helt hugged her.

7

Make a List

The scent of Mena lingered from the hug, her skin fresh from a morning scrub with that moss-and-cedar-scented soap she favored. Her scent had not changed. She was rough with her washing, in a way that had caused Helt, once, to take the cloth from her strong hands and bathe her gently, as if she were a child. The memory hurt. Helt had not touched her for—eight? Eight years?

Kybele's soil was her pride, pulverized, smooth-polished sand sifted and mulched and treated with micro-life painstakingly collected and hauled up on specifications designed by Mena's husband, Alex Aaronsohn. Aaronsohn had died on an Earthside trip, examining soils in the arid Sierra Tarahumara, a victim of a drug war, or anti-Semitism, or a target for someone who thought Earth had no business in space, but none of the usual suspects claimed credit for the killing.

Yes, Mena grieved for Alex. Helt had been part of that grieving, a shared time of relief from despair, of desperate love-making where joy and sorrow were united and the pain of death was held at bay, a time of passion in the face of unbearable loss. But when that time was over, Mena had pushed him away.

"Do you have another lover?" Helt had asked her.

"Not yet. But I will. So will you. Go."

She'd left him. It hurt and he had tried not to show how much it hurt. What hurt most was that she didn't break stride, didn't seem distressed, had gone on about her work with the same intensity and pleasure she had shown before her husband died.

If the occasional man came and went in her life now, that man was none of Helt's business. It hurt not to know if there was someone for her, but he hadn't asked.

As far as Helt knew, her loves were the grain fields in Center, the coffee and cacao that grew in lighted plots on Level One of Stonehenge, and the vineyards. She was particularly fond of the vineyards. Don't forget the stands of tea bushes, grown in a misty habitat on Level One, Helt reminded himself. First grain, and then stimulants. That's how we are.

He had an instant's memory of a *mareritt* night, a dream where the small boy Helt padded the length of a long corridor to a closed door he could not open, worried by sounds from within that he could not understand. He pushed the nightmare away.

In his office, he searched Legal's cache of boilerplate for the authorization he needed to let him solve a murder case. Special Investigator seemed to fit the job description. He spent a few minutes staring at the list. Examine records and locate links, identify case issues and figure out what evidence is needed, obtain and verify evidence. Interview suspect and witnesses. Fine, that's what an IA did. Perform undercover assignments and maintain surveillance, including monitoring communications. As *Kybele*'s IA, Helt had done that, but only by the request of the parties involved. Spy on ourselves, the execs had just said. The newly designated Special Investigator would be looking at Mena and Archer and Doughan in ways he hadn't before. He didn't think he was going to like that at all. It felt icky.

Helt sent the file to the execs for signatures. He wondered how closely they would read it. The document gave him a decidedly odd place in the power structure, but Helt could hope it was temporary, a set of powers that would vanish the moment Cash Ryan was declared a suicide. He profoundly hoped that moment would be soon, like today. Like now. The shortest route to that was Elena. He wanted her to fix this mess for him and for herself.

The wall of greenery behind him misted itself, on schedule. Helt kept the other three walls blank for projections. He turned them all morning blue, clean, and neutral.

The mist finished its cycle and sighed. He took a deep breath and called Elena Maury. She was in her lab, at a table barricaded by machines and glass, working with a camel's-hair brush and what looked like a miniature guillotine.

"Good morning, Helt Borresen."

"Good morning. Please pardon the interruption."

"Urrgh," Elena said. She flicked a flake of something or other away from the end of her brush. "I'm doing paraffin sections and you just made me ruin one."

"I'm sorry," Helt said. Mena had said it would take days to sort this out, and he was sorry about that, too. He wondered what part of Cash Ryan Elena was slicing up so carefully this morning.

Elena put her brush down and looked up at her view of Helt's face. "I knew you would call."

"How did you know that?"

"Mena. She said I'm the only recorded suspect NSS has so far."

Mena had gone to Elena with the news, then, as soon as she got back to Stonehenge. Maybe Mena had even told her a few things about Helt Borresen, and he had to wonder what she'd said. Elena might have been the person who last saw Cash Ryan alive, and she'd lived with him, probably slept with him, and those things made Helt angry at Mena, and at Elena. He tried to keep the anger out of his voice and away from his face.

"I would like to meet you and talk. This evening," Helt said.

"I've given a report to Severo."

"I know. But there are other things I need to know. I need your help." He would make it an order if he had to. "Eighteen hundred? Athens, if you don't mind making the trip."

"I don't," Elena said. "Eighteen hundred is good. That gives me time to finish . . . not finish. Make that stop work, get some food, and get to Athens."

He liked her cheekbones, although the balloon-shaped gauze bonnet that covered her hair looked like a bowl cover from his mother's kitchen, and was not flattering. She didn't seem nervous, and that scared him. She should be frightened.

"Okay," Helt said.

Elena picked up her brush again and nodded. Helt blinked her away from his screen and went to Jerry Beauchene, who had signaled him three times since 0900.

He got a view of the sole side of a set of bare toes. Jerry pushed back from the table in Nadia's office so he could put his feet on the floor and roll his chair closer to the screen.

"Interesting," Jerry said.

"Tell me," Helt said.

"I looked at yesterday's weather in Center. There were some of those twisty winds, the really fierce ones, starting around 1600. Sixteen to sixty kph. They died down by 1900, more or less."

"It was breezy when I went up there to meet Severo," Helt said.

The control of winds in Center was not easy and never would be. Drone earth-movers were constantly revising the berms that spiraled out from the north and south towers. Every degree of temperature change in *Kybele*'s manufactured seasons changed the wind patterns and the drones tried different configurations to control them, on specs that came from Navigation engineers assigned to Biosystems. There were windmills to catch some of the turbulence and change it to electricity. There were deflection sail drones as well, up where g was nil, spin was apparent, and most human inner ears insisted that their humans were required to throw up, right now, and get somewhere else fast.

"So I was thinking, remember when Calloway said Ryan might have tried to glide down? He could have just been caught in a wind spin."

"Heh," Helt said. "Passive positioning. That's good. I mean, it's something to think about."

"Does the stuff SysSu comes up with go to you, or to Severo?"

Helt took a breath. "I'm thinking." The execs had just made him the boss of this mess. However, the police work on it belonged to NSS, and would be their job until and unless Biosystems found a good case for suicide. But he had the job of collating what anyone found.

"I mean, I know Severo needs the information," Jerry continued, "but there's Archer, there's you."

"Not a clear decision tree, is there? Not yet. I'll try to come up with one. For now, send what you find to me and I'll cc Archer and Severo after I look it over. Your third call was?"

"Was that Nadia's going down to Venkie's for breakfast samosas. You want one?"

"I want three," Helt said.

"Yes, sir."

Venkie's kiosk offered a mix of fruits and nuts and spices plus a few choice nuggets of chocolate, wrapped in half-moons of yogurt pastry and baked. The kiosk was convenient to the Library entrance, and the pastries were expensive.

On *Kybele*, the highest salaries were paid for work done by human hands. The system meant that Venkie's pastries were pricey, and it meant

SysSu didn't have difficulties finding people to do manual labor, like, say, overseeing the machines that collected garbage. As a side benefit, the garbage collectors got plenty of material for sociology papers.

Venkie made things that people wanted. Venkie was going to be rich in a few years, and Helt wondered what he would do then. Or maybe he was rich already. Maybe he had come to *Kybele* loaded.

Helt checked. Venkat Raghava, PhD in linguistics, Cambridge, therefore probably not at all rich. He was a lottery winner, not a contract worker. He wouldn't be breaking down his kitchen and heading back to Bangalore.

But some of the lottery winners would not be staying. The unconditionally un-chosen were on Helt's off-list, the one Archer called Get Out Now. GON.

That task had a time frame and would soon end. The other part of his task—not his alone, everyone's task—would continue after *Kybele* was on her way, and would never end. Permit—no, *encourage* the living of creative lives; permit—no, *encourage* experimentation with social systems, family structures, ways of living with each other that didn't destroy the ecology. Experimentation would be a necessary condition for survival over time in this terrarium.

Meanwhile, give as much slack as possible to those who hear different drummers. Find or create enough space, physical and emotional, for people to live and grow and explore the possibilities of the genomes they expressed—new genomes, blended and mixed, and that led him back to Biosystems and the tinkering that would be done, must be done, in an environment where radiation damage and the necessity for ongoing repair was a given.

Elena's work had to continue. If she had to be replaced, someone would replace her, but Mena had called her a wizard.

Who needs to Get Out Now, Helt?

Being socially different was not necessarily a criterion for expulsion. Some of the best minds on *Kybele* were not well socialized, but they had dysfunctions that were not crippling, and were sometimes even charming. If you played nice, no one here cared much if your socks matched. Some diagnosable personality disorders, like depression, anxiety neuroses of various types, and obsessive-compulsive disorders, were well within the spectrum of tolerated behaviors. In fact, without a considerable number of OCD and high-functioning autistic nerds on board, *Kybele* probably had no chance of survival at all.

Helt used a lot of psychiatric terminology to structure some of the things he looked for, but he was no shrink. Last night's searches of protocols for dealing with suicide had included looking over something called a "psychiatric autopsy." Okay. He checked Jim's schedule. James Mair Tulloch, MD, was with a patient for the next five minutes.

Jim's office was here in SysSu, because even in this enlightened day and age—Helt added an overlay of irony to the term *enlightened*—a lot of people didn't want their need for psychiatric tune-ups known to all and sundry. So Jim was here, not in one of the medical clinics, Supporting Systems in his own way. As a planned side effect, he was also available for a quick chat now and again with the Systems Supporters themselves.

Helt topped up his coffee, walked through SysSu, a quiet, busy place this morning, and left the lobby via the corridor that led to Jim's office.

The door was open. Jim was in his chair, his long, thin body stretched out, his sandaled feet crossed at the ankles, his coffee cup in hand. His socks matched. They were red.

"Good morning," Jim said. "I never saw the guy."

"That leaves you a little short of material for a psychiatric autopsy." Helt closed the door, took the empty patient's chair, had a sip of coffee, and looked at the faded yarn-and-branch Medicine Eye hanging on the wall above Jim's head. Three square yarn eyes, actually. They might have been green and yellow once. Each of them faced a slightly different direction. "Did Jerry or Nadia send over what we have so far on Ryan?"

"They did. Charles 'Cash' Ryan didn't make a single visit to any medic during the past three years, except for the required yearly physicals. He turned in his radiation badges to his supervisor when they were asked for. That's all that's on record."

"Heh. I know better than to ask you what's off the record."

"You know I respect patient privacy. You know I'm required to speak out if someone is demonstrably a danger to self or others. I didn't see Charles 'Cash' Ryan as a patient." Jim Tulloch leaned back farther in his chair, locked his hands behind his head, and grinned. "I do so love a challenge. You want a psychiatric autopsy on someone who kept to himself, left no obvious warnings about suicide, in behavior or written records, and managed to spend three years here without making a single friend that we know about."

But the dead man had known Elena. Helt's fantasies of who Elena was and what she might become to him had lasted less than a day. One single day, and then she got hurt, got trapped in something terrible. It was enough to make him feel he was responsible for her forever, and that was truly nuts.

He didn't want to talk to Jim about her. He knew some of the reasons for that. A Scandinavian tendency toward keeping private things private was part of it. Nuts or not, he wanted Elena Maury to come out of this whole, sound, and happy. And he didn't want to tell Jim Tulloch anything right now.

Not now. Not yet.

"I'll do what I can," Jim Tulloch said.

"I know you will." Helt nodded, got up, and went back to his office.

The GON list, when he brought it up, gave him no comfort. Cash Ryan's name had never been on it. He had been expected to climb aboard the last shuttle without protest.

By design, there wouldn't be much time for protest for the GON people. The plan was that the division chiefs would give the off-listers the news in person. The plan was that NSS would march them to the shuttle while a team packed their personal belongs, up to the weight limit and not a gram more.

There were people in the world who didn't mind saying, "You're fired." Helt wasn't one of them. Parse it any way you liked, but the message remained the same. Your job performance doesn't meet the needs of the project. I don't want to play with you. I don't like you. You're not my friend. Or, no one likes you even if they don't say so. Go away.

The exits would be demeaning, ugly, and cruel, a model taken from the worst of corporate behavior. Ugly, but effective, or so the chiefs hoped, at diminishing possible threats to the ship's safety. Helt didn't like the plan and had no other to suggest.

Black letters on the white screen in front of him suddenly focused themselves. Nadia's biography of Cash Ryan had grown longer. This was his *second* tour. He'd been on *Kybele* thirteen years ago on a three-year contract. He had worked on the reactors at the poles then, under David Luo I, *Kybele*'s chief engineer during the first decades of her existence.

Whoa. Helt messaged David Luo I. He sent him the death report, complete with the video of Mena's announcement. He asked David I, retired, currently living in Vancouver, Earthside, for a conference time. A copy of the request, flagged, went to the execs and Severo.

David Luo I had been chief engineer twenty years ago. David Luo II, his son, *Kybele*'s current chief engineer, would have still been a college kid, working on various projects assigned by his dad as apprenticeship for the work he would do on *Kybele*. Helt cc'd David II as well, and looked up to see Archer, in the flesh, standing in the doorway.

"I've some information for Wesley Doughan," Archer said. "And you."

Helt swallowed the last bite of a samosa. He hadn't noticed he was eating one, and he didn't know whether Nadia or Jerry, or both of them, had put them on his desk.

"It's best if I discuss this in person with Wesley. Can you come with me?"

Helt nodded. He closed his screens, shrugged on a windbreaker, and put the remaining two pastries in his pocket.

Archer led the way through the lobby and out into the agora.

"Doughan's office?" Helt asked.

Archer nodded.

During the five-minute train ride, Archer said nothing at all. He was like that. Helt took advantage of the quiet time and rescheduled some of today's canceled appointments. Since most of them involved telling prospective colonists they hadn't moved up the list of hopefuls, he had mixed feelings about the delays. He thought it was only fair to talk to them in person, and he dreaded doing it.

Navigation's chief's office was in Operations, down on Level Two, a complex built next to the airlocks where shuttles came and went. Incoming shuttles docked at the far end of *Kybele*'s north pole, out where half her big engines were housed. From there, they spiraled inward through airless tunnels and ended their journey at *Kybele*'s waist, her equator. When they had unloaded and reloaded, they left via a drop tunnel that led to the surface and they fell away with a half-g boost from *Kybele*'s spin to use for going wherever they were headed.

Doughan met them in the Level Two departure lounge, empty, and led them past the Customs office, empty, and into his office.

"A personal visit," Doughan said. "I'm honored."

His office was dome-shaped and his desk was a curved affair smack in the middle of the room. The wall behind him showed blue Earth. The rest of the walls were live views of the near-real-time starscape outside, a display doctored by camera cuts so it looked stationary.

"Nothing's recording. Coffee?" Doughan motioned his visitors toward four empty chairs surrounding a table.

"I'll pass, thank you," Archer said.

"You, Helt?"

"Sure."

Doughan filled two mugs and brought one to Helt.

"SysSu is burdened by many things and one of them is banking." Archer pulled a small Huerfano, a self-contained unit not connected to any other device anywhere on the ship, and sent a display to a space on the wall, easily visible to all three of the humans in the room. Nine names appeared, none of them familiar to Helt and none of them on his off-list.

"We have seven people aboard who have received money from Seed Banker front companies in this past year," Archer said.

Huh? Helt knew of the organization. It was multinational, vocal, claimed to be pacifist, and raised funds for Earthside seed banks. It also bitched about *Kybele*'s existence, but that bitching was countered in world opinion by the fact that some highly influential people had cousins or sons or daughters here.

Doughan sighed, a quickly suppressed sound of exasperation. "What have they done here?" Doughan asked.

"Nothing," Archer said. "These seven people have been remarkably quiet for activists, if that's what they are."

"Your list says they're all colonists," Doughan said.

"Yes, colonists. If they stayed quiet, they would have decades to try to persuade us to change our deluded notion of going to the stars. Or pool their resources and buy spin doctors or whatever they think they need from Earth or the belt."

"Like a shuttle filled with technocrat commandos," Doughan said.

"We started gaming pirate takeovers years ago," Archer said. "The expert systems that watch political unrest haven't pinged a hot spot that could divert resources to stopping us for more than"—Archer looked at blue Earth for a moment—"six years. If we're at risk from anyone, it would have to be the Northern Coalition."

Archer paid close attention to Earthside politics, border wars, coalitions, hate groups. The northern circumpolar regions supported a couple of billion humans. Russia, whose boundaries with Central Asia had been forcibly rearranged, Europe, Canada, and the northern United States were players in the Northern Coalition. Those nations were divided on many things but, so far, able to find common cause in staying alive. The southern arable zone was smaller, as it had been before the big melts, and it had even less land now. South America's narrow tail was above water in some places, and parts of Africa were usable. Antarctic melting had changed the pattern of currents, and therefore rainfall, so that agriculture was pretty viable, with a lot of help, up to the Tropic of Capricorn.

Earth was alive. Her polar caps had almost vanished in the past hundred years, which was no surprise to anyone. The seas had risen, as predicted, and the coastline cities had moved inland, with predictable amounts of turmoil. The damage to the oceans would take centuries to heal, but Earth was still alive. For now.

Archer made note of shooting wars, the endless disputes that formed a band between lands that were still arable and watered and the ever-widening dry zones that girdled the planet below. So did Navigation.

"And the Coalition has spent considerable chunks of money on us," Archer said.

The Northern Coalition had coaxed the UN into funding a great deal of the building of *Kybele.* Contributions were tax-deductible from anyone or any company in any UN signatory nation. A lot of private funding was involved as well, and then there was the lottery. The lottery had been key in keeping a sense of involvement alive in the hopeful.

Doughan put the incoming shuttle's path on a wall screen, a white dot on a white line that stretched from China Station to *Kybele.* "When this last cargo gets here and leaves again, we're done with boarders, and anyway I know the pilot. Went to school with him.

"These Seed Bankers just don't give up," Doughan said. "Leave *Kybele* where she is, right up here in her nice stable LaGrange orbit; Earth needs a safe biologic haven off-planet." He vanished the diagram and looked again at the list of names on the Huerfano. "I don't see Cash Ryan on the list."

"He's not there," Archer said. "Three of these people work in Navigation, two in Biosystems, two in SysSu."

Helt recognized neither of the SysSu names.

"The SysSu people are both teachers." Archer must have seen Helt's slight dismay at not knowing who they were. "One teaches an ESL class,

English as a second language, at the University. The other's a colonist, a lottery winner. She's an archaeologist."

The University was essentially autonomous, but on flowcharts it was listed under the SysSu umbrella. It was autonomous, yes, but if the academics decided to teach classes only in, say, Ukranian, SysSu could and would challenge that decision. Helt hoped that never happened. He'd be the person to listen to arguments from both sides and try to keep things out of court. The arguments would be wordy ones. He wasn't certain of much, but he was certain of that.

"There's not enough information for Legal to make cases against any of the seven people on the list. They have done nothing on *Kybele* that is actionable in any way," Archer said.

"You're saying you and Legal can't get the work done before that last shuttle leaves."

"We'll keep working on it, but it's not likely."

"Three of them in Navigation. Let me see." Doughan pulled up the bios attached to the names from Navigation and gave a quick glance at each. "At least none of them work anywhere near the drive systems," Doughan said.

"And ours, in SysSu, aren't in position to do much damage. Although I suppose propagating bad grammar could be a sort of sabotage," Archer said.

Doughan leaned back in his chair and folded his arms across his chest. "I'm going to miss being a dictator, damn it. Once that first burn ends, the execs are up for votes of confidence and all the other checks and balances that we've built into our version of democracy. But for now, I can just offload these bastards, and I intend to."

"It might be that some of the people know—pardon me, *knew* Cash Ryan," Archer said.

"It might be that NSS might want to ask them some pointed questions," Doughan said.

Whoa, Archer. Helt frowned at his boss. Damn it. You just put me in charge of investigating Ryan's death and you and Doughan seem to have forgotten that inconvenient little fact.

"Are you going to tell them they're being questioned about a suicide?" Helt asked. "If you are, then it's about the Ryan case and I'll need to be there. If the Seed Banker problem is quiet white collar crime, and not related, then it's a purely administrative matter, of course."

"I don't plan to tell them Cash Ryan's death is a murder," Doughan said.

"We don't know which it is at this point, do we, Doughan?" Archer's voice was gentle. Anyone who worked in SysSu would have known that gentleness was a warning signal that said, "You've done something really, really, stupid, haven't you?"

Doughan picked up on the reprimand and found something interesting to look at on the wall behind Archer. "No," he said. "We don't. For this round of questions, I'll have a uniformed NSS officer with me, or—or someone from Legal, Archer. In face-time, or in real-time as observer."

The weight of unease Helt had been carrying since last night grew appreciably heavier. Damn. He wasn't sure how to parse that interchange between Archer and Doughan. Doughan had signed off on the document that named Helt Special Investigator, with all its odd privileges, but the two execs were talking past him.

"I don't know if that's needed," Helt said. "I'll ask Obrecht." Giliam Obrecht handled *Kybele*-Earth legal traffic. He wasn't a criminal law specialist; no one on *Kybele* was, but Giliam could find out what was needed.

Helt's discomfort came from an embarrassing sense of incompetence as well. None of the Seed Bankers were on his first tier of off-listers.

He called files from his State of *Kybele* construct, isolated them on his interface, and checked them against the list projected on the wall. He went down two levels of risk assessment and found one of the names. Only one, Andrea Doan, Biosystems, agronomist. He flagged the name so he could study her history. He'd need to use what he found out about her, about the others, to restructure some of his sorting mechanisms, because he'd missed a potential threat to the ship.

That job had to be done, and quickly. Also, as of right now, seven of the shuttle seats would be occupied by Archer's seven newly discovered off-listers, and seven contract hopefuls got to stay. Yves Copani would be among them, if Helt could manage it.

News of the death would ripple through the ship. The questioning Doughan planned to do would wake nightmares of unauthorized interrogation, of arbitrary eviction, old horrors set free to alter the spoken and unspoken social contracts of daily life. The fabric of how life would be lived here.

Helt's life, too. The death and the reactions of these two were threatening his sense of safe haven, coming to harbor, refuge. *Kybele* was a dream made real, and now the dream was in danger. He couldn't step aside. He couldn't fail, and he knew he might.

He forced himself to concentrate on the task of adding the seven names to the Ryan list on his pocket interface, under Contacts, more for Jerry and Nadia to cobble into Cash Ryan's biography.

There was nothing specific he could say to Archer, to Wesley Doughan, no words he could think of except to say, "This feels wrong." They had no proof of murder. They wanted suspects if murder had been done. Archer had found some people that looked suspicious to him, and Doughan was hot to turn them into killers. This chase might be worthwhile, or it might divert attention from the work Severo was trying to do.

Helt opened the NSS Station Log. NSS, as usual, made the sort of reports that would have been avidly read in a small-town weekly news site from the last century. Responded to call, observed whatever, arrested whoever, by name and alleged offense. The work on the death of Cash Ryan was on there but without fanfare. An unexpected death.

"I think Mena and I could keep these questioning sessions intradepartmental, at least in form," Archer said.

"As opposed to formal arrests, sure. But we have to look at these Seed Bankers. Maybe they know something about Cash Ryan," Doughan said. "No one else seems to have noticed he was alive."

"These grilling sessions you're planning. You'll be prepped on specific things that Severo will need. That *I* will need, I take it," Helt said.

"You're the Special Investigator," Archer said. "You'll do the interviews, of course."

"Of course," Helt said. Doughan looked surprised, but didn't object. Helt was not an exec, but he had the authority, in this instance, to do this his own way. So maybe Doughan had read the boilerplate, after all.

"This was Cash Ryan's second tour," Helt said. "We don't know much about what he did during either of them. We're working on his biography, and we need any info we can get for a psychiatric autopsy."

"Yeah. That second tour surprised me. Maybe David I remembers something about him," Doughan said.

"I sent a query to David I this morning," Helt said. David I had been in charge of the big kabooms that had blown a hunk of solid rock into a hollow sphere and filled it with breathable air. His crew had bored the tunnels of Level One and the Navigation spaces of Level Two. David I had hired Ryan for three years and might have known him; his crew had been exponentially smaller than the one David II guided now. The list of other people who had been on ship twenty—no, thirteen—years ago needed looking through as well. Engineers, certainly, but Biosystems and SysSu people had come on early, too. Someone must have known Cash Ryan then. Helt added that search to his list.

"If you set up a link for a conversation with David I, I want to sit in. I haven't talked to him for years," Archer said. He stretched and stood up. "Also, I haven't been over to Stonehenge for a long time. I'll go give the names to Mena."

Archer stared at his little Huerfano and flicked its controls until they pleased him before he put it in his pocket. Mena came from Stonehenge to Athens for face-time work and never complained, but the travel took time away from her working day. Archer would spare her a trip, have his lunch there, and probably go up into Center for a walkabout, a taste of this and a bite of that, fresh from the fields in Center or the specialty crops grown on Level One.

Doughan tapped his left ear. "Severo's back. He just cleared the airlock."

Archer sat down again.

Helt took another sip of coffee. It was hot, and he hadn't noticed Doughan refilling the cup. He hadn't noticed the pastry in his hand, earlier, and now the coffee. He needed more sleep.

Helt's tired eyes remembered the picture of a Ferrari. Yves Copani, the miner, now had a better shot at staying, at being one of the new colonists whose Earthbound seats would be filled by the Seed Bankers. Copani belonged to Navigation, but he was well down the chain of command from Wesley Doughan.

Helt tried to tamp down his irritation at Doughan. Doughan's stage-set office was part of Helt's resentment, even though Doughan had had nothing to do with its design. The executive decision to get rid of the Seed Bankers was efficient; committee discussions would certainly have lasted well past the last Earthbound shuttle's departure—and any committee would probably have ostracized the Seed Bankers, in the full ancient sense of the word. Banished them; in this case, permanently. Even so, at the moment, Helt didn't like Wesley Doughan at all.

Helt's personal worldview had taken a sudden lurch. He suspected it was a result of recent sexual arousal mixed with a threat to his world as he knew it. What he wanted to do, right now, was to challenge the alpha male who ran Navigation. He told himself to stop it. He would think about the implications in his Copious Free Time. Right.

Doughan pushed the lock buzzer. Severo came in wearing his NSS uniform but something of the Big Black clung to him, a slight temperature difference on his skin, perhaps a few molecules of canned cold air, or maybe just the excitement that could come upon a man when the large spaces inside *Kybele* suddenly fell into the real perspective of time and distance and became tiny and mortal. Something.

"They didn't mind talking to me at all," Severo said. "You know how it is, a crew, how they stick together. They didn't post their reactions to the death when they learned about it, but they seemed pretty standard—irritation, maybe some grief. They were cooperative, but they can't help us with what Ryan did yesterday after he left shift."

"Did they notice anything unusual about him? Any change in behavior in the past days, or weeks?" Helt asked.

"They thought he was more relaxed than usual yesterday. They said he had a week off coming up, and maybe that was why."

"You'll look at that more closely," Helt said.

"I'll talk to each of them, separately, sure," Severo said.

Helt opened his palm screen and entered the info. It was data for the psychiatric autopsy, perhaps.

8

Elena's Story

Helt sensed, rather than heard, Severo nearing the door of the murky dark bunk room in Sysu. It seemed only minutes ago that he'd left the NSS office, left Severo listening to more reports from his officers. They'd been sent out to talk to some of the people who had been in the same video screen with Cash Ryan, anywhere, anytime in the past three years. To narrow the field a little, Jerry and Nadia had put together a partial list of people who might have known Cash Ryan. They were still working on it, unless they'd gone home for a break.

"I'm awake," Helt said.

"Coming in, then."

Helt raised the light level in the room, sat up, and looked under the bunk for his shoes. One was there. He grabbed it so it couldn't get away and looked around for the other one.

"Here." Severo lifted Helt's other shoe from the edge of the sink and handed it over.

"Why was Ryan happy last week?" Helt asked.

Severo leaned back against the edge of the sink. "You've had a nice little nap and it grieves me to have to tell you NSS hasn't found your answer while you zeed away in here."

Helt shifted on the bunk and rested his back against the wall.

"And where did he go after he left work?" Severo asked. "Straight up Athens tower so he could jump off? And how many hours is it going to take for us to find out?"

"Heh. I wish I knew," Helt said. "It takes seventy minutes to get back to Navigation offices from where he was working. At least we know that. And he came in with his work crew. Last they saw him, he had changed into civvies. So there's one hour and maybe twenty minutes when we know he was still alive."

Sleep was a wonderful thing. Helt assessed how his muscles felt and how his bones fit into their sockets. This had been a particularly hard and deep sleep, dreamless, healing. He assessed the state of his teeth and tongue. They could use some help.

"We need to get this nailed as a suicide," Severo said. "That's a quote. You said it."

"And if we don't get a good enough case from Biosystems to call it that?" Surely some more lab was in by now. Helt reached for his interface, but it was in his shirt pocket and his shirt was on the back of the chair in the far corner.

"Then it would be really fine to find Ryan's personal info stash. We don't have to ask it questions," Severo said.

"You said his interface wasn't on him when they stripped his body at the clinic. And you haven't found it in his quarters. And SysSu hasn't located whatever he turns off to keep things private, but everyone has something like that, somewhere. So where is it, Severo?"

"I even had one of the engineer guys scan the walls in his rooms, looking for hidey-holes. All rock, all the way. We're doing a fucking archaeology search from the tower to where we found the guy. Could be Ryan kept his interface in a Faraday pouch, one of your techs said. So we're sifting dirt under that tree. As soon as we know where he was before he hit the ground, we'll look there, too."

"There's spook tech we could be using that I don't like to think about," Helt said. "Surveillance bots. Mini cams. Long ears, Wi-Vi to see through walls. Eyes on everyone who's on the streets, day and night, full-time monitoring of where people are and what they're saying and doing. It's one way, but the monitoring we do, have been doing, has always been with consent."

"You're the IA," Severo said. "What you're talking about will get you what people are doing *now*. What they did last week or before that we can look at if it's recorded. Not if it isn't."

"Maybe suicide stuff is in his interface," Helt said. "Recorded. We can hope. Join me for an early dinner, Severo? I have a meeting coming up after that."

"You'd better clean up before you go meet anyone. I brought you a sandwich. Look at the time." Severo flashed the time onto the wall.

"Ouch," Helt said.

"Is it a woman?" Severo asked.

"Yeah."

"Maybe you should shave." Severo hauled his bulk off the bunk and made for the door.

Helt got up and looked in the mirror. Severo was right. Helt felt like an underachiever adolescent, sleeping in. He hadn't done that for years.

"Thanks, Severo," Helt called down the hall.

"Don't forget your shoes," Severo yelled back.

Helt met Elena at the Athens train station and they walked toward the agora. Elena paid attention to her surroundings, to the paving, to the walls of the buildings carved into the rock on either side of the street, the doorways she passed. She walked as a woman walks on rough ground, as if wary of pebbles that might slip beneath her foot.

When he'd talked to her in Center he'd felt comfortable with himself. Boy meets girl; let's see if we want to meet again. Helt wasn't comfortable now. Boy meets girl again, girl is either wrongly accused of a terrible crime or innocent of it. He had sworn, long ago, to stay away from women with dark secrets, terrible pasts. Maybe Elena wasn't like that at all, but it was possible, because of Ryan's death, to add layers of darkness to Elena's words, her actions, even if none existed. It was possible he wanted to do that.

The street was dark, the dark of a cloudy night in a quiet town. The night lights on the doorways and the ones high overhead were set for that particular effect, and Helt didn't know where to start.

"I don't know where to begin," he said. "I've never seen a woman carve an old lover into precise little pieces before."

At the edge of the open space of Athens agora, she paused, a deer at the edge of the clearing, or a predator looking for game. A street sconce backlit Elena's dark hair with silver, as if she had suddenly aged.

She looked up at Helt and smiled. If he'd been looking to shake her confidence, he hadn't managed it. She had wrapped a red shawl around her shoulders against the chill, like one of those Russian dolls that have other dolls inside them. Matryoshkas? Something like that.

"Let's say I was living with Cash Ryan before he fell," Elena said. She began to walk again, toward The Lab, a combination restaurant and bar. Scattered lighted windows marked rectangles of yellow on the pavement of the Library portico. Muted, the lush sounds of a string quartet drifted past the columns. The Anachronistic String Quartet was in rehearsal; Brahms, Helt thought. Archer Pelham was sawing away on his cello tonight. The music stopped abruptly and then resumed, repeating the same passage.

"I wasn't," Elena said, "but let's say I was. Even so, I would have been dealing with a cadaver, an exercise in pathology, no longer a living thing, and I would have distanced myself from the memories of the man I had known. Who was not there anymore. It's something I know how to do, but so do you."

And that was true enough. Compartmentalize. Do the task. If there is a cost to pay for putting a reaction aside, pay it in the middle of the night. That night, or a night years later, for sooner or later, the bill came due. Helt nodded, but he wasn't sure she saw the gesture.

"I'm the only person on *Kybele* right now who has experience with autopsies in real time," Elena said. "Calloway found my name when he asked the system for an assistant. Should I have refused, because I had known the man in life?"

It was a rhetorical question and he didn't answer it. He waited for two steps.

"We live in small towns now," Elena said. "We'll be living next door to our morticians, our bakers, our butchers. It's not a new pattern and perhaps it will be easier for us than cities were."

The Lab was almost empty. They picked a booth near the bar and sat down. Elena slipped the shawl from her shoulders, and the curve at the base of her throat was lovely and her skin was flawless and must feel like silk. Helt wanted to rest the palm of his hand on her throat, to see the contrast between that shade of creamy tan and his own pale hide.

Elena ordered brandy. So did Helt.

When it came, she cupped the big snifter in both hands to warm it and stared into the liquid as if it were a mirror.

"Are you tired?" Helt asked.

"Yes. I'm tired and I'm worried."

She looked up from her drink. The booth was dim, only a candle burning in a red glass to light it. Her eyes, in this light, were the color of clear Baltic amber and a tiny reflected flame burned in each of them. She didn't look worried. She looked relaxed, calm, tolerant. She looked as if she wondered if Helt would do a good interview. "Did you sleep last night, Helt Borresen?" she asked.

"Some. In the bunkroom in the office. And I napped there just before I came to meet you." Helt reminded himself to be cautious, to guard himself against liking her too much. He should be looking at this woman as someone who might be trying to deceive him, an actress using very effective tools to distract him; her eyes, her graceful hands, her apparent honesty. Helt pushed his brandy aside, unrolled his screen, and stiffened it. "You know I'm going to ask questions. Shall we begin?"

Elena made a space for her own screen on the table and read the file he sent to her. "Unexpected death. Mena didn't say suicide, or murder, or accident. Our leaders are cautious."

She scrolled down until she found the section with her name on it. "So that's how you found the connection," she said. "We were at the same college. You found split restaurant charges and then, later, rent charges from the same apartment address. Yes, we lived together for a short time during my last semester at MIT."

"Roomies or lovers?" Helt asked.

"Lovers," Elena said. She leaned back against the padded fake leather of the booth and looked directly, calmly, at Helt's face. He had known this, and he didn't want to know it. She was so cold, this woman. His sudden fear made him want to gasp.

She'd said he knew how to compartmentalize. He had to prove that, right now, right here.

"Tell me what you knew of him," Helt said. "Tell me things the records won't show."

"For the record," Elena said.

"Yes. If this was a jump, a suicide, an accident, so be it. But I don't want to find out it was a murder and find that the perp is still on this ship after that last shuttle leaves."

"The perp. You've been reading protocols, or genre mysteries."

"Yes. Protocols say that kin murders kin, and as a prior lover, you're kin. Sort of."

"Do I need someone here from Legal?"

"If you want. I'm recording."

"I don't want anyone from Legal."

"I'm not a cop. I'm the Incident Analyst, and because this death was definitely an incident and, as Mena said, unexpected, my job is to find out how and why it happened. So you're on the record. Be careful."

"I'll be careful. For the record, Cash Ryan has been a ghost to me since I left MIT," Elena said. "I knew he was hired for some engineering work early on. I knew he was gone before I came up here. I saw his name show up three years ago but I ignored it because he was on a three-year contract. He would finish his work and leave. I'd be staying."

"Would you have left *Kybele* if you thought Cash Ryan would be a colonist on her?" Helt asked.

She shook her head. "Absolutely not. I wanted . . . it was my life, dreaming of this place. My only goal. Everything I've ever done was done for this." She looked at the stone ceiling as if she saw through it to the hollow heart of *Kybele* above them.

Helt couldn't stop watching her hands, the way her fingers cupped the brandy snifter as if it were infinitely precious, something to be held safe, protected from harm.

"You didn't hate him enough to give this up," Helt said.

"Hate him? That's your phrase, Helt Borresen, not mine. When he came up here, I found him highly avoidable, and I avoided him. But I wasn't going to give up a dream because of that. A little social discomfort, a little stepping out of the way, would not cause me to lose the chance to help shape this tiny world and go to another one." She smiled into her brandy snifter. "Every day, I wake surprised to find I'm not dreaming this, that the dream didn't vanish while I slept. We're so lucky, we dreamers, so immeasurably lucky."

She looked up. Helt smiled at her. To spend life here meant living a dream, and there was no one on this ship who did not share some version of that dream. A wonderful thing, but dreamers can be dangerous. "Yes. We're lucky." And I have a job to do, Helt reminded himself, although he did not want to believe this woman capable of murder. He wanted the death to have never happened. He wanted to know, to understand, the dreams of a woman who was literally shaping life for Biosystems. Was she lonely? Did she have a lover now? Would she be as careful with Helt as she was with that glass? He didn't ask any of those things.

"You've been here ten years."

"I've been here ten years. I didn't know Cash was on board again until about three years ago when I saw him in Center. I ran for my lab and closed the door."

"Did he see you?"

"I don't think so."

"Did he ever try to contact you?"

"No. He didn't bother me. He didn't try to renew our relationship. But you know that, if you looked for times and places where Elena Maury and Cash Ryan were in the same place at the same time on this ship."

He was still looking. He'd found none as yet. "Did that seem odd to you? Not even a chance meeting? Not even a 'Hi, how are you?' Did that surprise you?"

"You're good," Elena said.

She knew techniques for psychiatric interviews as well as Helt did. But the techniques work, and if Helt couldn't hack clients who were intellectual peers, or brighter than he was, he had been in the wrong job for a long, long time.

"No, it didn't surprise me. I told you, I had decided having one weird dude on this ship as a short-timer was not going to spoil my days. And the Cash Ryan I knew years ago was one weird dude."

"From what I've found so far, he didn't have close friends," Helt said. "He had coworkers. But he tested close enough to be socially acceptable to get a job here. You were lovers. Why? Will you tell me?"

"Because it may help lay the ghost? That's what the post-trauma protocols say. Talk it through." Elena took a generous mouthful of brandy and swallowed it. "Okay."

Helt motioned to the bartender and he brought refills for both of them.

"MIT. Cambridge," she said. "I noticed him because we hung in the same places but we didn't get together until my senior year. Just knew who he was. Pretty curls, an intent look, and he talked with his hands. I'm rambling. Is that what you want me to do?"

She looked amused, as if she had reviewed the strategies for the game they were playing before she came here. Probably she had.

"Yes. Elena, the man is dead. Once we know why he's dead, all of us can get back to the dream. Until then, dead or not, he's in our way. Please, ramble."

"It was the slam poetry that suckered me in."

Her smile brought out her cheekbones beautifully. She didn't have dimples. Helt decided it didn't matter.

He wondered briefly if he should let her know how intently SysSu had looked for a connection between Elena and Cash, and decided to go for full disclosure. "We found a line or two. The ITs in SysSu found it, I mean. Was he really a poet?"

"Ah, even better than that, a stealth poet. So they found his net name for those years. Penny Dreadful, he called himself. He did the occasional guitar gig, but he never read at the slams. Just watched, intent, motionless, with a look of . . . frustrated pain? Something like that. More like he was looking at aliens and was lonely because he couldn't communicate with them. His face made me think of . . . Poe, perhaps. But he was healthier, at least physically. Some sort of Byronic throwback.

"Cambridge, and the club was a dark cave, not off Harvard Square but in a quiet rundown area that had been a working class district. When it rained, when the air was wet, you got whiffs of ancient sweat and beer outgassing from the brick walls. Not that there wasn't plenty of new sweat and new beer as an overlay."

Helt's own student bar had not been like that at all. He saw, so clearly, polished white pine walls, a girl's fingers stroking the stem of a glass of colorless wine. Kirsten. Her name came to him now, and the memory of her hair, the color of ripe wheat, her tense shoulders, her straight back as she walked away.

Yes, it had hurt.

"The poetry was full of passion and political outrage and poignant reactions to leaves, waves, and the open beaks of poisoned birds. Like that. And we were all young and brilliant, of course, and no one had ever loved or suffered as we loved and suffered.

"Throw in pheromones, and that Cash could really play that guitar."

Even if pheromones are not as noticeable to humans as they are to, say, ants, Helt believed in their efficacy. The invisible scents floating around the red glass bowl of the candle on the table made him believe that the promise of that first meeting with Elena, out in Center, would survive the rude statement Cash Ryan had made with his death, whatever it had been meant to say. But he couldn't love her and then find out she was a murderess. He wouldn't.

"Set and setting count in love affairs," Elena said. She paused, smiling again.

"They do," Helt said.

"And I suffer from an unworthy attraction to tall, silent men."

Tall and silent when he could be, Helt suffered a momentary fear Elena would find some of his old poetry someday. Can't hide. But she would have a hell of a time getting him to admit what his net name had been in those years.

"I said Cash Ryan was quiet, and he was. There's a time, in talking, when the conversations wander toward parents, high school crushes, old girlfriends. I got answers to direct questions, but after a time I noticed that there were never any calls home or messages from Mom, or from old friends. That every reference to family was oblique, and the subject got changed fast.

"There were never any plans about the future, either. I wasn't looking for marriage, at least not on a conscious level. There were shared daydreams, of course. How life would be on *Kybele.* Whether we would both make it. I was short-listed already; Cash never actually said he was but the implication was there.

"And of course he wasn't on the colonist short list. I found that out after I had started graduate work at Stanford."

"His doctorate is from MIT," Helt said.

"I was accepted at both places. Cash wasn't. He decided I couldn't leave him. I decided I could. I did."

"Was he abusive?" Helt asked.

Elena developed an intense interest in her brandy snifter. She set it down with measured deliberation.

"If you require physical violence as a parameter for abuse, no. If you're looking for emotional blackmail on the level of 'I'll kill myself if you leave me,' no."

"You just tensed up. I don't think you're lying. Are you protecting him?"

Elena looked for eye contact with Helt, and got it.

"No. I'm not protecting him. I'm talking to you, Helt Borresen, and I'm telling you everything I know. Pay attention."

Held as motionless as a stalked rabbit by the depths of her amber eyes, Helt could only nod.

"He was suspicious. If I said I was at the lab, he would call the lab to make sure I wasn't out screwing somebody else. He was curious about my sexual history and assumed every friendship I had, man, woman, or critter, was for sex. I'm making this sound blatant but he was subtle in his insinuations. It's not always words; body language and speech patterns can make you squirm."

Helt was reading hers as best he could. She was a little more rigid than she had been at first, but not much. She used standard media English, but there was that tiny hesitation before some of her words, that hint of indrawn breath. He'd never heard anyone do that and he couldn't place where it came from. He was breathing her air, breathing deeply to catch her scent and his own, and his hindbrain liked the mix. A lot.

"He left sometimes and didn't post anything anywhere that I could find, and didn't answer his interface. Sometimes for hours. Once or twice for days. I began to think he was dealing, or part of a Mafia family, or something.

"But everything was subtle. I said that. I never found any specific thing about him that I could say, definitely, This is wrong, illegal, immoral. But he made me uneasy, and I left.

"We parted friends, technically speaking. I had his offer to come to me if I needed him. And I went off to Stanford and I never saw him again."

"Until three years ago."

"Yes."

"Do you—from what you remember of him—do you think he would have committed suicide?"

"No. Never. Not the man—the boy—I never really knew."

"Could he have become a killer?"

Elena pulled her shawl a little closer around her shoulders. "Because every suicide contains at least two things, both the killing of the self and the murder, in some magical way, of an other? I don't know. I think the construct I've made in my mind, my imagined Cash Ryan, could kill someone who got in his way."

Sociopaths, make that psychopaths, could kill and never look back, except to see if they've been found out. That's what the books said. Helt suppressed a shiver.

"But I don't know about his life, not before, not after he charmed me for a while. I don't know, Helt Borresen. Do you think people can change? Change in fundamental ways?"

"I don't know," Helt said.

"Neither do I.

But she did. And so did he. Injuries change people. An injury had changed his mother in terrible ways.

Helt looked at the woman who sat across the table, someone new in his life, someone who knew a hell of a lot about nature and nurture, about genetic manipulations and therapies for warped brains and bodies. She had access to treatments that worked now and could be redesigned to work better. On *Kybele*, in a real way, children, human children, could be, had to be, designed to thrive here. Helt felt the hairs on the back of his neck tingle. "Elena vets every embryo," Mena had said. That meant she discarded the ones that didn't meet her standards.

Elena sighed. The curve of her breasts rose and fell. Her skin was beautiful, her hair, the shape of her smooth arms, the contours of solid muscle under her creamy skin. Her amazing hands were hypnotic in their deliberate grace; she pushed buttons that Helt had never known he had. She wakened longings for a time and place, a woman, that somewhere, in some dream or memory, he must have known. She was terribly, achingly familiar, and she was a stranger.

Helt wanted to know her, mind, body and bone, and he knew, in some part of his brain that analyzed and assessed and would not leave him alone, ever, that he would never know her at all. Never, really, understand anyone. At all.

Helt reached for his screen, collapsed it, and put it in his pocket. "Okay. It's enough. Thank you."

"Is that it? Am I interviewed?" Elena asked.

"For now. For tonight. Would you like another brandy? I'm buying."

"Yes. But not tonight."

So Helt walked her to the train station.

"No one has come to the clinic to ask about Cash Ryan. No one is planning a memorial service for him," Elena said.

"I know," Helt said.

The doors opened and the train told her to watch her step.

"What name did you use for your poetry?" Elena asked.

"I didn't tell you I wrote any. Am I that easy to read?"

"Yes."

"I'll have to know you much, much better before I tell you that," Helt said.

She smiled and sank into the padded upholstery of the seat closest to the door.

How, why were his responses to this woman so strong? Had he been lonelier than he knew? It was the damned death, perhaps only that, a major glitch that had interrupted plans for a departure, but he couldn't stop it. When the ship moved out, it would mark paid to any doubts about the life he'd been so busy choosing all these years. He would feel the big engines fire up to move them out; every human on board would feel them, every animal, probably even every fish. He would feel in his flesh the reality that there was no turning back, no retreat to Earth, ever. There would be no way to test another set of options in the list of What I Want to Be When I Grow Up.

So he wanted retreat, shelter, the safe haven that can seem real for a time in a bed where someone else breathes beside you. And he had just met a remarkable someone. And she was capable of murder. Helt had no doubt about that at all.

Helt watched the cars slide out of his visual field, traveling toward Petra, toward bed, rest, solitude, sleep. He could go home. He could get his laundry out of the bunkroom at SysSu and then go home. It seemed like a lot of bother. When half a block of walking was too much work, it was time to go to bed.

"Helt?" Mena's voice asked his pocket.

"I'm here," Helt said, through a yawn he had in no way planned. He was still standing on the stone floor of the train station platform and his feet were getting cold. Helt hauled his interface out of his pocket and blinked at Mena, apparently in Stonehenge, apparently wide awake.

"Cash Ryan was drugged. There was scope-and-speed in his bloodstream and in his stomach when he died."

"What does that mean?"

"It means—it means he took some stuff or someone gave it to him, and it means we aren't going to talk about it until morning. You look like hell."

The next train slowed. Its door opened on an empty car. Taking drugs didn't mean Ryan hadn't played "jump off a tower and see if you live." Really, it didn't. Helt wasn't really sleep deprived. Three hours last night, two this afternoon, that's five. It should have been enough.

Ryan had been drugged when he died. Damn. Oh, damn.

"Thank you, Mena."

"Good night, Helt," Mena said.

9

Last Meal

A ladder, legs, a feminine rear in jeans with a knot of canvas tied at its waist, and from there on up Mena was hidden by the leaves of an apple tree.

"That you up there?" Helt asked, although he knew the curve of Mena's ass and could have identified it in a lineup. Or he thought he could, anyway. He wondered if anyone had tried to ID people that way and wondered if it might be more accurate than looking at a row of faces.

"Just a few more and I'll come down," Mena said.

Uh-huh. She would pick every apple she could reach without tipping over backward.

His neck would get tired if he just stood there squinting up at the sun, so he looked for windfall on the ground. He shuffled an array of leaves and twigs with his foot and found a couple of brown saggy apples whose intact parts were red and green.

"What are these?" Helt asked.

"McIntosh. Do you want one?" Mena asked. She shifted on the ladder and Helt saw that the knot at her back was attached to an apple picker's apron, a heavy thing bulging with picked fruit, a botanic pregnancy of sorts.

"Sure."

He caught the tossed fruit, polished it on his sleeve, and bit in. The apple was sweeter than he expected and juicy, a New England autumn in one bite. He remembered the glory of sugar maple leaves in October, red oak and white oak in full color, white trunks of birch bright against the green-black of pine and hemlock, colors almost painfully vibrant in the muted brightness of a south-traveling autumn sun. He had scraped his knee that day, scrabbling in rattling leaves in colors he had never seen before, on a long-forgotten journey with his father. His blood had been no more red than a maple leaf beside him and he had not cried.

His mother was nearby, in that memory. In that memory, he knew she would have been proud of him. It was before a shard of granite slammed into her brain and left her unable to love him.

Something large, warm, and hairy nudged Helt's shoulder. It smelled like horse, and he liked the smell of horse.

It was not a tall horse, but its eye was as big as an egg and right next to his ear. It had the damnedest mane, pale at the base and tipped with black, clipped neatly into ridges like a dragon's crest. It was a fjord horse, a small draft horse or a big pony, depending on how you felt about the appropriate size for horses.

"Who's this?" Helt asked. He raised his apple to shoulder height. The horse lipped it politely and then lifted it away from his palm. The orchard was so quiet that the breaking of the apple sounded like a pistol shot. After some determined crunching, the horse explored Helt's palm with its lips and, finding nothing but a little apple juice, gave an exasperated *whuff.*

"Eple. That's her name." Mena backed down the ladder. Eple's long, cream-colored back brushed Helt's arm as the horse moved toward Mena's apron.

Mena tugged at her apron strings.

"Could you help me with this?"

"Sure," Helt said. The knot came loose with a few tugs. Helt took the apron from her. It didn't hurt as much to be close to her as it had once. Helt chided himself for being fickle. A new woman was taking away old pain, unless she was going to cause more.

The apron strings made a handy strap, so he slung the weight over his shoulder. Mena picked an apple off the top of the batch. The horse noticed this.

"A bruised one, just for you." Mena fed the mare an apple. "No more, pretty one. Enough. Come with us."

Mena led horse and human to a gate, not the one Helt had entered by, which was people-sized, but a bigger one. Beyond it, in the great shallow bowl of *Kybele*'s croplands, black plowed fields were furred with the first sprigs of winter wheat. In a circle of vivid green winter rye, the monoliths of Stonehenge guarded their bed of parent stone. The remnants of this morning's mist blurred the horizon.

Someone whistled and Eple trotted toward the sound, her shod hoofs almost silent on the black gravel of the road. Her back was almost white in the sun and then shadows from the latticework of the pillars of Stonehenge tower, high above her, marked it with stripes. Helt saw a human leading a matching horse, far enough in the distance to seem that the road was climbing. Mena and Helt turned the other way, toward Stonehenge tower. A cluster of low buildings and tall barns huddled close to the central shaft and its elevator.

"Why are you breeding fjord horses?" Helt asked. "To get a harvest in if the power goes out?"

"We have more people than horses," Mena said. "But if I ran out of willing human labor, sure." Mena gave very literal answers to questions, sometimes, but then, she was used to people whose knowledge of farming was all theory and no reality. "Eple and her partner Eikenøtt are breeding stock; the breed is thousands of years old and a good size for this climate. They live a good life, those two, and their trainer has willing apprentices."

"For down the line."

"Down the line." Mena frowned. "They are test subjects, bless them; big, long-lived vertebrates—they can live twenty or more years—good candidates for testing radiation damage therapies. So far, so good; they are six years old and healthy, and we have harvested a few embryos."

A breeze came up, cool air from the poles moving down beneath the sunny air rising over the sun-warmed fields. To say that the Biosystems Headquarters complex in Center was unassuming was an understatement. Mena's office was in a low building that connected a lab complex to a barn. The barn was a well-kept barn, but if you closed your eyes in Mena's office you could get an unmistakable whiff of hay and manure.

"May I have the apples?" Mena asked.

"Sure." Helt stuffed a couple of them in the pocket of his jacket. "Carrier fee."

Mena smiled at him and carried her apron through the lab-side door. When she came back she closed her office door and braced her shoulders against it, her hands behind her.

"This is what I know about the scope-and-speed in Ryan's blood. The levels were high but not toxic; scopolamine ran 400 picograms per mil; dextroamphetamine 40 nanograms per ml; that's in high therapeutic range. Scope-and-speed is an old mix for motion sickness and it's in Medical's formulary. Scopolamine for nausea plus dextroamphetamine for alertness is the original formula. You should talk to Elena or Calloway about their experiences with the drug if they've used it, or seen it used. I haven't."

"Why didn't you send me to *them* first, Mena?"

"Because Elena is analyzing the contents of Ryan's stomach this morning, and I want you to be here. There are so many possibilities—" She was facing him, but her eyes looked through him or past him, focused on grim scenarios he couldn't see, histories he didn't know. A breath, and she returned to the present, to the now.

"Let's take the stairs," she said.

He didn't want to see a stomach on a plate, or what was in it. He wanted to follow Eple up the road and play in sunlight, at least for an hour or two.

The ceiling of the Level One corridor was four stories above their heads, this near the tower and the elevator. The plan was to build the Stonehenge complex from the top down, but for now, one-story construction, entered from corridor level, served for the labs and the few dwellings. The four-story ceilings over the crops that grew behind closed doors, far down the corridor, gave plenty of height even for fair-sized trees.

Elena's lab was cut into the rock of Level One, close to the elevator, close to the stairs. There was no stomach on a plate to make Helt feel squeamish, but there was a screen on the wall where small objects floated in a clear yellowish fluid, pushed around by a giant, blunt probe.

It was actually quite tiny, a needle with a sharp point. Elena sat bent over a binocular microscope, guiding the probe through a thin layer of liquid on a glass slide. She lifted her head and pushed her chair back from the lab table. The projection of fluid on the wall screen continued to tremble, Brownian motion setting up tiny currents that nudged its contents from one place to another.

A greeting is an assessment. Elena looked at Mena first and then at Helt, her attention on each of them in turn. Everyone does this, Helt knew; everyone gauges the status of someone who comes near, to make a guess if they friend or foe, to see if they are happy or angry, if they are in a mood to hug or to hit. But because he knew Elena was a trained physician, as well as a geneticist, he felt the texture of his skin and the little veins in the whites of his eyes and the ease of his breathing had been thoroughly evaluated.

His own assessment was that Elena looked rested this morning, and that her amber eyes were bright and her skin, in the lab's light, was a color he couldn't name, but it looked like satin and it was beautiful. There was a hint of golden-pink color under the pale tan of her face. The color was similar to the olive of Mena's Greek Mediterranean skin, but it was a shade or two lighter and, well, younger. He deliberately did not look at Mena, did not want to analyze the effects of ten years' difference between her skin and Elena's. He didn't want to be rude.

"Good morning," Elena said, and she offered her visitors a nod of approval. Helt felt he had passed his physical. "Would you care to sit down? I have another chair here somewhere."

Mena reached for a chair Helt hadn't noticed at the table behind them, rolled it over and motioned for Helt to sit. Elena stepped back and leaned against the edge of the table where she'd been working. She wore a lab coat, a soft, faded red one, and Helt admired the way it tightened over the slight indentation where hip met table. Not too much flesh, obviously well toned, but soft enough to dent.

Mena took the chair Elena vacated. "I don't think he liked veggies, Mena," Elena said. "I didn't find carrots or spinach floating around." Mena had a tense musculature, as always, but Helt thought he sensed a slight lessening of tension in the muscles of her back.

The screen blinked abruptly and the fluid was replaced by a list of names and levels. "Here's what we have so far from the liquid analysis. He ate a few fruits; there's apricot and grape residue. The grapes probably weren't wine; there are no wood tannins. Probably raisins."

"Or really cheap jug wine," Helt said, to make Mena bristle. Mena had strong feelings about good wines.

"Sheep protein, yeast, and wheat, so probably lamb and bread. There's turmeric, it would look bright yellow in a dish. Some other spices, cardamom, cinnamon, cumin . . .

"And the alcohol he drank is certainly there. It was probably gin; there are some juniper oils. And then there's scopolamine and dexedrine. My best estimate is that he ate three or four hours before he was found."

"That's as close as you can get?" Helt asked.

"I think so," Elena said. "There are so many variables. If there's a lot of fat in a meal, it stays in the stomach longer. Alcohol is absorbed through the stomach lining itself so the concentrations often match blood levels pretty closely. Ryan's did. The scope-and-speed would have speeded up the gastric emptying reflex, but stress would have slowed it down. Stress, anxiety, fear; they change everything."

Mena seemed lost in reading the wall screen.

"Mena. Something about carrots worries you. What is it?" Helt asked.

"I was thinking about vegetable residue, not carrots," Mena said. "The substrates—the basic compounds—of amphetamines and scopolamine come from plants. Scopolamine is a belladonna alkaloid. Belladonna is a plant, but the compound can be grown in many plants. I didn't think this Ryan person would have chewed raw Datura or made himself a toxic dose of Mormon tea to get his speed. If he had, he would probably have vomited and been too sick to jump off a chair, much less a tower. But I had to wonder if someone is growing those plants, or others, for a private lab. Not that it's illegal, but nobody's applied for a license yet."

"And if they do, *Kybele* wants the tax revenue," Helt said.

"Let me run some signatures," Elena said. She suctioned some fluid from a jar into little vials, set them in a cabinet thing, and entered some parameters.

Those hands again. Helt couldn't stop watching them. So beautiful, so sure. Mena didn't look at her or at Helt; she searched screens while she waited, looking for?

"There aren't any signature proteins for Datura or Ephedra," Elena said. "His drugs were purified to at least a kitchen-lab level."

"And the compound was dexedrine, not meth," Mena said. "Meth is easier to cook, so it shows up in homemade drugs. So he took drugs because he wanted to. Or he was drugged by someone else."

Jim Tulloch ran recreational drug assays on his patients if he thought it might be helpful to them. The common ones were legal, licensed, quality checked, and available over the counter, although routine drug assays were part of the requirements for any job on ship that required motor skills. Don't work when you're stoned was an old tradition, and a sound one. *Kybele* enforced it. The tradition was an old one.

"Now we know that much," Helt said. "It doesn't help, though. And we know he managed to jump off Athens tower, with or without assistance from someone else. That's what we know." It wasn't enough. The suicide versus murder question remained unanswered.

"I think it's safe to say the drugs should not have killed him and that the fall did," Elena said. "Did Severo find my fingerprints up there, Helt? Or his?"

Helt didn't want to tell her.

"Yours are," Mena said. "So are traces of lots of other people. Severo's tech is still sorting."

Ryan's fingerprints were remarkably absent. Helt knew Mena knew it.

Were there gloves in Ryan's clothing list? Helt wished he had a screen inside his eyes, so that he could blink and look, right now.

"And I'm still a murder suspect," Elena said. "I don't like the feeling." Her eyes showed hurt and an instant's bewilderment.

Helt rolled his chair closer to Elena and turned it so he could face her. "My dear Dr. Maury, I'm a murder suspect, too. So is Mena. What sort of luck put you on Athens tower then, anyway?"

She looked closely at his face, intent on reading something from his expression, or maybe just looking at his nose or his eyebrows. "I was up there late because I was at work late because I was noodling around with a gene sequence in an arctic char. That's a fish."

Helt had eaten a few of them. They were pink-fleshed, but not salmon. He liked salmon better. Neither would be part of his future, unless enough people requested them and aquaculture could get some good strains adapted.

"But I remembered it was time to check tower flora, so I went up to smack Petri dishes against the walls and the floor, to see which little bacteria and fungi have managed to colonize the towers. We follow that over time."

"Is there anything interesting in the batch?" Helt asked.

"I don't know yet. The process isn't that rapid. Things reproduce at their own pace. Some microcritters, fungi, for instance, can take weeks or even months to grow in culture media."

"But you logged your samples into the lab," Helt said.

"I did."

"Time and date."

"Yes."

Which would be a great alibi, if anyone could prove she didn't have the samples stashed, ready to log in at a convenient time. But it would have been weird if she had planned and executed a murder and then managed to get herself on camera in order to be the only human in camera proximity to the victim shortly after he died.

"Mena, are you covered for the hour?" Helt asked.

She shook her head. "I was at home, but I have no proof of it. The reports from NSS says there's a lot of time to cover before Ryan's death."

"There is. Cash Ryan left his shift at 1500. No one reports seeing him after that until the SysSu techs found his body at 2044. Severo and his crew are doing everything they can to fill in those five hours—no, only a long three, because it takes ninety minutes to get back to Nav offices and his work team was with him—but we don't know yet where Cash Ryan was after that, or who knew him; don't know anyone who even saw him after he left work. We've scheduled a psychiatric autopsy, but Jim—Dr. Tulloch—tells me he can't do a good one unless he has more personal data, more narratives, for the guy."

"I have none to offer you about his life on *Kybele*, because he never tried to approach me. Perhaps that's odd in itself," Elena said.

She could be lying. Helt, you idiot, you know she could be lying and you don't want to believe it.

"But you didn't approach him, either."

"No. I don't test well on social skills. I didn't really want to talk to him and I didn't want to think about how I would keep him at a distance if I did."

Helt was not finding her social skills to be inadequate in any way. The name for that fine blend of gold and red in her cheeks came to him. It was apricot. He wanted to see if it deepened when she blushed, or ran, or became aroused in other ways. He wanted to know her. He didn't want her to be someone he'd met briefly, and then sent away forever.

The golden apples of the sun were apricots, someone had said. There were apricots in Cash Ryan's last meal. Helt thought he knew where he might have eaten them.

Helt got up and pushed his chair under the table beside Elena. "I'm going to be late to meet Severo if I don't get out of here. I don't know if this is an aha moment, but I think I want to see a man about an apricot first."

"Is it important?" Elena asked.

"I hope so."

"It's a hunch, then. Good luck, Helt," Mena said.

10

Cold Equations

Severo, pacing the platform at the Athens station, wore his NSS coveralls. He looked ready for inspection or ready to inspect anyone or anything. Helt straightened his shoulders as if to snap him a salute, realized what he was doing, and grinned.

"How were the ladies?" Severo asked.

"Fine. All three of them were just fine." Helt reached into his pocket for an apple and handed one to Severo, and then he took off his windbreaker. Athens felt too warm after the cool morning of Center.

"Three?"

"One's a horse."

"A horse. You like horses?"

Helt thought about the question as he strolled with Severo toward the agora, thought about the twelve-year-old boy he had been, invincible and fearless until he hit the ground after an incident involving a gelding, a breeze, a blowing plastic bag, and a steep trail. His left hip sent him a slight twinge to say it still remembered.

"Yeah. I do."

"You'll like this, too. While you were out—"

"On business—"

"While you were out apple-picking, we cleared twelve minutes of your time during the SM hour. You're on the surveillance camera at the Frontier Diner. An omelet and a salad, that's healthy, but you could have had a burger with green chile fries."

Helt didn't argue about green chile. It was futile. He liked green chile, but Severo didn't think he ate enough of it.

"Twelve minutes, eh? I think I have time and date markers in my SysSu interface from then on."

"Yeah, you do. I've looked at them myself, and so has Doughan. You're clear, but Doughan wants to know what your thing is with the Ferraris."

"None of his damned business," Helt said. "Severo, have you talked to Venkie?"

"The empanada guy? About Cash Ryan? No."

"It's worth a try."

Severo and Helt walked toward Venkie's kiosk. It looked deserted at this midmorning hour. The scent of spices and frying bread reached out to them as they bellied up to the counter. If there was a culture on the world spinning below that did not fry bread dough in hot fat and eat it with pleasure, Helt had never heard of it. This little kiosk smelled wonderful.

The proprietor was turning bell peppers into a pile of perfect little green dice with a very large cleaver. Cleaver in hand, Venkat Raghava met them at the counter, and nodded first to Helt and then to Severo. Venkie was dark, and lean, and taller than Helt. Helt was tall, and noticed when he was looking up at someone rather than down. He was definitely looking up at Venkie.

"I have food, if you wish. I regret that I am low on information, however, Chief Mares," Venkie said. "Your officer Evans has exhausted my supply."

"Evans. She had some questions, did she? I suppose she took your security camera records for review," Severo said.

"She did. Even though everyone its eye has seen is with her, she continued her questions. She will give them back?" he asked Severo.

"She will."

"I am relieved. There are some interesting accents on the voices in that record."

"What's for lunch today?" Severo asked.

"Samosas. Vegan or chicken?"

"Chicken." Samosas, empanadas, pasties, Severo didn't seem to mind what they were called. "I'll buy Helt's, too." Severo pressed his thumb against the pay screen.

"You, sir?" Venkie asked.

"Chicken," Helt said.

Venkie put the cleaver down on his worktable and retrieved two very fresh samosas from a hot box, triangles of pastry big enough to fill a man's palm, nestled in folded paper triangles.

"Thank you. We haven't met, I think. I'm Helt Borresen, from Systems Support."

"Venkat Raghava. A pleasure, sir."

"Mrrph," Helt said, his mouth full of samosa. "Thank you. This is very good. I haven't tried lunch here. I've had the breakfast ones, though, and I really like them."

"I am not a purist in many ways. The addition of chocolate to a sweet eaten for breakfast is not traditional to the cuisine on which my foods are based, but people like them that way," Venkie said.

Helt munched a mouthful of gently browned onions, sweet raisins, spices, and chicken, rich and meaty. He looked at the contents of the pastry crust and spied something orange. "Apricots?" he asked.

"No. Mango, but it is not fully ripe, so it has a firm texture. I use dried apricots in the ones I make with lamb. They add a bit of acidity to counteract the richness of the meat."

"So Evans asked if you knew Cash Ryan," Severo said.

"She did."

"There's so much to fill in about his death," Helt said. "Biosystems found out, this morning, that he ate lamb and apricots and spices on the day of his death."

Venkie's eyes narrowed and he moved away from Severo, a millimeter of withdrawal quickly arrested. "Did he? Are you thinking I provided his last meal?"

"Perhaps," Helt said.

"If so, I am distressed." Venkie stepped back from the counter, cupped his hands together and stared at them.

His utter stillness made Helt wonder if he should offer some sort of reassurance, but he wasn't sure what he would say.

Venkie dropped his hands. "Perhaps I should take it as a gift to this Cash Ryan, from me, a gift someone gave him on my behalf. I will do that. Three days ago, I made lamb samosas then, yes. But Dr. Ryan did not come here on that day."

"Evans asked you about that," Severo said.

"Yes. Repeatedly. The officer—Evans—showed me a picture of Dr. Ryan's face. I did not recognize him. She put him in a Navigation suit, and I still could not be sure. She found a video of him walking, and then, yes, I knew him to be someone who has come to my kiosk."

"You knew his walk?" Helt asked.

"Not until I saw him walking away," Venkie said.

"Was there anything special about the way he walked?"

"No. But then I knew I had seen him, in his Navigation coveralls, yes. The parts came together? Yes.

"People live here in Athens, they walk by on their way to the train, they go to Navigation offices, engineering, to Stonehenge to work growing mangoes or almonds, wherever they go, and they pass by here. This Ryan man wasn't a talker, and that's really all I know about him. He came here, bought his food, and went away."

"You picked this location because it's a good place to sell food?" Helt asked.

"No. I sell food here because it's a good place for people to walk by."

"Your degrees are in linguistics, Dr. Raghava," Helt said.

"Yes. The material! To record the beginnings of a unique language that will develop in centuries of isolation! There are little shifts in intonation, already, that are not present in the river of public speech that flows up from Earth. Vowels are shifting in their placement in the mouth. For the A, some hays have changed to hahs, but also the consonants, b, v. They are already shifting. And word usages are changing rapidly, how we speak of direction, of distance. Also we, here, are appropriating words from different languages at a remarkably rapid rate. There are so many accents, so many languages, all becoming one. So soon!"

Venkie's face, in the shadow of the awning, glowed with the delight of the chase, with the excitement of evidence supporting theory.

"Will we become incomprehensible to Earth?" Helt asked.

"Except in written words, yes, almost certainly. Helt Borresen, humans are often incomprehensible to one another, even when we share the same language. That has been one of our tragedies, I think."

To put it mildly. "I would very much like to discuss tragedies with you, Dr. Raghava, and comedies as well. I would say over a drink, but you might not be a drinker."

"Of course I am not a drinker, but I enjoy comparing the different flavors of Dr. Kanakaredes's explorations in the fermentation of varietal grapes. I look forward to such a conversation."

"As do I. Do you know everyone on this ship?" Helt asked.

"Not yet. Many of them, not well. I am, in my way, a miner. I mine my customers for narratives. For speech patterns. I admit it. It is, perhaps, devious of me. I have made it my goal to become acquainted with as many people as possible," Venkie said.

"You're also an excellent cook. Chef."

Severo nodded agreement and stepped away from the kiosk.

"Thank you," Venkie said.

Severo turned to scout the agora for safety and threat. Helt nodded to Venkie and caught up with Severo on the way toward SysSu headquarters. Students and shoppers glanced at Severo's NSS uniform and responded, however minimally, in their various ways. Some glanced at him and then avoided eye contact. Some looked through him as if he didn't exist. A few people caught his eye and smiled.

One was a dark-haired woman about the same height as Elena, a little less muscular. "Severo, could Elena Maury have picked Ryan up and thrown him over the guardrail?" Helt asked.

Severo frowned. "I dunno. I mean, I haven't tested it. What are you thinking, IA? That we should ask her to try? You crazy? If she did it, she could fake that she couldn't."

"Sure. I'm crazy. But I'd still like to know."

Helt had planted the idea and he waited for Severo to decide what to do about it. It was police work; it was Severo's turf, and Helt's job was to use what NSS found, not to direct what they looked for, unless it was something he needed to do. But Helt was going to stage a reenactment of what might have happened on that tower, if Severo didn't.

Helt glanced back across the agora. Five people had lined up at Venkie's counter by the time Helt and Severo entered the SysSu office building.

"So someone else bought Ryan's lunch for him," Helt said. "Or . . ."

"Or he had Venkie's food in his fridge," Severo said.

"Yeah. I'll add the info to my lists, anyway." Helt led Severo through SysSu and into Nadia's office. Nadia's office had become Jerry's and Nadia's office, at least for work on the "unexpected death" of Cash Ryan. A curve of tables and several more workstations had been added, all with good views of the wall screen, divided at the moment into columns.

TIMELINE | AUTOPSY | PSYCHIATRIC AUTOPSY |CONTACTS | ALIBIED PERSONNEL

Cash's last samosa went into place on Day One of the timeline, and the information was cross-referenced under Autopsy, with its sub-column of biographical data. That list was only slightly longer than it had been yesterday.

Helt looked for remains of lunch on the tables in Nadia-Jerry's office. There were none. He hoped they had eaten something, somewhere.

"Hi, Helt. Severo," Jerry said. "What did you bring us?"

"Alibis for the Navigation crew that worked with Cash Ryan," Severo said. He sat down and pulled a keyboard into position. "Where do you want the videos?"

"In the Cleared list, right, Helt?" Nadia asked.

"Sounds right," Helt said.

Severo linked the records to the list. "Three people, and the clearance cost us eight Security hours," he said. "Ryan wasn't bad to work with, they said. Quiet. Did his job. This crew seems sociable enough but they don't hang after work that much. It's all on here." Severo folded his arms and leaned back in his chair.

"Alibied for the SM hour, I take it," Helt said.

"Alibied for the evening," Severo said. "We cross-checked. That took another couple of hours."

Venkat Raghava's name flashed into view in Contacts, just beneath Wesley Doughan, David Luo I, and David Luo II.

Severo was going to need to multiply those hours of investigative time if the Seed Bankers went under 24/7 surveillance. But Doughan wanted to keep them as his secrets for now, so Severo might not know about them. The hell with that.

"Severo. Jerry. Nadia. It seems there're some new suspects and they'll need surveillance. Seven of them."

"Say what?" Severo asked.

"Archer found seven colonists who have Seed Banker funds in their accounts. They're in the Contact list now. Let's keep that quiet; Doughan wants them interviewed before they know they're in trouble."

"I don't have enough people who know how to do 24/7 surveillance," Severo said. "It's a skill set. You don't get it from watching cops and robbers shows. The real stuff is different."

"Not saying it wouldn't be," Helt said. "But I'm wondering. These people have jobs. If they are at work and doing them, it seems like we could just set tags to tell us when they move. Nights, too. If they're in bed asleep, they can't do much damage, and if they're awake sending messages around, we can look in at those. We can do that from SysSu."

"Meaning all I'd need is maybe . . . one or two live bodies to get out on the street per shift. Times three central locations, maybe. Athens and Petra, for sure. Any one of these suspects live in Stonehenge?"

"Two," Helt said.

"We keep someone up there. Some *one*, I said."

"Trains?" Jerry asked.

"We haven't, but we could."

"We could camera them full-time really easy," Jerry said.

"Yeah." Severo looked like he wasn't happy with the new information at all. "So part of NSS is now over here," Severo said. "I don't know if I like that."

"We could move the surveillance ITs to NSS offices," Helt said.

"There isn't room," Severo said. "Not really." He shrugged. "Okay. I'll let it happen. But only if you set up how you're going to do the handoffs from shift to shift and show me first. And show me that the system will let some of my people sleep once in a while."

"I'll do it," Nadia said.

"Good. Anything to keep shaggy SysSu nerds out of my public space," Severo said. "It's not the image we need over there."

Relief was the sensation in Helt's chest, but he didn't give an audible sigh. Severo was the best kind of macho there was, the real genuine article, the kind that could delegate authority and not fret about it.

"Anything new for the psychiatric autopsy?" Helt asked.

"The chiefs have sent the notice of death to Cash Ryan's mother," Nadia said. "Mena asked if I would copyedit it for her. It went out this morning."

Mena hadn't mentioned it.

"Ms. Ryan is not required to respond," Nadia said, "but perhaps she will. If she does, we'll send her response to Dr. Tulloch."

"So says the Personal Assistant to the Incident Analyst," Jerry said. "I thought that was my job."

"It is. I'm helping you anyway." Nadia aimed a kick under the table at one of Jerry's feet. Jerry had his shoes on, Helt noticed, and he dodged the kick without looking up from his screen.

Severo was looking at her with a calculating eye. Nadia was noticeably smaller than Elena. "You're strong," Severo said. "I think I'll deputize you."

Nadia looked at him, startled.

"The thing is, Miss Tay, we need to find out how easy it is to toss someone about Jerry's size over a guardrail."

"Huh?" Jerry asked.

"You're deputized, too," Severo told him. "Maybe you should bring a parachute."

This much closer to the sun, the air was hot. Nadia left the elevator first, and a breeze lifted her hair. She brushed it back from her face and it settled slowly, underwater hair, a swimmer's hair.

The observation platform surrounded Athens tower, a saucer tethered to a down-curved spray of transparent pillars. The pillars were made of glass fused to a steel core, massive ribs that supported the platform and the roof above it. Helt looked out and up across the glass brick guard wall to the matching platform on Petra tower, just visible through the water haze of midday. Its cover sparkled in the sun, a hollow dandelion puff held upside down, or maybe it resembled a frozen waterfall. As was true of most of the engineering in *Kybele*, there were more pillars than were needed to support the mass of the platform. *Kybele* was overbuilt, overengineered, as secure and durable as possible. The glass pillars were made of money, really, like everything else on *Kybele*. The platforms were money transformed into transparent, fused silica.

Severo walked toward a specific place on the spinward guard wall and gripped it with both hands. "From his trajectory, he went off somewhere about here."

Nadia found a clip in a pocket and knotted her hair out of the way as she followed him. In this light g, it was four giant steps to the wall. Slight changes of timing and balance lent a dancer's grace to every motion of her arms, her torso. Down was still down, this high on the tower, but barely so. Jerry glided like a big, lethal cat; Severo moved his considerable bulk with an economy of motion that made him look like a drone torpedo on a deadly mission. Helt watched the trio line up at the glass brick wall and walked over to join them. He realized that he moved with ease, that he no longer had to think about changing his gait or the flex of his knees or the force of his foot's push against the floor. He was long past making a newbie's unplanned kangaroo leaps.

The wall was solid and reassuringly thick, the width of his forearm from elbow to wrist, a cubit's worth of reinforced glass brick barrier between him and the world below. Beyond the wall, the platform extended three meters to the sheer drop of the edge, and was transparent. From where he stood at the rail, you could see, high up the curve of the world, the ruffled surface of Second Sea at the far edge of the Athens wilderness.

Severo made a minuscule leap and positioned himself to sit on top of the wall.

"Okay, anyone can get up here."

"He was drugged," Helt said.

"Yeah, a little more than most people who work out on the skin," Severo said. "Whole universe spins by once every seven minutes, and it's hard to ignore. Ryan was used to working out there, but his stomach never adapted. That's what his team told me."

"He was drugged more than a standard dose and he had a drink or two." He'd been lured up here, or carried up here.

"Yeah," Severo said. "So let's see how hard he would be to haul. Nadia, Jerry, show me how that could work."

Nadia slipped one hand into Jerry's armpit, grabbed him just above the elbow with her other hand, and lifted. Jerry squawked. He stretched up on tiptoe; his toes remained in contact with the floor; he twisted to face Nadia and his free arm grabbed her in a bear hug. Nadia let her knees sag and then pushed up like a weight lifter. Jerry's feet left the floor, but came down again. Nadia threw herself against Jerry's chest and he simply stepped back on one foot and lifted her. They must have watched a performance of the Ballets Russes at some point in their lives, because Jerry kept on lifting. Nadia sorted out how to balance her torso on his lifted hands and held her arms wide, her back arched and her legs curved up behind her, a woman diving toward an invisible pool. Jerry turned beneath her and displayed her imaginary wings to the audience. The backdrop for the performance was a panorama of the distant curves of Center and the bars of shadow that sectioned the distant terrain below. Two of the four curved legs of Athens tower could be seen from this part of the platform, now a stage, in this sky, rising through the blue air to intersect at an unseen point far above.

Nadia giggled and cued Jerry to put her down. He did, and the audience of two applauded.

"My ribs are going to hurt." Nadia gasped.

"Oh! I'm sorry!" Jerry's look of alarm and regret was completely unfeigned.

"Not from being thrown around. From laughing," Nadia said.

"So much for the theory that you can haul someone around if they don't want to be hauled," Helt said. "Okay, next plan." He walked to the elevator, opened its door and set it to stay open. "I'll go limp, Nadia. As in, really limp. Show me if you can get me from here to the wall and over it if I'm out cold."

Helt stretched out on the floor of the elevator. His perspective changed to views of feet and trouser legs and little lights in the elevator ceiling.

"Ready?" Helt asked.

"Sure," Nadia said. She knelt near his head.

Helt closed his eyes and felt the radiated warmth from Nadia's thighs on either side of his face. In other circumstances . . . never mind. He opened his eyes and stared up again.

Nadia braced her feet on the floor. With her knees high on either side of his head, she slipped an arm beneath his neck and then slid both arms down his back until she had an elbow under each of his armpits. He could feel her breathing against his neck. She pushed both forearms against his ribs and tried to lock her hands together over his chest. Her arms weren't long enough for that, so she locked her elbows at right angles. She duck-walked backward until she hauled him out of the elevator and then managed to stand in a crouch, her arms still tight against his chest, and she backed up until she reached the wall.

Helt had been dragged, semi-sitting, his head lolling forward over his chest, over the smooth floor. His belt had kept his trousers more or less on, and Helt was grateful for that.

"Just like practice rescue sessions," Nadia said.

Helt kept on playing possum. Nadia managed to work her arms around his torso so she faced him, one leg on either side of his torso. She hauled him up so his back rested against the wall.

Feigning unconsciousness requires thought. Helt thought about floating in salt water. He wondered whether a truly unconscious person would sag to one side or the other and slide down into a fetal position, or whether that would require some voluntary motion on his part. While he was thinking about that, Nadia lifted both his knees and pushed them toward his chest. She leaned her chest against them and he didn't slide anywhere.

"Don't hurt your back," Severo said.

"Won't." Nadia grabbed Helt's torso in a bear hug, inhaled and lifted. She scooted his back up the wall and he tilted forward, ending up slumped with his head over her right shoulder. Nadia sighed.

"Okay, now what?" Jerry asked.

"I don't know," Nadia said. She let go with one arm and got it under one of Helt's thighs. He let himself sag in all directions, an unwieldy bundle of arms and legs with its back against the bumpy surface of the glass brick wall. Nadia held him against the wall and pushed him up it, but then she stopped pushing and let him slide to the floor, gently. "I could roll him up the rest of the way, maybe," Nadia said. "But I don't want to hurt him."

Helt, the him in question, said, "Don't hurt me, and don't hurt you, either. I'm ready to stop this." Nadia backed away. Helt pulled himself up and sat with his back against the wall. It was a comfortable enough place to sit and he wanted to come back at night, sometime, and watch the world sleep from here.

"I could do it," Jerry said.

"If Nadia can get him that far up the wall, a larger woman could get up to the top and push him over," Severo said.

Elena could have. Helt remembered the look of defined muscle beneath her soft, smooth skin. She had been on the Athens elevator that night. Ryan had been her lover, and her stories about that interlude were too unemotional, too distanced; they bothered Helt and he couldn't say why. She could have rolled Ryan up the wall if she was cold and calm about it, more easily if fear jacked up her adrenal output.

The elevator door began to beep.

"I think you just need a little practice, Nadia," Jerry said. "Tonight, at home? I'll be cooperative, I promise."

"Men." Nadia sighed. She went to the elevator door and released it to go get whoever waited below.

"I think Dr. Maury could have done the job," Severo said, "if Ryan was unconscious. She could have had a harness or something along with her."

"Heh," Helt said. "Yeah. She's a doc; she would know how to package an unconscious man for transport. Two people could do it, easy, if the guy was unconscious. Two people could toss him over, even if he was awake, do you think?"

"You and I could," Severo said. "Thing is, we didn't."

The elevator door opened. Calloway stepped out.

"Hi, doc," Severo said.

"Hi, yourself. You guys, too." Calloway nodded to Jerry and Nadia. He ambled over and sat down beside Helt.

"I went over to SysSu and they said you were out sightseeing. Damn, it's hot up here." Less than a minute, and the big man's forehead already glowed with a fine film of sweat. "I wasn't sure you wanted this public, so I thought I'd tell you and let you decide. Here's the deal.

"Remember when Elena put her hand in Cash's chest and said he was cold? He was cold, all right. We went through post-mortem cooling files. You can only measure the rate of cooling after death by being there and measuring it; and if you aren't there to do that, everything's a guess. Cold air, cold room, cold soil if somebody's outside, different body mass for each case, every variable changes every time. And then there's stuff like even a fever before death, that sort of thing would change the rates of cooling. Clothing. Water immersion. Too many factors. But there's some data that says the cooling rate of an undisturbed corpse at room temperature can be estimated at one measly degree Fahrenheit per hour."

Severo was frowning. "You're saying—"

"I'm saying you can't get a man that cold, alive or dead, by throwing him on the ground for an hour."

"The scope-and-speed? Tell me about that, Calloway," Helt said.

Calloway found something interesting to look at way, way in the distance.

"We don't talk about it much. The PA who looks after the surface crews has a quota that he gets from Pharmacy. It's not good for people, but it's less harmful than hurling inside a closed suit, maybe."

"Would the cold alone have been enough to knock him out?" Helt asked.

"Oh, yeah. If he was alive when he got up here, he was way too cold to be functional. Let me put it this way," Calloway said. "In my humble and recently researched opinion, no way he could have made it off this elevator by himself."

"I think I hear you," Severo said. "He was cold, and you can't walk when you're even halfway that cold. He was drugged and part drunk, and you can maybe stagger around when you're drugged and part drunk, but not if you're drugged, part drunk, and cold. Any way you look at it, somebody helped him get dead," Severo said. "It was murder."

11

In Absence of Directives

***Going down.* The elevator** didn't say that aloud once its doors were closed. Helt stared at the wall and felt down get more defined during the controlled fall of the elevator cage inside its shaft, felt his feet and the muscles of his legs begin to adjust again to the job of balancing his seemingly increasing weight upright against the floor. One of the bright and beautiful and lucky who lived down there had murdered another, and ridden this same elevator, down, after the job was done. He had a video of one woman who might have done it.

The silence was heavier than the air.

"I'm sorry I spoiled the party," Calloway said.

"You didn't," Severo said.

"Did, too." Nadia looked up at Calloway with an exaggerated pout. "I was planning to put this away and spend more time helping Martin with a project he has going."

"Martin? Martin Kumar? He's supposed to be studying pathology any time he's not on duty as my clinic grunt. What's he up to?" Calloway asked.

So she meant Martin, the night tech on duty for the autopsy. Of course he was Calloway's apprentice; Calloway had said so. The professions on *Kybele*, of necessity, would be taught in a sort of guild system, apprentice, journeyman, master. The system had worked in the past, and worked well. The problem was that strong personalities, willingly or not, imprinted their biases on what was taught.

Some IA, someday, would have to adjust for that. Visions of darkened rooms, chants and candles and incense, and magics born of wishful superstitions drifted up from Helt's cache of remembered histories. But new diseases, new neuroses, would develop over time in this milieu of the unknown, and perhaps the fight against them would exert enough pressure to keep the rational alive.

Helt realized he had just made a case where some future human might need to get exotically sick to improve a database. Develop an alternate scenario, he told himself. Simulations? Sure. Simulations at the level of metabolic pathways. Was Biosystems already on this? Surely. But he would ask.

"Martin's designing neuro-prosthetic interfaces for some appendages humans don't need yet," Nadia said. "But someday, somewhere, we might."

"I'll be damned," Calloway said. "I guess I'm not pushing him fast enough. He's already testing out at second-year med student level, and he's doing his thirty hours a week in the clinic. If that's not keeping him busy enough, it's time to put him back at the books." Calloway's pride in his apprentice was a clear subtext in his grumbling. "I want a look at these things. What's he building? Arthropod legs? Gills? I've always wanted gills."

"You'll have to ask him." Nadia looked away and smiled.

Jerry, Helt noted, did not look pleased. Helt suspected jealousy. The elevator touched down and opened on a bright afternoon that felt cold.

Jerry was first out the door. He headed back toward the SysSu building. Nadia hurried to catch up with him.

"Love," Severo said. "I guess it's never easy. Don't know if I would want my Sonia in the same office with me all day, though."

"What are you going to tell your guys in Security?" Helt asked.

"Nothing, for now," Severo said.

"Heh. Yeah. It's going to take some careful wording."

"And some careful timing. We're going to get different answers about Ryan if people know they're talking about a murder, not a suicide." Severo nodded to Helt and Calloway. "Later, guys."

"Calloway, about this hypothermia—" Helt began.

"Gotta get back to the clinic," Calloway said. "Mena's coming over for Ryan's interment, and I don't want Martin to be the only person around for her."

Oh, damn. "No, of course not. She shouldn't be alone. I'll come with you," Helt said.

"If you'll stay, I'll get back to work," Severo said. "Doughan wanted at least six people at the service; you'll make the right number. Calloway says he wants his student there. Me, I've seen more funerals than I want."

Calloway led Helt to a room in the Athens clinic, not far from the morgue but not adjacent to it, not a chapel, not anything else but what it plainly was, a room with a door for the living to enter and the closed doors of a low rectangular elevator, centered on the opposite wall, to serve as a final exit for the dead. Its ceiling was blue and its lighting calm. The wall murals suggested greenery and distance. In the room was a gurney, and on the gurney was Cash Ryan's body, wrapped in a covering that seemed to be woven of reeds. On one side of the gurney, Martin Kumar stood at a sort of parade rest, looking stoic. On the other, Mena continued to loosen the wrappings that covered Cash Ryan's head. She glanced up at Helt and Calloway and looked past them, to nod at Archer Pelham and Wesley Doughan as they entered the room. The newcomers watched in silence as Mena reached into her pocket and pulled out two coins, paper-thin, gold, placed them on Ryan's closed eyelids, and smoothed the wrappings back into place.

"I've searched his papers, Mena. He left no directives and his papers list no religious preference," Doughan said. Doughan walked to stand near Ryan's head and fixed his gaze on the closed elevator doors just beyond the body's feet. "As the executive of Navigation, who held his contract, it's my duty to be here, and to speak for him. I'll be brief."

"Thank you," Mena said.

Helt had never seen Doughan look like this. His posture was imperial. He was impeccably groomed, as if he had shaved and combed his hair moments before. The left front of his Navigation uniform was loaded with medals Helt had had no idea he had earned.

Helt was suddenly aware of how much sweat the heat of the tower had brought to his skin, now thankfully dry in the carefully monitored Athens air, and of the grubby windbreaker he wore. He wanted to rub his hand over the possible beginnings of afternoon stubble on his chin, but he didn't.

Doughan held a tablet reader in his left hand. He glanced at it, briefly. "People have come to *Kybele* from many cultures and many places. However different from one another we may be, we are alike in our love of challenge, our pleasure in examining and enjoying the complexities of life, our longing to understand and make known what is unknown. Charles 'Cash' Ryan was one of us, and worked with us, and is no more.

"A prophet said, to every thing there is a season, and a time for every purpose under heaven."

It was the old language of the King James Bible, part of the history of the West.

"A time to be born, a time to die; a time to plant, and a time to pluck up that which is planted. A time to kill, and a time to heal . . . a time to weep, and a time to laugh, and a time to mourn . . ."

A time to kill. That was in the text. Helt listened to the stately rhythm of the old words.

". . . A time to keep silence, and a time to speak. A time to love, and a time to hate; a time of war, and a time of peace."

Wesley Doughan straightened his erect shoulders a fraction more and took a deep breath. Archer Pelham kept his sharp gaze on Doughan's face. Mena's eyes were bright with the shine of tears. Her face was stern. Calloway and Martin looked neutral and attentive.

"In the midst of life we are in death," Doughan said. "Privileged as we are to witness and cherish the miracles of birth and death, with humility we commit the body of Charles 'Cash Ryan' to our ground; from our Earth to this new earth, ashes to ashes, dust to dust. Part of the air, part of the soil, he will be part of *Kybele* forever."

Doughan stepped away from the body and marched to the wall. He pushed the button near the rectangular doors. They opened on a dark tunnel with solid walls.

"Will you assist me?" he asked the room in general.

He wanted six, Helt realized, because that's the traditional number for pallbearers in Western culture. Doughan, Mena, and Archer took their places on one side of the bundle of reeds that was Cash Ryan's last shelter, Martin, Helt, and Calloway on the other. Doughan nodded, and the six of them, three on a side, rolled the gurney to the edge of the open, waiting door and slid the reed-wrapped body into darkness.

The doors closed. Doughan raised his eyes and looked pointedly at the door that opened to the hallway. Calloway, as if on prior orders, opened it and motioned the group out into the hall.

The body would stay in its cupboard until the mourners were gone, and then it would be dropped into a tank for reclamation. Probably Calloway would push the button for that.

In the hallway, Mena took one hesitant step toward the clinic waiting room. Archer stepped to her side and put his arm around her waist. Doughan caught up with them and slipped his arm around her waist, too.

"The coins, Mena. For the ferryman?" Archer asked.

"For Charon, yes," Mena said. She spoke softly.

"Are you going ethnic on us?" Doughan asked her.

She looked up at him and Helt saw her smile, the smile of a woman who has found her facade of resiliency and competence and has glued it firmly in place. "I do, now and again. I wanted my roots for this. Reassurance, guidelines, tradition."

"Your traditions shaped the West," Arthur said.

"They had some effect, yes. But I was relieved by what you chose, Wesley."

"Thank you," Wesley Doughan said.

"I like it when you feel Greek," Archer said. "The side effects, like the *galaktoboureko* you baked for me Wednesday night, are agreeable. Let me amend that. Superb."

The group reached the doors that led back to the agora and stepped out into a light that had deepened to the deep blue of late afternoon. Tints of rose edged up from the sky's horizons. Helt felt a mild claustrophobia vanish in the wide space and the cool air.

Wednesday was when the cameras went offline and hid Cash Ryan's murder. So, Archer and Mena were visiting each other that night. Helt remembered Archer shuffling into SysSu in cardigan and slippers, hardly a costume for wooing a woman like Mena, if that's what the old boy had been doing. What a concept. Archer Pelham was getting on toward seventy.

"Anybody want a good stiff drink?" Doughan asked. "That's also traditional, isn't it?"

"I'll buy," Archer said. "As an appreciation of your stellar performance in a required, but hopefully not-often-practiced, executive role."

"Nothing like a script. A good one obviates the need to think."

"Impressive, all the same," Archer said. "Helt, you coming?"

Helt's pocket interface was in his hand and it showed that the announcement of time and place for Ryan's interment was right there in Community Events, next to listings of Friday evening entertainments of various kinds. Another keystroke showed that Elena was still in her Stonehenge laboratory.

"Uh, thanks. I'd join you but there's something I have to do. Good evening," Helt said.

He started off toward Athens station. If Elena wouldn't see him, he would try to catch up on other things that the day's events had pushed down the list.

Surely Archer hadn't made an attempt at an alibi for Mena and himself. It was just too clumsy.

". . . *Book of Common Prayer*," he heard Archer say.

"Nope. Army Chaplain's manual, modified," Doughan answered.

12

Comfort

The main corridor of Level One in Stonehenge stretched into the distance, its length marked by lights at the entrances to underground farms. In them, individual dwellings were centered in crowded plots of food crops. The people who grew them wanted to stay close to their gardens, day and night, and the architects hadn't argued.

Near the elevator, doorways were closely spaced. The door to Elena's suite of labs was closed.

"Elena?" he asked the door.

She buzzed it open and came to meet him, backlit by the open door to her office, walking through the dimly lighted atrium of her lab complex in a flood of music, voice and strings, rich and somber. She still wore the dull red lab coat he'd seen this morning but the balloon hat was gone, replaced by a headband light, turned off.

"How's Mena?" she asked.

"She's drinking with the other execs," he said.

"That's good. She dreaded this."

"How are you?"

Kyrie eleison, a baritone voice sang in long-voweled plainsong, a plea rising over rumbling sorrow, *eleison*.

"I didn't want to be where Mena is. So I'm here," Elena said.

"Working?"

She sighed. "Housekeeping. I've learned not to try head work when I'm distracted by—other things."

Her voice was dull and tired.

"Fewer errors that way," Helt said.

"Yes. Now you know he was murdered. Calloway said he would tell you about the cooling."

"He did."

"Why are you here? What do you want from me?" She crossed her arms over her chest, her hands gripping her arms so hard that it must hurt. "Did you come see how a murderess responds to the funeral of her old lover?"

Yes, in part, he had. But he wouldn't have come here for only that; not to satisfy a voyeurism that could only be ugly and cruel. He had come because he didn't want her to face this night alone, no matter what had happened.

"Did you bring a BCI rig? Saline pads? You'll see a spike at P300 if I see his face. You know I knew him. But that's so primitive I'm sure you have something more sophisticated in mind. A special set of visuals, perhaps, tailored from what you learned from me last night."

Helt looked beyond the goading and saw outrage mixed with hurt and fear, saw a trapped animal attacking a cage. He didn't want her to hurt like this.

"I came here to offer comfort, if I can."

"Comfort? When you come here to tell me you've found something, somewhere, that removes my name from your list of suspects, then I'll be comforted. Am I alibied yet? Am I?"

"No," he said. "Can you help me do that?"

She lifted her head and those amber eyes scanned his face as if to memorize every detail of it, from eyelash to chin stubble. "Dear God. I think you mean it."

"I do," Helt said.

Elena turned away. "There's no proof I can give you that I didn't kill the man, nothing recorded, nothing to show except my trip down that elevator."

"There must be something else. Somewhere."

"I've tried to think. I was here, alone, in these labs. I've looked at the lab stamps on those samples I carried down from the tower but they only show when I filed them in the incubators, not when I took the plates out of the lab. I went home when I finished work. I've relived that evening in so many different ways, where I was, who might have seen me or heard me. But I was alone, until Calloway called me for the autopsy."

"We'll find something."

Her eyes narrowed. "Something."

She turned her back to him, and the line of her neck curving down to meet her broad shoulders was a powerful and lovely line, even if covered by the faded rough cotton of her work coat. She stared at the atrium and looked from one lab door to another. "I should close down in here. I'm tired and I'm hungry."

"I'll help," Helt said.

The music switched tempo, a jazz drumbeat, pianoforte, bass guitar. *Christe eleison*, the voice sang, meandering through major and minor keys with each iteration.

"There's not much to do," Elena said.

"May I look over your shoulder?" Helt asked.

"These are just labs. You're a curious bastard. Explorer type, right?"

"I am that." He was an explorer of his own senses, at least. Because he lived in his flesh and no matter how good a simulation is, to ski fresh powder is a different experience than observing someone else doing it. The totality of the physical experience, the ultrafine bite of ice crystals on a cheek, the transcendent clarity of frozen air, thin, breathless, air-hungry, the flex of muscle, the reassuring bite of edge on snow was a total immersion in a time and place, but that reality was gone forever. Sometimes the loss of the mountains woke him in the middle of the night. Sometimes he knew what he had left behind.

For skiing, add a gambler's rush of fear; the cost of a single error could be so high. A man might fall very far and be hurt very badly.

Elena's music glided into an intricate counterpoint, flute against flute; its tempo almost giddy.

She went to a door that led into a lab where racks of tubes and stacks of Petri dishes stood cloistered behind the glass doors of incubators, where hoods and sinks and light microscopes and rows of reagents lined the counters.

Elena turned out lights and then the darkness glowed with little pips of color, indicator lights for processes Helt knew only in theory, some of them blinking offbeat, some in unplanned synchrony with the pervasive music.

"See how pretty?" she asked him. "Night lights so the germs won't have bad dreams."

"Anthropomorphic fantasy, my dear Dr. Maury?"

"Certainly not. I know when the little guys are happy," she said, with an absolutely straight face. She closed that door and two more. The next one was doubled, like an airlock, and the exit from it was solid black with a red warning sign.

INFRARED PROTOCOL BEYOND THIS POINT

"What's that for?" Helt asked.

"Multicellular embryos. Daylight, sunlight, stimulates eye formation.

You get bug-eyed monsters, for real. The wombs are UV shielded and we have lighted stations where we work if we take them out for any reason. But if we're not working in there, we keep the room dark." Elena pushed some buttons inside the light-lock cubicle and closed the outer door.

"In vitro babies?" Helt asked.

"Some of the embryos are human, yes. We take them to the blastocyst stage. We don't have the tech to go farther yet and when we do . . . I'm not so sure. Someone would have to convince me that the whole complex process of a nine-month pregnancy isn't worth the trouble. Hormonal factors, bonding, and all that. There's evidence that the mothers of preemies who are machine-grown, essentially, for weeks or months . . . the relationship is not the same for mother or child, but the parameters of what's different are elusive, hard to measure."

She vets every embryo, Mena had said. Therefore, as part of that vetting, she destroys the ones that fail her tests.

Beneath a glissando of flutes, in this humid, warm air, the quiet white noise of humming machines tended the examined lives in Elena's care, and Elena, the living, lush inhabitant of an archetype called Great Mother, stood before him.

A man might fall very far.

"I'm ready. Let's go."

"Your headband," Helt said.

"Oh. Infrared, for the embryo lab." Elena pulled her headlight off and put it in her pocket before she took off her lab coat and hung it near the door. The lab coat had covered a deep red shirt, unbuttoned far enough to reveal a hint of cleavage. Elena grabbed a dark jacket from the rack.

"Can we bring the music? I like it." Helt said.

"Sure," Elena said.

In the corridor, the bubble of sound transited to vocal, *Kyrie eleison*, the solo voice keening high in its register over a heavy rock beat. *Eleison*, an ethereal chorus echoed in seeming distance as they stepped on the train. They were alone. The music ended when they sat down.

"Was that Greek?" Helt asked.

"Dutch. Tease von Lear. I don't want to go to Athens," Elena said.

Helt glanced at the screen on Elena's interface, and Tease von Lear became *Thijs van Leer.* "I was ready to buy you wonderful food and intoxicating wine."

"I'll settle for packaged homestyle and house red in the Petra canteen."

"Why?"

"Because I don't want to run into Mena and the others."

"Okay."

They were the only passengers. The trains were designed to a population that wouldn't exist for a long time. Some of the seats were arranged in fours, two facing forward and two back, with a table between. Someday, the tables would vanish. All the seats would be turned forward and the spacing between them would shrink. People would know the taste of each other's breath. Not yet.

Helt stretched his legs in front of him. Elena stared out the window at the passing kilometers of slick, barren black stone, and all was quiet save for the hiss of wheels on rail. Her blink rate was high, fighting fatigue or maybe tears. Helt suspected both. But he could feel her relaxing beside him. He wanted to slip his arm around her shoulders and let her rest against him, feel the weight of her head against his chest, but he didn't.

"Blank slate," Elena said.

"The walls?"

She managed a little smile. "The world."

"What would you put here?"

"On the walls? Beautiful things . . ."

Whatever she was going to say segued into a stifled yawn. The train began to descend the grade into Petra station.

"I wouldn't have the courage," she said. "So easily marred, so difficult to restore."

"The world?" Helt asked.

"The tunnel."

The décor in the Petra canteen was split, laminated bamboo and the food was continental, if by continental you meant, pick a continent, and there will be one entrée from it on the night's dinner menu, more or less. Elena didn't even raise an eyebrow when Helt brought a full carafe of house red to the canteen table. She ate her paella like a good girl, down to the last grain of rice. She drank her first well-filled glass of wine while Helt kept pace on food intake with his lamb tagine.

Compared to Earth below, they ate like billionaires. Meat was a luxury for the few. *Kybele* kept live animals, and ate them, a food chain cost outweighed by the need to perpetually harvest good tissue against the certainty of radiation damage. But still, every meal here was a sacrament of sorts.

Elena sipped at her second glass of good, sturdy dark red, thank you, Mena, while Helt shelled pistachios for her and dropped them in her palm. They hadn't said much, little bits of chitchat, wry observations on the other Friday night diners. Many of them were single, some partnered for the evening, or the weekend, or lengths of time as yet unknown.

"There's a different energy in here," Elena said. "I mean, different from most evenings. More people sitting together. More talk."

"Gearing up for the big move," Helt said. "Leaving Earth orbit is a marker."

"It's not that far away," Elena said. "Do you worry about it much?"

"Sure. Renunciations, final good-byes, points of no return, all that. It's a biggie, but we'll wake up the morning after and still be able to ignore the latest scandals in Denver and Jakarta and watch today's game in Barcelona."

"Is your family giving you a hard time about it?" Elena asked.

"Not really," Helt said. He wanted to leave it at that, but she kept looking at his face. "My dad's gone. Mom?" His mother had gone away on business when he was young. She came back as someone who didn't know him. "We talk, remote. We've done that for years."

"No brothers or sisters?"

"No. You?"

Elena smiled. "I'm an only child, but I grew up in an intentional family. There are three generations at home now, so there's always somebody to talk to and somebody who is willing to distract you if you'd rather not talk to one or the other at the moment."

"How many people?" Helt asked.

"I think . . . around thirty? But only seven or eight in residence at one time. A good thing, too. Sometimes several batches show up at the same time, and that gets really noisy." Elena was smiling at old memories.

The idea of that many people who had grown up together, who had aunts and uncles and cousins, who were young together and got old together, was one Helt hadn't thought through.

He'd learned to make friends fast, but once they were gone, they were gone. It was part of his father's travel. Doughan said he acted like a military brat. Military brats, hell, military people, Doughan said, made friends fast. When they moved on, they tried to leave the impression of friendship even if they didn't like the people they were leaving, because someday they might meet up again. Helt had sort of done that, but he had never known whether it was a good or a bad thing.

"What do you do with newcomers?" Helt asked.

"We pretend they've been around forever. We pretend they share our memories and know our—traditions? I guess that's what they've become, little things over the years, shared jokes and remembered griefs. Eventually, they do, because they've added some."

Helt wanted that. No, he wanted to have the sense of self that could come from that, but then he'd be a different Helt.

"Will they miss you?" he asked.

"Every one of them. I'll miss them, too. But they love me, and I love them. They're rooting for me, Helt."

Elena covered a combination smile and yawn with one hand.

"You didn't sleep last night," Helt suggested.

She shook her head as if to clear it. "Wrong. Didn't sleep two nights."

"I'll walk you home."

She shook her head again. "I'm not sleepy. I'm tipsy. That's different."

Uh-huh. She was both, although food and wine had wakened some buried reserve of tightly wound energy. "Stay right there," Helt said. "I'll get go-cups."

She had finished her dinner like a good girl, so Helt cleared the table like a good boy and took the dishes away. He poured the rest of the wine into cups, and brought them back to her.

"Where?" he asked.

"I want to walk for a while."

They left the canteen, cups in hand, and paused at the edge of the shopping area that surrounded the station. Beyond its roof, the cliffs of Petra rose steep and high. The sky over them was programmed for waxing moonlight. It lighted the bridges that arched the river and whitened the leaves on trees in the courtyards.

"How well do you know this place?" Elena asked.

"Petra? I know how to get home. Lady, you don't get to win the workaholic competition with me without a fight. I get off the train, I grab food if I'm too tired to cook. I stagger to bed."

"You're in fairly good shape for a nerd," she said.

"Sometimes I go up to Center and wander around the wilderness to look for some of the new creatures Biosystems turns loose up there. When I need to think about things, I climb rocks, or trees. Keeps up upper body strength. That's working, right?"

"Do you brachiate?"

"Heh. Yes. It's a quirk of mine. But I stick with one tree at a time. No swinging from one to the other. I'm a cautious man." He tried to be, and knew sometimes he wasn't. "Your muscle tone is not shabby for a workaholic, if I may say so."

"Thank you."

"What do you do?"

"I do stoop labor for Mena. I weight-lift boxes of cabbages and things, part of the job. And I wander around and look at rocks. Seeking the animal in the mineral."

"Bio-po-morph-izing," Helt made the word up on the spot, "our nickel-iron. I suspected as much."

"Give me lichen and I will make loam from sand."

They were past the last of the houses, one of them as yet only a rectangular maw of shadow in the cliff wall. The street became a path of flat stones set in the black sand that bordered the river. Nothing was planted here yet. Stone, water, air, and darkness existed here, and that was all. The canyon was a preview of where humans would first live on Nostos, a canyon with a water supply that could be purified, a roof over it where air could be filtered, a testing ground for what could and could not be grown in the new place. Dwelling in caves by rivers was an ancient strategy. Its efficacy was proven.

"I haven't been here before," Helt said. "Not this far up the canyon. I've seen the plans. We're in a space that's planned to be left unbuilt, I think."

Elena nodded. "The next group of houses will go in beyond that bend." She pointed ahead. From here, visually, it seemed they were nearing a wall of solid rock.

What blocked the view ahead was not a wall, but a massive stone outcrop, a triangular wedge that jutted out from the side of the canyon and climbed the entire height of the gorge. The river lapped its pointed foot. Helt stopped and looked up. There were no setbacks, not even near the top.

Elena was well ahead of him when he brought his eyes back to the ground. He thought she was walking into the water at the base of the wedge, but he saw her foot find a stepping stone, and another. Helt, when he reached the river's edge, stuck his fingers in it. The water wasn't quite ice and it was only ankle deep this near the shore. Beyond the rock barrier, the valley widened. Elena stayed on the path that ran close to the canyon wall. She climbed a waist-high mini mesa of sharp-edged stone, a mega-shard that had obviously fallen from the rim during the violence of the canyon's recent birth, and stepped into shadow.

"Where'd you go?" Helt called.

"I want to show you something." Her voice rang, not quite an echo, but the sound held the suggestion of a hollow space.

Someone had cut rough steps into the big fallen rock that had hidden Elena from his sight. The steps led down to the canyon floor and into a little setback in the canyon wall, tucked in against the back of the outcrop. It was large enough to be a generous courtyard, floored with the ubiquitous black sand of Petra. The wind had shaped its surface into waves that looked liquid in the moonlight, although the night was blessedly still. The air was getting colder.

Someone had sculpted part of the back wall of the space. A column of intertwined, stylized figures, perhaps, no, surely aquatic, rose from the sand. They sheltered beneath a stone tree whose roots spread out from a point on the rock wall three times a man's height, although some of those roots seemed to be creatures as well. On the trunk of the tree, creatures unknown to zoology texts climbed and played. Above them, their offspring climbed higher and higher, jumped or leaped or napped in niches or on branches, if those were branches and not arms. Higher up, very high, birds spread sheltering wings over the creatures below, or those wings were leaves of this thing, lifted in an unseen wind or with a will to soar.

It wasn't any historic style that Helt knew. When he blinked, he wasn't sure it was a sculpture. There was something organic about it, and his mind brought him the concept of an accident in the breaking of this stone, a byproduct of explosions that had cut the canyon into *Kybele*'s hide, but no. That couldn't be. He walked up to one of the aquatic things and laid his hand on its hide, and felt the familiar cold smoothness of laser-carved asteroid. He turned away.

Looking out from this alcove, the view was of canyon walls marching on upriver, roofed with stars. From here, the waterfall at the far end of the canyon could just be seen, a white, vertical, silent slash on black.

Elena had returned to the steps and she waited for him on the lowest one. She didn't look impatient, but she looked as if only an act of will was keeping her on her feet. She had jammed her hands into her jacket pockets and hunched her shoulders against the cold.

Helt walked back and stopped on the sand below the first step, to be, for a little while, exactly Elena's height and no taller. "It's magnificent," he said.

He watched traces of anxiety in her face soften into an expression that seemed a little more relaxed. He took a drink of his wine, hoping she would copy him. She did. Her hand trembled on the cup.

"You're cold," he said. The cups were empty. He reached for hers, flattened both cups, and stashed them in a pocket. "I would stay longer, but we should go back." It wasn't so far. It wasn't far at all to return to warm rooms and soft bedding. He climbed the steps and they walked away.

"Except for the sky, it feels like an old, old cave in there," Helt said. "Lascaux, or Altamira."

"This isn't in your blueprints, is it?" Elena asked.

"No. I would think photos of this would be everywhere. How long has it been here?"

"I don't know. I've been watching it change as it's worked on, for months."

They reached the stepping stones and Helt kept quiet until they were both back on dry land.

"Are you going to report it as vandalism?" Elena asked.

"Hell no," Helt said. "Not a world-tree like that. We've used that motif since Minoan Crete."

"Longer. Assyria," Elena said.

"Egypt."

"The Parthenon, stone columns scored as reminders of tree bark."

The walking had warmed Helt a little, and Elena wasn't shivering any more, at least not that he could see. "Yggdrasil. I think I saw Ratatosk in there."

"Who's that?" Elena asked.

"He's a squirrel. A messenger, runs up and gets gossip from the eagle, runs back down to tell the snake gnawing the roots. Gothic cathedrals," Helt said. "The arches in those old churches look like a forest with really high branches, some of them."

Lamps on either side of the river marked the approach of the town named Petra.

"Gaudí," Elena said. "I want you to note that I did not say phallic. Not once."

"Noted," Helt said.

Elena smiled up at him. They continued past the empty house-to-be, and walked by silent, dark courtyards. "My house is the next one."

They stopped at her door.

"Who's the artist?" Helt asked.

"The people who know about him say he calls himself a welder."

A welder. The sculptor was Yves Copani. It had to be him. I will not have us keep a Cash Ryan, Helt decided, even a dead one, and send this artist away.

"That's all I know about him," Elena said.

"Not his name?"

"No. There are some things I want to know but I save them until I can savor them."

Well, damn, Helt thought. He was just tipsy enough to have thought for a moment that delayed gratification, tonight, was a bad idea.

"There are things I know that I wish I didn't," Elena said. "That river."

Helt looked over his shoulder at the river, black, its ripples silvered with manufactured moonlight.

"I know which waters feed it; I know it to be pure, drinkable; I know how it's purified. I know the sources of the reclaimed nitrogen that will enrich Mena's fields someday, but most of the time I can forget. When I'm here," she said.

Helt knew exactly how it was done, the schemata for the holding tanks in the rock beneath the Athens clinic and in other places, the carefully monitored bacteria in the water where Cash Ryan's body floated in the dark now, the deadly brightness of the banked UV lights that burned away the water's life when the sludge had been mined for its values and stored away. He knew, and he wished he didn't.

Elena held up her hands, palms forward, as if to push him away. "There's another thing. When you find whatever you find that gets me off the suspect list, what if it's something that has only your word to verify it?"

"Why do you ask?"

"Because I think we could become lovers."

She said what Helt's body knew. He could not read her statement as an attempt to seduce. It was an acknowledgment of shared reality. Helt thought of himself as honest, but her honesty was less cautious, and perhaps more real, than his.

If Elena Maury needed to kill someone, she would make her reasons known, loud and clear. A still small voice said, She's got you, boy. You want to believe anything she says.

"If we are lovers," Elena said, "will your word be as believable as if we are not?"

Well, yes, and then again, no. Her thinking was a little paranoid, but then again, she might have something there.

"I suffer from excessive caution," Helt said. He knew, as well as anything he had ever known in his life, that if he hugged her, if he held her close, she would have no defense against his desire or hers; she was too exhausted for that. "So we will find proof you didn't kill Cash Ryan, and then we will find a way to verify that proof. Even when we are lovers."

He knew one thing he could do to reassure her. If it didn't seem reassuring to her, but a threat, then possibly she had things to hide from him. That would be terrible, but it would tell him a lot. "Let me see your interface."

She looked up at his face and frowned, but she reached into her pocket and gave it to him. She was so alone, facing this suspicion. There was risk in what he was going to do, but the risk was hers more than his—if she had anything to hide.

Helt entered the access codes that would reach him, day or night, at SysSu, at home, anywhere.

"You can watch with me, work with me, see any file I see when I see it. I will not hide from you. I will not do that."

She took her interface back and left her palm open, her fingers wide as if she were afraid to close them, as if the little machine might bite them.

"You can delete the codes if you want," Helt said.

Elena nodded.

Helt closed her fingers over the interface and kissed them.

He turned and walked away, no easy thing to do, and heard the sound of her door closing, and looked back to see that she was safe inside.

13

The Sane Suspect

At some point in the night, Helt put his hand on his cold face and felt moisture on his cheek. It was dew, so the dawn would come soon, and it was cold out here. He blinked at the night sky and burrowed deeper into his sleeping bag, hoping the waking dreams would stop.

If that's what you called them, the incidents he never realized he remembered until they replayed in half sleep when he was waking or trying to drift into sleep. They came razor-sharp, complete with every emotion he'd felt at the time, shame, or guilt, or anger, raw and unmuted by the defenses a waking mind uses to get through a day.

"I'm trying to *reconstruct* how it felt," his mother said. "I'm trying to act as if I love you. But it's an act now. Don't ever think I mean it. If it weren't for the boy . . ."

"Once he's older. Once he's older, we won't bother you again." Jørn Borresen's voice came from the depths of the green armchair where he sat in the evenings, close enough to tend the fire, but this was summer and noon, and nothing was right and maybe Jørn wasn't in the chair but on his way to the door.

"He knows, doesn't he? He knows I don't love you. He knows I don't love him," his mother's voice said.

"Of course he knows."

"He's becoming as stoic as the man I see now. A cold Nordmann who will be trained to be polite and honest to a fault, and never let anyone know whether he loves them or hates them or could care less. Just like you. Leave me for a while. Leave me. *Please!*"

The chair belonged at home, not in that tiny apartment with a door that opened on this long hall with a nursing station at its end. Helt felt the shame of eavesdropping, but he hadn't meant to. He was in the hall waiting for his father and the walls were thin. He felt ashamed that he had wanted to pull away from the kiss on the cheek his mother had offered, because she was following a script that says a mother should be fond of her twelve-year-old son. She didn't know, really, who he was. Not in any way that counted.

And now he really was awake.

A terrorist's bomb had sent a shard of granite from a carving on a Quebec stair into Lily Borresen's head when Helt was ten years old. It had been tiny, and sharp, and it had obliterated a small part of the medial temporal cortex in the right side of her brain. He remembered, ten years old and lonely, looking up the words and the pictures of his mother's brain that went with them.

Lily Borresen had memories of her husband and her son, but her emotional memories weren't tied to current experience then, not even two years after the injury.

Things got better, or Lily built memories of love that she thought she *should* have for her husband and her child. She moved back to Helt's childhood home in Maine, and brought the chair with her. But things weren't better enough, and his father's restless travels from consulting job to consulting job started then. Helt went along. One year, two years, for so many cities. He'd learned to make friends fast and learned they would be gone soon.

Helt turned over in his sleeping bag and reached out to stroke the chilly stone beside his pillow. He was on top of a cliff that was just the right distance, a ten-minute jog, from Petra tower. It was a good place to look down at whatever came by. He'd come up here after leaving Elena, after tossing and turning for a while, after wishing he could put his hormones in storage for a few hours and get some sleep.

He had kept on thinking about certain human imperatives, like sex. No, not just sex, but sex in the context of love, a complicated endeavor.

He wanted superlative sex, the striving and the tenderness and the release and the profound relaxation that followed. Well, for a while it followed, but, as with the best of drugs, hunger always returned. He wanted to play the war game of sex with a worthy opponent, with points scored on either side in conscious and unconscious artistries of surprise and delight, triumph and surrender.

He wanted someone he could trust, up close and personal. He wanted to talk without censorship on either side. He wanted a sympathetic ear when he needed one and he wanted to be strong for the vulnerability of a cherished other, and he wanted someone who would surprise him and lead him into explorations of new territories in the art of living, things he hadn't thought about yet, and. And resilience, and the ability to give him the occasional goad, and laughter, and, and. And his list was far too long, and he knew it. And he knew people could change, and never be the same again.

He'd been thirty-five when he decided that whatever happened would have to happen on *Kybele.* His imagined partner would have a good mind, of course, and he forgave himself for knowing she needed to be beautiful, at least to him. About common interests, shared recreations, he wasn't so sure. He didn't care if she liked the seashore and he liked the mountains. If it didn't work out, he couldn't try to hide from it by traveling from place to place, like his dad had. Not here.

He just wished the woman who was currently filling his fantasies, if not his arms, weren't a murder suspect.

He pulled a corner of his sleeping bag over his nose.

The pool table sound of cracking antlers startled Helt awake in predawn light, but he didn't get a look at the battle. While he stayed quiet and tried to find some sign of where the herd was this morning, the rest of his brain woke up, bitching.

His protocols had missed the Seed Bankers. That was scary.

Some way had to be found to spend time with Elena, to learn everything he could about her.

He climbed down from his flat rock and went home, showered and ate breakfast, and went back to SysSu.

This early on Saturday morning, SysSu was deserted. Helt made himself a pot of coffee in his office, set his interface display full-wall, sprawled in a chair to sip a cup, and looked for his deer herd.

GPS locators found them; they had already moved away from Petra and were traveling toward Second Sea, following a migratory pattern they made up for themselves.

A migratory pattern might serve for chances to talk to Elena without compromising her or him. Just happened to run into you. Right.

It was too early to wake anybody if they were working day shift, and certainly too early if this was a day off. He sent a text to Yves Copani.

Helt. Could we meet face-time today about your request to stay on board?

Helt's search programs found a few nodes of speculation about the "suicide." Not many, and Severo's folk had sifted the individuals in those speculations. All of them had been alibied for the missing hour.

The police log showed very little activity last night. People were busy with departure tasks, or they were behaving. Or they were getting surprise visits from the execs, for all Helt knew. Ripples would spread from those interviews, but so far, *Kybele*'s folk were doing what they usually did, except for the ones who had Things to Do in the run-up to the first firing of the big engines.

Helt, reassured, still felt a nagging discomfort about Doughan's plans to interview Seed Bankers without telling them they were busted.

The GON list created serious discomfort for him anyway, and now it included people Helt hadn't considered, hadn't found. Archer's Seed Bankers were secure, dedicated, vetted colonists. None of them had set off alarms anywhere. Vetted? Yes, by Mena, by Archer, by Doughan. And knowing that it hadn't been Helt's job to look them over didn't help one bit. How far should preemptive justice go?

Once upon a time, hungry five-year-old children who stole a loaf of bread were hung by the neck until dead, and crowds came out to enjoy the show. Witches were burned at the stake. What a person thought and said about God, or a king, could draw a death sentence. *Ugh* was the reaction to that sort of justice now. What were they thinking? Why were they so cruel?

He wondered how history would feel about what Helt Borresen was helping his bosses do here.

In the past, people got in trouble, and were sometimes executed, because of sex. Forbidden sexual practices were culture-specific, which could cause real trouble if you didn't know the local rules. The punishments for indulging in forbidden sex had always been terrible and sometimes bizarre, and had forever been remarkably ineffective at changing behaviors.

Helt, he told himself, you're back to sex again. Something must be done about this.

Okay, Helt told the future population of *Kybele.* I tried, with imperfect tools, to select people who could survive one another's company in this little egg, and if you're alive to complain about my work, I did my job.

He poured himself another cup of coffee and then pulled up the GON list and looked through it. It was short a murderer, if he could find one to add to it.

The data streams on Cash Ryan's murder were full of stuff that might get overlooked, even this early in the game. Helt set up a sphere with a dot called Ryan in the center. Murder Management? Okay, at least it was a filename. He set fields for method, motive, suspects, with suspects at the periphery for now. Motive? Elena had one, maybe. Time. Four hours to deal with, including the dead camera hour between 1900 and 2000. The sphere was all too empty, but it was a framework. Helt moved alibied personnel outside the sphere, leaving Elena lonely in there, still near to the periphery but closer to the center than anyone else.

He went back to his off-list and stared at the names. Making it had been his most unpleasant daily discomfort until now. Going back to it felt almost like relief. Scanning the names, he felt secure that the people who were currently on it had earned their way off-ship. It contained a few unfortunates whose psychoses had surfaced on *Kybele*, the ones Jim Tulloch couldn't ease back into any semblance of function. Embezzlers, mischievous unauthorized hackers, and other white-collar thieves, the ones who'd been caught, anyway, had always been shipped off by their division chiefs when found, and some had been found for this off-load. Some of the lottery winners were just flat miserable and wanted to go home. They would.

Ask people if they want to go to sea and they say they do. Ask them if they want to spend their lives in a submarine. Well, not so much, when you put it that way.

But these Seed Bankers weren't planning on leaving. They were all colonists. They expected to spend their lives here. And perhaps they planned to make those lives short, along with the lives of everyone around them, to make a point.

He pulled up the Seed Banker bios and looked through them, searching for any sort of connections between them, for any incidents that might have clued him, or anyone, that they wanted to cause trouble. The agronomist woman, Andrea Doan, the only one whose name was on his second tier of possible off-listers, was there because she'd been shifted from team to team several times by Mena, and he'd asked Mena why.

"She's a lottery winner, and she's an expert brewmaster. A polymath of sorts," Mena had told him. "I can use her anywhere, nurseries, fields, lab work. But people are happy enough to see her go somewhere else."

"Bossy?"

"Not obnoxiously so. But she's resentful about getting bossed. It's not uncommon; most of us have authority problems. There's something else, something bitter about her, people say."

Helt had let it slide. He wished he hadn't. Doan's mug shot showed a plump woman with a determined expression, dark hair slicked tight to her head, older than most colonists, a lottery winner. Doan had once been Doãn, the tilde a victim of net-induced standardization. Her surname was Vietnamese and he was beginning to scroll through her bio when he heard someone in the hall. He switched his screen to a news feed.

The someone, Doughan, arrived at his door.

"Let's talk to a Seed Banker, IA."

"Okay." It was a relief to hear that Doughan hadn't spent his night playing tough cop, but his assumption that Helt would drop everything on the instant was irritating. Mildly. At least Helt would have a chance to structure the rest of the interviews, if not this one. "Which one?"

"Kelly Halkett, electrical engineer. He's a good one, too," Doughan said. "It's early, and he's not on duty, so we don't have to rush. Might I have some of that coffee?"

"Sure." Helt poured coffee and tossed his trusty windbreaker off the visitor's chair. Doughan hung his windbreaker on a hook and made himself at home. For Saturday time off, he looked like a movie cowboy, shoulders braced on the chair back, butt on the edge of the chair, legs full length and ankles crossed. He was wearing a denim-blue T-shirt, jeans, a totally disreputable leather belt that featured some sort of Native American silver buckle, fair-sized but not in the least flashy, and well-worn boots, the rough leather kind called "roper."

Kelly Halkett's bio flashed up on the wall screen. He'd come up on a ten-year contract. He had worked on some of the step-downs from the big generators, both fusion and "solar," meaning the power captured from *Kybele*'s quartz sun and the turbines that caught and distributed winds from the poles in Center. Halkett had designed some generators, smaller and simpler than the originals, to capture a few joules from the spin of the wheels under the trains, and that had earned him a colonist upgrade seven years ago.

"I don't see any red flags on it," Helt said. Kelly Halkett was a native of the Scots highlands, educated at Edinburgh, sometimes teased with the name "Scotty," a persistent homage to eighteenth-century age-of-steam engineers. "What does David II have to say about him?"

"I'll ask him after we talk to this Seed Banker. David II's coming over here," Doughan said. "So is Engineer Halkett."

"Here," Helt said. "When?"

"As soon as David II and said engineer finish soccer practice. We'll record everything, of course. The lawyers can sort it out later."

Helt checked the Cleared List. The station cameras showed Kelly Halkett going home after shift, and they didn't show him anywhere after that until the next morning.

"He's pretty much accounted for on Wednesday night. I'm not prepped for this. I wasn't planning on becoming an interrogator so soon."

"You'll do fine," Doughan said. "Think of it as low risk. After all, Halkett will be off-ship no matter what. And all we need to know from him is if there's a connection between him and Cash Ryan."

"Right," Helt said. "Get the info but don't spill the beans and let the man know he's been found out. Doughan, I am not good at lying. I'll do what I can, but I'll use any info I need to use. That's how it has to work."

"Accepted," Doughan said.

"Damn. What you're saying is that you're going to be evaluating my interview performance, and you've given me no preparation time at all. At the very least, I want to look through whatever bio we have on the man. And I'll want to do the interview in here, please."

"What about the conference room upstairs?" Doughan asked.

"It's too big for four; those empty chairs make people want to perform for an audience, and they get too much space to set their distances in. I'd say Nadia and Jerry's office is the right size, but I don't have time to vet the clutter in there. I'm sure there's nothing too perverse left out, but something in the mess might clue the guy that something big is up."

I sound like a fussy guy with OCD, Helt realized. But these things count, damn it.

"I'll get some chairs," Doughan said.

"Thank you," Helt said. He scanned on down Kelly Halkett's history on *Kybele*. Relationships. Nothing much on *Kybele*. Heterosexual, a wife and son in Scotland, deserted forever after Halkett got his colonist bid. Hmmm. Helt moved Halkett's name into the scrutiny of his interaction sorters, some individuals in it newly overlaid with a sickly orange glow of Seed Banker funding. He found, in addition to the money highlight, a cluster of activity centered at a site devoted to playing variable-g football. Okay.

He heard voices in the lobby. Doughan put down the two chairs he was carrying and went out front. Helt stayed put and heard quick intros and some comments about the condition of the turf in the Athens stadium.

Both David Luo II and his guest were freshly showered, dressed in jeans and black team jerseys, and hauling gym bags. The logo on their shirts was a pair of robotic hands with prominent nuts and bolts, cradling a stylized *Kybele*, an oblong spheroid floating in a spindle made of the struts of the plasma shield.

"Helt, this is Kelly," Doughan said. "I don't know if you've met."

Kelly Halkett was a knotty-looking man, mid-sized, mid-forties, with sandy hair going gray, fair skin, and blue eyes that darted here, there, and everywhere. Big hands, big knuckles, but he shook hands with a firm medium-strength grip that was courtesy and not a challenge. Kelly Halkett moved quickly and looked tightly wound. He took the chair Helt offered and settled his gym bag beneath it, precisely centered in the square formed by the chair legs.

David II sank smoothly into his chair. The word *smooth* always entered Helt's mind when he was around David II. The engineering boss might have been made of some advanced polymer whose characteristics included resistance to chemicals, fire, and psychic distress of all kinds. He was always calm, pleasant, and polite, as far as Helt knew. He was a handsome, athletic, ethnic Chinese, and he was horribly talented. People worked themselves to exhaustion for him.

Doughan resumed his good ol' boy chair slouch, but with his arms crossed so that he had a firm grip on each bicep.

"What's up?" David II asked.

Oh, great, Helt thought. Doughan hadn't clued David II about his plans for the interview.

"Trouble," Doughan said. "I'll let Helt explain."

Halkett's eyes darted from Doughan's face to David's to Helt's, and then went back to David's again.

"It's about Cash Ryan, the man who died in Center." Not about your sudden windfall, Dr. Halkett, and although Helt watched for any sign of relief or relaxation in Kelly's face and muscles, he couldn't spot one. "NSS is pretty sure he was murdered."

Halkett gave Helt a quick glance. He looked back at David II, who displayed no startle response at the news and offered Kelly no suggestions about how he should respond. After some silence, in which responses like

"I'm sorry to hear that" or "Am I under suspicion?" didn't get said, Helt figured that Electrical Engineer Halkett probably didn't have much innate capacity in verbal social interactions and bailed the guy out.

"Cash Ryan didn't leave us much information about himself, and he didn't seem to have many friends. Did you know him?"

"I knew his name."

"But not the man?" Helt asked.

"I knew he worked for Navigation as an engineer," Kelly said.

"Have you had any contact with him in the past three years?" Helt asked.

"Very little. When he came aboard, he was assigned one of the three tunnel crews I was supervising then. He requested a transfer a couple of weeks after he got here. I okayed his request."

"You didn't talk to him about it?" Helt asked.

"I did not."

"Do you, usually? Talk to someone about why they want to move?"

"The answer to that would have to be yes, and no," Kelly said. "The crew Cash Ryan was working with told me he was thinking about asking for a transfer. Sometimes that means a newbie is shy and afraid asking for a transfer would make trouble. Sometimes it means the crew doesn't like the newbie. In either case, it's better to have crews who are comfortable with one another. So we don't question a bit of shifting around when someone is settling in."

"Ryan's record doesn't give us much that would clue us on why someone would want to kill him. Engineer Halkett, at this point we're just looking for people who have any information about Cash Ryan, about what he did when he was off work. Anything that might have gotten him cross-ways with anyone. Who brought this death to your attention?"

"I think it was Birdy who said something about him."

"Oriol?" David II asked. "Oriol Bruguera?" Oriol Bruguera was on the Seed Banker list. David II had a gift for giving nothing away. Nothing in his voice or posture indicated anything but polite interest at hearing the name.

"Yes," Kelly said.

"Did Birdy know him?" David II asked.

"He knew who he was, anyway," Halkett said.

"Birdy works on one of the reactor crews, Helt," David II said. "What did he say?"

Halkett looked as if he were trying hard to pass an exam on a difficult subject and knew he hadn't studied. "Birdy said he remembered that Ryan worked with his crew for a few days and then got transferred somewhere else. He said he didn't remember his face but he recognized the name when it showed up."

"Anything else?" Helt asked.

"Not much. Birdy started talking about the guy's trajectory off the tower. He said he looked at the GPS coordinates of the roped-off area NSS put up and he tried to calculate how he got that far away, and the figures don't work out."

"Tell him it was windy," Helt said. "Wait a sec, I'll give you the numbers." He looked at Jerry's notes about the weather that evening. "Sixteen kph with gusts to sixty."

That got him a quick eye contact from Kelly Halkett.

"Oh. I will." Halkett stared into infinity. Helt could see the calculations going on and waited. "Yes. That works. I'll tell Birdy."

"You and Birdy are on the same football team. Do you play variable-g with him as well?"

"Oh, sure. Birdy's good at both. I'm better with the virtuals."

Helt smiled. "Is gambling involved?" The question got the reaction of puzzlement that Helt expected. Kelly looked as if he couldn't decide whether to be alarmed. Gambling wasn't prohibited, but if you ended up on Basic Support with debts to pay, medical would give you a gentle nudge about psychiatric help. "You don't have to answer that."

Kelly thought it over and decided it was okay to smile back, quickly and briefly, and some sort of barrier went down.

"Do you play, Dr. Borresen?" Kelly asked.

"Helt. No, I don't. I played the live game as a child. I just looked at the home page, though, and it looks like the virtual game could eat my lunch really fast."

"Aye, that it might." With that single phrase, the Highlands came through and Helt realized the man's lilt had been there from the beginning. "There's a beauty in it. It would seem an enjoyable thing, to take the great games of the past and play them again by recalculating impetus and trajectory for every move the ball makes. The concept is to end with the same score as the original, and it's possible. But try it at a g and a half, or a quarter. There are sets of scores, one set based on your accuracy at calculating the force applied and the direction of the ball to keep the scores as they were in the original games. Then, for taking a player's initial position and playing the game de novo at that same altered g. And that is when things get a wee bit more complicated. We've upset many a championship in our own version of alternate history."

This time the grin was wider and not so quickly hidden.

"More complicated than the live games you're playing," Helt said.

"Not so. Not so, Mr. Borresen." Halkett sighed. "The variable-g games, now, when a man enters a direction, a point of impact, and a force, the ball goes where it should. Out on that field, a man's muscles don't always do what they're told."

"You trust the numbers," Helt said.

"That I do."

A corner of Helt's screen strobed. He gave it a quick glance. Yves Copani. Coming to your office.

"Pardon me," Helt said. Helt. OK 30 min, he replied, and vanished the info.

"Sorry about that. Tell me, Mr. Halkett, the probability that we'll get to turnover without a stray rock getting past the plasma shields."

David II shifted in his chair. If his expression changed, Helt couldn't see it.

"Any size rock?" Kelly Halkett asked.

"One big enough to kill the ship."

"At a tenth light, with our hide made of four kilometers of nickel iron, something the size of a soccer ball would burn down to a size I can hold in my fist."

It was an impressive fist, clenched hard enough to pale the man's knuckles.

"Even so, such a rock would blow a hole about—I say *about*—two kilometers square. That it would."

"The probability?" Helt asked.

"The probability is something I cannot"—*canna*, Helt heard—"calculate without more data. There's a lot of faith in those pulsar navigation systems we'll be sending out ahead, but. We'll do our best to aim for empty sky, that I trust. But we don't know enough about interstellar dust, now, do we? We don't know where it is for a certainty and how many dinguses of what size there might be in it. But we know it's out there."

Doughan raised his head and stared at the electrical engineer. "You're a mathematician and a gambler. Why did you choose to gamble on *Kybele*?"

"The probability is that I'll be long dead before a rock hits us hard enough to do damage. By my calculations, it's a better risk than the risk of getting killed by a stray outlander in the Highlands."

They kept coming, the outlanders, coming out of the dry south, armed, desperate, seeking a place to drink clean water, plant a crop, stay alive a little longer. Most were killed. Some got through the cordons and into the hills.

"You left your family behind," Helt said.

This time those blue eyes looked directly at Helt and did not shift away. "With their blessings on me. I may never forgive myself for that."

The man's pain was obvious.

"I'm sorry. You've been very helpful," Helt said. "Thank you."

Doughan accepted the signal that the interview was over and got out of his chair. He and David II ushered Kelly Halkett out of the office. David II went with Kelly to find Birdy. Doughan came back in.

"What did you learn from that?" Doughan asked. "I can't say I didn't enjoy your exploration of this guy's little pleasures, but what purpose does any of that serve?"

Doughan didn't curse in public and he didn't curse now, but the air was thick with unspoken expletives. He'd said once that he'd learned that if you don't say the words in private, they won't come bursting forth to haunt you in public. It was a skill learned by politicians, diplomats, and people who didn't want to get in trouble with their superiors.

Even so, Doughan was a master at speaking italics and even all caps. Helt was still practicing the art. He didn't always succeed.

"He's likable, isn't he?" Helt asked. He was pushing Doughan's limits with the statement and he knew it.

"He's a traitor." Helt watched a vein pulse on Doughan's forehead and estimated his pulse at about 90.

"That was decided before he walked in the room, but now we have some useful information from him. We have a lead to someone who knew Cash Ryan and is also a Seed Banker."

"And what did the other stuff tell you?" Doughan asked.

"Kelly Halkett will not betray a friend if there's any reasonable way to avoid it. He gave us Birdy's name only after he chose to believe we were simply looking for contacts who might have known a murdered man—with the goal of solving a murder in which Kelly Halkett is, in my best estimation, in no way involved. He's a true and honest child of the Enlightenment;

he believes in reason and he trusts his numbers, his probabilities. He has a naive belief that reason will triumph, eventually. He may be a Seed Banker at heart, but he doesn't plan to harm *Kybele*."

"You can't know that." It was almost a snarl.

"I'm extrapolating and I know it. But I'll lay odds he has what he wants for his future. He has time. A lifetime, to try to persuade the rest of us to use reason and keep this treasure available to an Earth that is in sad need of the resources we've hoarded here."

Doughan slowed his breathing and relaxed some key muscles. It was an effort to bring his temper back under control, if Helt read him right.

"You have a major character flaw, Helt Borresen," Doughan said, and his voice was flat. "You would have sympathy for the devil himself."

"Accepted," Helt said. "I have another problem as well."

"I'll bite. What is it?"

"Kelly Halkett is sane. It's difficult, with the tools I have, to find threats to this ship that come from people who are sane. And I don't have a lifetime to spend at it."

Kelly Halkett had left a wife and child on Earth. His gamble had to be that he could convince *Kybele* not to leave the local system—and then he could go back to Scotland. If there were a way for him to cripple the ship, would he use it? Or had he only thought to spend his life here, hoping to convince the ship to stay at home, even if his efforts lasted until everyone in his family was dead? Had he planned to be that sort of martyr?

Whatever he had imagined made no difference now. Kelly Halkett was going home.

14

The Sculptor and His Girl

Yves Copani was in SysSu's lobby, pacing from monitor display to monitor display in the otherwise deserted space. His hands were gripped behind his back, the art gallery posture of someone who really wants to touch something.

"How long have you been here?" Helt asked.

Copani turned and smiled, a flash of white teeth. "Ten minutes."

Helt motioned toward the hallway and Copani followed him. "Did you see Doughan leave?"

"I saw him. I'm not sure he saw me. He looked like he was in a hurry."

The extra chairs were still in Helt's office. Helt motioned for Copani to take the visitor's chair beside his own, the one Doughan had just vacated.

"Why didn't you tell me about the sculpture?" Helt asked.

Copani's alert enthusiasm changed to posture of limp despair, a deflation so theatrical it had to be, in part, feigned.

"I'm busted."

"Busted for what?" Helt asked. Not the murder. The man in Helt's chair had been in the diner, begging for a place on board, when Ryan died. Busted for the creation of unauthorized art? Not if Helt had anything to say about it.

"Vandalism," Copani said.

"Is that what you call it? Damn it, man, that area of Petra canyon is marked as home sites, and now that has to change. Your World Tree, if that's what it's called, is magnificent."

Yves Copani's hands relaxed their grip on the arms of the visitor's chair. "The area was gonna be lazed into rubble after I left. I figured I'd just start the process a little early."

"It has to be that everyone who's seen it has kept it secret, a treasure of their own," Helt said. "No images are up anywhere; I looked. That response is unusual. May even be unique. I'm wondering when the first captures will go viral."

"Me too," Yves said.

Helt read a quickness about the man, a restlessness, a sense of controlled purpose. The sculpture was a challenge. Copani decided to show us what he can do. He wants to stay on board; he's said that. What else did he want? "You're an architect. You didn't put that on your résumé when you signed up as a welder, and you've completed more projects than any of the guys working here now."

The dejection was gone. Sometime during Helt's admiration speech, Copani had decided he was not in enemy territory. He had fitted into the visitor's chair as if he'd spent hours there, shooting the shit with an old friend.

"You had architects working up here already. The position of 'welder' didn't have that many applicants, so that's the one I asked for. I figured I'd lay low about the other stuff."

"The last big verbal punch-out the architects had was about twelve years ago. That's a few years after the megaliths went up in Stonehenge. The—discussions—got a lot of media time," Helt said.

Copani glanced at Helt to see if the two of them were sharing the same subtext. There had been some battles royale over Biosystems' choice of a monumental work. Any Earth-based architect could find who said what to whom in the chatter behind the journal articles and published plans, and obviously, Copani had.

"The designs wakened some strong post-colonial sentiments." Copani's tone was a calculated neutral, a reversion to the formalities of academe.

Copani was just showing he could speak diplomacy-speak if the situation needs it, Helt decided. "That's nicely phrased. They did. I remember." Helt grinned.

"But in the aftermath, *Kybele* convinced the world that the climate wasn't all that would change up here. Buildings, homes, walkways, megaliths, you name it—everything can be torn down and rebuilt, if enough people want to, always." Copani talked with his hands, building and trashing castles in the air with swooping gestures. "I like that. I really like that."

"It's a hope," Helt said.

"You were still Earthbound. That PR was your work?" Copani asked.

"Looked me up, have you?"

"Sure. You're the man I need to convince, so I did some homework before I talked to you the first time."

"Okay. But I didn't do the PR. I was working IA for *Kybele*'s lottery office in Oslo then."

"But you pushed the PR guys when the flap started. I'd bet on it," Copani said.

Helt didn't deny it.

"What sold me that you guys up here had your act together was that abandoned structures will get filled in with rubble. Clean slate for rethinking."

Even without haunted houses, the ship had already made a ghost. Stories of the missing miner came up now and again in idle discourse, and the differing certainties about where his body was, and why, were urban myth, nothing of concern. This was not a superstitious population. Yet. But the plan was, David II's crews had decided, to fill in abandoned structures. Yes, Helt had nudged them a little bit in that direction, but it hadn't taken more than a nudge.

Helt nudged, sometimes, and sometimes he had hunches. He had one now. "You know where the dead miner is," Helt said.

Copani's eyes narrowed, assessing Helt's face. "Some things are secret. The tunnels are ours," Copani said.

Heh. The miner died in the tunnels and the body was never found. But it was here, somewhere; Copani had just told Helt so. Where? Why did they hide him? Was he frozen close to the surface where it's really, really cold? They didn't put him in one of the seed vaults. Those vaults were monitored 24/7. Did they carve out a private mausoleum for him?

"Ours?" Helt asked.

"Well, there's hardhats, and then there's everybody else."

Everyone else meant nerds, meaning SysSu and some of the Navigation brains, or farmers, meaning Biosystems. "I thought so," Helt said. "David II wonders about class divisions sometimes, but no one knows whether to worry about them. So, Yves Copani, you're telling me an 'us and them' spirit is alive and well in the tunnels. David II thought he had staved it off by having everybody sleep and eat on Level One."

"All that going upstairs for food does is piss us off," Copani said.

"What's it like, living in a stratified society?"

"It's good. It's easy; we're not feeling excluded. Some women, you know, like men who work with their hands, and vice versa. I don't know if I'd want to mess with the way things are now."

"But if, if, I say, it comes time to mingle Level One with the underworld, could you do it?"

Copani frowned, probably thinking about traffic flows, destination structures, light and sound. "I think so," he said.

"Look, the list of people who will be departing on the last shuttle has changed. I'd rather you didn't ask why. But I'm wondering if you would send your portfolio to David II. I've looked it over, quickly, and I'm impressed. I think David II will be, too.

"And be sure to send him some of the stuff you've thought up since you've been here." Helt wanted, very much, to see if the time-striding resonance of Copani's world tree carried through into homes, parks, stadia, whatever he wanted to do here. Did Copani paint on canvas, on wood, did he make lightscapes? His online portfolio showed only buildings.

"I'll send a few things."

"I'm looking forward to it. Did you know Cash Ryan?"

"The dead guy? No. Never worked with him. Most of what I do at my day job is weld conduit and supports in the new tunnels as we go. This guy worked outside, is what the story is. You think he killed himself because he didn't want to leave?"

Killed himself was the current assumption, then, still holding through the morning. Helt wasn't good at lying, and he didn't want to. "I can't answer that."

"Okay," Copani said. "I wasn't trying to push. You execs deal with whatever happened. I haven't heard anyone else say they want the job."

"Do you know anyone who knew him?" Helt asked.

"Only one person."

"Who?" Helt asked.

"I don't want to say *know*. I know only one person who could recognize him on the street. She says she was at a club with some friends and this guy Ryan tried to talk her into a date. She thought he was creepy, and told him, no way, never, go away."

"Navigation is tracing every contact the man ever had. If you could help them . . ."

"Susanna knew what he looked like," Copani said.

"Your girlfriend?" Helt asked.

"Susanna Jambekar, the best midwife on *Kybele*."

"Your girlfriend."

"The love of my life."

Oh, shit. Yves's girlfriend was one of the two people in Biosystems on the Seed Banker list. Hide your damned reaction, Helt.

"Creepy, how?" Helt asked.

"Wouldn't stop staring at her. I can't blame him for that; she's beautiful, but there's staring and then there's staring, you know?"

"I think so," Helt said. "We'll want to talk to her soon, then."

Yves tensed up.

"You didn't rat her out. Security tells me she was in the same street camera view with Cash Ryan a couple of times, so she was on the list already." That much was true. Helt didn't mention the Seed Banker funds in her account. He didn't mention that she would be booted back to Earth. Would Yves Copani follow her? "Thing is, the guy was a loner. We're looking for anyone who had any contact with him. We're trying to put it all together, that's all."

"You better be nice." It wasn't a threat. It was the real thing. Be nice to her or I will hurt you; a message sent loud and clear via a sudden increase in the bulk of the muscles in Yves Copani's neck and arms. Helt was suddenly aware that this was a man who carved and chiseled rock for pleasure—and did it after a hard day's physical work. Copani's reaction was controlled, but very real. His face looked friendly, so the message was only a message—but not one to be taken lightly. He'd been sitting with Helt during part of the dead hour, but only for part of it. He had to go on the suspect list.

"We will," Helt said. "So, you'll send files to David II? I'll tell him they're coming."

"I'll do it," Copani said.

As soon as Helt was alone again, he grabbed the videos Navigation had culled that showed the combination Susanna Jambekar/Charles "Cash" Ryan. The captures were brief. One showed Susanna entering a hairdresser's shop in Athens, Cash Ryan behind her, walking past without a glance. Another, Susanna exiting the Athens clinic and turning up the street that led to the plaza and the elevator. Cash Ryan was walking the other way on that street and didn't seem to notice her.

Wait. Helt replayed it.

Susanna Jambekar had dark hair tied in a knot at the back of her head. A dull red lab coat slung over her shoulder. She walked—

Wait. "She found a video of him walking, and then, yes, I knew him," Venkie had said.

Helt looked for a view of Elena walking away from the camera's eye and found one.

Helt viewed, split-screen, Susanna walking away from the camera, walking away from something she had finished at the clinic, Elena walking away from the camera in the Level One corridor near her lab. Susanna Jambekar and Elena had the same sort of stride, that careful placement of the feet. Graceful but cautious. Not the same, but. But add the lab coat and wishful thinking.

Over a rising fear, he searched the Athens plaza cameras on Friday morning for Severo and himself, and found the woman he had briefly thought looked like Elena. It was Susanna.

This was discovery, this was a lead, but which one of these women had hated Cash Ryan enough to kill him? Please, not Elena. Please, don't let Yves Copani be in love with a woman who would kill a stalker.

Helt wanted to run. He wanted to go to Mena, right now, to tell her to wait, wait, before she scheduled Susanna's interview. There were specific things to ask, very specific things.

He took a deep breath and looked at the rest of the Susanna Jambekar/Cash Ryan footage. They had both exited the train at the same time on a couple of occasions. The times of the encounters were scattered over three years. Views of the Stonehenge elevator platform, Cash exiting or entering as Susanna crossed the platform going from one place to another. If you went back in time and forward in time from those same views, would you find places where Cash Ryan had been nearby but had avoided camera capture?

Helt didn't have time to find out. He called Mena.

"I'm having lunch," she said. The background wasn't in focus. Mena seemed to be standing in front of some sort of cloth. In the foreground, he saw a wineglass, a pitcher on a table.

"Where? Where are you? I'm coming there right now."

"In a tent in the vineyards. You'll see it," Mena said.

15

Privacy

Helt ran. He made good time through the deserted SysSu lobby and dodged past shoppers in the plaza. He paced back and forth until the train slowed and stopped at Athens. He paced up and down the car while it traveled, stared at the Stonehenge elevator lights as if glaring at them could speed his ascent, thumped the opening door, but not hard enough to hurt it, and ran for the tent he saw at the edge of one of Mena's pet vineyards. His path led him between rows of stripped vines, their severe pruning apparent through yellowing leaves. They looked tortured to him, only two twisted, recently unburdened arms left on each to cling to the supporting wires on either side of their trunks. The scent of ripe grapes grew richer in the warm midday air.

His eyes, in the shade cast by the canvas, took far too long to adapt. Skiing into black shadow now would be risky—but he wouldn't be skiing the *fjells* again, and he shouldn't expect to have a teenager's near-instant adaptation to changes in ambient light. He was too old for that.

Those bulky cylinders in the shadows were vats on trailers; the long white-clad tables set up for this morning's harvest crew were to his left, and there was Mena, sitting at one and staring out at a field as yet unharvested. She saw him coming and turned her head to watch him pant his way toward her. Elena, seated across from her, looked up, frowning, and he wondered how the big, sweaty, anxious nerd interrupting her lunch looked to her today. Helt stopped beside Mena's chair.

"What is it, Helt?" Mena asked.

"More on the murder." Helt would have sworn he saw Elena's eyes strobe from amber to yellow and back to amber again when he spoke. It was a quick flash, and he didn't know how to read her eyes. He had no clue whether what she signaled was fear, or anger, or pleasure at seeing him. Her expression was pleasantly neutral, one of polite concern.

Elena's presence here was a complication. Either she was privy to everything Mena knew, and knew the execs were keeping the Seed Banker information to themselves, or she wasn't in the loop and didn't know. And then there was the question of recordings going on right now, documentation of the harvest, possible listening ears.

"Pardon me," Helt said. He grabbed his interface and checked; there were four cameras recording in the tent but none of them were close enough to catch conversation from this point. But he wanted this recorded, every word, every gesture, because Elena was here and he wanted there to be no secrets, nothing hidden from possible review, no private moments between them until she was no longer a suspect. He set the controls on the nearest camera to pick up their speech and send the footage to his SysSu files and nowhere else. "Okay, we're on camera. For the archives."

"Helt! Slow down! *Sit* down." Mena pointed to the chair beside her.

Helt sat. Lunch for the grape pickers must be mostly over. A few people were still seated, deep in conversation. Two men carried emptied plates to a cart near the door. A few crumbs littered the white cloth in front of him. Mena and Elena were eating late; skewered lamb and dolmades. His view of the beauty of Elena's face, her throat, her hands, was enhanced by a non-barrier in the center of the table, a bowl filled with clusters of ripe grapes in ice and water. There were several kinds of grapes; pale greens and purples and reds, but one cluster was almost black, another tawny gold. The colors seemed to have been chosen by an Old Master to set off Elena's skin.

He looked at Elena, and Mena beside him was a flood of memory, of her body, her sensuality, her ability to demand and to satisfy. He felt her assessment of what might develop between him and Elena. It was generous. It was right as Mena saw it. It made him hate time, that he and Mena were separated by it.

"There's some information Doughan wants kept quiet for a while. It will be public soon. Elena—"

Elena pushed back her chair. "I'll let you talk in private," she said.

"No! Don't leave! This may concern you, and I want you here."

Beside him, Mena had shifted away from him and lifted her shoulder as if to guard against a blow. She stared at him over that defensive shield, her dark, unblinking eyes as observant as a hawk's. The tiny lines at the corners of her eyes were deeper than he remembered, and Elena was on her feet and walking away.

"Stay with us, Elena," Mena said. It was a command, but her eyes never left Helt's face. "Forgive me," was what he thought he saw. And because Mena asked it, he could not do otherwise.

"Please," Helt said, speaking to the woman leaving them, "I want you to know everything I know."

Elena stopped and turned back toward the table. He knew she had heard, and Mena had heard, everything he implied with that statement, every truth that was in it. Mena looked down at her plate with a tiny, knowing smile. Elena came back and sat down again.

"It's this information, for now, that I want you to hear. The implications bother me," Helt said. "Elena, there are seven Seed Bankers on board. There may be more; we don't know yet. The seven are all colonists and in the past year their backers have sent them money. A lot of money. One of them is Susanna Jambekar, and—"

Elena frowned. "That's nuts," she said. "It fits nothing I know of her."

"I'm sorry," Helt said. "All seven of these people will be questioned by NSS or by me, or both. All of them will be sent back to Earth. Mena, I came here because I must interview Susanna Jambekar myself. Preferably with you there."

"Of course." Mena stared hard at him for a minute. "Oh. You assumed I would grill her, get answers, and guard her from Doughan and NSS? You are wrong. I want this cleared up as much as you do, I can promise you that." Mena looked exasperated. "Oh, Helt. Is that why you ran all the way up here? And have you had lunch?"

"I want you there. You might see things I might miss. I ran because I was afraid that you might be already talking to Susanna."

Mena waved to one of the men near the cart. He nodded and went away somewhere. "No. I won't talk to her without you. I wouldn't do that," Mena said. "But what worries you about this particular woman?"

"I've been looking at records on Susanna Jambekar. She knew Cash Ryan, at least a little, and her boyfriend says she didn't like him. It's possible he was stalking her; I don't know that yet for sure. Elena, in some ways, to some degree, she looks like you."

"Stalking? Oh, that's ugly," Elena said. "No, she doesn't. She doesn't look like me at all." Her fingers explored the texture of a slice of bread on the plate beside her unfinished lunch, but her thoughts seemed to be elsewhere. "Except for dark hair, and our skin tone is fairly close. She's thinner than I am."

You are lush and there's not an ounce of fat on you, Helt wanted to say. "You walk the same way. Sort of," Helt said.

"Really?" Elena asked.

"Really," Helt said.

"So, do you think she killed Ryan because she didn't like him?" Mena asked.

"I don't know," Helt said. "I don't know if he could have been that much of a threat to her, or if she could have hated him that much. I don't know the connections between the Seed Bankers." He didn't know a fraction of what he needed to know about this, and he could fail, and he wanted help and didn't know where to find it. "I don't know if Cash Ryan was one of them. He didn't get funds from them here; we know that. At least one other Seed Banker knew who Ryan was, and Doughan is finding out more about that, probably right now.

"If there was a connection between Ryan and the Seed Bankers, what did he do, or not do, to mark him for murder?" Elena asked. "If they didn't want him around, all they had to do was wait and he'd be out of their hair. Out of Susanna's hair, too, for that matter."

And out of Elena's hair as well.

Mena curved forward, stretching her back, and then straightened. "I suppose this Ryan man could have threatened to expose whatever plans the Seed Bankers had to sabotage *Kybele*, if they had any. Or threatened simply to expose them to get them off-ship and leave him here. And then they selected Susanna to do the deed of killing Ryan because she didn't like him? Helt, this is wild speculation."

The smell of sizzling chunks of lamb grilled over oregano stalks drifted up to Helt's nose from the plate that had magically appeared in front of him. The dolmades, wrapped in fresh grape leaves, added a hint of citrus.

"Next you'll be speculating that Susanna killed him in self-defense because Cash Ryan was so delusional he thought she was me, and he tried to hurt her," Elena said.

"And attacked you, except it wasn't you, it was Susanna," Helt said. "Do you think he hated you that much?"

"I don't know!" Elena's amber eyes changed color, to black-centered gold. "I told you, I knew him when he was a student. I know nothing about his life since then, except that he showed up here and got himself killed. How many times must I tell you and your damned archives that that's all I know?"

“I’m sorry,” Helt said. “I didn’t mean—I wouldn’t—I won’t—Please forgive me.” He still blushed, when he felt this chagrined. His face was hot and bright red.

“Okay,” Elena said, and her eyes were amber again.

A glass of ice water had appeared when the lamb did. Helt raised it to Elena in a grateful toast.

“Thank you,” he said.

“Hmmm,” Mena said. “We need to get this settled. I think the person to ask about whether Susanna hated Ryan is Susanna.” Mena retrieved her interface from a pocket, hesitated, and laid it on the table. “What are the rules for this? I should be present when you talk to her?”

Helt nodded. His mouth was full of lamb.

“Wait!” Elena said. “Could this possibly be delayed a day or two? Susanna has a primip in early labor. Can’t this wait until the baby is here?”

“Primip?” Helt didn’t know the word.

“Primipara. This will be her first child,” Elena said. “It’s a matter of trust, Helt. Susanna’s done all the prenatal care, and the mother knows her and will be more comfortable with her than with anyone else.”

“Is it Zhōu? Any problems?” Mena asked.

“No problems,” Elena said.

“I didn’t know she was this near term. That’s wonderful!”

Helt watched the two women smile at each other, smiles that held the worry and hope that burdens every childbirth, smiles that spoke of concerns that began when a particular primate species developed a bipedal gait. He was an intruder in archetype country. He sat very still.

“Well,” Mena said. “This requires us to be adaptive. ‘Where’s my midwife?’ ‘Oh, she couldn’t make it today. She’s under investigation for treason.’ Put that speech in Calloway’s mouth. No. That conversation could upset any patient,” Mena said. “What’s the risk of delay, really, Helt?”

“We have watchers on all the Seed Bankers. I don’t know what she could do that wouldn’t be noticed,” Helt said.

“It’s settled, then. Zhōu will have her baby without disturbance. The grilling of Susanna about Cash Ryan can wait for a few hours.” Mena pushed back her chair and got to her feet. She put her interface in her shirt pocket.

“Now, if you’ll pardon me, I’m going to the fields. There’s a small planting of Moschofilero that may be ready for harvesting tomorrow, but I want to be sure of it.”

She took a few steps toward the pulled-back canvas that served as a doorway and then turned to look back at them. "You don't need me as duenna, you two. Let the cameras do the work. Finish your lunch, Helt."

Helt watched Mena walk away, her posture so erect you could forget how tiny she was because she walked tall, always focused on the work going on around her, always focused on the next thing to do and how it would be done. He watched her leave the blue-gray of canvas shadow and step into the soft golden light of an early autumn afternoon.

"You still love her," Elena said.

"Of course I do." He would never know what women talked about or why, but now he knew Mena had told Elena about Helt, about shared intimacies. Whatever she'd said, it hadn't sent Elena running, at least. "But the time of being lovers is in the past now."

"If she needed you, you would go to her."

"Never doubt it," Helt said.

"I never will." Elena smiled. "Particularly now that it's on the record."

"Ouch," Helt said. A great weight lifted from his shoulders and he felt very, very good. Elena didn't hate him. He smiled to let her know she had scored a point, but hadn't hurt his feelings.

"It would work. The camera thing. I'm not saying it won't feel weird. I've never thought of myself as an exhibitionist," Elena said.

"It's only for documentation if it's needed," Helt said. "I hope it won't be," and then some of the things that might end up on that record became very clear to him, and he blushed again.

But everyone was on the record, sometimes when they knew it, sometimes when they didn't, and a certain sort of anonymity came from the sheer bulk of what was available.

Someday he would tell Elena that she was more beautiful now than she had been at eighteen, caught in public videos when she accepted awards in high school, when she went on that school thing to Europe, when, in her early twenties, she defended her dissertation for a committee that tried to look dispassionate. But they had been pleased. The videos showed that.

The contours of her face were more defined now; her eyes seemed larger and wiser.

"I'll be fidgeting around my lab all day," Elena said. "I'll drop by Zhōu's house as the obstetrician on call, but I'll be in the background. My job is to stay out of the way and let Susanna do the work. So I'm going to be distracted. I'm sorry."

"I have to get back to SysSu. A conference. If you're finished before midnight. No, before two a.m. Let me know. We'll have a drink." Which didn't sound suave or debonair at all. Helt felt like an idiot, but he didn't much care, because he thought she knew what he meant.

Elena looked carefully at the bowl of grapes and plucked a particular one from the cluster that was almost black.

"For you," Elena said. She leaned forward with it and Helt, obedient as a baby bird, opened his mouth. The flood of its juices was sweet, musky, rich with complicated darkness and spice. Her fingers brushed his lower lip. She drew away and stood up to leave.

"If it's past two in the morning, I won't take the risk of waking you," she said.

16

Manipulated Objects

Helt set a true color image of Rodin's *The Thinker* on the display stage in the center of the SysSu conference table. Testing, testing, one, two, three. He aged it with verdigris, rotated it, slowly, and then grew it to the size of a man and a half.

Severo, in a T-shirt that was fiercely pink, and David II, whose team's black jersey still looked impeccable, were already seated, their backs guarded by the curve of wall behind the round table. Both of them were intent on whatever they were looking at on their table screens. They had good views of the door and of the plaza below. Severo never put his back to a door if he could help it.

Helt rubbed his lower lip. It was slightly chapped, a little rough. He licked it, but he couldn't taste grape, or Elena's fingers.

Down on the plaza, maybe twenty people formed a shifting amoeboid pattern, pseudopods of two or one or five of them stopping and talking or coming in and out of the Library or the shops. Another twenty or so sat at café tables, drinking, munching, and talking. The umbrellas that shaded the tables from summer sun were furled so they wouldn't block the afternoon warmth. It would be so nice to be down there rather than up here. It would be so nice to laze away the afternoon.

Jim Tulloch ambled in, his hands in the pockets of a pair of disreputable chinos. His mud-colored T-shirt looked equally battered. He wore his signature sandals. On a Saturday afternoon, he had opted for socks that didn't match, or he hadn't noticed they didn't. One was green and the other a sort of blurry yellow-and-blue tartan.

He looked as if he'd be more comfortable in a kilt. Something about Dr. Jim Tulloch reminded Helt of a slightly warped ad for single-malt Scotch.

Helt vanished the statue. Severo looked up and nodded at Jim Tulloch.

"It's your show, Jim." Helt motioned to the chair he'd left empty between him and Severo. "We're all here, except that David I has a slot with us. Archer's still fine-tuning him; he'll be here when he's happy with the signal."

"Doughan? Mena?" Jim asked. He took the empty chair, peered at the table screen in front of him, and tapped its keyboard.

"Doughan can't be here," Helt said. Doughan was looking for Oriol Bruguera. The official fiction was that only the execs were supposed to know there were Seed Bankers on board. That little deception wouldn't last, and Helt felt uneasy about it, but there wasn't really time to explain it right now, or a way to get the three execs together and agreeing to let the information go public. Not right now. "Mena's not coming. A woman's in labor, and Mena's guarding the mom and Elena Maury and the midwife from, I don't know, the harpies or invisible bears or something. You're here for Biosystems."

"Okay." Jim Tulloch pushed back from the table and brought his tartan-socked right ankle up to rest on his left knee. It was a relaxed pose, but Helt knew him well enough to know he was paying sharp attention to everyone in the room.

"The idea is to re-create a personality with a particular set of traits that caused another personality to murder him."

"Make that plural," Severo said. "Personali-*ties*. Could have been more than one person."

"Granted," Jim said. "I take it we all agree to dismiss the theory that Charles 'Cash' Ryan was simply in the wrong place at the wrong time, saw something he shouldn't have seen, and was killed for it."

"How often does that happen, Severo?" David II asked. "Historically, I mean."

"Depends on when and where you look. Different times, it happened more. Somebody misses a target; bystanders die. That was Earth. Here? An innocent victim would really piss me off," Severo said. "I don't even want to think about that can of worms."

Because, Helt thought, however improbable it might be, if Cash Ryan turns out to have been killed by mistake, we'll have to get really creative about why it happened and who wanted to kill whom.

"So we won't go there," Jim said. "What we need to do varies from the standard model. Psychiatric autopsies were often, historically, a method for psychiatrists to mourn a colleague who had committed suicide. Because, in the bad old days, a lot of psychiatrists were depressives. Or they had other neuroses. They were people who went into psychiatry to try to heal their own wounds."

"My understanding is that they still do," Helt said. He'd heard Jim relive some of those wounds, war stories from his time as a medic in the Northwest Passage. Then med school, then a residency in neurosurgery, then back to academe for a psych residency, because that was where the pains were that he couldn't fix, not for himself, and not for his patients.

"Yup." Jim Tulloch grinned. "I am the well-adjusted, sociable exception that proves the rule."

Severo sighed.

Jim looked away from Severo and kept talking. "To review the tool we're using, the procedure developed as a way to look for clear warnings of suicidal intent, so we could try to prevent the next one, but also it was used as a way to expiate some of the guilt of realizing, after the fact—I should have known. I should have seen."

Tulloch's baritone voice was mellow and relaxed. He spoke in the conversational cadence of a prof at a graduate symposium, colleague to colleague. It was a practiced strategy that implied that the listener, whether she was a Psych 101 student or one of Severo's beat cops learning crowd control, knew all about the subject at hand. Helt admired the technique. He tried to use his own version of it from time to time.

"But we're dealing with a murder victim, not a suicide. The job, this time, is to rebuild his personality out of fragments of fact, and then sort out what about that reconstructed personality made someone take the risk of killing him."

"Kill him and then try to make it look like suicide," David II said.

"Yeah, when it would have been easier to tuck him into a side tunnel and shove some rocks over the entrance," Severo said. His eyes did a quick scan of the activity in the plaza, the faces of the others in the room, the stillness of the open door into the hallway. Apparently satisfied, he looked down at his desk screen. "Later for analyzing the perp. Sorry."

"I've wondered about the tower toss myself," Jim said. "It seems fairly impromptu to me. If we had access to where he kept his personal confessional, his diary, whatever, we could do a lot more. We don't have it."

"Not yet," Helt said. "We have his e-mails. They are scant in number and mostly about business. We haven't located a data storage device of any sort. We know there's a stash in the cloud somewhere, under some name or other. There has to be one. We haven't found it yet."

That Ryan hadn't used the table interface in his quarters for anything like that was odd. But he hadn't. The money was on the missing pocket interface.

Severo turned his head from side to side, slowly. His mournful face made the "no" gesture more emphatic.

"So we're searching public data, all of us," Jim said. "I hoped to have some of the flavor of Ryan's childhood for you. Early history helps; I hoped to talk to his mother and flesh out the school records and such we have on him. So far I've failed to make contact with her."

"You ended up with that job? I was willing to sign off on the death announcement," David II said. "But Doughan said that because it looked like a suicide, and it did, at the time, the death announcement should come from Biosystems."

"Yes, because it seemed to be a medical death, Mena sent a formal announcement to his mother. That's who was listed as next of kin. My name was given as the contact on *Kybele* for a more detailed account. I waited forty-eight hours and then tried to contact Ryan's mother. I tried several times. She didn't respond." Jim was looking out the window, mostly, while he talked, but he was keeping track of David II's expression. It was neutral. Helt wondered if the two of them had ever discussed family relationships. David II's were complicated.

David II had been born in Singapore, a clone child of David I. When you saw the two of them together, they looked like father and son, closely related but not identical, but because they were clones you looked for identity—and sometimes found it. That the younger David was a clone had not been mentioned until David II scored higher than anyone else on the set of exams and interviews for David I's position.

The cloning problem, Mena had said twenty years ago, was a nonproblem. No, *Kybele* didn't plan on cloning humans; maintaining a heterogenous population was the idea, certainly for several generations. But David I wanted to retire, and the observations of David II's life would be interesting. Denying the position to the best candidate was foolish. End debate.

"Go on," Helt said.

"I poked around a little, and found that a Cynthia Ryan lived in Idaho, where the records said she lived. She's the right age. I didn't know why she wasn't interested in her son's death. Most mothers are. I came over to talk to you about it, Helt, but you weren't here, and Nadia saw me wandering, so she helped out. SysSu had already put tags on all e-mails that mentioned Cash Ryan, and she was able to tell me that the message to Cynthia Ryan had been opened at destination, not just trashed."

"Tagging is standard for some situations," Helt said. "Every mention of Cash Ryan's name is tagged for recovery and has been since the night he died."

Of course we did that. Helt felt defensive for no good reason; the practice was common, routine. Surely no one alive assumed that e-mails were private. But, he realized, we didn't announce that we were doing it. Transparency is a sacred cow for us, but we're hiding stuff. Since this death, SysSu has been making too many assumptions about what SysSu thinks is a given. SysSu and the execs.

So it's time for another round of announcements about what we do, time to bore people with announcements of the obvious. But they won't bother to read them anyway.

Helt knew Jim had noticed that he'd tensed up with that statement. The psychiatrist was a damned good clinician, and he might ask Helt to tell him what was going on, later. Or maybe he wouldn't.

"You can be angry at your son for a lot of reasons," Jim said. "You can never want to hear from him again, although that's not so common. I wanted to know what was going on between this mother and son, so I asked you, David II, what Cash's severance pay was going to be."

"You did," David II said. "I sent the figures over."

"And I used them as a bribe. 'Talk to me and money will come to you.' Just like a lost fortune scam, except with *Kybele*'s verifiable insignia all over the communication.

"The message was viewed by the recipient. So far, there's still nothing."

It was fishy. It felt fishy to Helt, and he knew it would seem fishy to Severo and David, too. They sat impassive and kept on listening.

"As far as facts go," Jim said, "I can tell you that Charles 'Cash' Ryan switched schools several times between age eleven and age fourteen, and that his mother kept the same address during those years. Dad? I don't know whether he was around or not. His name was Charles James Ryan and he died four years ago. So I can assume adolescent turmoil, but it's an assumption. I don't personally know a clinician in Caldwell who might have seen the kid in those years. I'm working the Old Boy network to try to find one."

"Jim, you'll need waivers and stuff to open the records if you do," Helt said. "I'll see if we can preempt the permissions." He did a quick draft of the request to *Kybele*'s UN ambassador.

"Thank you," Jim said. "Let's take a look at our subject, Helt."

Helt put Cash Ryan onstage, courtesy of videos Jerry had tweaked into holo displays. A boy with dishwater blond curls, maybe ten or eleven years old, shifted his feet and craned his neck to look up at something. He was a well-built child with big feet and big hands; probably he would be a little clumsy until the rest of his growth caught up with his feet. Just a kid, Helt supposed, handsome, but not beautiful enough to be obvious pedophile bait. He was utterly expressionless.

"What was the context, Helt?" David II asked.

"A school trip to a local museum." Helt retrieved the original flat video, a group of children nearing the turmoil of puberty, looking up at a sort of wagon with red wooden wheels taller than they were. Its bare wooden carriage seat was perched over a cylinder that looked like a bomb.

"That's a Stanley Steamer," David II said. "No, it's not. It looks like a homemade version."

"Looks dangerous," Helt said.

"Ryan's high school records show he was bright; no surprise there," Jim said. "Advanced placements in physics, math—No disciplinary kerfuffles that show on these records. He was bright enough to get into MIT when the time came. Show us more, Helt."

Jerry's displays showed Cash walking, slowly, through snow and black-trunked trees, water in the background the color of steel, a blurred wall of buildings beyond it. The tag read "Back Bay." He was alone, head bowed, hands stuffed into the pockets of a dark green puffer jacket. He was bareheaded, the blond curls of childhood now a brown mop, and he'd grown a beard. He looked at the camera once, unsmiling, and then walked on. He's posing, Helt thought. The artist as a lonely young man.

"At MIT, Cash Ryan majored in engineering, minored in instrumental music. Applied for colonist status on *Kybele* but didn't make the cut."

Onstage, the young Cash Ryan, obviously tense, hunched over a guitar and played for an exam. He was good.

Archer came in and sat down next to Helt. Helt started to tap controls and close down the music, but Archer shook his head, no.

Cash Ryan's fingers, long enough to look spidery, walked the neck of a guitar. The recording caught the man's breathing, a sharp intake before some apparently difficult fingering at about the three-minute mark. The solo was a wistful piece, slow in tempo, melodic with a late romantic feel.

Helt was beginning to like the guy. He didn't want to. Cash Ryan had been in bed with Elena, long ago and far away, so Helt wanted to hate him. But he came across, in his music, as shy and sensitive, someone who wanted approval. It was possible, just possible, that Elena had been intrigued for good reasons.

It was just possible that Helt was not going to be objective about Elena Maury until he knew her better.

The music ended. Helt faded out the display. Next up in the queue, if Jim stayed with a chronologic order of business, were captures of Elena and Ryan together. Helt wanted to hide them, brief as they were, but they had to be shown, and anyway, Severo had been through them. Probably Jim had, too.

Archer pushed his white eyebrows down and lifted his nose to squint at the empty stage. "I'm sorry for the delay," he said. "David I wanted to review what you've done so far. If you'd care to have him join us, Helt."

"Now is fine," Jim Tulloch said.

Helt brought the Vancouver link from David I's home office to the stage. There would be time delay, but it was such a familiar one that the use of it had become almost an art form.

"I believe Ryan's piece was Villa-Lobos, *Prelude Three*," Archer said.

Which meant he knew damned well what it was. Helt sharpened the focus on David I's smooth dark face and softened the setting, a cordovan leather overstuffed chair placed in front of a window. The light outside was the deep blue of evening. The view from David I's window was a forest of distant skyscrapers with a snow-capped mountain in the background to dwarf them. It looked cold out there. "It's a good choice for a student recital," Archer said. "Andante, so careful practice can get you through the arpeggios even if your speed isn't up to virtuoso standards."

David I nodded serenely. "I bow to your superior knowledge of the subject. Did he play it well?"

"He didn't play it like a Spaniard. He played it like someone who's spent time listening to Spaniards."

David I smiled. "Archer, please introduce me to your colleagues. David II and I are well acquainted, of course."

David I and David II nodded to each other. The synchrony of muscle motion, the so-similar faces and expressions were bothersome but by no means a match, and one face was definitely forty years older than the other. Watching the two of them should have been no more intriguing than watching identical twins, but it was.

Archer said names; everyone nodded to one another, including David II.

In the spaces between intros, Helt checked the info on the music anyway. Villa-Lobos, as Archer had said.

"Thank you for joining us, Dr. Luo," Jim said. "So, we have the young Cash Ryan, a disappointed colonist. This is when he knew Elena, right, Helt?"

Here it was, damn it. This had to be done. He put up a still of Cash Ryan with a mike in a Cambridge coffeehouse, the young Elena at a front-row table. Her face and those beautiful amber eyes looked up at the poet with rapt attention. "They met at the beginning of their senior year at MIT," Helt said. "They shared an interest in coffeehouse poetry. Here's what Elena said."

He showed her in the Frontier diner with a glass of brandy.

"The poetry was full of passion and political outrage and poignant reactions to leaves, waves, and the open beaks of poisoned birds. Like that. And we were all young and brilliant, of course, and no one had ever loved or suffered as we loved and suffered.

"Throw in pheromones, and that Cash could really play that guitar."

"We've heard him do that," Jim said. "I've listened to Cash Ryan's poems. You have the transcripts."

"Do we have to listen to them?" Severo asked.

Helt wasn't sure Severo was delivering a straight line. Apparently everyone here had read the poems, or skimmed them. To Helt, they seemed much as Elena had described them. They seemed young and anguished. Lines from one of Ryan's poems came back to him.

The curve of your sleeping back
Sweats tears of past surrenders

"No," Jim said. "But you have to hear what I found in them. I ran them through a speech pattern analysis developed for terrorist screening. It doesn't work; too many false positives, but it's a workaround for reviewing concerns a therapist might miss hearing. Even I, as well adjusted and sociable as I am, choose to brush off certain kinds of problems if I can get away with it. But I know I do it, so I check myself now and then.

"Cash Ryan's poetry uses these words, or close alternatives, fairly frequently." Jim put them onscreen.

HAUNT
BURN
SEVER
RIP
BLACKEN

"His usage is well within the frequency of other angry poets, and within the convention that action verbs are important. There's a different usage that's more bothersome."

CRUSH
ENSNARE
DELUDE
DEVOUR

"His point of view is always that of the outsider, the alien. The fantasy that we're changelings, dropped into the wrong family by mistake, is common enough in the struggle to grow up. But Ryan seems a tad more alienated than most, someone who studies people's responses in order to use them.

"How long did his relationship with Elena Maury last, Helt?"

"Three months." His voice sounded detached and clinical and he was pleased with himself for pulling that off. "And then she went to Stanford for a couple of graduate degrees. Cash Ryan stayed at MIT and left, ABD, all but dissertation, four years later. Dr. Maury has stated, several times, that she had no further contact with him until she dodged contact here on *Kybele.* Three years ago." Helt wondered if anyone here believed she had managed not to run into him, except for that single incident of seeing him once in a crowd. Helt wondered if he believed it himself. But so far, the public video records confirmed her story. There were a few captures where they had crossed the agora at the same time or traveled on the same train, but never in close proximity to each other.

"You hired him, David I, right after he left MIT. Why?" Jim asked.

The time delay from Vancouver made David I's answer seem more carefully composed than it probably was. "I hired him," David I said. "I brought him up to do manual labor, essentially. His qualifications were no better than many others, but his humility, his desire to touch the stone of *Kybele*, to be part of her birth, convinced me that he was willing to take on humble tasks, that he wanted to be proud of his work. I was, perhaps, overinfluenced by his video interview. I remember him as an intense young man."

Pause, while the link synced voice and face and the next batch from Earth arrived.

"Cash Ryan worked hard. He was assigned to the construction crews that were assembling the reserve reactors, the ones that are mothballed now."

"But you didn't extend his contract." Jim said.

David I's eyelids were at half-mast. If expression resides around the eyes, his expression was well guarded. "We wanted to offer as many people as possible the opportunity to be a part of the building of *Kybele*," David I said.

That was the spin speech the execs put on sending someone away, in those years, and would repeat, even with this last pruning, to avoid saying why some were chosen to stay aboard and some were not.

Jim didn't challenge David I, didn't ask for his reasons, and Helt wondered why. Respect for an elder authority? An attempt to do something to David I's head? Perhaps, for surely *Kybele*'s former chief engineer was ready with an answer to the unasked question, "Why did you send him away, really?"

David II was not looking at anyone in the room. He was intent on something on his desk screen. Severo leaned back in his chair and linked his hands over his stomach. Archer's fingers were busy on his keyboard, which was standard for him in any meeting. He never seemed to look up, but from long experience, Helt knew he missed very little.

"David II, what do you have on the years between Cash Ryan's first and second tours?" Jim asked.

David II's hesitation lasted only a microsecond, but it was there. "He didn't complete his PhD. I didn't know that when I hired him, but I know it now because you sent me the records, Helt. He worked reactor maintenance at Svalbard for a couple of years, and then he worked on the building of the Kitimat reactor in BC."

"Do you have anything on his personal life before you hired him? Relationships, peer review reports?"

"No."

"Severo?" Jim asked.

"Nothing from those years. We're looking," Severo said. "Why did you hire him, David II?" Jim asked.

"His qualifications were good. He'd been here before, so his ability to work in low g was known. There would be no period of adjustment to the conditions on *Kybele*." David II looked up from his desktop screen to the life-size image of David I. "His interactive interview with me presented energy, longing, and humility. I found him charming, much as I think you did, sir. He was, as you said, an intense young man."

David I nodded. "He had a degree of charisma, yes. I will be extremely interested in what you find about his recent activities."

"Severo?" Jim asked.

"He never ended up cited by NSS for anything. Public cameras show that he went to work and came home. The neighbors in his compound never complained about him. They knew him by sight. They saw him come and go. None of them report any conversations with him that were more than standard greetings.

"He ate in the canteen and in restaurants in Athens. He went to the stadium for *futbol* games sometimes. He played pick-up games with a couple of engineers, Oriol Bruguera and Masaka Ueda. We'll be talking to them."

Severo looked at his reports on screen. "We know that Cash Ryan went to work Wednesday, four days ago. His neighbors didn't see him come home after work, which doesn't mean he didn't. We just don't know. A couple of hours later, someone, or probably more than one person, tossed him off the Athens tower. We have some blank spaces to fill in." Severo kept the flat cadence of someone reading a report. Hours of overtime and calling in off-duty personnel were part of the equation Severo didn't mention. "The cameras in Center were offline for an hour, and it's likely the fall happened in that hour," Severo said. "Dr. Elena Maury was the first person seen leaving the Athens tower elevator after the death and after the cameras came back online."

Well, Severo had to say it. Elena was on the elevator after Cash Ryan died. She'd been his lover once. Four days after the death she was still the only person on *Kybele* with known personal links to him.

"She's still a suspect?" Jim asked.

"Yes," Severo said. "Dr. Maury didn't like the guy. She's said that. There's another woman on board who didn't like him. We've only known about that since last night. Her name's Susanna Jambekar. Susanna's a midwife. She hasn't been questioned yet, so we don't know why she didn't like him."

And right now, Elena was hovering in the background while Susanna Jambekar kept watch over a woman in labor. Elena, Susanna, Mena, they worked together. Helt wondered how close they were, wondered if they shared that friendship thing women had sometimes. Women shared intimacies about the physical state of their bodies and the ups and downs of their emotions sooner than men did, was Helt's impression. As an outsider.

"Do you think either woman could have killed Cash Ryan?" Jim asked.

"Anything's possible," Severo said. "I hope Susanna didn't. She delivered my daughter, for one thing. She kept me from getting scared while she did it, for another. Well, at least I wasn't so terrified I went ballistic, anyway, and that took some doing."

What Severo wasn't saying was that Susanna Jambekar, who didn't like Cash Ryan, was on the Seed Banker list. Did knowing that make a difference to Severo? Would it make a difference to David I, or to Dr. Jim Tulloch, if they knew? Not much, Helt figured. The Seed Bankers complicated things but the knowledge that there were some on board didn't change the reconstruction of Ryan's personality. Severo might get upset if he knew Doughan's order was disobeyed, even with the group of people in this room, who had to know sooner or later. While Helt tried to weigh pros and cons on speaking out, Jim leaned back in his chair and rubbed his eyes.

"And that's where we are," Jim said. "Cash Ryan comes across as a secretive man, a loner, and before his death he hadn't managed to form a successful relationship with a woman, or a man, as far as we know. We know we need more information about him. I certainly do, before I can say anything helpful, much less brilliant."

"I have learned a few things that might be of some slight value in your efforts," David I said.

Archer's fingers stopped their keyboard dance. He looked up at David I.

"Please," Jim said. "Go ahead."

David I leaned forward in his chair. "I became interested in Charles 'Cash' Ryan when *Kybele* informed me of his death, doubly so because David II had hired him to work on board again."

"I didn't mention it to you," David II said. "Of course, now I wish I had."

"I would have had little to say, because he had not come to my attention after leaving *Kybele.*

"Cash Ryan made several trips to Svalbard from his home in Palo Alto, but the time he spent in Norway was less than six months, all told. I was unable to find where he was actually employed during the years he lived in Palo Alto, if he was. He moved to Vancouver after four years in California. He did not work on the construction of Kitimat until three months before you hired him and brought him to *Kybele*, David II."

"I would have to say that your information is of rather more than slight value," Archer said.

"He faked his résumé," David II said.

"So it seems," David I said.

"The feat is not easy to accomplish," Archer said. "Or rather, it is, but it's difficult to do it well. I'll see if I can sort out how he managed it, and who, if anyone, helped him."

Helt reached for his pocket interface and pulled up Elena's fact sheet. After her time at MIT, the record showed:

> MD/PHD IN MOLECULAR BIOLOGY, STANFORD, PALO ALTO, CA, 2185
> RESIDENCY, INTERNAL MEDICINE, VANCOUVER GENERAL HOSPITAL, VANCOUVER, BC, 2187

She had worked in Vancouver for two years and then spent a year splicing genes in London before she came to *Kybele.*

Oh, damn. Helt felt muscles in his shoulders tighten, felt his jaw tense up. It seemed pretty clear that Cash Ryan had lived where she lived, moved when she moved. He had stalked her. Helt felt a sense of revulsion that made even the cold, digital facts about the man disgusting.

"Helt?" Jim asked.

Helt put the dates up for them with David I's addresses for Cash Ryan during those years as sidebars. "It looks like he followed Elena to Palo Alto. It looks like he followed her to Vancouver. I think it's possible we'll find him in proximity to Susanna Jambekar on *Kybele*, once I set up the parameters to look through the records. I think he might have been a stalker."

And if that's what he was, and Elena knew it, would that make it more likely, or less likely, that she killed him? What about Yves Copani? Would he have killed Ryan to protect Susanna from his attentions?

"Someone who had the balls to fake a dossier to get himself employed on the most publicly examined construction project in human history," Jim said. "Someone no one knew, or seemed to want to know. Someone whose communication records are a little too bland to be real, or so Nadia tells me. Someone who may have stalked two women. Do the women have anything in common, Helt?" Jim asked.

"They both have dark hair," Helt said. "They walk the same way, if that means anything."

"It might," Jim said. "We don't know enough. We know we don't know enough, but, as a working hypothesis, I think it will not be harmful for us to look for the killer of a well-integrated psychopath. Not a sociopath, but the big brother of the syndrome, a psychopath.

"It's hard to get inside the worldview of a psychopath, but it seems that, to them, other humans are only objects to be manipulated. Many of them enjoy causing pain. Psychopaths don't develop the neural circuitry for empathy. Some of them learn to fake it, because they want to avoid punishment. Some are extremely charismatic.

"They are good at deception. Lies mean nothing to them. They assume everyone is lying because they do. They tailor their stories and their personalities to fit what they think their victims want to see, want to hear. And to them, all of us are potential victims.

"They have definite goals and they will do anything, anything at all, to obtain what they want. I think we should find out what Cash Ryan wanted, and why he wanted it. And then we can get on with the business of finding out who thought the only way to stop Cash Ryan from doing what he wanted was to kill him."

"This psychopath worked on our reactors, and then on the stabilization engines out on the skin," David II said. He looked like he wanted to check every one of the systems that controlled every one of them, right now. He looked like only courtesy was keeping him in his chair.

"We have work to do," Jim said. "Helt, you'll call us in again when we know more. And we will." Jim grabbed the arms of his chair in preparation for getting out of it. "Thank you, gentlemen. Good hunting."

17

Chimeras

David II went to look for Doughan after the meeting. Helt set his system to alert him if they made contact.

If Doughan had found this afternoon's Seed Banker, the man named Oriol Bruguera, he hadn't posted it. There wasn't any capture of Doughan's day, either. He was supposed to keep his interface live, and he wasn't doing it. Maybe he had good reasons and would explain them later. Maybe he hadn't thought about turning it on.

Safety inspections and drills are an interruption of anyone's work schedule and the most boring things in the world, unless they aren't. Navigation's records for the systems Cash Ryan might have known about or touched were up to date and unremarkable and had been done on schedule. Doughan and David II would certainly look everything over again, and Helt knew staring at equipment or specs for most of those things was not his job, because he didn't know what he'd be looking for unless someone coached him.

Helt went looking for a stalker.

Good old Bayesian probability. His search for situations where Cash Ryan and Susanna Jambekar were found in "near-miss" proximity on *Kybele*'s public space cameras paid off. Ryan had been in too many places just before her, just after her, for chance to be an explanation.

He did the verifications with his own eyes, capture after capture, with any and every view of the surrounding areas and events near those times examined. He kept going until his eyes felt sanded, and the theory held. Helt sent the stalker hypothesis to the Murder Mess construct, stretched his arms wide, and felt the knots in his shoulders complain.

There was still Elena Maury and her history and the time spent in Vancouver and Washington state, in the deserts west of the Cascades, briefly, with side trips into faces and friendships captured in passing, and the music of the years when those faces had been younger. Her family surprised him. It was a company, with maybe monogamous pairs in it and maybe not but it was hard to tell from the outside.

He was still in his chair in the SysSu conference room. He was thirsty.

He looked for David II and the locator found him in Doughan's office. He didn't call him.

"Helt?"

It was Jim Tulloch's voice, out in the dark hall.

"Here."

Jim brought a tray with him, loaded with containers that smelled good. A wine bottle was on it, lying on its side, and two coffee cups. One had a logo of a cracked pot on it. The other featured Victorian cover art for *The Secret Garden.*

"Is that coffee?" Helt asked.

"No."

Helt looked at the contents of the cracked pot cup. It was filled to the brim with red wine.

"Thanks, Mom."

"Don't thank me. Thank Nissa. We were talking over dinner and my dear companion thought I seemed distracted. I told her I was worried about you, so she kicked me out with food. She told me to come back when I could pay attention to her for a while." Jim picked up the other cup. "Cheers."

Helt raised his cup and drank some of his wine. Nissa was an engineer, Russian, and had been a soldier in the Arctic when Jim was stationed there. They hadn't met until Nissa came on *Kybele* as a colonist. Their memories of the north and the conflict there were so different, Jim said, that they had material for arguments to last at least another twenty years.

"Please thank Nissa for me," Helt said. "Ryan was stalking the midwife."

"That's good," Jim said. "I mean, I'm glad it fits with what I thought I was seeing, through a glass, darkly. The brain slides may tell us if there's anatomic evidence to back me up. Psychopaths sometimes have anatomic markers. Deformations and decreased mass of the amygdala, that's common. So is increased activity in the ventral striatum, bilaterally, but that won't show on an autopsy."

"Could you unpack that a little?" Helt asked.

"Oh. The amygdala does a lot of things with emotion, and one of the things it does is tell you when you're afraid. So psychopaths don't fear punishment much. Parts of the ventral striatum make up the pleasure center.

Psychopaths anticipate pleasure more than most of us. A sort of addictive behavior, actually."

"Thank you," Helt said, but he was thinking of Elena and her frozen sections. She was doing the work as fast as she could, he knew that. She would tell him the instant she found something like that.

Nissa had sent a large portion of pasta topped with red sauce. Helt tucked in. Jim unwrapped some garlic bread for him.

"How is it even a couple of bites and I feel better?" Helt asked.

"It's not Nissa's sauce Bolognese, it's the secret powers of glucagon and insulin," Jim said. "The buzz isn't in the sauce. You made the endorphins yourself."

"Please tell Nissa I'm grateful for the high. I only hope it lasts."

Jim rolled one of the chairs nearer so he could use it as a footstool. He kicked it into the position he wanted and stretched out with his cup resting on his belly. "We can segue directly into your postprandial depression, if you like. You never really thought everyone would play nice, just because we have a new world to play in and plenty of food, and bright, capable people to play nice with."

"No, I didn't."

"You knew something like this would happen sooner or later."

"We all knew that. It's part of what we work on, SysSu, Biosystems, the execs, all of us. We'll have varied climates so life, and diet, for that matter, won't get too boring, and construction that will never be finished. We'll maintain a balance of head work and muscle work, and neither will ever be just busywork. The work is completely reality based; without hands-on maintenance, *Kybele* will die. Research. That won't stop and we think we have the cerebral mass and the materials to keep on doing it. A shared destination. A shared goal."

"And we've known it won't be enough," Jim said.

"Sure. Most of the gloom and doom scenarios for generation ships were played out by science fiction writers long ago, and they always came down to the same ugly thing. It's not the machinery that will be the problem. It's the people."

"Warlords. Feudalism. Slaves. Cannibalism for kicks. Am I missing anything?" Jim asked.

"Corrupted information, religious fanatics, and inquisitions. Right now, right here, I'm watching power games get played, secrets kept in violation of the transparency we said we would keep. We aren't. I'm worried, Jim."

"People keeping secrets from you?"

Doughan wasn't playing by the rules on recording what he was up to, but that shouldn't be a problem once Helt let Doughan know the gaps were showing. He had to do that soon.

"Probably not consciously," Helt said.

Jim glanced at him and then away. "But you'll call them on it."

"I will."

"Another risk for isolated populations is terminal boredom," Jim said.

"I don't think we're in danger of that this week," Helt said. "Once we get the Matter of Governance nailed down so we can survive each other's company for a couple of hundred years, then, maybe, I'll get bored."

"There's this matter of a murder to solve first." Jim produced a bottle of wine that Helt hadn't seen him bring into the room, and refilled Helt's cup and his own. "The prime suspect so far is a beautiful woman. What's bothering you about Elena Maury?" Jim asked.

You bastard. Not now, damn it. Not now, not ever. We aren't going there. "What the fuck do you mean?" Helt heard the anger and frustration in his voice but the words were out.

"I mean you showed some tension when Severo brought her up."

"Well, yeah." Helt leaned back from the table and looked out the curve of windows toward the agora, a ploy to calm down a little. Night had fallen. Saturday night, and Helt was at work, alone, as he'd been so often for so long. So it *showed* that he wanted to protect her, would have spared her the wounds these suspicions had given her if he could.

He saw, whenever he closed his eyes, the texture of her skin. He felt the warmth that rose from her throat when she looked up at him to see his reaction to that sculpture in the canyon. He felt the hurt this suspicion had caused her. He feared that he would never know the woman she was before this because now she wasn't that woman anymore. Did that show, too?

Jim was sipping his wine, his eyes at half mast and his attention, apparently, on the night outside. The bastard was going to wait him out.

"She says she was up there getting samples from the platform," Helt said. "She says it was just bad luck that she was there then. And I want to believe her. I really want to believe her."

"Elena's a good woman. I work with her, you know."

"I hadn't thought about that," Helt said. Naked, seen half-hidden through a door left ajar, Tulloch's bony shoulders, Elena's hair fanned loose on a pillow. The imagined scenario was instant and painful. "Do you know her well?"

"Don't bristle," Jim said.

Bristle, hell. Helt wanted to punch him out.

"She's a colleague." Jim said, quietly and reasonably. "She's not my mistress, and the answer is, no, we have never made love. To break one of my sometimes-broken privacy rules, I will tell you that she's never been my patient, either."

It helped to know that. A little. "Do you think she could have killed Cash Ryan? I mean, it looks like he was stalking her, and we know they were lovers."

Jim sighed and took a sip of his wine. "It's an interesting question. She's in charge of human reproductive strategy here, and if we don't have a good one, we're toast. She culls embryos before they're implanted, but it's not the same thing as culling a fully developed adult who's been out in the world for forty years or so."

"I don't know her," Helt said. "I don't know who she was before this happened."

Jim nodded and his eyes were looking at something farther away than the starscape on the ceiling above Athens.

"I've spent hours learning what I can about her. There's so much damned *stuff* around about people if you look for it. I know a lot of drivel about her family." It was an eclectic collection of people and had been from the beginning, a business of sorts, and documented more than most families were at the time. He knew the names, Pilar, and Jared who died, and Signy and Paul Maury and the others. Elena was the granddaughter of a doc named Jared but Jared had never known he'd fathered a child, any child.

The next generation of the Maury family, and that's what they used as an official surname, continued the family business model of finding something that needed doing and then picking up the skills to do it. People came and went for years or decades or lifetimes.

"I know her grades in elementary school and what her professors said about her—for the record. But I don't know what anyone thinks about themselves or the world around them once they become a suspect in a murder case. I don't know what damage that does even if it turns out they had nothing to do with it."

"Your question may be—I'm not saying it *is*, but it may be—what the old-timers would have called overdetermined," Jim said.

Meaning, your question is about this woman and about at least one other. Jim knew who, in Helt's life, had been hurt and damaged and stayed damaged.

The scars on Lily's scalp were covered with her thick dark curls and never mentioned. She never again said Helt reminded her of his father and she couldn't love him because of it, and Helt wasn't supposed to have heard that conversation anyway. His parents had stayed married. Jørn had traveled as much as he could in his younger years, Helt with him at one school or another. Later, the quiet man who was Helt's father stayed home as long as he could stand it, and then found another desalination plant in need of his services, somewhere, anywhere in the world.

There had been two households in the old saltbox high on a cliff in Maine, but only the boy who had known the unity that was there before Lily's injury knew how separate those households were. Lily was still there, and polite when Helt called. Jørn had died fifteen years ago, climbing *Perito Moreno.* The glacier face was unstable and he had known it.

"Damn you," Helt said.

"This is a single trauma for Elena, psychic, not physical. Single traumas leave a lot less damage than multiple ones. You've studied PTSD as much as I have, I think."

"Yeah," Helt said. "Probably." Sequelae of parental loss was a topic Helt had read a lot about, too, even though his loss of a parent was different from the death of one.

"You say you'll never know who she was, and that's true."

"Damn Cash Ryan for that, if nothing else."

"You need to know the Elena she's becoming," Jim said. "Elena Maury culls defective embryos. In some ethical systems, that's a form of murder, and she does it every day. You need to find out if she could or did cull a rogue human, Helt. My suggestion is that you get to know her well enough to know for yourself what she is capable of doing and not doing. Not in the past, but in the now. You're the best person for the job."

"I'm falling in love with her," Helt said.

That Jim knew it showed in his face, and he didn't look at all surprised or dismayed by the news, although part of Helt was surprised and dismayed that he'd said it.

"Yes," Jim said. "But are you going to hide evidence to protect her if she killed a man?"

Helt had been thinking about that while he stared at camera captures of Susanna, while he worried about Doughan's response to Seed Bankers, while he made the occasional side trip to look at the painfully thin data points around Cash Ryan's last hour.

"No," Helt said. "I won't do that. I'm not capable of doing that. How did I get stuck with this mess anyway?"

Jim grinned at him.

"You got stuck with it because the injury to your mother gave you a caregiver neurosis, sometimes known as a hero compulsion. You got stuck with it because whether you like it or not, people like you and trust you and talk to you. If you're going to get information out of them, that's a skill set you need."

"You talking to you or to me?" Helt asked.

"I'm a psychiatrist and I can do one-on-one. You handle groups with that same concern, with the ability to listen to everyone's narratives and try to get a benign result out of them. I learn from you, Helt."

Well, damn. That's what Helt had been doing with Jim. He saw him as a peer, yes, but more than that, as a mentor. "Yeah. I learn from you, too." He said the words slowly.

"You're good at your job, you poor bastard. You're afflicted with a certain rigidity of ethics, too. You're in love, and you're in danger of going batshit crazy if you don't get some sleep." Jim picked up the tray and the cups and the bottle. "Help me wash the cups. You didn't drink your wine."

Helt knew what Elena was doing tonight, and he knew he wouldn't see her, so he might as well sleep, except he couldn't. He picked up the tray and led Jim toward the lounge.

"I need to talk to Obrecht," Helt said.

"Why?" Jim put the dishes in the sink and looked hesitant and confused. Helt nudged him out of the way with an elbow and grabbed the detergent. He handed Jim a towel.

"Because we don't have an established crime force and we're not following the rules. There aren't any reflexes in place to protect witnesses, or suspects, or the crew who's looking for the criminals, for that matter. Rules, sure. Reflexes, no."

"It's too late tonight and I want to be rested when I sit in on that discussion," Jim said. "Building in reflexes takes practice. Can't be just theory, and I don't want to think about what sort of practice is needed for learning that skill set, not right now."

"Gaming," Helt said. "A cops-and-robber game where we get points for not ever falling into the Stanford prisoner trap." It had been an experiment where the theorists set up a situation with some people as prisoners and some as guards. It got ugly fast, and the experimenters had shut it down.

Jim polished the cup he held, for far longer than it needed. "Might work."

Helt took the cup from Jim's hand, stacked it and the wine, corked, onto Jim's carry tray, and handed it over.

"This means you're going to quit for the night, right?" Jim asked.

"I need to close down."

"Which means you're not quitting but you don't want to lie to me about it. You're an idiot," Jim said. "At least get a little rest before you do the next thing, okay?"

"Good plan," Helt said.

He was back in the data flow, staring at a blinking light that said David II had left Doughan's office. Doughan had pulled the file David II left, the locations where Cash Ryan had been on work crews this past three years, and then Doughan had gone home. He lived in Athens, close to his work.

Helt had opted for Petra, not Athens, because he liked to separate work from home, and because a roofed canyon habitat was the plan for the first settlement on Nostos. Not that he'd be there to see it.

Elena was in the clinic lounge with Mena. They were talking about papoose boards. Papoose boards? Helt wanted her to finish the pathology slides, but she had to have time. He wouldn't dare rush her.

The camera at the Athens station showed Doughan getting out. Helt traced him into the residential section where he lived.

Jim was gone. Helt didn't notice that until he blinked and realized he was alone in SysSu.

He might as well sleep at home.

In the agora, on his way to the train, he seemed to sense Level Two, the shuttle port, and Navigation offices below. He thought he felt the spin of the world beneath his feet.

18
Key Words

Sunday morning's crew of vitriol-peddlers on Earth below had exhausted the value of railing about resources lost on the construction of *Kybele.* Now they were trying to drum up hits from the idea that firing *Kybele*'s departure engines would, pick one or several, cause tsunamis, earthquakes, volcanic eruptions, or, Helt's favorite so far this morning, blow up the moon.

Thirty thousand people lived on *Kybele*, and as far as Helt could tell, maybe eight thousand of them had a secret itch to be Hollywood moguls and six thousand were closet actors. So far, three studios were up and running, and they made good money on made-for-Earth exports. Films produced on *Kybele* had earned a lot of film festival awards, usually for Art Direction. The mise-en-scène was spectacular, and the half-g effects added a certain something.

At least four thousand people on board made music, with varying degrees of skill. From bluegrass to sitar, you could hear it live. But the real money was in docudramas. Silkworms were a hit. Go figure.

Were the silkworms, proudly brought from Suzhou, China, thriving? An artisan co-op there had pooled donations and purchased three lottery tickets. The Province budget committee had gone a little nuts and increased the number of tickets to three hundred, and three Suzhou people scored.

Were the colonists thriving as well? We are, the Suzhou colonists assured them, and camera crews followed their settling in, and later, the growing romance between two of them. The birth of Zhōu Xifeng's son on *Kybele* in the wee hours of Sunday morning had been celebrated with fireworks and dragon parades in Suzhou.

That meant midwife Susanna Jambekar was now available for questioning. Mena would call before that happened. Maybe Elena was asleep now. Maybe she would call when she woke.

Helt told the audio feeds to pick up buzz words from the crowd chatter of the past two days and got up to get his next cup of coffee. He'd slept hard and deep last night, with no dreams at all that he could remember. He felt almost rested.

Murder, the wall whispered, murder. In the Athens agora, in the restaurants and bars that sent their feeds to Security, in the Petra canteen, in the barns at Stonehenge and all over social media. Coulda been murder. Cover-up. I hear Navigation is doing some serious grilling of some people. In face-time. What are the bosses hiding? Cover-up. Who was that guy Ryan? He was murdered, no question. What if it's a serial killer? But there's just one victim. Cover-up. Will we be safer in crowds for a while, or should we stay out of them?

Was this part of the "different energy" Elena had sensed in the Petra canteen?

The police log showed very little activity, less than usual. People were busy with tasks that could best be done while *Kybele* was still in Earth orbit, or they were behaving. No one wanted to end up arrested and shuffled to the off-list this late in the game. Severo would be busy getting morning reports about now, but Helt decided to interrupt him. It was time for disclosure.

And it was time to talk to Giliam Obrecht about legalities and money. Helt sent a request to him.

Helt. Legal advice, please. Anytime, please, but soon.

He asked the interface for Severo and got a view of the waiting room at the Athens office, NSS's miniature version of a bull pen. Helt watched the backs of two people in plainclothes leave for the streets and the working day, orders presumably in hand. Officer Evans, she of the maple-colored hair, the woman who had insisted on chain of evidence precautions with Cash's home interface, she who had apparently been quite authoritative with Venkie, was talking to Severo.

Helt let Evans leave before he buzzed Severo's pocket.

"You on my case already? I was looking forward to a Sunday that would only be twice as much work as usual. You're going to add to the load, right?"

"I hope not," Helt said. "This shouldn't be a biggie. Severo, the public wants to know why the execs are hiding a murder. It's time to go public or we'll have paranoia all over the place."

"That's going to foul up Doughan's idea of private interviews before the facts are out."

Severo's eyelids were puffy. He looked like he wanted to be stubborn just to be stubborn.

"But the news that it's a murder is already out there," Helt said. "The street already knows about it, and the information will only get more garbled if we don't put the facts on the record. You want me to send you the camera captures?"

"No. But I'll have to clear it with Doughan."

"Let me do that." If you want to curse someone, give them responsibility without authority. Doughan was playing that game with Helt, consciously or otherwise. "I'll talk to the trio. As soon as they clear it, then putting the info on the police log becomes an order that came from the top. I'll draft a statement for them."

"Okay," Severo said.

A slight edge of the stubbornness Helt had sensed in Severo seemed to have been put aside.

"Have a good one, Severo."

"Bueno, bye."

It was 0750. Helt looked out through his open door to the hallway, hoping Jerry or Nadia would come by, even though it was Sunday morning.

Helt's opening paragraph to the execs said that the public was aware that the death was probably a murder. He added quickie links to show the resultant unease and the need for putting the facts in the data stream. He sent it to the execs and to Severo. He followed that with a proposed murder announcement. Ongoing investigation has now determined that the death of Charles "Cash" Ryan was most probably a murder, investigations are proceeding, and so forth. Mena sent back an okay. Her interface, and presumably Mena, were at her home.

Helt poured two cups of coffee and carried them down the hall to Archer's office.

It was dark in there, except for the glow of the desktop screen. Its light traced Archer's profile, his craggy nose and clean-shaven authoritative jaw; it highlighted the icy paleness of his unblinking eyes and his smoothly combed white hair.

Archer's shoulders were slightly hunched beneath the shelter of his blue cardigan. He looked his age, and usually he didn't. He looked old and frail and sad.

Helt put Archer's coffee cup on his desk. The text on the screen was the murder announcement.

"I see," Archer said, without looking away from the screen.

Helt sat down in the chair next to Archer's desk and waited.

Archer shut off the announcement and the room went dark.

"I went along with the delay," Helt said. "But now the fact that Ryan was murdered is news, and it's everywhere."

Archer sighed. His programming lighted the room with a large window that seemed to look out at the morning agora, on mute. The display was on the north wall. The agora was south of here. Archer liked it that way. "You disturbed my searches for right-to-forget dodges that might have been used to create Charles 'Cash' Ryan's faked life."

"I'm sorry," Helt said.

"Don't be." Archer's fingers continued their dance on the keyboard. "News? The apt term seems to be 'leak.' Do you have any ideas about who talked?"

"No," Helt said. "It could have been anyone in medical who knew Calloway was looking at hypothermia files. Calloway's girlfriend, if he has one. Jerry, Nadia, Severo, they were with me when Calloway brought us the news. I doubt they said anything, but we didn't mark the information Top Secret."

Archer leaned back and took a sip of his coffee. "You think it's time this went into the NSS public log."

"I do."

"Make your announcement. You have my approval. That's one of three."

"That's two," Helt said. "I sent Mena and Doughan a heads-up on this. Mena says to go public."

"But not Doughan."

"No," Helt said.

"He hasn't seen it yet. You sent it"—Archer glared at the info on his desktop screen—"less than ten minutes ago."

"I hope Doughan okays it. You and Mena make up a majority," Helt said. "But I hope I don't have to play that card."

Archer spun his chair so he was facing Helt. He took a sip of coffee and looked at Helt over the rim of the cup, scanning him as if he were a malfunctioning program. "What's wrong?" Archer asked.

A lot of things, like Helt was not at all sure he could do this job, and his innocent wish that *Kybele* would be a peaceable kingdom where he could live happily ever after was broken, and he was mad at himself for wishing for something like that, which was obviously an unrealistic, childish dream. "Chain of command. Severo looks to Doughan on this and wants to go through Doughan on everything. We have time constraints, and waiting for his go-ahead could be problematic. But the fact is, Doughan tagged me for the oversight job. The Special Investigator."

"With the relieved approval of Biosystems and SysSu, I seem to remember. Why are you here?"

"Either Doughan lets me do the job, or he's an obstacle. I don't like that, Archer. I don't know how to handle the problem."

"I think you do. That's why you're here, bothering me," Archer said. "So what shall I say to Doughan to make your life a little easier?"

"Heh. Tell him Severo needs to hear that Doughan will be happier if information comes to me first and goes to Doughan after I've vetted it. It would save some time, and I get the feeling Doughan's happier looking at updates than wading through stuff himself. That's what junior officers are for, right? I suppose I suspect a military mind-set and I'm accusing him of being limited by it. I don't know him well enough to say that."

"So you've noticed our Navigation exec is fond of concise reports and well-defined hierarchies."

"You know him better than I do and you've known him longer," Helt said.

"That's been my analysis of him in the past. It's a character flaw and it's cost him at times."

"Because you've used it to manipulate him?" Helt asked.

"Of course I have."

Archer didn't elaborate, but some of the history he must be remembering caused a smile to visit the corners of his mouth. It was quickly chased away.

"Talking it through with you helps," Helt said. "I'm going with him to interview the midwife this morning, so I think I have a framework to use to state my case."

Archer turned his chair and nodded to the simulated agora. "IA, you're good at what you do. This death is an interdepartmental problem, to put it mildly. I give those to you. Solving problems that won't stay in one department is your job description. I wrote it. I knew quite well you would end up stepping on toes, and you have. But I knew you could figure out how to step off them again. And you have."

"Remind me of that when Doughan balks, if he does. You began by doing all of SysSu's liaison work yourself," Helt said.

"I did. Now I confine myself to the internal conflicts in SysSu, as best I can." Archer leaned back in his chair and stared at something in the direction-reversed agora. "And I watch the pressures coming to near-space from Earth. I've tried to encourage rumors about more intensive colonization of Ceres, the project that the Northern Coalition made so much talk about before the triple eruption a couple of years back."

Iturp, Karynsky, Lascar, those three volcanoes in Earth's Ring of Fire, had belched a lot of smoke.

"The cloud cover over the Northern Hemisphere mitigated some of the heating in South Asia," Archer said. "End result, the Northern Coalition's been pretty quiet about us. We may even get away without too many sabers rattling."

Russia, Northern Europe, Canada, and the United States had found many common interests as the planet heated. They had water and arable land; much of the world didn't. In the south, the Pampas were irrigated farmland, now, not grassland. The tongue of Africa that remained temperate was intensively vertically farmed and constantly at war.

"And here," Archer said. "Here in the luckiest, most improbable place a human can be, I grow old. I suppose I had the fantasy, once, that keeping communications easy and open would be enough, that interdepartmental problems could be solved using the obvious tools of transparent, accessible communications and common sense," Archer said.

Helt tried to imagine an Archer that young, that naive. He couldn't.

"It was ridiculously rational of me to think that," Archer said. "I would say, modestly, that I've done a good job with communications. Common sense, however, still seems to be in short supply. So I picked you to run interference between the departments. You have a gift for accepting the irrational."

"Thank you," Helt said. As compliments went, it was a little bothersome.

"Have you picked my successor, Helt?"

"What?" Helt scanned his mentor's face for signs of illness, incipient death, or clinical insanity. Archer displayed none of the above. He looked both competent and healthy. "What are you asking me?"

"You know SysSu will need a division chief when I retire."

"Retire? Are you planning to do that?"

"Not this week. At some point I'll want to get rid of the administrative load and just sit in a quiet corner and play with code. That skill set seems to be holding up, even now in my dotage. Clean code is my version of art, I suppose."

It was his strength, certainly. Jerry called him a cautious, careful, deliberate developer. His code was lean, tight, and concise. Archer couldn't tolerate kludgy messes of spaghetti code. He rewrote the sprawling epics of others until they were pared down to tight, elegant haikus of code that achieved the same results. His work took anyone else a week to read and understand, but, oh, did it work.

Archer's pet project was capturing images of Earth-based systems and storing them for comparison to *Kybele*'s.

As a precaution, Archer pulled Earth-based systems for storage on *Kybele* at measured intervals and filed the results, for *Kybele*'s internal operating systems were diverging, rapidly, from Earth-written programming.

It was much like Venkie's documentation of the speed of language changes, Helt supposed. *Kybele* was a bottleneck that created, or perhaps forced, wide divergence from parental sources.

"Quite selfishly, I want to know we're on our way outsystem before I step down, though," Archer said.

"But I thought—"

"Certainly you didn't think you would be next in line. It's obvious that you have to stand outside SysSu's turf to do what you do."

Well, yes. And yes, he'd been looking at Jerry and Nadia, evaluating how they would fit in his place, in Archer's.

"Nadia Tay, now, she might do well at it. She's a calming influence, even on me. Your young firebrand, Jerry, would not be happy as a division head. He lets himself go off on tangents, and he pursues a problem until he's beaten it into submission, and pays attention to nothing else while he's doing it. Nadia's better at pacing, at looking at temporality. At looking around to see what's happening."

"The big picture," Helt said.

"That's your specialty, I know. You have a fascination with currents, ebbs and flows, initial conditions." Archer nodded to something on the wall.

"The ebbs and flows of currents, a butterfly's wing that sets up a storm. Initial conditions. We have a lot of those," Helt said. "Unintended consequences, now, those are a heck of a lot of fun to extrapolate. But if you're aware of possible consequences, are they, then, unintended? I worry about the answer to that question, sometimes."

"You urge us to caution. We need that. I like watching you work, Helt."

The compliment startled him. Archer didn't give them often and now he'd offered two in one day. "Thank you," Helt said.

"You're almost a separate division, something apart from SysSu. Sometimes I worry about that." Archer waved his hand in Helt's direction and focused on his desk screen again. "Now go back to work. I'll say something rude to Doughan."

"Thank you," Helt said. "May I bring you more coffee?"

Archer looked around for his cup. It was on his desk, half-hidden by a Koosh ball, a baby blue one to match his cardigan. Nadia must have brought it to him, or Jerry. Helt wondered which one had thought to do it.

"No, thanks. Go away."

"Yes, sir," Helt said.

19

The Midwife

Helt's shoulders were sore. He stretched them on the way back to his office. So Archer had Nadia as the next IA, Jerry as—what? SysSu exec. Jerry had the people skills. The tangent thing was manageable. Everyone in SysSu went off on tangents, some more frequently than others.

If Jerry didn't control them himself, Nadia would call him on it. That would leave Helt as? As the former IA who didn't solve a murder in time. Maybe Mena would put him to work. He could troll for fluctuations in residential methane production secondary to changes in the canteen menus. Well, hell. It would be useful information.

Archer's speech about tangents sent him wandering on a tangent of his own, a long view on transfers of power, the human need for hierarchy, a SysSu whose scent would be different than Archer's. No help for it, a designated leader leaves marks on everything, and the pack sniffs them and behaves accordingly. Or picks a different leader.

The methods used to pick leaders on *Kybele* were designed to balance merit and approval, an effort to keep the power of personality checked by the reality of competence. Merit, in that a seeker for a job had to test out as able to do the job. Anyone who wanted, or would agree, to represent a group at any level of a division's hierarchy was elected by coworkers via secret ballot. Approval was involved in that. And on up the chain of command, so that division heads were selected, essentially, by their future replacements, by people who were qualified to do the boss's job but weren't doing it yet. Approval, for division chiefs, also meant that every three years they faced a ship-wide Vote of Confidence.

Doughan's obvious replacement was David II. David II would fit so well for the years past Saturn, years of constant, steady acceleration via systems that would need careful tending but, fate willing, not much else. There would be years, decades, for building and sculpting and "moving in" in a real sense.

When Ryan's first tour came up in the psych autopsy, David II had gone on full alert about Ryan's possible exposure to anything related to the propulsion systems, but Cash Ryan hadn't worked on any of them. Maybe David II had talked Doughan into checking them anyway, yesterday afternoon.

But David II had gone to Doughan's office, and as far as Helt knew, they hadn't begun to check hardware. He'd ask Doughan about that.

It was past time for Helt to set up the information scatter on Ryan's death to suit himself. He built a planetary system of the NSS and SysSu factoids about the murder, centered on the enigma that was Cash Ryan. He watched as swarms of data dots aggregated into more or less two groups, one of possible motivations, one of personal relationships. At the scale he used, the construct told him that what was *known*, as opposed to surmised, about Cash Ryan and his death was at about an Oort cloud distance from a solution.

Helt nulled the display on his screen, leaned back in his chair and locked his hands behind his head.

Setting the murder aside until the doors that led to Earth were locked would be such luxury. Once *Kybele* was on her own, legal blueprints were clear on the matter of murder, of treason. Keeping the culprits on board to face *Kybele*'s nascent justice system would happen by default if they weren't found before departure.

If only putting the Seed Bankers on the shuttle wasn't the easiest way to get rid of them. If only it were possible to start out without a killer, or killers, on board. If only there wasn't pressure to look good to the Earth that had put so much into this edifice of stone, seeds, and hopes.

Favors could be called in to keep the Seed Bankers' sudden appearance on the off-list looking like just another transfer back to Earth, despite the last minute shuffling of names.

There had never been a desire, when someone left *Kybele*, to bring attention to people's failures, to publish the reasons they were leaving. There had never been a turnover of seven or more people charged with treason or murder before, either.

Media hounds would go into a feeding frenzy if *Kybele* were locked up and on her way having sent their troublemakers back to Earth. The news would harm nothing and no one here, but information and data sets from the ship were part of the expected payback to her parent planet.

The way *Kybele* would handle this mess was an example, fortunate or otherwise, of how a society forms itself. It would be ungrateful, distasteful, *wrong* to hide information on how well, or how badly, it was done. But hiding information about the Seed Bankers was the plan. No charges, no explanations, just "You're fired."

Fine, great, so the alternative would be to keep everybody here, sort out the Seed Bankers and trace their connections, if any, to Cash Ryan, in a calm, slow, deliberate fashion.

Helt needed a time travel device. He needed to go ask a living Cash Ryan why he got himself killed. Or at least he needed the man's personal data stash. Helt shrugged his sore shoulders and began to look for it, again.

"Boss?" Jerry was slumped against the doorframe of Helt's office. His hair was after-shower damp and tied into a sort of braid that hung over his right ear. His ragged Levis had gone mostly white and his Henley shirt had seen better years. Maybe it had been neon green once. Faded seemed to be this year's high fashion. He dangled an empty coffee mug by the handle. "You got coffee?"

"Sure. Come on in."

Jerry poured himself a cup and slouched into Helt's visitor chair. "You're working," he said.

"I'm looking for Cash Ryan's personal cache. We need his interface, since his access codes to it weren't on that desk unit Archer has stashed in his office. We don't have them," Helt said.

"You've traced the sites he went to," Jerry said.

"Oh, sure. You and Archer did, too, Wednesday night. Work, work schedules, recreation, poetry sites, porn. That's what you found. He had to have a personal stash, encrypted, that he accessed with an alias."

"Yeah, the alias," Jerry said. "Usually it's letter substitutions or something in a biography. Nickname or whatever. We didn't get in because he didn't access his stash from his home screen. He used his interface; that's obvious."

"You here to work?"

Jerry's lack of enthusiasm was marked. He looked sad and tired.

"If you are, I appreciate the help," Helt said. "I may have to add extra shifts all over SysSu. I'm going to ask Legal to research a bunch of stuff for me that's not directly related to the murder, but I need it."

He wanted to see how Legal would play keeping the Seed Bankers on board and charging them with treason here as one of the first court procedures on *Kybele*. It was such a good idea, except for the little problem that

Cash Ryan, or one of the newly scheduled off-listers, might have sabotaged something that would go boom before the shuttle even left.

"For collating the info on the murder scenario, putting together what NSS finds and what SysSu comes up with, there's you and Nadia," Helt said. "You're working too many hours already."

"She's with Martin this morning, something about feedback circuits to modify axon potentials. I want to truly not like that guy, but that sort of stuff intrigues me in spite of myself."

Suspicions confirmed. Jerry was losing his girl. "So you're alone," Helt said.

"Yeah."

But, damn. If friction between Jerry and Nadia butted into the work they were doing on the murder, the fact was that Helt couldn't shift them off onto anything else. Not without a considerable cost in time and efficiency, and he didn't have wiggle room for it, not now. He could leave it alone, or he could push the envelope of a friendship that was too new, that might not survive if he overstepped Jerry's limits of trust.

"Martin's the problem?" Helt asked.

"How'd you know that?" Jerry asked.

"I didn't know it. I guessed it when we were coming down from Athens tower." Helt wasn't going to tell him that Severo, too, had nailed it. The look on Jerry's face when Nadia talked about Martin had been as clear as a shout.

"You guessed right. Sucks."

"Has she moved out? Have you?"

"No, we're still roomies. We haven't staked a formal claim on a building site. But we've looked at plans. Architect's blueprints, floor plans. We figured we'd spend a year or two thinking about them. Those things are time sinks, you know?"

"I do," Helt said.

"But we haven't done much of that lately," Jerry said. "It's like she's around, but she's not."

"That bad?" Helt asked.

"Worse. She spends her time with Martin, or daydreaming about Martin. She wants to do him, well and truly, but she won't until I say it's okay. I think. I mean, she looks at him like she wants to get laid. I know that look. She used to look like that a lot when she had a crush on you," Jerry said.

She *what*? That kid? Helt had never really paid attention to her in any way before this. His surprise must have shown on his face.

"I didn't know," Helt said.

Jerry grinned. "You really didn't, did you?"

"But . . ."

"You should take a look at hunk.com sometime. Password Kybelefem. All of us sexy bachelors are on it."

"I don't . . ."

"I know. Don't worry, Helt. I love that look Nadia gets. But I haven't found the time or the place to let her talk it out. To let *me* talk it out."

Helt leaned back in his chair and rubbed his eyes. Okay, he'd decided to push, and learned something about himself doing it, so he had to lay out a trust-offering in payment, at least that. "If I offer any advice, you should be aware it's coming from a man who's besotted with the ship's primary murder suspect."

"Are you? Dr. Maury? No shit?"

"I'm afraid so."

"She's beautiful," Jerry said. "Do you think she did it?"

"I really, truly don't know." Helt wondered if Elena was awake yet. He wondered how she looked, waking, dark hair loose on the pillow. He could almost feel her blanket-heated skin. He could imagine her amber eyes blinking to focus on the day. He wondered if at some point she and Mena had discussed, or would discuss, what sex with Helt Borresen was like. It was a markedly uncomfortable concept. It was also a turn-on.

For an instant, Helt saw the hollow sphere of *Kybele* paved with interlacing tendrils of loves desired and pursued, nodes of loves in flower and stable loves going stale, dull, old branches of loves lost and connections unraveled. In such a construct, relationships that ripened and endured would be nodes of stability, continuity, perhaps. Or they might become lumps of resistance to change, to innovation, cages made of the inertia that sets in when we find what we want and hold on to it. Is there an optimal number of long-term relationships in a community, a town, a world? Could there be too many, too few?

The data would be worth looking at, over time.

"Helt?" Jerry asked.

"Oh. Sorry. Spaced there for a minute." Telling Jerry he would survive this and become more resilient because of it would be stupid, and also it would end the conversation. Helt looked at his choices and decided to gamble. "What do you dread most about talking to Nadia?" Helt asked.

He saw a momentary flash of anger on Jerry's face. Helt had just challenged Jerry's courage, but Jerry recovered and accepted the question.

"I think she's going to cry. I hate it when she cries."

"Heh. Can't blame you for that. If Martin were there, do you think she would cry?"

"What?" Jerry shook his head, and then thought about it. "Wow. That would be highly weird."

"I mean, he may have things he wants to say, too."

Jerry looked in the general direction of the espaliered pear tree on the back wall of Helt's office. Yellow blades of fallen leaves were scattered on the floor; the sweepers hadn't claimed them yet today. Jerry picked one up with his bare toes and tossed it toward the corner.

"You know, if Nadia weren't in the picture, I could like the guy. He's really, really bright, and there's that oblique British humor, the stuff that comes in from the side and you catch it two, three sentences later if you catch it at all.

"I introduced him to Nadia, actually. We were drinking a beer and he started talking about what he was working on. I thought Nadia could help him."

"It might be worth talking out, the three of you. The concept of that sort of honesty—I don't say I'd be brave enough to try it," Helt said.

He had been that brave, in those times where the desire to know something overcame the possible losses from knowing it. He'd done that with Mena. He still hadn't completely integrated her honesty.

He'd been deliberately sought out, she'd told him, as a sort of therapeutic agent. A drug to assuage grief, a cocktail made of new friendship, new intimacy, new sex, and then she'd sent him away—set him free, she said—because he had a life to live and it would be better lived without the burden of an aging partner. Because she was at risk of falling too deeply in love with him, she'd said. Because she had a job to do, a living world to build, and her love for it, her duty to it, had to come first.

She was Mena, and she was superb at what she did, but he still felt resentment at the role she'd given him to play. Help me heal, and then step aside. But, to play fair, to look back at who he was then, he'd run the numbers on loving an older woman. Male thirty-something and female forty-plus had been one set, easy to deal with then. Try male fifty-something and female past sixty. It might have worked. Mena was still, by any standards, a sexy woman.

Helt wanted to tell Jerry to stay in the background for Nadia, to wait this out until it quit hurting. Someone else would arrive in Jerry's life, or

Jerry would be there if this attraction faded and she wanted to come home again. She might, someday.

Helt didn't say that. He couldn't speak with authority about long-term relationships. The real thing was just not going to happen for him.

But then he thought of the three of them together, Martin having sex with Nadia and Jerry good with that, or Jerry and Martin lovers, and of Nadia with two lovers at the same time. He didn't know how Elena felt about open relationships and he knew at some point he'd have to ask her.

He couldn't stay in this place in his head a single second longer.

Not Helt, the hopelessly heterosexual guy. Couldn't go there.

"What's Martin working on?" Helt asked.

"Long view stuff. Literally," Jerry said. "He's had a pet project for a couple of years, seeing if he can adapt human vision to the spectrum we'll have at the new place. I mean, human eyes are really fine, but there's a few things missing, infrared and so forth. He has the theory that we could train visual cortex neurons to see colors we don't see, if the signals were morphed into a different frequency. Adaptation to low light levels—we'll be living with a lot of those."

"Calloway seemed to think he was working on different ways to connect up prosthetic claws or something like that."

"That was last month," Jerry said. "Rock-climber stuff. Grip and let go signals, brain to cleats. He sent it to some Earthside buddies to do up some prototypes. He could get rich on the patents, if the systems work out."

"Earthside. We'll be so close for so long," Helt said.

"Close enough to reset Martin's grippers for half-g climbing, once they're up and working on Earth. Scuttle up the Petra cliffs in minutes and throw down water balloons, or other responsible shit like that. I like outsourcing," Jerry said.

Mena appeared on Helt's screen. "I've asked Susanna to come to my house," she said.

Doughan's sigil blinked as well. "I'll wait for you at the Petra station," he said. "Two hours from now. Mena, set the time for this."

Jerry got up and made for the door. "I'll get after Cash Ryan's data stash," Jerry said. "If I start looking beady-eyed and evil, tell me, okay, Helt?"

"I'll do that," Helt said.

He asked his interface for Giliam again. There was time to find out what Giliam could tell him and get to Petra.

"Your office or mine?" Giliam Obrecht's voice asked.

Helt pulled up a visual and caught Giliam in a full yawn. He was walking across the agora and a trick of morning light turned his generous crop of carrot-red curls into a saintly halo. "Yours," Helt said.

"Come on, then."

Like Jim Tulloch, the ship's in-person Legal Chief had chosen his office location so that people could pretend to be going somewhere else when they came to see him. Helt walked past the vacant tables on the agora and caught up with Obrecht in the Library lobby, a marble-floored, high-ceilinged expanse of calm, and followed him to an office suite on the second floor.

A thick, intricately patterned gold-and-green rug, a view of the agora below, two big armchairs. Obrecht sat down in one of them. The chairs faced a wall screen that showed rows of books bound in leather and gilt.

Obrecht's bicycle spandex and layers of shirts didn't quite match the ambient décor. He didn't look like a lawyer. He looked like a large cherub. He was the same age as Helt.

"I am hurt, *hurt*, I say, to be this far down your list," Giliam Obrecht said. The cherub had a basso voice.

"I'm sorry," Helt said. "I've been scrambling." Giliam didn't look like his feelings were hurt. He looked delighted to find an opportunity to tease Helt about his tendency to apologize for anything and everything.

"And I, barred from the inner circle, I've been carefully following only the public feeds. I've been noticing NSS has been spending what seems to be an excessive amount of time on this suicide. If that's what it was."

"Not a suicide," Helt said.

Obrecht nodded, slowly. "I've seen no records of arrests. I've not been asked to represent anyone."

"That means you've had a few nights of undisturbed sleep to get ready for an onslaught," Helt said.

"And you haven't. Okay, Special Investigator. Tell me what's bothering you."

"How did you know I'm the Special Investigator?" Helt asked.

"It's in the minutes of the exec meeting Thursday morning. Along with the boilerplate of your job description."

Helt pulled out his interface and shut off the mike. The locator function would still know where he was. That was okay.

"It's quiet in here." Giliam waved his arm around the room.

"Has anyone asked you about providing legal counsel for the people Doughan wants to question?" Helt asked.

"Not yet. Isn't questioning people your job? And why isn't Severo asking? I know his troops are out talking to people."

"Severo's looking for people to talk to, mostly. Cash Ryan was a loner. And NSS is recording every encounter they get. There are no arrests as yet, on or off the record."

"If you're recording, you don't need one of us there. Can't imagine why you'd think of it unless you were worried about what you're doing. Are you worried? Is that why you're here?"

"Yes. I'm worried. Archer found some suspects for Doughan to focus on. There are seven people on board that Archer's tagged as Seed Bankers."

"Seed Bankers? And Doughan thinks they're involved in a murder? What are they, contract killers?"

"Damned if I know," Helt said. "All I know is that Doughan jumped on them as suspects and he wants to ask them about their connections to Cash Ryan."

"Helt, it would be most convenient of you to find a single murderer, not seven, please. We have three lawyers on board, and that's all we have. Seven charges of—of what, Helt? Murder? Conspiracy to murder? We're not set up to handle that at this point in time."

"I doubt you'll be asked to represent any of them," Helt said. "Doughan and the execs plan to send the case, and all the Seed Bankers, back to Earth."

"So *that's* what's bothering you," Giliam said. He rested his elbows on the arms of his chair and looked down at the carpet.

"Yes," Helt said.

"It bothers me, too. It can be handled like that, yes, but it may not be wise. I need time to think about this.

"Jurisdiction. Venue. All this arbitrary go and stay ends once we're moving," Giliam said. "The switch to sovereignty is really quite arbitrary, actually." He sighed. "No, we couldn't ask for the rules on dismissal to change before we depart, could we? They *do* change at that instant."

He was talking to himself, his rumbling voice feeding Helt a few hints about his chain of thought, but not the whole picture.

Giliam had been deeply involved in the wording and structure of *Kybele*'s constitution, a compilation of evidence-based structures gleaned from millennia of trials and errors. The successes and failures of any government that had ever recorded them on planet Earth had been examined and mined, beginning with strategies tried in Sumeria and ancient China and from then on, including the several attempts and failures in the restructuring of the UN.

Kybele's constitution was based in part on the protoype of the U.S. Constitution, with several major changes in the areas of franchise (universal in electing electors), qualifications for office (specific, and qualifying exams were part of that), and entitlements (*Kybele* would always provide basic levels of food and shelter and health care. She could not afford not to).

At all levels, it included people who were chosen by lot, and there were strong inducements to do your public duty if your number came up.

Its overwhelming concern was consent of the governed and its foundation was fear of governance run amok. And it was as brief as it possibly could be, for which many thanks to Giliam and his peers and predecessors.

"We don't have much time," Helt said. "Five days, counting this one."

"This is going to be terribly difficult, isn't it?" Giliam asked.

"Yes. Giliam, would you look at what Archer's put together about these people?"

"If you request this in your role as Special Investigator, then it's an order," Giliam said.

Giliam had the expertise to sort out the Seed Banker finances and what they might mean. That meant he'd become part of the prosecution, not of defense, and that limited the ways Helt could use him. So be it.

"It's an order. I'm sorry."

"You're sorry. That's twice in this conversation. You apologize too much, Helt."

"I'm sorry. Oh, damn."

"All Scandinavians apologize too much."

Giliam waved him out of the office.

Jerry in one office, Archer down the hall, and Helt in his, with a timer set to tell him when to leave for Petra and three screens up.

Helt went to the biography he had on Susanna Jambekar for a quick review.

He set searches for Seed Banker interactions and found football and not much else, and about twenty things he needed to search but maybe he could send those to Nadia. The third screen was archives of Elena's childhood. He looked at a few baby and childhood pictures before he filtered those away and focused on interactions she had with the adults in her family. He wanted to find out how Elena responded to frustration, how she'd been taught to deal with anger.

The damned timer beeped.

Doughan and Mena would influence this Seed Banker interview and be players in this Seed Banker interview. Mena's interface said she'd gone to Stonehenge this morning, after a quick visit to Athens—probably to look in on the well-being of the new human baby, Helt figured. She had left the clinic at 0312 and she was back home now. Doughan's interface had been firmly inside Doughan's house during the night and he was on his way to Petra station now.

The locations said he had worked at home all morning.

At Petra station, Doughan greeted Helt with a curt nod. "I signed off on your announcement," he said.

"Thank you."

Doughan didn't look angry. Helt was a little surprised. The exec had probably viewed the data stream and seen for himself that rumors of murder were widespread. Helt didn't know whether to worry that Doughan wasn't showing any upset about it, or accept that the man didn't fight reality when he knew it was there.

They walked the Sunday morning street, bright imitation sunlight from the roof high above, joggers out on the walkways in this deep valley with its village carved into the rock walls on both sides of the river. Bare cliffs above waited to be honeycombed into dwellings as the generations passed. The palette was a spectrum of reds and golds, autumn leaves against black cliffs, their vivid glow mirrored in the glazed surface of the black river. Helt had a sudden, aching longing for the colors of limestone, sandstone, marble, granite, blue-gray sand beaches. Not here. Not ever again until someday, there, and he wouldn't be around to see them.

"She'll know it was murder, then," Doughan said. "If she didn't hear it on her own, Mena will have told her. You ask the questions, IA."

"Why not you?" It was warm out here. Helt shrugged out of his windbreaker and slung it over one arm.

"Because this investigation belongs to you and NSS."

"About that," Helt said. "It would help me a lot if you let Severo know that information comes to me when he gets it. He wants to clear everything with you first. Don't slow me down, Doughan. Please."

"I should have thought of that," Doughan said. "Okay. I'll tell him."

It was almost too easy. Helt felt a little hurt that he hadn't had to battle for that particular piece of turf.

"You'll get all the reports anyway," Helt said.

"Yeah. I'm the Navigation exec, so I'm responsible for the performance of NSS, but from a different place. We missed the Seed Bankers. Archer found them. We should have."

"I should have," Helt said.

"You're the go-to man for problems between divisions, and not in charge of any of them. The Seed Bankers aren't an interdivision problem. I'm not sure who they should have belonged to."

They were a problem Helt hadn't seen because he hadn't looked for it. He could have; he had tools that might have worked.

Helt had started to game interaction problems inside SysSu years ago, to search out nodes of irritation where efficiency dropped, where work slowed down, where work schedules got shifted to avoid someone or some problem. The early visuals had been ripples in a stream, then beds of sand where repulsions or attractions moved pebbles from place to place as if pushed by tiny ants. At first, he took his prototypes to Archer. Archer would glare at them for a while and then pick up his coffee mug and go walkabout. A question here, a nod of approval there, and most often the flow pattern around the perceived irritant returned to normal in days. Now variants of the program ran for Mena, for Doughan, for Severo. Helt's own version of the Irritant Watcher ran for public spaces, non-work hours, where the divisions met and melded. The Seed Bankers hadn't caused a ripple in any of them.

"They're an infrastructure problem, damn it. I made the faulty assumption that one of the secure pillars, one of the strongest bonds for us was the common goal of getting somewhere else," Helt said. "It was a blind spot."

Every colonist had signed a contract that included an obligation of shared responsibility for the well-being of the ship and its journey, an edifice made of language. Venkie would have the linguist's expertise to predict how the document might be interpreted after a hundred years of isolation. Isolation in a culture where even the definitions of up and down were already changed. Up, inward, central. Down, outward, peripheral.

The Seed Bankers were a blind spot. There had to be other blind spots, things that no one was looking for. And if we set a watcher, Helt wondered, and if I end up being the watcher, the question remains, who watches the watcher?

"Okay, so it's your bad," Doughan said. "Be prescient from now on. I'll have Archer write it into your job description."

"Give me a sound database that predicts shifts in human moral imperatives and I'll extrapolate," Helt said.

"You do that. You'll have to build the database first, I take it."

"I'm afraid so."

"Later," Doughan said. "For now, you've been tagged as the behind-the-scenes ax man for the off-list, but the execs still have the job of sending people away. You don't. They'll hate us, not you. But I, for one, won't lose sleep over the Seed Bankers. Sending them away is the only reasonable thing to do." Doughan's right foot took careful aim at a maple leaf on the path and punted it out of his way. It circled in the air and came back down inches away from its original position.

"Is it?" Helt asked. "There's going to be political fallout about this, whether it's that one, or several, of the Seed Bankers faces murder charges, documented, and Earth has to deal with them, or one, or several, of them were sent away simply on suspicion of being Bad Guys, undocumented, because of membership in a lobbying group. Earth is not going to be able to slap our wrists for that, but they will want to."

"I know," Doughan said. "I know. But you'll get this sorted out, and send the facts along with the people. And until our doors are closed for good, we can send anyone back to Earth for any reason at all."

"I still don't like it," Helt said.

"I know." Doughan slowed his pace. They would be a little early, anyway. "However. This can of worms, this murder, is on your plate, IA Special Investigator. I'm just the Navigation presence while we interview this woman. I'm glad I'm not asking the questions. I'm scared of women."

Was he, really? Doughan had a history of one divorce, much earlier in his career. If he was looking for a partner here, now, Helt hadn't heard any gossip about it. *Kybele* was short on State Dinners and many other public spectacles, so choosing a companion for one wasn't an issue. It was long on documentaries designed for Earth audiences, but that wasn't the same thing at all. Helt wasn't sure women liked Doughan up close and personal, but he'd seen women who didn't know him do that posture thing, a slight straightening of back and tucking down of chin, when Doughan came into a room. Women smiled at him a lot, and Doughan smiled back, a lot. Doughan didn't fit "afraid of women" definitions as Helt knew them.

"I've never seen evidence that you're scared of women," Helt said.

"Let me put it this way," Doughan said. "My past history suggests that at times I haven't been scared enough. It was an ugly divorce, Helt."

"I'm sorry." They walked on, quiet for a while.

"What if I miss something?" Helt asked.

"Then I'll chime in."

Doughan might or might not have read Helt's brief on Susanna Jambekar. He might or might not have noticed that Helt hadn't said anything about her relationship with Yves. There was no reason Doughan would know about that unless he'd looked for it.

"I'm dreading this interview," Helt said.

"Don't make me doubt you," Doughan said. "Don't go soft. You have the job and you'll do it well. That was the assumption Archer made, Mena and I made. Don't prove us wrong."

Doughan seemed to be trying to bolster Helt's confidence in himself, in his ability to do the job. A tiny, nagging suspicion rose in Helt's mind. Doughan was distancing himself from the data stream on these Seed Banker interviews and Helt wondered why. And it seemed that he was trying to tell Helt he trusted him to do his job well.

But the bastard had just called him a coward. Helt felt macho tropes try to take over his bloodstream. What did the guy want him to do? Go punch everybody out? Helt figured he would begin with Doughan. The tiny, nagging suspicion rose—they picked me because they think I can't do it.

But they were only steps away from Mena's courtyard gate, and the concern that showed on Doughan's face, the pleading, looked completely real.

Helt rang the bell. "I yield to your wisdom. You've just showed me an effective motivational technique, or one of them. A challenge and then a call to battle, a variation on carrot and stick."

"What?" Doughan asked as Mena came to them through light and shadow. She wore dark slacks and a coral shirt, loose sleeves tight at her wrists, rough-woven fabric with a gleam in its threads when the light caught them.

"That meant thank you," Helt said. He smiled down at Mena. "We were discussing donkeys."

"They're fine," Mena said. "Come in."

She led them through the interior courtyard, past the tiers of wall plantings and the central fountain, into the sitting room at the back. It smelled of fresh coffee, black tea, white musk, and leather. Its walls were plastered in white and crowded with paintings. An icon of Saint Phocas, pruning sickle in hand, guarded the door into the kitchen.

The icon was very old and very small, hauled up from Earth by Mena. The other paintings were gifts from a society of Greek antiquarians, meticulously imaged on Earth, meticulously 3-D printed on *Kybele.* A plethora of colored cushions were piled on divans and chairs. Helt knew from experience that all the seating was comfortable and that all of it was arranged to give a view of the courtyard. He hadn't been here for years, and everything was the same, and everything was different because the time he'd spent here was over.

He'd spent long, lazy hours in this room, with books and music, getting lost in idle cloud searches that came from shared words or random memories. He remembered those hours so well. The comfort of shared meals, shared touches, the comfort of caring and being cared for. Damn, he missed how that felt.

A woman rose from a chair in the shadows near the back of the room. He thought he would be seeing a motherly figure, a clucking hen, perhaps. Not so, this woman was more of a shore wader, an egret or a heron. There was no softness in her flesh. She was as lean and ropy as a long-distance runner. As she stood, a cushion, patterned in the black and gold of some ancient shield, fell to the floor.

Helt's view of Susanna Jambekar was overlaid by what he thought Yves might see when he looked at her. She was taller than Mena by a head, but almost everyone was. Low, straight-line black eyebrows guarded her eyes. There was a hint of beak in her finely modeled nose. She was a native of Goa, but if there were traces of Portugal in her face he hadn't seen them in captures and he didn't see them here. Wary, guarded, and weary, she stood her ground. A caryatid, that might be what Yves would see, the weight of the Petra cliffs on her strong, uncomplaining shoulders.

He looked for a resemblance to Elena. Other than black hair, nothing. Nothing in her face, and her eyes were much, much darker, deep cordovan brown.

"Susanna, this is Wesley Doughan, and Helt Borresen from SysSu," Mena said. Doughan and Helt nodded in turn. "Have you met before?"

"Not in face-time." Susanna looked from one to the other, and then back to Doughan.

"Let's begin. Please sit down," Mena said. Her coffee table was loaded for company with coffee and tea and a tray of pastries that smelled of cinnamon and butter.

"You know why we're here," Helt said.

"I think so." Susanna Jambekar gripped both arms of the chair and sat down slowly, cautiously, like an old woman. She lifted the cushion from the floor and wedged it into place beside her. Her fingers kneaded a portion of the gold braiding at its edge. She stared at a point somewhere between Helt and Doughan, through the window toward something out in the courtyard or at some unseen monster.

"We'll be asking questions," Helt said.

Susanna took a deep breath and sighed. "That's what Mena told me." Her voice was mid-range soprano, pleasantly pitched, but Helt imagined the potential edge of a knife in it. Susanna laid her interface on a cushion beside her. Its little lens would be set for voice activation and move from face to face.

Mena poured for them, her brutal hands quiet on the mug of coffee she handed Helt, on the handle of the silver holder beneath the glass of steaming tea she filled for Doughan.

Helt laid his interface on the arm of his chair. "We'll have two records, then. That's fine." His audio picked up the clinking of Doughan's spoon stirring cherry jam into his tea. Mena placed a glass of tea on the table in front of Susanna. Her pendant earrings gleamed coral and gold, moved forward as she leaned down, swung back to bring attention to the pure Attic curve of her throat as she straightened.

Susanna looked at the tea as if she didn't know what it was. "I—" She reached for the glass.

Doughan cleared his throat, a sharp, harsh sound. Susanna's hand jerked, a startle response quickly stifled.

"You know Cash Ryan was murdered," Helt said.

"I didn't know it until this morning."

"We're combing every record we have to find people who knew him, talked to him, worked with him. The two of you got off the Petra train at the same time, several times." Twice, they had ridden the same car at the same time. Twice wasn't several. Let her think there were more captures, let her fears grow. There was so much he needed to know, so much he needed to learn about her, about who she was and what she was.

Her future on *Kybele* was over, no matter what happened here. Mena would send her off-ship because of the Seed Banker money in her account and because Doughan wanted that to happen. Yves might leave with her, whether or not he'd helped her throw Cash Ryan off the tower.

Helt didn't want Yves hurt, but if this woman had killed Cash Ryan, or Yves had, then the searching, the suspicions, could stop.

"Anything you could tell us about him, and I do mean anything, might help us find out who killed him."

He picked up his coffee, freshly ground, freshly made, medium roast, medium strong, richly fragrant. Mena brewed it for his American tongue. What she brewed for herself was thick and strong, a pharmaceutical-strength potion to be served in tiny cups.

Helt let the silence lengthen. Mena had the ability to turn feral mother for her own but she showed no hint of doing that. She looked as compassionate as a carved Great Mother, and as stern. Doughan's relaxed posture was that of a hunter in a duck blind, motionless in meditative, patient awareness, primed to move on the instant. Scary.

"It was almost three years ago."

"Yes," Helt said.

Susanna looked at him and blinked. "The first time I saw him. I went to the Frontier with some people from the clinic for happy hour that one evening and Cash Ryan came up to say something to a woman he worked with."

Helt checked the NSS records for Cash's coworkers. Zaida Krupin. She was a third-generation Russian spacer, an engineer trained in Germany. "Zaida?" he asked.

"Yes," she said. "She invited him to sit down."

Happy hour at the Frontier was one of ship's meet-and-greet places, where the world below and Level One Athens sought each other within the guidelines of an unstated contract. Like all contracts, it had rules and disclaimers. Zaida's invitation meant "He's available," and implied "I've vetted him."

Helt pulled a security clip from the Frontier to his interface. The camera he was interested in was positioned to give a shoulder-level view of the tables, and its motion-capture function was set for wide gestures—impending fisticuffs or sudden departures. When it wasn't alarmed, it panned back and forth from table to table in slow, lazy arcs.

"Yes, she did. I see her, I think. Let's look at this," Helt said. "Mena, would you put this on a screen for us?"

Mena gave him a curt nod and unrolled a screen to stand on the table. Doughan shifted his chair so he could get a view of it.

Four women sat at one of the Frontier's round tables. A man bent his head and said something to one of them. It was Cash, scrubbed down after a day shift, dressed in a gray chambray shirt and new jeans. That must be Zaida, black curls clipped close to her skull. Human voices buzzed, but individual words were hard to catch. The drone of voices was interspersed with bangs from the kitchen, metallic rattles of cutlery, footsteps of the waitstaff coming and going. Helt hadn't realized how noisy the place actually was.

Susanna leaned forward a little and stared at the screen. Helt watched her eyes widen. She was beginning to realize how closely NSS had looked at her. He circled the curly-haired woman's face with a pointer. "Is that Zaida?"

"Yes," Susanna said.

Zaida shrugged and indicated an empty chair. The camera panned away to other tables and showed an inevitable student lost in contemplation of his screen, a booth where a couple shared a single platter of pasta, a bridge game with its aura of studied nonchalance that fooled no one, certainly not the players.

When the view drifted back to Susanna's table, Cash was seated but Zaida was on her feet. She picked up her rucksack and left.

"She didn't stay long," Helt said.

"She told us Cash Ryan was a newbie. She introduced him, and then she left," Susanna said. Zaida's face implied that she worked with him but he wasn't her thing.

He glanced again at Zaida's name on his list. Her hour was cleared and

Severo had talked to her, but her store of information might not be exhausted.

"What did you talk about?" Helt asked.

"It's hard to remember," Susanna said.

Helt doubted that. "Chief Mares tells me a lot of businesses set their audios so that normal conversation sounds blurred, but shouts or screeches come in clearly. It's a privacy thing for their customers, and it makes the records easier to review if anyone needs to review them. I don't need word for word, just your impressions of the conversation."

Susanna Jambekar stiffened in her chair and gripped her right knee with both hands. She lifted her chin and closed her eyes for a moment, and then blinked them open. "Before he came, we were laughing about Dr. Calloway. He had a bruise on his lip and he wouldn't tell us how he got it, so we made up theories that got pretty wild.

"And then they started talking about a historical drama, the one set in Greenland before the melt."

"Did you like the film?" Helt asked.

"I hadn't seen it. I don't have much time for movies," Susanna said.

"Then Cash Ryan showed up," Helt prompted.

"He listened to the chatter about the film and said some of the music was by—I thought he said Cigaruss? And that they were from Iceland, and that was probably okay, but that the outdoor shots were from New Zealand."

Sigur Rós, warrior rose; sad, weird music; the Icelandic group had been a passing fancy of its time. Helt remembered Archer's theatrical wince when someone had played a clip of the sounds of a bowed guitar.

"He seemed angry about that, because he thought they should have combed the cloud for archival footage of the old island. But he didn't say much, really."

"Was there more?" Helt asked.

"He—we didn't talk much longer after he came there. He was new, so we were polite, but he wasn't one of us, and . . ."

They waited her out.

"And I didn't like him. We were all women, that day at the table, and he looked at us like we were . . ."

Her eyes narrowed.

"Go on," Helt said.

"He was disdainful. Cold. That was the impression I had of him."

"He left when you did," Helt said.

"I told him I was going home. He said he was, too. We rode the same train to Petra."

Helt showed the captures of them leaving the Athens station, getting off at Petra.

"Did he sit next to you?"

She shook her head, no.

"Do you know where he lived?"

"No. I don't."

"He lived in Athens. Do you know if any of the other women who met him that night became friends with him?"

"If they did, I haven't heard about it. When we get together, we talk about the people in our lives, women, and men, too."

Helt nodded. "Susanna, if they had other contacts with him, you can't protect them. We'll be questioning them, anyway, because of this first meeting."

"I told you the truth! His name just didn't come up again! Are you going to bother everyone on this ship?"

"Yes, if we must," Helt said. "Let's look at this."

On a different date, Susanna Jambekar and Cash Ryan stepped into the Athens train, got off at the Petra station. "This was a year later."

"I remember," Susanna said.

"Tell us."

Doughan and Mena sat like statues, saying nothing, watching everything.

"He just appeared beside me. He sat down beside me on the train. He asked if I remembered him, and I said I did. He said he was not a colonist, he had no chance of that, but that before he left he wanted to get to know me. Sometimes you can get an 'ugh' reaction from that if it's just a clumsy way to ask for sex. This wasn't that feeling. It seemed like an honest request for a friendship. This time he just seemed shy. I asked, why me? And he said because I reminded him of someone who had been very special to him."

"Who?" Mena asked.

Unexpected, Mena's question gave Helt a quick jolt of irritation. He had a plan for what he wanted to hear from Susanna. He didn't want her to talk about Elena, and he wanted to steer her away from mentioning Yves, if he could. Susanna turned her head to look at Mena. Surely I'm not abandoned to these wolves, the midwife must be thinking. My boss is here. She'll protect me. "That's what I wanted to ask him, Mena. Who?"

Helt could hear the relief in Susanna's voice, the slight lessening of tension that came from believing she had an ally in the room. "And what he said was, 'I'm sorry. I wanted to protect her, and you. It won't come up again. I hope I haven't disturbed your evening.' Those were the words he used. At least they're very close to what he said."

To Helt's ears, the meaning of Cash's words was far too clear. He knew who the *her* was that Cash wanted to protect. The expanded search that would show Cash trailing Elena wasn't done. He had to look at it as soon as this interview was over. Had to.

"What was your response to that?" Helt asked.

"I didn't know what to say. I just wanted to get away from him. I said something, told him I wasn't disturbed, even though I was. I looked around to see if there was anyone on the train I recognized but I didn't see anyone. If I had, I would have gotten up to sit by them. I was sitting next to the window, and he would have had to get up to let me leave. . . .

"I didn't want to risk that he wouldn't move. I told him I was meeting Yves for dinner."

"Yves?" Doughan asked.

Okay, Yves was in play. That his name would come up had probably been inevitable. "Yves Copani. He's in Navigation," Helt said. Not now, Doughan. Later. Please.

Susanna looked away from Mena, back to Helt. He watched her process the realization that Helt knew about Yves, knew about their relationship. And if he knew that, then he knew about the Seed Banker money. Or she feared that he did. Her pupils grew in size. All her attention was on him; she would read threat or promise in what he said, she would do her best to decipher the subtexts that might lurk in his voice, his muscles.

The Scots engineer, Halkett, had not been frightened of Helt when they talked. That was before the rumors of murder swept through the ship. That was when Ryan's death seemed a suicide, unfortunate, but in no way connected with Kelly Halkett. The man had become uneasy as the questions continued, but Susanna's fear was different, a primal fear kept at bay by the trappings of civilization in this room, by her own expectations of how she should act. So this was the power inherent in the inquisitor's robe. It was not Helt's power, but his to use for now.

He looked away from Susanna, looked at Doughan and Mena to see if their silence, their acquiescence to what he was doing, came from set and setting, or from an unfamiliar script, the arousal of hunter-prey roles that were no longer considered decent in civilized behavior. Except for war, and perhaps this was one.

Doughan seemed to be trying to hide in a cave made by the curve of his own shoulders. Helt felt him peering out of it, evaluating, considering, reconsidering. Mena was watching Helt's face with a fascination that didn't seem to be fear. More the full attention she might offer a test subject that was exhibiting unusual behaviors.

" 'I wanted to protect her, and you.' What do you think Cash Ryan meant by that, Susanna?"

"I thought it was a threat. I thought if he ever came close to me again, I would speak to NSS about it."

"Did you have any conversations with him after that? Ever?"

"I never saw the man again until the announcement of his suicide." Her voice clipped off each word. "Now you say it was a murder."

"Cash Ryan left none of the warnings, the indicators, that usually precede a suicide. NSS began to treat this as a murder within hours of the death, and now it's certain that the man was killed," Helt said. "Did you tell Yves about this . . . encounter?"

"Yes."

"What did you tell him?"

"I told him I had a disturbing conversation with someone on the train. I went through what the Ryan man had said, and I told Yves I knew I was making too much of how I'd felt about the interchange. He looked at me for a moment and didn't say anything. We talked about something else."

She forced her eyes away from Helt's face with what seemed to be deliberate effort. She stared down at her hands.

"I hadn't known Yves very long then. Now I would know to worry if he went silent like that about something."

"Because . . ." Helt said.

"Because when he doesn't say anything, that means he's really, really angry." Susanna smiled, a fond little smile that vanished quickly.

"I want you to see this." Helt played the clips he'd found when he'd increased the time window around the appearance of Susanna Jambekar on public cameras. Susanna going into a hairdresser's shop, Cash Ryan on the street outside. Susanna leaving the Athens clinic in her lab coat, Cash Ryan walking by its door minutes later. Cash Ryan leaving the Stonehenge station on the train before Susanna, Cash Ryan stepping into the train just as Susanna left it. This was new information for Doughan, for Mena.

Doughan spread the fingers of his right hand, made a fist, opened his hand again. Mena took a deep breath. Her nostrils flared.

"There are more of these," Helt said. "Twenty-seven instances, total. You say you didn't talk to him again."

"I didn't!" Susanna lifted her head and met his eyes again.

"You didn't see him again."

"I did not see him! I did not talk to him!"

"He was stalking you, Susanna. How did you not know it?"

She tried so hard to read Helt's face. "How despicable," she whispered.

"What?" Helt asked.

"You make it difficult for me to be sorry he's dead. But I did *not* know! I would have gone to Security if I had known." Righteous anger lent weight to her every syllable. Righteous anger is a secure place to be.

"I'm sure you would have." Helt propped his elbows on the arms of his chair and tented his hands, fingertips together. It was a gesture Archer sometimes used. "Susanna, I believe you. I believe that you did not know you were being stalked. I am telling you that everyone who had any contact with Cash Ryan, however minimal, will be asked where they were on the evening he died. You will be asked to document that time for us."

And where had she been? She would be reviewing the evening of Ryan's death now, wondering if she'd been alone, if she'd been on a public camera somewhere, if Yves had been with her and could back up her story. But he hadn't been, not for all of the missing hour. He'd been making his plea to Helt for part of it.

"We are reasonably sure that more than one person was involved in Cash Ryan's murder. We don't know if anyone else was stalked by him. You're the only person we've found." That was not quite true. Helt was almost certain Cash Ryan had kept close tabs on Elena, but in ways that public cameras hadn't found. Yet. "We're learning that he was an odd man, perhaps a dangerous one. Perhaps dangerous to the ship. We're worried about sabotage, about funding, transfers of money, things that may have required more than one person to accomplish."

Helt looked beyond his fingertips and focused on her eyes. He watched her eyes widen as her comprehension of what he had just said struck home.

He had just told Susanna he knew about the money and she must be thinking he was keeping his knowledge secret. She was building possibilities about his silence, about what he could or would do or had already done with information that would change her life. He felt her terror, a shadow in the room. She had to be waiting for a question about the Seed Banker money in her account. She had to be praying that no one knew about it, and now this death, her connections to the man who died, brought attention to her that she surely didn't want.

He could ask her anything now, prompt her to make any response he wanted to hear.

He had never had this sort of power over anyone, not a lover, not an enemy. Sitting in the chair next to Susanna, a woman he had loved observed him closely, and he knew that even in the strivings of sex, in the art of orgasm delayed or hastened, Mena had been less helpless than the stranger he questioned now.

Shiva danced with transcendent glee to the drum of the pulse in Helt's ear. Conquer this or embrace it. Now you know. This feeling is only a hint of what's available to you.

Mena's good coffee became a nauseating chemical presence in his gut. Helt let his hands fall to his lap. "I'm sorry. I believe what you've told us. I'm worried for you. I'm worried for all of us. I'll want to talk to you again, but this is enough for now."

Mena looked out at the courtyard and got to her feet. "Someone's at the gate." Mena placed Susanna's interface in her hand. Susanna looked at it as if she had never seen it before. Her eyes followed Mena as she went to the door, opened it with a jerk, and closed it firmly behind her.

Doughan unfolded himself from his chair with deliberate slowness and stood. "Miss Jambekar. I am sorry we had to meet in circumstances like this. I would like to tell you that everyone on the ship appreciates your valuable work."

Doughan meant it, Helt was sure, but the unspoken part of that statement was something like, "We'll miss you when you're gone." Helt got to his feet. Susanna took her cue and rose as well. Her dazed eyes darted to the courtyard and back to the men in the room. She did not look at Helt's face, or at Doughan's.

Helt heard the click of Mena's shoes on the courtyard stone, coming back to the door.

"It's Yves," Mena said. "I'll take you to him."

Doughan and Helt stood aside as Mena walked past them, took Susanna's hand, and led her away.

20

Mena and Doughan

Doughan went to the window and scanned Mena's courtyard as if it were enemy territory. He held his right hand behind his back, like a reverse Napoleon. "What about this boyfriend?" he asked.

"His name is Yves Copani. He's an overqualified welder on David II's miner crew. He's an architect, among other things."

"What other things?" Doughan began to pace, three steps from the window to the door and back again.

"He's a sculptor and an acute observer of the influence of geometry and habitat on human interaction."

"Is he a friend of yours?" Doughan found a water spot on Mena's window and rubbed it away with his thumb.

"I met him the night Ryan was killed," Helt said. "He came to ask how he could stay on board with Susanna."

"But he's on contract."

"Yes, he is. I've seen some of his work." A minor piece, worked the full height of the Petra cliff. "My advice to him was to take a portfolio to David II."

"And what will be your recommendation to David II?" Doughan asked.

"I think we need him," Helt said.

Doughan left the window and took the three steps back to the door. "That good, eh?" He opened the door for Mena.

"That good."

"I think she'll be all right," Mena said. She walked past him and leaned down to the screen, which was frozen on a view of Susanna in half stride at the threshold of the opening door of the train. "Enough," she told it. It went dark. Beside it, the untouched pastries waited on their tray. Doughan grabbed one. Mena handed him a napkin and rolled the stand to the back of the room. "I have no idea what she'll tell Yves. Sit down, both of you."

Helt did. Doughan went to the window again, munching baklava and lost in some private reverie far away from this room and its inhabitants. "Mena, you know her and we don't," Helt said. "I thought she was telling the truth, that she didn't know she was being stalked. Do you?"

"Is that all the information you have about this stalking?" Mena settled herself in her chair. "Come back, Doughan. Stop fidgeting. You're making me nervous." Mena didn't look nervous. She looked determined and patient and durable. The hollows under her eyes were deeper than Helt remembered. An inverted parenthesis of frown lines was beginning to show itself between her eyebrows, tiny lines. Helt's fingers didn't remember them, although they remembered tracing the silken wing of her eyebrow, the delicate softness of her temple. He didn't remember seeing those lines in the harvest tent so long ago. Yesterday, when Elena was there. Mena's relaxed calm seemed to be a veneer of determination and patience over what looked like crushing fatigue.

"That's all," Helt said. "I searched for captures that show Cash Ryan near her door, in groups, concerts or the bars and so forth. I looked for her near his quarters as well."

"Really," Mena said. "Near *his* quarters. I hadn't thought about that. It had to be looked at. Of course it would."

"I scanned for messages, of course, but those are never private and Ryan wasn't stupid. He didn't make that mistake. What I have are camera captures, those twenty-seven times they came and went in close proximity. The number of near connections, near misses, is above random, but not by much. It was what she told us today that makes the stalker hypothesis viable."

Doughan came back to his chair and sat down. "So did she know about the stalking, Mena?" he asked.

"I think not," Mena said.

"But now she believes she was stalked, whether it was real or not," Doughan said. "Now her boyfriend knows, this guy Helt is pushing us to keep. Or he knew before, and did something about a man who was harassing his woman. He just went high on my list of suspects."

"Let me talk to him," Helt said. "We have a degree of rapport. If you're going to ask me whether he's capable of murder, my answer is I don't know yet but I doubt it." That Yves was capable of anger, Helt doubted not at all. The guy could punch someone out, no question, but Helt didn't know the man's parameters for the use of physical violence, didn't know what codes he had for its use. He had protective instincts about Susanna. Helt had roused them when he told Yves Susanna was on the list of people NSS would be looking at. No question about the protective instincts, either. And he was a contract worker. If he wanted to off Cash and thought he could get away with it, the days before he got shuttled Earthside would be his last chance.

"You turned Susanna Jambekar loose with the news that we're worried about sabotage," Doughan said. "That will result in false alarms to answer, tests to be run on equipment, food, you name it, by Security Personnel who are supposed to be spending their time finding a murderer. What led you to fantasize Ryan was a saboteur?"

"That's a hypothesis from the psychiatric autopsy."

"Hypothesis. You let loose a sabotage scare based on a hypothesis."

You're the one who just brought up sabotage, not me, Helt didn't say.

"Susanna's not a gossip," Mena said.

"But she's a Seed Banker." Doughan's glance at Mena was full of reproach. "And everyone talks to someone. This boyfriend of hers, for instance." Mena set her jaw and stared at the chair Susanna had occupied so recently. Doughan returned his attention to Helt. "You still haven't shown that Ryan got Seed Banker money. Or did he?"

"Not that we've found," Helt said.

"I am relieved to hear that," Doughan said. "You told her we're on to 'transfers of funds,' is how you put it. If that isn't a heads-up to the other Seed Bankers, I don't know what would be. What, exactly, are you trying to accomplish?"

"I want to solve a murder and we're running out of time. If we could keep the Seed Bankers on board until we know if they killed Ryan, we also might have time to sort out whether or not this ship is going to blow up, and when."

Doughan's hesitation could have been a pause while he deliberated what to say. The corners of the exec's eyelids narrowed for the briefest of instants while he sighted on a target across the room. "They have to go," Doughan said. "They have to go on schedule."

"The shuttles can keep coming and going until the poles are powered on." Helt meant the statement to be a blunt challenge to Doughan's authority, a test to see how much power the execs had turned over to their

IA. Their IA knew that in a less stressed situation, he would have offered his challenge after more planning and hopefully at less risk. Let me do this or fire me, was one way to look at what he was doing. Please, let me just go hide in a corner, was another.

Doughan looked at Helt as if he were a tool, a wrench that could be repurposed to hit something, hard. "I won't list the fuel costs if we don't power up when we said we would. Or the remote, but very real, danger of piracy."

Mena frowned at Doughan. "Archer says the Northern and Southern Coalitions are quiet for now," Mena said.

"For now. But the sooner we can turn on the plasma shields, the better off we are."

It was definitely time to back down. "Understood," Helt said.

"If we don't have these bastards in hand in time, that's when to think about delays. Not now."

It was a sort of concession, or, Helt figured, it would be wise to accept it as such.

The paired lines between Mena's eyebrows deepened. She glanced from Doughan to Helt and back to Doughan, evaluating them for signs of incipient battle rage, or something like that.

"I accept that," Helt said. "If possible, before they go, I want to see connections between the Seed Bankers. If they're a terrorist cell with a mission to kill this ship or keep her where she is, they are extremely skilled at not leaving traces. I haven't found friendships between them, or messages, or even physical locations they've been to that might serve as drop-boxes. Two of them, Kelly Halkett and Oriol Bruguera, play on the same soccer team as David II. We haven't talked to Bruguera yet."

Doughan had been on his way to see Oriol Bruguera with David II yesterday, right after the Kelly Halkett interview. Okay, he and David II had gone somewhere else.

"He's due to come down to Navigation tomorrow with David II," Doughan said. "I wanted him to have a little time to worry."

"I don't mind that at all," Helt said. "I want the Seed Bankers to be nervous. The Security people tailing them might get some useful information that way. So far, there's been no communication between these seven people since Cash Ryan died, not via interface, not in person."

"None?" Doughan asked.

"None."

Doughan moved in his chair, the motion of a man with a backache who wants the cushions to be where they aren't, exactly.

"We know about the Seed Bankers now but they almost slipped by us," Helt said. "What about other people with other agendas we haven't even thought about? It's in our interest to give people space to be themselves, to have private loves and hates, but which loves, which hates, should we be on watch for?

"You asked me what I want to accomplish. I want us to leave system with a chance to get where we're going. I don't want to burden us with the lifetime sequestering and care of two, or maybe even three or four killers. And I don't want to purge us of creative, perhaps quirky, perhaps irritating people who may make our journey richer, not for fears that have no basis in fact."

"The Seed Bankers are traitors. End story," Doughan said.

"Ryan wasn't a Seed Banker," Helt said.

"Biosystems is supposed to deal with crazies," Doughan said. "They missed Ryan."

Mena's hurt look was momentary, but there.

"To be fair, so did NSS," Doughan added.

"Tulloch and his associates are as accessible as they know how to be." Mena's voice was dull and flat. "NSS intervenes only when a person's behavior interferes with the physical or mental well-being of others. Cash Ryan didn't set off any alarms, even when he stalked Susanna. I wish he had."

She poured Doughan another glass of tea and smiled when he reached for the cherry jam. "If you doubt the ethical concerns of Biosystems, I might ask you to review a meeting where we discussed how many roosters are needed for the optimal emotional health of hens. Interminable discussions, but perhaps humbling," Mena said. "Medical and NSS did the jobs they are authorized to do. But they are not Thought Police."

Doughan raised an eyebrow in her direction. He looked sad and thoughtful.

Willingly, consciously, or not, Mena's Biosystems and Doughan's Navigation were marked with the individual stamps of their personalities, their priorities. Mena's Biosystems was filled with curiosity and tenderness. Doughan's Navigation was all confidence and competence. Archer herded cats, quirky ones, with bemused skill. Helt liked their versions of the way things should be, the versions he dealt with in his work, in his life here, in the comforts that came from them.

Backlighted by the window, Mena's profile belonged on a Greek coin. Doughan's face was suddenly, clearly, despite the few generations his family had spent in Texas, a face carved on an Assyrian gate. He was Lebanese, a child of the city once called "the Athens of the Mideast." No longer.

Helt's ideas of justice didn't match Doughan's. Due process, rule of law, was supposed to be how things were. But. But this bending of procedure was obviously something Doughan would do because it fit his version of protecting the ship. The Seed Bankers would be sent away with no criminal charges, no blots on their records. In many ways, they were scheduled for a soft landing. If they stayed here, they'd end up in jail. In many ways, what the execs planned wasn't cruel.

A culture finds its way toward new behaviors, new, hopefully more adaptive, versions of right and wrong, slowly at best. Humans didn't bait bears now—well, they didn't in most places. In others, they did.

"I'll tell Severo to put a tail on Susanna's boyfriend," Doughan said.

Mena shook her head as if to clear it. "Doughan, to phrase this very clearly, it's not your job to do that. We gave this investigation to Helt." She tapped her fingers on the arm of her chair, twice, and then looked away from Doughan and sought Helt's eyes. "Yes, Archer told me your concerns. I support you," was her clear, unspoken message.

"Susanna is a suspect," Doughan said. "So is her boyfriend. Many a man has killed another because of a woman. He needs tailing. He needs to be questioned."

"He will be," Helt said. "It would be such a neat, tidy, explicable solution, wouldn't it? 'Jealous boyfriend and outraged victim kill stalker.' I won't believe it until I can prove it."

Mena came to a sort of attention in her chair. "If that turns out to be so, I'll accept it. However, if she's not a murderess, I want to keep my midwife," Mena said. Her voice was brighter, sharper, deliberately, and falsely, lighter in tone. "In order to do that, I'd like to see her cleared of a murder charge, and if it's possible, the matter of this Seed Banker money must be resolved. Until I know why it's there I'm going to think of it as a smoke screen, placed in her account to draw suspicion to her, something false."

Doughan put his tea glass down and stared at her.

"Doughan, I remind you that unless criminal charges are filed against her, I am within my rights to keep any colonist in Biosystems."

That little bombshell delivered, Mena stood up and stretched. "It's time to go pry Archer out of his cave. We're scheduled to have a relaxed chat, in the plaza, for some documentary people." Her voice held an edge of near hysteria. This was not a Mena Helt knew, this person who seemed determined to make light of what she'd just said.

The documentary, at least, explained the pretty blouse and the earrings. Mena never wore dangly earrings when she worked. He remembered Mena washing her face in his steamy bathroom, a soapy thumb and finger on a naked earlobe. She didn't fancy having Calloway stitch up a rip in one, she'd said.

"Oh, the pastries. This whole business kills the appetite. Maybe the camera crew will eat some of them. Let me get some boxes." She walked past St. Phocas and disappeared into the kitchen.

"She's gone nuts." Doughan stood up, following his dismissal signal like an automaton. "She doesn't mean that."

Helt had never stood in front of a prompter and watched the words scroll by. He hadn't read this screenplay. He didn't know his next line. If Mena broke ranks and said, "No, my people stay," could Archer and Doughan override her decision? Would they?

Mena came back with paper boxes, scooped equal portions of the pastries into them and handed one to Doughan.

"While you're at it, Helt, I want to keep my best gene-splicer as well. It's really time for you to find an alibi for Elena."

She gave Helt his box and kissed his cheek, a quick, emotionless brush of dry lips on his early stubble. "Take these to her. She's waiting at the gate.

"Doughan, wait just a minute. I forgot something." Mena hurried off into the hallway that led to her bedroom.

21

Retracing Steps

Outside Mena's gate, Helt thumbed his interface to catch real-time audio from Mena and Doughan, but got nothing. He was eavesdropping. That he was doing it disgusted him. Anything they recorded would go in the SysSu records anyway. Voice activations were time-stamped and would show if they blocked what they said, so there was really no reason to keep their feeds coming to his pocket.

His screen stared up at him, blank, waiting for notes. The list was growing too long for his distracted memory and he hadn't made any during the Susanna interview. He hadn't wanted to break the tension in the room. Everything they'd said was recorded. He could review it all later.

Helt walked past the gate, his goodie box in one hand and his interface in the other.

Elena waited at the far end of Mena's wall, her black-and-white plaid shirt striped by shadows cast by the maple overhead. Bloodred leaves drifted down in singles and pairs. Her shoulders braced her against the wall. She leaned against it with one ankle crossed over the other, her arms wrapped across her chest, a cowboy drifter waiting for something to happen.

The strangeness of Mena's challenge, of Doughan's determined passivity in the face of Helt's unplanned—mostly unplanned—defense of the turf they had given him flashed through his mind, replaced by fascination with what was coming next, what he would say to Elena, what she would say to him, what they would learn from each other.

Through light and shadow, Helt carried Mena's pastries toward the unknown person who was Elena, slowly, so he could watch her unaware of him for a few more moments. She kept her eyes on the interface she held in one hand and didn't look up at him.

"Hello," he said.

She turned and stared at him. Her hair, gathered in a clip at the back of her neck, fanned across her left shoulder and caught red highlights from the maple trees behind her.

She wasn't smiling.

Helt tried to read her face, tried to see signs of anger, of apprehension, of curiosity about what they might have said about her when she wasn't there to hear. What he saw was the blank face of a student in a lecture, an appearance of attention over concerns that were far, far away.

"You're wondering what we talked about," Helt said.

"Yes," she said.

She looked down at the interface in her hand.

"I asked Susanna a lot of questions. I think her answers were honest, but I can't be sure of that." The aggression he'd felt with the midwife was gone now. He felt lost.

"Did you scare her?" Elena asked.

"I think so."

"Did you need to do that?"

"I think so."

"I'm sorry," Elena said.

"For Susanna?"

Her answer came slowly. "For you, I think. And for Susanna. I'll hear about it. You know that."

"I know it now. I thought you would talk to each other. That's okay," Helt said. But he didn't want to talk about Susanna. Elena was still looking at the interface in her hand.

"Mena said for me to clear you from the suspect list, today."

Elena turned her interface so its screen faced him. He saw himself, his hesitant walk and the worried look on his face as he approached her. His uncertainty about the response she would give him was clear on his face.

The interface display was a challenge to his vanity. His walk would be there for anyone to see, the tensions in it; he looked like a kid expecting to get yelled at.

"You're playing by the rules," Helt said. "No moment undocumented."

"Yes," Elena said. Her face was impassive, on guard against him. "So you're going to get me off the suspect list. How do you propose to do that?"

"You've been through the blank hour."

"Over and over again. I was in the lab. I left it and went to Athens tower. I was on the train for most of it."

"Okay. Let's go to your lab. Let's walk it through. Between us we'll find something, something that can't be argued away."

She put her interface in a pocket and fell in step with him. They walked with their heads down, scuffling through the leaves on the path that led to Petra station. Her boots had round toes and thick soles. They looked like a child's boots. He liked that. He hadn't found anything about her he didn't like.

He didn't know her. She was not yet formally accused of murder but she knew that NSS and the execs on this ship knew her links to Cash Ryan, and her proximity on Tuesday night to where and when he was killed. That had to hurt. She had to be deeply hurt by this, already. Helt, again, regretted that he hadn't known, and now would never know, the Elena she was before this happened.

"I suppose it's a place to start," Elena said. "Although the reality is, you'll be looking for evidence that I was *not* innocent of this murder."

There was no denial he could make that wouldn't be a lie. Anything he said now was going to be wrong. There was no help for it.

"I can only . . ." He wanted to hold her. He wanted to explain who he was and what he was and why, and what he hoped for and what he feared. ". . . promise you that if you killed him, you'll have to prove it to me. You'll have to give me hard proof, because I'm going to be hard to convince."

She didn't smile. What he thought he saw in her face was concern for *him.*

"That's fair," Elena said.

"You are not the only woman on this ship with connections to Cash Ryan."

"Susanna?"

"Cash Ryan found her interesting, at least. You know I suspected it. I told you and Mena I did."

"And now you have proof."

"More than I wanted. I'll show you." He reached for the interface in his pocket. "When we're on the train." Notes, notes, he needed to make them.

"Wait." He stopped short. "Just a moment . . ." Helt hauled his interface out of his pocket.

ZAIDA

SEVERO TAIL FOR COPANI

ELENA-RYAN NEAR-MISSES

DAVID II DOUGHAN'S SATURDAY AFTERNOON

"Please forgive me. Homework."

Her hand covered the little screen of his interface. He looked at her reproachful face. "For one, that's rude. For two, you're avoiding talking about Susanna."

"I'm sorry. Yes, I'm avoiding talking about Susanna." He pointed to his screen. It's listening. So is yours.

She nodded. He put the interface back in his pocket. "The notes—the work's for you," Helt said. "Things I don't want to forget. In part, it's for you . . ."

"Because Mena told you to clear me."

"Not just that. I have other reasons."

"But you'll have to give them nonverbally."

"If I can." He was closer to her than he'd been when they started walking. He wanted to brush her hair away from her throat, but he didn't.

"You're on the record as promising that." This time, Elena's smile was genuine. "Are you hungry? Is that why you look like you want to be nipping at my neck? I mean, have you had lunch?"

Oh, Elena. Yes, let's search for at least the appearance of something normal here. Thank you. "No. Maybe that's why I feel shaky."

They were close to the Petra canteen.

"I thought you were trembling for other reasons," Elena said while they examined today's food offerings.

"Perhaps I am. You want to guess what they are?"

"Not for the record, no," Elena said.

Helt admired a beef burgundy, but that was messy eating. "One of these days I'm going to cook," Helt said.

"One of these days I'll let you," Elena said, and that sounded like a promise. Helt liked the sound of it. They stashed hand meals, a picnic of sorts, in a canvas rucksack from the counter supply. Elena liked half-sour pickles, Helt noticed. So did he. She liked kalamata olives. He didn't. In the picking and choosing, some of the tension between them went away. They could have been carefree; they could have been exploring each other's tastes, in the simple way new friends do. But they weren't that. Still, he wanted to believe they could happen, even now. Helt added Mena's box to the rucksack.

On the train, the familiar sensation of free time, suspended time, came back for an instant, a space in his head created by familiar upholstery, the accustomed feel of the seat back, by neutral views of cut stone and distance rushing past. It was always quiet except for the rush of the wheels, a space where he moved effortlessly toward work, or went toward home and rest. It was twenty minutes of free time, time for daydreams.

Not today. A warm, beautiful, perhaps dangerous woman sat beside him, breathing mysteries. Helt sighed and pulled his interface out of his pocket. "We have to look at this," he said.

"At what?" Elena asked.

"Camera captures of times and places where Ryan was in the same space with Susanna." He scrolled through a few of them. "It happened too often to be random. Did she know it? Do you know if she knew him at all?"

"She didn't." Elena's words were flat, a statement of fact. "She would have said something while we were waiting for Zhōu's baby. The news about the death was out then. But we didn't talk about him at all."

"Okay. Camera captures of times and places where Ryan was in the same space with you, before or after you were there. I've asked for the data but I haven't reviewed it. This will be new for both of us."

Elena leaned forward for a better view of the little screen in his hand. He moved it to the support of the armrest between them. She pulled his wrist to change the angle of the screen and let her fingertips stay on the back of his wrist.

The set covered Elena's appearances on public cameras, plus captures of Cash Ryan taken by the same camera, plus or minus ten minutes. Ryan was there, in the corridors of Level One on Stonehenge, at the Petra station morning and evening, on the wide stone circles at the base of Petra tower, Athens tower. Helt looked at captures of Elena when she was unaware of being observed, Elena yawning, tired after a day's work, Elena going somewhere for an evening, her careful, sure-footed walk. He watched as Cash Ryan bought food at the Petra canteen after Elena left, as he drank coffee in the Athens plaza at tables Elena had vacated minutes before his arrival. The man's casual stride, his glances at this or that, seemed studied. There was no way, now, that Helt could evaluate Ryan's actions with an impartial eye. Ryan was good-looking, okay. He moved like a cat, long strides and then sudden, momentary pauses.

Elena's hand fell away from Helt's wrist.

In the next capture, Cash Ryan followed Elena on her way home to her quarters in Petra, but he slowed and stopped, well away from her door, to stare at the river as if something in it had caught his eye. He turned back as if he'd seen what he had come to see.

Helt watched the dates scroll by. The captures were thick three years ago. He paused the display.

"The number for the convergence of two people who don't live in the same town is around eight per year," Helt said. The train slowed for Stonehenge. "We'll finish this in your lab."

"I could use a break. This isn't easy to look at," Elena said.

Helt located Susanna Jambekar and Yves Copani on the PS functions and set up a constant feed of their locations to NSS, with a note to Severo.

Helt. Surveillance on Yves Copani and Susanna Jambekar. Fleshtime if necessary. Warrant follows asap.

He'd look for a boilerplate surveillance warrant later. Helt shoved his interface back into his pocket as the train stopped.

They went down to the corridors of Level One at Stonehenge, deserted and full of Sunday calm. Elena led him into her lab, a quiet place today except for the white noise of motors and the occasional gurgle of fluids. The lab lights were balanced for work, not daylight. Center, above them, seemed far away. If you added a heartbeat, this could be a well-lighted womb. They sat side by side at Elena's desk.

Helt savored the closeness of her, the little things he was learning about the texture and shine of her hair, the shape of her long, tapering fingers, the ovals of her matter-of-fact short nails, the pace of her breathing beneath that soft flannel shirt.

"That first one," Elena said. "The very first one. I saw him and turned away before he saw me. That's what I hoped, anyway."

Larger, on Elena's screen, Helt replayed it.

"See? It's so clear now. I was about to get on the train for home and I turned and went back to the elevator. I went up to Mena's office on some excuse or other. I didn't tell her why," Elena said. With Cash Ryan's eyes on her back. "Twenty-four of these captures would be random. We haven't seen that many. You're telling me there are more."

"There are more."

"Let me see them," Elena said.

In the second year, the captures stopped abruptly in June. After that, the next one was in late September. Helt went back to June to check.

"What are you doing?" Elena asked.

"Watching time and date stamps," Helt said. "What happened there? That gap of time?"

"I went to Puget Sound. The family's there."

"To say good-bye," Helt said.

"To my mother, of course. To the elders. To Pilar, especially, a sort of grandmother."

Helt knew her name, and a little of her history. A brief phrase of her music had flashed by, this morning, startling him because he didn't know the versions he'd heard of that song were covers.

"She's gone now . . ."

"I'm sorry," Helt said.

Elena smiled. "She sent a keepsake. I'll tell you about it someday." Meaning, I'm not recording this for the world, not this little personal thing.

"Okay. Elena, you don't have to watch all these. We're on the downhill slope now."

"I want to see them."

At the end of it, she shuddered.

"It's not the numbers, is it?"

"No," Helt said. "You okay?"

"It's feeling like an object. It's like being observed by a squid or something. Not that I have anything against squid. I accept their worldview as being different from mine."

"A giant squid. One who wanted you for lunch."

"Yeah. By the numbers, this *could* have been chance," Elena said.

"It wasn't. You know it. I know it. It's not the frequency, it's the distribution. No way these are random. Look at this."

Dates only. The frequency of the encounters dropped after Elena's return. It was if Ryan checked in from time, but had been content with what he saw. In the past year there were four captures of Ryan-Elena. Only four.

"He stopped hunting me," Elena said.

"Heh. Let me look at something." Side by side, he put up columns of the dates of capture for Elena-Ryan, Susanna-Ryan. Ryan had found Susanna shortly after Elena went Earthside, and his attention stayed on Susanna from then on.

"He found a substitute," Elena said. Her voice was flat.

"We could look at more of the Susanna-Ryan captures. They're much like yours, only there if you look for them."

"No. Poor Susanna. I once heard a woman say—she was a counselor, worked in the pit in Chicago, in shelters, with battered women and she'd lost one, a woman murdered by a man she'd run from. The victim—I really hate that word—did all the right things, changed her name, left the state, warned everyone she knew not to have contact with him. He found her and strangled her with an extension cord.

"The counselor was giving a lecture to a bunch of MDs and she said that one strategy for a battered woman to stay alive was to find a new victim for the abuser. She ground out the words as if they were forced. You could see her struggling with her conscience when she said it. Horrid, isn't it?"

"Yes," Helt said. "Elena, you didn't do that."

"Damn! He was sicker than I thought! If I'd known. If I'd looked . . ."

"You thought he was leaving for good. He did nothing, nothing that could have clued you, or anyone, about his problems while he was here."

"Or if he did, no one's said so."

"If anyone knew how he spent his time and can tell us, I'll be listening," Helt said. "I'll be listening very carefully."

Elena got up. "I want this taste out of my mouth." She grabbed bottles of water from a fridge and brought them back to the desk. She tipped her head back and drank. Helt admired the curve of her throat. He watched her eyes close. Her lashes were so black, so thick. He looked away, back to the screen.

In the three weeks before his death, there were no paired captures of either woman. Damn. Ryan knew something was up or he was busy planning whatever he planned, too busy to keep track of Susanna or check on Elena.

"Clean water," Elena said. She opened his bottle for him and pushed it into his hand. He was here, in part, to look at her resilience to trauma, to help her grieve, if he could do that, and she was taking care of him.

"The universal solvent," Elena said. "It helps." She blinked and looked at the screen, but Helt had vanished the dates, with that intriguing gap at the end.

Helt drank. The water was icy cold, a shock to his throat. "If Ryan was only an abuser, then we're safer. *Kybele*'s safer, I mean. But then there's the deliberate manipulation he did on his credentials. On what his work history was."

"He changed stuff?" Elena asked.

"Yes."

"And he got away with it."

"That he got away with manipulating records is one of the scary parts about this. Jim, Jim Tulloch, is willing to call him a long-term plotter, a planner. Jim's word is "psychopath," and that bugs me. Someone hated him, or feared him, enough to kill him, and I don't know why, much less who. Someone thought he was dangerous enough to kill, and they are still walking around."

"Ugh. You make me feel very safe."

"Sorry. If Ryan was murdered by self-appointed vigilantes—"

"Like Susanna?"

"—like Susanna, whose reasons would be hard to argue with by some standards, we're still in trouble until we find his killer. Killers."

"Killers who could have just waited for him to be gone forever. That's crazy. If only they waited. He was leaving!" Elena said. She looked down and squeezed her water bottle a little, watching the liquid inside rise and fall. "That's the plan I had for him. To stay away from him until he left."

"I believe you just wanted to write him off. We don't know about the sanity of his killer." Helt was getting a firm bias toward the belief that Elena hadn't killed Cash Ryan. Her reactions just didn't have the ring, the feel, of someone trying to hide something. Proving she hadn't done it was the challenge. If he couldn't, if she'd killed him, his belief in the validity of his own perceptions, his belief in his ability to see people and patterns, would be thoroughly shaken. It would be a difficult lesson, and he didn't want to have to learn it. And that meant he had to watch out, be careful, try to make sure he wasn't overlooking things in an effort to push his internal narrative into an unfounded edifice that left Elena innocent if she wasn't. "You, however, seem to be sane. To you, he was just an unfortunate incident of your wanton youth, and he wasn't bothering you."

"I've never been much of a wanton, really. I've been a deliberate loner," Elena said. "I wanted to scatter my wild oats up here. I wanted a lifetime to live in my work, and to find richness in love outside it. For the pleasure of whatever love does, of course, but it fills the well of energy for work, too. So I've heard." She spoke as if she had known him for years. The glimpse she offered into the cost-benefit analysis of her worldview startled him. It was an intimacy she had no reason to offer so soon, not to someone who might hold her future in his hands. She seemed to like Helt and trust him, and he hoped it was not just the best acting he'd ever seen. It felt real.

She shook her head, chasing away cobwebs. "Dreamer," Elena said. "I dream, always. The dream I'm living right now is a nightmare."

Mareritt, mare-ride, nightmare was an old word and hadn't changed much. "I'm sorry," Helt said. "You said you didn't sleep those first two nights. Are you sleeping at all, now?" Are you damaged? Will your work suffer because we've doubted you? Will you heal?

"I don't have nightmares while I sleep, not that often," Elena said. "And then, like most humans, I dream of things that happened long ago, scrambled and placed out of context and into strange places. Right now, these past couple of nights, I've been sleeping at night. Nights are okay."

Helt wondered if they really were. His doubt must have showed on his face.

Elena looked into and beyond a monitor screen, now blank. "It's the waking hours that are hard. I'm catching myself obsessing about what's happened and when I do that I'm about five years old. Like, 'I didn't *do* it! It's not my *fault*! It's *his*! He started it!' " She used the voice of an outraged five-year-old, and then she looked embarrassed and she smiled a rueful little smile.

"In my family, the speech that followed was always, 'I don't care who started it. Just stop it,' " Helt said.

"Mine too." Elena's smile changed to one of memory and nostalgia.

"But I am *not* asking that of you. It is not your job to stop anything at all."

She nodded. "Except the obsessing. The doubt that shows up, sometimes, I could be guiltless in this. I found him attractive once. That must mean I thought what he was, who he was, was good, beautiful, worth having sex with, even. What does that tell me about *me*?"

He couldn't let her stay in this space, but to make this go away, she needed to talk. "Perhaps that you, like many people, find physical beauty . . . well, beautiful?" Helt asked. He was afraid she would stop talking, but she seemed to hear that fear in his voice, or maybe it was the ache to comfort that she sensed.

"I even wondered, once, if I had some sort of fugue, some variety of psychotic episode, and killed him. Even that." Her voice was flat, exhausted, bitter. She shook her head as if to clear it. "But I knew, even when I was that terrified, where I was that night and what I was doing, and I knew that particular fear was irrational." She spun her chair and looked at him. "That's what you walked in on, when you came here before. After the funeral. I'm sorry. I wasn't at my best."

"I'm sorry I wasn't with you then."

"You had a job to do," Elena said.

"Yes," Helt said. "Guilt, shame, don't accept them from yourself or from anyone else. It is not your job to make this go away. It's mine."

"Can you do that?" Elena asked.

Helt's list of undone tasks nagged at him. Get the Seed Bankers out of this picture. Talk to David II about what Doughan thought was more important, yesterday afternoon, than interviewing a Seed Banker. There was Zaida the coworker, who might know something about Cash Ryan, and even if Severo had cleared her Helt wanted to talk to her. He hadn't looked over Severo's first interview of Zaida, or the interviews of the others in Ryan's work crew, either.

"I don't know," Helt said. "I'll try. Let me see the work you've done on your missing hour."

Elena pulled a list to the screen and even as the data came up she was all business, clinically detached, and apparently relieved to get on with it. "Nineteen hundred to 2000, that was the SM, right?"

Helt nodded.

"I looked through the other tower cameras for that hour as well," Elena said. "They're not there. The hour isn't there. They were turned off, too? No one told me that."

"It's not public knowledge yet. The space where the tower elevator videos should be has had a lot of hits," Helt said.

"Are you monitoring who's looking for themselves?"

"There's a count. Yeah, the names are filed." Nadia had reviewed them. The elevators from Level One to Center didn't get much traffic at night, usually. Nadia had stories from people who said they'd been there. All of them checked out as business as usual.

"You said you were here in the lab and then you went to Athens to get samples from the tower. There weren't any entries on anything in here during the missing hour." Helt waved his hand at the lab.

"I was on the train for most of it," she said. "The trip to Athens from here runs around forty minutes. No one got on or off at Petra. I was alone on the train."

"But there's no entries for"—he checked again—"forty minutes—before 1900, either."

"I got a sandwich out of the fridge at around 1800. It was grubby," Elena said.

Helt must have frowned.

Elena smiled at his frown. "I mean, the fridge was grubby. Not the sandwich. So I ate the sandwich and then I cleaned the fridge. Then I remembered it was time to get samples from Athens tower, and I grabbed a rack of plates and left."

"But the time, as far as the records go, is still blank. We need something else. You were working late . . ."

"Not really. I'm always here by seven in the mornings and I stay until lunch. After that, sometimes I come right back, but sometimes I don't get here until thirteen, fourteen hundred. I sleep, or walk, or . . . after lunch or after a nap is when I clean up, shower. It gives me a second day, is my theory."

"On Wednesday?" Helt asked.

"Susanna came by after lunch. She'd checked on Zhōu, and she was a little exasperated. Zhōu wanted to deliver at home; almost everyone does. But a primip—the first birth is the hardest, a test run, if you like. We have the veterinary surgical suite up here, but the only full operating theater for humans is in the Athens clinic for now, and the risk of losing a mother or a child trumps getting to deliver at home."

"I thought hospital deliveries were ancient history," Helt said. "A relic of the bad old days when clinicians were cold and uncaring."

"Maybe we still are. C-sections are rare now, but the fact remains that if you need to do one because the kid's brain is dying from anoxia or the mother is bleeding to death, you need to do it fast."

"And we can't afford too many damaged children," Helt said. Or life imprisonments, for that matter. He thought about the plans for prisoners on *Kybele,* confined to their homes under electronic surveillance, permitted visitors, fleshtime, only at specified times and with supervision, year after year after year.

"No. We can't," Elena said. "Anyway, Susanna took Zhōu over to the birthing suite at the clinic. They counted chairs, and brought in extras, and tables so visitors could bring in food and play those gambling games her friends like so much. Twenty-five people stayed at the clinic for those twenty-three hours of labor, Helt. It was cozy."

"I take it that's an understatement."

"No, not really. It was colorful, people in dress-up clothes, and candies and treats. Some women were sewing little red clothes, silk clothes for the baby, by hand. Some people were painting banners. It was tribal. It was good. I stopped in now and then."

"Mena stopped by," Helt said.

"Of course she did."

Both of them in the background, but close to the clinic. Just in case. And Elena hadn't slept last night, either, although she said she was getting enough sleep. She seemed to be recovered now, but she was running on reserves, had to be. Helt wanted to see her rested, truly relaxed, not working on habit and courage, not spending bitter coin on maintaining an appearance of normalcy when she could not possibly be feeling normal.

"But Wednesday afternoon, Susanna got her talking out. She left around 1600, I think. That's why I was doing rounds on my blastocysts in here a little later than usual." Elena glanced at the closed doors to the embryo lab with what looked like longing and regret. This could be lost to her; someone else could be working here all too soon, unless.

"I worked for a while in the embryo lab. I'm trying to build a baby for a couple in Stonehenge. They're both too damned bright, of course, and they said random material from the vaults is okay for the third parent addition. This new little colonist will be all human this time, no totem animal components, which should make it easier. But both birth parents' genomes display strong tropes for osteopenia and that's just not going to be a good thing here. We keep bone mass up but it's borderline, even with the daily cocktails we pass out. I want to mute that, and it's tricky without getting into other traits that I'd like to keep."

Her voice was different when she talked about her work. Her words came more easily, free of the choked tensions she'd been trying so hard to hide.

"I can put a cell or two into a neuron-derived matrix now. I do that rather than let the test blastocysts go on and develop until there's enough cell mass for me to work with." Go on developing as an embryo with all its potentials, she meant.

Elena looked at him, and Helt watched the hurt come back, the realization that she was still under suspicion as the possible killer of an adult human. She was aware of taboos and how tenacious they are. She must know that a considerable portion of Earth's population thought that she and her colleagues committed multiple premeditated murders, a lot of them. Jim had said it yesterday. "Elena culls defective embryos. In some ethical systems, that's a form of murder, and she does it every day."

"That's what I was doing Wednesday evening," Elena said. "And then I thought I might go over to Athens and look around Center. The place where I'd seen you watching me. I thought you might be up there again."

"I wasn't there," Helt said.

"Neither were the deer. They'd moved. So I didn't go up."

"I was going to take a stroll up there, but then Yves—Susanna's boyfriend—came to ask if I could turn him into a colonist with a wave of my magic wand," Helt said.

"Have you?" Elena asked.

"I'm going to try." He could tell her that Yves had done the sculpture on the Petra cliffs. He decided not to, not yet, not here. "He's a talented man and I hope we can keep him. And get you free of this mess." If we don't, Helt didn't say, you'll be leaving, too.

She winced.

"Elena, the cultures from that night. You said you have time and date stamps on the ones you brought here."

She screwed the cap down on her water bottle and gave it an extra, impatient twist. Helt wondered if it could be opened again without a wrench. "I'll show you. Maybe you can see something I don't see." She got up and opened the door into Bacteriology. "They're in here."

The microbiology lab was a vast space. Its walls were covered with supplies and incubator cabinets above counters with sinks and hoods. There were enough workstations for twice the five people who were assigned to it now. Helt recognized light microscopes at desks, but some of the other gadgets and machines, large and small, were unknown to him.

Elena went to a keypad and queried for Wednesday night tower samples. Their locations glowed red on a 3-D view of the lab cabinets. It was an answer to the eternal question, "Now where did I put that?" Not so easy to do with the files SysSu dealt with.

"If I'd thrown some of the plates away on the way back here, there would be no way to trace them, but once they're here, they're on record. Some are in different locations now. We pick them up on transfer media, and then move them to different substrates. How's your bacteriology, Helt?"

"I think I remember that anerobes won't grow very well in room air, and that funguses, I mean fungi, grow slow."

"Some do, some don't. We monitor the tower platforms to see what the wind is moving up there, different soil organisms, things that grow on humans and cows and chickens and wheat. You name it. This batch isn't showing anything out of order in the bacterial spectrum. It will be weeks before we can get much out of the fungal cultures."

"NSS tells me you've looked for DNA in this batch," Helt said.

"Severo called in the roster of people who had some background in forensics that night. They took samples all over the tower, but that was after I came down. We've scanned for concentrations of it, from the handrails and the elevator doors, everywhere."

"You didn't find any," Helt said.

"We found traces here and there, but there were no collections of fluids left in one place, spit or mucus or whatever, no scraps of skin or teeth or hair that could be traced back to an individual. There're fingerprints. Mine, for instance."

"Most of the prints were smeared, the techs said. The rails get washed down now and then and they were cleaned two weeks ago. Yours and Evans from NSS were clear enough to identify. Evans made security rounds up there on Monday; her visit is verified. There was another set. One of Mena's people came up to get infrared photos of plowed fields. He was up there Tuesday."

"When we were in the meadow?" Elena asked.

"No, earlier."

If there was anything else to look for in here, Helt didn't know what it might be. He was on his feet, and he turned in a circle, looking for inspiration, but he didn't find it.

"We're finished in here?" Elena asked.

"Sure," Helt said. "Let's go up to Athens tower. Show me what you did there when you went up to get the samples."

"I don't want to go back there." She motioned Helt back into the office and closed the lab door behind her.

"We might see something, think of something."

Her deep breath wasn't quite a sigh. "Let me check the embryo lab before we go. Everything was fine when I left this morning, but. But I may not get back here until tomorrow. Do you want to come in?"

"Sure. What do I need to do? Wash my hands or something?"

She took both his hands in hers and looked down at his palms, the backs of his hands, his fingernails. He caught a glimpse of her impish grin again. "I don't think you'll contaminate anything." She dropped his hands and opened the outer door of the embryo lab. Helt followed her into the small passage that served as a light-lock.

"Close the doors, please." He did, and closed away the light. Elena opened the inner door. The lab wasn't pitch-black; it was more a gloomy cavern, with little pips of indicator lights starring the darkness. She handed him a pair of night-vision goggles. "I want to do a quick check on some ova I fertilized this morning."

Her matter-of-fact assumption of the role of a man or a rooster startled Helt. A bit of male insecurity might just have surfaced there, but then he'd never spent much time in a genetics lab so he wasn't desensitized to the concept. He wondered what nouns and verbs about the process would go colloquial, like, "I knocked up twenty geese this morning. It took me five minutes." He'd have to ask Venkie about that.

Highlighted with weird infrared colors, Elena opened the door of what looked like a cabinet fridge and took a covered Petri dish to a microscope nearby. "I should have around eight cells in the good ones. I'll send a view to your interface."

Helt looked at a blob on his screen, yellowish, trembling. Elena fiddled with the focus depth, and he saw six translucent grapes. No, eight.

"That's a take," Elena said. She sounded relieved as she jerked the plate away from the microscope stage and put it back in the black box, not a fridge but an incubator. "If there's one healthy one, there are likely to be more."

"What was I looking at?" Helt asked.

"An oyster." In this light, Elena's nose was white, her cheeks and throat were red, and her eyes circles of yellow and blue. She looked up at Helt's puzzled face. "No, really. We have Bluepoints and Kumamotos, but Mena wants to start some beds of Belons. European Flats. The tidal pools are working so well, so well. Maybe someday we'll have salmon."

Helt doubted salmon could possibly taste right this far from the fjells and fjords. But by the time Biosystems grew them, they would probably taste wonderful because he would have forgotten the originals.

"I thought boy sea critters just spread their wealth in the water," he said. "Didn't require human intervention."

"They do, but the waste is amazing, and we don't have that many samples in the vaults. If these blastocysts develop normally, I can put them in a liquid medium and then they can grow into little critters and swim off into their cozy tidal vats. Sans oil waste, sans fecal bacteria. They're going to taste so good, Helt."

"I was getting hungry until you got to the fecal bacteria part."

Her face developed a faraway look. "I shouldn't stall anymore. We have to go to the tower. I have to do this."

"Yes," Helt said.

On the train to Athens, he could tick off more of his to-do list.

Elena closed the two doors behind them and got the rucksack out of the fridge. She added bottles of water to the stash and started to lift the bag.

"Allow me," Helt said. He took the rucksack.

Helt went back to his interface once they were on the train. Elena didn't object. She pulled out her own and they were separate for a while, following the passenger etiquette that takes over in close, anonymous spaces. He got lost in Oriol Bruguera's CV. The guy had worked at Svalbard for a while, on the pebble bed reactor that kept the place cold in summers.

Even so, he was aware that she was beside him, within reach, and he liked the feeling.

He checked the Athens agora cameras and looked down at Mena, Archer, and Doughan, sitting at a table with cameras, cranes, and assorted crew around them. The overhead view reminded him of ants nibbling at a cookie. He listened to Mena's feed and caught a few phrases about how arbitrary it was that the canteen chefs were assigned to Biosystems rather than Systems Support. It was standard documentary chatter.

Helt glanced at the screen in Elena's lap but he couldn't see the text. After a few minutes she leaned back and closed her eyes.

"Did you see me on Wednesday night?" Elena asked. "At the station?"

"The cameras were dead when you got on the Stonehenge elevator. Stonehenge, Petra, Athens, all the cameras were offline. The next thing we see is the view of you coming down"—he checked—"at 2026."

"Right," Elena said. "I must have stopped somewhere to get Cash Ryan's body. I must have stashed it somewhere close to the tower." She didn't try to hide the sarcasm in her voice. "I hauled it up to the platform and shoved it off. Then I collected my samples and hung out to come back down when the cameras went back on."

"Because you had checked for the SM and wanted to make sure you'd be seen afterward," Helt said.

"Oh, Helt, no one looks at those schedules but you."

"Not even me, sometimes." He hadn't looked for the timing of Wednesday night's SM. According to the log, neither had Elena.

"Really?"

"Really," Helt said. "I didn't look at the notice. It's routine. It's boring. Sorting out who *did* pay attention to when the SM was going to happen doesn't tell me much. The list includes everyone who has some responsibility for keeping systems running."

"That's a lot of people. That's all the execs and a lot of other key players. And me," Elena said.

The train slowed and stopped at Athens Level One.

They walked to the elevator. It didn't stop at Center as they rode it up. When the door opened to the observation platform they stepped out, side by side, into cool air, a breeze. The curve of the world below, the secure lacework of the pillars that held up the sun held him spellbound, as mountain skylines, as wide swathes of desert, as the sight of islands rising from the sea had always held him spellbound. A few clouds moved anti-spinward, gold-topped in the afternoon light. Their shadows were black on the ground.

Elena glide-walked without hesitation to the rail, to the exact place on the circumference where Severo said Cash had gone over. She pushed both palms against the glass bricks. Helt felt his breath catch in his throat. She had stood there, almost exactly there, on Wednesday night. That's where her fingers had left a complete set of prints. She had watched Ryan's body catch the wind and spiral away, limp and helpless. It must have been a pleasant surprise that he fell so far away from the base.

Helt put the rucksack down, close to the elevator doors.

Today's breeze loosened a strand of her hair and she brushed it aside. "It was breezy, but I didn't think I would go sailing off . . ."

The wind had been dangerously high Wednesday night, high enough to carry Cash Ryan's falling body half a k from the tower. She had fought against it, Elena and her partner, if there was one, must have fought against it, fought to keep their balance up here.

She had killed him.

"I looked for where the deer had been when you and I were talking. Over there." Elena pointed out and down. "The deer weren't where they had been. They weren't by the creek. They went over there after we left."

She pointed out and down to the dark green mass of ponderosa where Cash Ryan's body had landed. "They moved into those trees."

She knew where he'd fallen.

She knew because. Because she had been standing right here Wednesday night, breathing hard from the exertion of lifting Cash Ryan's body over the guard wall. He felt the fear Elena must have felt as she fought the wind and dragged Ryan's body to the very edge, the unprotected drop, and pushed it over.

She knew, had to have known, that Ryan was a sick bastard who could not be permitted to be here, and she had culled him and gone back to work. She would have waited for the dull soggy sound of the corpse hitting the ground and heard, instead, the sharp cracking of the branch that had impaled him. She'd climbed back over the guardrail and looked back from right here, safe behind the barrier of this wall.

An instant later he realized Elena had viewed every report, seen every capture of the man in the tree, probably more than once. It should be no surprise to him that she could point out the exact location where he came to ground.

Elena looked at the tower, the landscape, the trees below as if she wanted to memorize them. Tears were standing in the corners of her eyes. "It's so beautiful," she said.

She was saying good-bye.

"Severo didn't see any deer," Helt said, as gently as he could. "He would have told me. I didn't see any sign of them when I was running that night, when I was on my way to see where the body had come down. But I doubt I would have. There had been people in the area before I got there," Helt said.

He didn't *know* she'd killed him, he didn't know anything for certain except she had left the Athens elevator at 2026. "Did you see anything at all in the trees that night?" Helt asked.

"You mean damage? No. I didn't. Nothing shows from up here, does it?"

They turned and walked back, following the curve of the guard wall, and looked down again at the ponderosa.

"No," Helt said. "That's what Jerry and Nadia said Wednesday night after they came back up to Center. They went to the staked-off area and when they came back they told us nothing had changed. Everything was calm and peaceful again."

"No visible scars," Elena said. She gripped the top edge of the guard wall. The tendons on the back of her hand stood out in high relief. She turned her head away so that Helt would not see her face. He watched a muscle in her jaw tighten.

"There are scars if you know where to look," Helt said. "Broken branches. A white circle where they sawed off a limb to get the body down. Look at me, Elena."

She turned and faced him. Those golden eyes blazed in her face. "So you can see my scars? Scar tissue takes time to form. I'm not sure I'm at that stage yet."

"We didn't find an alibi for you here. Not yet. I hoped we would."

"So did I. We found nothing." Elena walked to the elevator and stabbed the Down button. "Let's go home."

Helt stood beside her. They stared at the closed door. "Anything I say is going to sound wrong," he said. He picked up the rucksack and wanted to choke it by the throat.

"Anything I say is going to sound angry," Elena said.

"With good reason. I don't know who murdered Cash Ryan. You're right to be angry with me. I'm angry at me. If I'd figured out who the killer is by now—"

"By now? You've had five whole days to sort this out," Elena said.

And he knew so damned little.

The elevator doors opened. They stepped in and turned so they faced the door. There were only four buttons to watch, Tower, Center, Level One, Level Two.

"That's not right." Elena looked down at the floor and shook her head. "You've had five nights and four days to sort through information that's been hard to find, at best, about a man who lied, we've now learned, about anything and everything if it suited his purposes. You're doing everything you can. No one can do more than that. I wish I could help you."

She wasn't crazy, and she knew Ryan was leaving. If she'd killed the man, he might never know her reasons. There must have been a compelling need to do it, if she had. He believed that.

"You came down this elevator after Ryan died. That's a problem." He watched her jaw tighten again. "I won't rest until I know that you were only doing your job up here."

She looked up at him.

"You knew Cash Ryan. That's a problem, too," Helt said. "That's one I won't ever be able to solve. But I won't rest, I won't stop, until I know what happened up there."

"And if that's not possible? Elena asked.

He was up against it. It was too soon to say this. It was a decision he must have begun to make when he wondered what Yves Copani was going to do when he learned that his Susanna would be exiled. It was a decision Helt had made over years, made in the process of sorting his still unanswered questions about sanity, loss, love, and the limitations of reason. It was a decision finalized in his sleep. It was a decision made today, here, while he watched a woman stay on her feet and maintain her dignity, her courage, even her sense of compassion, while her eyes caressed everything around her and said good-bye to it.

However it had happened, he knew what he would do. He knew that what he was about to say was the absolute truth. "I'll go back to Earth with you," Helt said.

He could see a no begin to make its way toward her mouth. He dropped the rucksack. "Please. May I hold you?" Helt asked.

He didn't wait for an answer. In the circle of his arms, he kissed the *no* away. Elena was warm and her lips were soft and her hair was warm. He pushed a strand away from her throat and kissed the silken resilience of the skin it had hidden.

Elena slipped her arms beneath his jacket. He heard the clatter and bounce of her interface hitting the floor. She slid the palms of her hands up his back and pulled his shoulders forward to bring him closer.

He kissed her again.

The elevator door beeped to tell them it was tired of staying open.

Elena backed away, leaving a cold space on his chest where her warmth had been. She picked up the rucksack and her interface. It probably wasn't broken.

Helt followed her out of the elevator, into the afternoon chill of Athens plaza. No one was outside at the tables and he didn't see anyone strolling in the shadows beneath the Library colonnade. Venkie's cart had been rolled away somewhere. He wondered if the string quartet would move inside this evening for its Sunday concert, and now, he was saying good-bye, too.

He retrieved the rucksack and took Elena's newly freed hand in his. He pulled her to his side, too far away but at least a little closer. His office was just across the agora. He should go there. Jerry was probably still there, working.

"No," Elena said.

"No, what?" Helt asked.

She must have seen him glance toward the SysSu building. "No, not back to work. Not yet." She tugged him toward the Athens station. "I want to go home now. I want you to stay with me for a little while."

22

At the Roots

The windows on *Kybele*'s trains were large, designed to offer a good view. The route the train followed through raw stone wasn't scenic yet, but someday it would be, with pillars of stone left as supports and wide vistas of fields, crops, play lands, dwellings, landscapes not yet imagined, beyond them.

The large windows of the train that waited at Athens station made it easy to see Mena and Doughan, seated at one of the four-place booths. The seats facing them were empty.

Helt slowed his steps. "We could turn around," he said.

"There's no way they haven't seen us," Elena said.

"Can you handle a casual social conversation that's going to be loaded with subtext?" Helt asked.

"The question is, can you?" Elena asked.

"Sure," Helt said. He let go of her hand and shrugged the strap of the rucksack to a more comfortable place on his shoulder. "Maybe. But I don't like to ride backward. And besides that, I had a plan for the trip and now it's changed."

"Tell me?" Elena asked.

"The plan involved an empty car where no one would watch me kiss your earlobes and then your throat, and your shoulders, and then . . ."

"Stop it!" Elena said, but she smiled. "I can do this. Really, I can. You leave my subtext alone for a while, okay?" Bright-eyed and looking for all the world as if she'd been having nothing more than a pleasant chat with a friend, she stepped into the train.

A few other passengers were aboard. None of them looked up. Mena and Doughan, however, didn't pretend not to see them. Their expressions were pleasant and quizzical, the neutral, practiced masks worn for social greetings, and both of them were watching Helt and Elena like hawks watch rabbits. Helt followed Elena to where the two execs sat.

"Please join us," Mena said.

"Helt, Dr. Maury," Doughan said. "Have a seat."

Doughan's skin looked preternaturally natural. His social mask was, in part, makeup, professional maquillage done subtly for "outdoor" light and done well. Mena's fatigue had been carefully disguised. Mena and Doughan were still camera-ready; polished, perfected versions of themselves, but Mena's eyes focused on one thing and then the other a little too quickly. She was on high alert about something.

The film crew was missing, and if they had known the setup they would be gnashing their teeth. *Kybele*'s execs, her Special Investigator, and a—and *the*—highest-ranking murder suspect, gather in face-time, to discuss—discuss what? Helt watched Mena brace herself to take the lead, set the tone, of the interchange.

"I'm so sorry," Mena said. "You haven't found what you need yet. It shows on your faces."

That shows, and signs of frustrated lust, Helt figured. It was kind of Mena not to point it out. Elena, seated directly across the table from Doughan, looked straight at Navigation's exec. In the working-spectrum light of the train, traces of darkness beneath her eyes showed clearly, signposts of fatigue, of sleepless, worried nights. She and Mena were both on edge, and Helt felt a moment's sympathy for himself and Doughan. No way to duck and cover.

"Yes," Elena said. "It seems I'm still the prime suspect. It's not comfortable for me. It hardly makes for easy conversation, doesn't it?"

If Doughan was surprised by Elena's candor, he didn't let it show. He looked at her with an expression that conveyed both sympathy and admiration.

"Dr. Maury." Doughan crossed his arms and met Elena's eyes. "I haven't had that many conversations with you, easy or otherwise. Mena keeps you locked up in those labs of yours. She admits it."

"Of course I do," Mena said. "If I didn't, I'd have no one to hear my side of the story, uncensored, when I get exasperated about one thing or the other. I need you, Elena, and I was hoping you and Helt could find some tiny thing, some detail of documentation."

Elena's eyes didn't leave Doughan's face. "We didn't. But thank you, Mena."

"Because I don't know you," Doughan continued, "this is going to sound strange. Irresponsible. Something the Navigation Executive should never say, but I'm going to say it. If I could, I would declare this death an accident and get on with business. The more we learn, the more it seems the world is better off without this man walking around in it."

Huh? In other words, Doughan was saying, If you killed him in self-defense or in defense of the ship, good on you. Which meant that either Doughan's ethics were way less informed than a leader's should be, in a way that worried the hell out of Helt, or that Doughan might be hiding information from Helt, from NSS. Information about what made Cash Ryan worth killing. And that couldn't stand.

Helt had to call him out, to know what Doughan feared, but he didn't know how he was going to do it. All he knew was that it had to be soon.

Elena hesitated a little before she responded. "But that really wouldn't solve anything, would it?" she asked. "Someone killed him. I'd like to know who did. And establishing that I'm not a murderess has become strangely important to me."

Elena spoke without a trace of irony, without a single tell to mark the anger Helt knew must be there. Helt decided he would never, ever play poker with her.

"I'm so sorry," Mena said. "I'm horrified that you're having to go through this. But I can't see a way around it. The Rule of Law. I don't want it in my face, in your face; I don't want it to hurt you or anyone. It should be in the background, always, as dependable and sturdy as—as the stone walls that hold up my ceiling. It isn't. It's a tissue of assumptions, glued together with hope, at best. Since this death, this murder, I've been forced to remember what's happened, over and over and over again, if the Rule of Law is permitted to crumble. Remember the rubble that's often all that is left when it does."

Mena shook her head. "I'm so sorry. I'm an old Greek woman, still grieving over broken pillars and barren sands."

For a moment, she looked the part, her back curved and her neck bowed from years of gleaning what the harvesters might have missed.

But she straightened her shoulders and was Mena again, strong and alert and in her prime, and her smile was designed to show she knew the irony of what she was about to say. "It won't happen here."

And that's why I love you, Helt thought. You, Mena, and Archer, and maybe even Doughan. You're bright, and you're good at what you do, and you don't waste anyone's time with idle chitchat, especially your own.

"The Rule of Law. Due process," Helt said. "Those concepts tend to get shoved aside under the pressures of clear and present danger. Is that what we're facing, Doughan? Clear and present danger?"

"I don't know. Sometimes it's my job to play paranoid." If Doughan was lying, he was lying with determined bravado, and his control of voice was superb, the threat in it carefully modulated. "I'm doing that. When I'm not interrupted by documentaries made to reassure the good folk on *Kybele* and below, designed to tell the people who funded us that all is well."

Yes, there may be danger to the ship, and no, I'm not talking about this here and now, Doughan was saying.

On the instant, Mena supported his shift toward a lighter topic. "I thought the interview was bland enough," Mena said.

"Sure, all is well. That's what we told them," Doughan said. "Dr. Maury, I don't know if it helps, but the people who know you have been discreet. They must have been deflecting questions. It seems the news hounds aren't particularly interested in you."

Helt imagined the headlines. *Prime Suspect Autopsies Murdered Lover*, and worse.

"I haven't looked at news coverage or gossip sites," Elena said. "I've been afraid to. I'm surprised that I'm not being pilloried."

"We were braced for the usual scandal questions, conspiracy speculations, and so forth," Doughan said. "I gave a canned statement that we're looking into all possibilities and went down the list, blah, blah, and so forth. I put homicide in the middle of the list and kept going, accidents due to hypothermia, reckless behavior, and so forth. The interviewer went somewhere else."

"Your distaste for the subject was apparent," Mena said.

"You mean I scared her." Doughan didn't look abashed about it.

Mena looked at the ceiling.

"She was more after emotional stuff, feelings about leaving, regrets. She wanted to know what we'd miss most," Doughan said.

"What did you tell her?" Helt asked Mena.

"I lied," Mena said. "I told her I'd miss the balalaika. I don't even like the jangly things, and I could see Archer's eyebrows do that frowny thing he does."

"You're afraid he's going to make one and serenade you in the middle of the night," Doughan said. "He probably will."

"What will you miss?" Helt asked Doughan.

Elena sat so quietly and so close. We'll be off this train soon, Helt wanted to tell her. Hang in there.

"I followed my peer's example and lied, too. Don't bristle like that, Mena."

Mena hadn't.

"I told her I'd miss Longhorn cattle. I figured Mena wouldn't grow me one for a pet," Doughan said. "They're too ornery to let loose."

"Are they?" Mena asked with feigned innocence. "At any rate, we got through it. Archer said he missed having time for cello practice, not on Earth but right here, and it was time for him to go do that before tonight's concert. So he got up and left."

"So that's why there were just the two of you when I looked in on the filming," Helt said. Two of you, who deploy white lies like weapons, who excel in the art of courtesy in its original sense. Court manners. Polite lies in words and behaviors, designed to maximize the chance of staying alive around kings. And you're offering a united front to your audience of two right here. You've closed ranks, and it's hard to believe it's only because Elena is here. You've closed ranks against me as well.

"You're always on the job, aren't you?" Doughan asked.

"I can't seem to stay away from it," Helt said. "I wanted to get Elena off the suspect list this afternoon and I didn't manage it. I want to. I am not objective about this."

Doughan leaned back in his seat and got his interface out of his pocket. "Let me quote what Dr. Maury said." He paused, searching his interface, and then found what he wanted. " 'We live in small towns now. We'll be living next door to our morticians, our bakers, our butchers. It's not a new pattern and perhaps it will be easier for us than cities were.' " Helt's memory brought him Elena's voice, the lilt and the hesitations, as Doughan read her words. She'd said them when he walked beside her in the quiet, dark agora. That first interview seemed so long ago now. Doughan had reviewed it. He'd found time to do that.

"Even if it's not easy," Doughan said, "you'll do what you have to do. There's no one on this ship who could do this better."

Doughan was telling him he was reviewing the NSS records as they came in. That he was looking for any slip Helt Borresen made. That Doughan was on this 24/7, too. "Back off, Helt. I'm doing my damned job, too," was one of the meanings. But Helt wasn't going to back off.

"Since I haven't found an alibi for Elena yet, I'm back to reconstructing where everybody was on Wednesday evening," Helt said.

"Screening everyone on the ship is a method that requires thirty thousand separate entries," Doughan said. "It's labor intensive, Severo tells me."

"I know," Helt said. "However, it's not a linear progression; one sure location can delete multiple names associated with that location or activity. It runs parallel to gathering data sets on some selected people. Your Seed Bankers, for instance." Helt left the implication that he'd found some other selected people to be of interest hanging in the air.

Doughan reached up and rubbed his cheek and then stared at his palm. "Makeup. I need to wash this off. David II might find it alarming."

"I doubt he'll think you're flirting with him," Mena said. "I think it's more likely that he'll worry you're getting absentminded."

"That's all we need," Doughan said.

The train began to slow.

Helt got to his feet before it stopped at Petra station.

"Don't forget our lunch," Elena said. She handed him the rucksack.

"Bye, guys," Mena said. She wasn't out of her seat yet. She was giving them time to escape. Helt was grateful for that. Or she and Doughan were going on to Stonehenge.

Helt followed Elena out of the train, past the canteen, out onto the path beside the river. She was so strong, so resilient. Jim had said it; one injury one time is something that a lot of people can get past with few scars. "Did you say something about food?" Helt asked. He glanced back. Mena and Doughan weren't behind them. He wondered what David II was doing in Stonehenge, and what Doughan's plans were for the remaining daylight hours. If David II was in Stonehenge. Helt checked. He wasn't. He was down in Athens Level Two near the shuttle port.

And then, on a hunch, he reached for his interface and went hunting for where David II had been last night. And found him, near the train station at Petra, at 0300 this morning. The Petra station videos showed two men walking into the dark, hunched into their jackets, their collars up, their faces turned toward each other in what seemed to be an interesting discussion.

". . . not going. It's just a bruise."

It was Doughan's voice.

"You must be hungry," Elena said.

"I am. Let's pick up a bedroll from my place."

"That's forward of you. Surely we could eat first," she said. "At a table, perhaps. I have one of those."

"Table? That's a concept," Helt said. "But I'd like to go back to the stone tree. I'd like to see it in better light."

"It's a little cold for that," Elena said.

"Therefore, the bedroll." Because he was pretty sure Elena's house was bugged.

"My place is on the way," Elena said. "We could pick one up there."

The light was dimming. The anti-spinward side of the sky would glow, soon, in the designated west, with the simulated colors of sunset. The unfinished part of the canyon, westward, was fitted with power for lighting; its faux moonlight had let Helt and Elena see the sculpture, the water, when they walked there together Friday night. There was no reason the sculpture itself couldn't be bugged, but it wasn't, in all probability. So few people knew about it yet.

They stopped at Elena's door.

"We're going blind," Helt said.

"I beg your pardon?" Elena asked.

"Selectively blind. We're almost at the point where images that aren't recorded don't exist."

Elena looked at her door and opened it. "You're saying anything we don't want to see can be hidden. Clutter, for instance. I wish it were true."

He followed her down an entry hall that opened on a great room of sorts, smaller than Helt expected. It didn't look cluttered. Its floors were bare black stone. Its walls were rough, pale, sand-colored stucco. A dome-shaped fireplace occupied one corner. A gray rug patterned in geometric red, white, and black lay in front of it, and pillows.

"I'll heat some cider," Elena said. She went into the kitchen. Helt watched her from the door. Elena retrieved a container from the fridge. "New harvest," she said. "It's really good." She set the jug in the nuke. "Oh, the bedroll."

Helt stood aside to let her pass. "I'm saying that if something isn't recorded, it effectively doesn't exist."

"Well, yes. That's why I'm in trouble, isn't it?" She didn't go toward a bedroom. The bedroll in question was in the hall closet. The microwave beeped. Elena tossed the bedroll, rolled tight in its dark blue cover, toward the front door and came back to the kitchen. She located insulated cups, big ones, in the second cabinet she opened.

The cider smelled good when she poured it. Helt was thirsty. He was hungry. He wanted to explore Elena's bedroom, with a tour guide. He wanted sex and there was no way to lie to himself about it.

"I'll carry the bedroll," Elena said. "These will fit in the rucksack." She tightened the lids on the cups and brought them to him.

The rucksack was still on Helt's shoulder. He took the cups from Elena and bent down to kiss her cheek. "Let's go," he said.

Outside, a few people walked the paths or raked leaves. The windows of the houses carved into the rock on either side of this narrow section of the canyon looked out at them with lazy, sleepy eyes. Helt's legs weren't sore, but he felt a faint trace of lactate burn in his calves and his thighs as they walked, an artifact of tension, not of exercise. A breeze came from anti-spinward and ruffled the surface of the river.

Elena had said nothing yet. Helt hadn't, either. When they were past the last house, he broke the silence. "Your house is bugged," Helt said. "Mine, too, I think. Wait a minute. I want to check."

He went into NSS feeds. Yes. Both houses were there, and the access showed up in the Murder Management files in SysSu. So far so good. He looked for feeds from Mena's house. There weren't any. Archer's place, no. Doughan's? No. Uh-oh. It was the sort of thing Severo might not think to do, might need to be ordered to do before he would do it. He should take care of that right now. But Mena's interface and Doughan's and Archer's were live. He knew where they were. It could wait a few hours.

"Yeah. We're both bugged. I asked Severo to do it. Because, when things that aren't recorded aren't real, then anything that's recorded is real whether it's real or not."

"Does it make a difference?" Elena asked. "There's nothing ominous in what I've said or done. Or anything you've said or done, either. We've recorded every interchange, every conversation we've had at work or at home, even every snore."

"Do you snore?" Helt asked.

"I don't know," Elena said. "Do you?"

"I don't know. I could listen to what I sound like in my sleep, but I might not like to find out."

They walked a little farther, side by side, not hurrying, exactly, but not with the slow, easy amble of people with no destination in mind, either. "I didn't say I'll disable the bugs," Helt said. "We need them, you and I." He could look later to see when they'd been placed. Severo might have sent a tech to put them in place that first night, even before he told Helt that Elena had been on the tower. Or Doughan might have.

Severo had said Doughan was home and would meet them at Ryan's apartment. But Doughan could have gone somewhere in that time, could have done all sorts of things. Helt and Severo hadn't seen Doughan that night until they met him on the street outside Ryan's quarters. "But I'm going to have to check on who ordered it done, and when. Bugs aren't legal without a warrant. I can find out when they were placed, and if the feeds are only going where they should go, when I get back to SysSu."

"Tonight. You're going back tonight." Elena had moved ahead of him and he couldn't see her face. Her voice was carefully neutral. They were nearing the wedge of stone that diverted the river's flow. The stepping stones looked a lot less difficult to walk this afternoon than they had in the dark on Friday night.

"I'll have to," Helt said.

Elena made no reply. Helt concentrated on not falling into the river. The water lapped at the stones, patiently working to dissolve them in a few thousand years or so. The water had no deadlines to meet, the lucky, mindless stuff. He followed Elena around the sharp-edged foot of the barrier rock, back onto solid ground. She reached for his hand and that simple token of trust startled him away from everywhere else but here.

Everything but this could wait for a few hours.

Hand in hand, they walked the rough-cut steps that led down to the canyon floor and entered the courtyard where the stone tree grew.

No footprints marred the patterns the wind had rewritten on the black sand. The contours of the strange beasts on and of the stone tree were a trap for the eye and the senses because some of the creatures seemed to move, to grow and change in the waning light. Helt forced his eyes away from them and looked west. The waterfall marked its single vertical stroke of white at the canyon's end. The sky above the black line of the cliffs was green, an echo of the evening color of the moist air in Center. The weathermen would shape that water into clouds before morning. It might rain up there tonight. The breeze brought clean, living air to chill his face.

He could capture this landscape, trap it in pixels, the cool tones of autumn light, the canyon, the sounds of the breeze and the river; replay them someday in an effort to tease back memories of his arousal and hunger, his body's anticipation of desires slaked.

He would not. He wouldn't trap the ghosts of this moment in images and recorded sound and look back, and wish he were here again. He would not.

Elena pulled her warmed hand away from his and tugged at the strap of the rucksack on his shoulder.

"Oh. I'm sorry. I was lost."

"Food," Elena said.

"Where?" Helt asked.

She scouted the roots of the tree and found a place where the wall of the canyon rose up sheer from the sand, where something like a dolphin's back angled forward from the cliff face and offered shelter from the wind.

Inside the alcove, Helt looked up at the massive canopy that roofed it. The branches of the carved tree diminished in mass and size as they rose, spaced and spiraled in a semblance of individual striving toward light and space to grow. There were creatures up there, half-seen, graceful, elusive.

Yves Copani was a fucking genius. It occurred to Helt that he wouldn't tell Elena he knew who the sculptor was, not today, not unless she asked. Yves had made this. There was too much baggage that went with knowing it; Yves, Susanna, the boundaries of what was lawful to create in public space and what wasn't. Helt realized he no longer thought of the tree as the creation of a single man. Its reality existed of itself now. It just was.

The spaces between the branches let in shafts of cathedral light from the evening sky. At Helt's feet, the black sand was dappled with geometric shards, green stained-glass light. Undersea light.

Helt knelt and helped Elena spread the bedroll. It was a double. Good. They sat with their backs braced against the dolphin's side and attacked the contents of the rucksack. Helt's ham on rye was good. He wolfed down half of it and then tried the hot cider. It was wonderful, a roomful of apples in a swallow. The second half of his sandwich wasn't going to be enough to fill him up. He slowed down a little.

Elena tucked up her legs to sit like a Buddha or a Navajo. Her knee touched his thigh and she left it there while she rummaged in the rucksack. He read the touch as seduction, and was a little alarmed. He read it as an invitation, and that was simply, completely wonderful.

"I've never been so hungry," Helt said.

"You can have half my sandwich," Elena said. She handed it over and brought a packet of olives out of the rucksack. "What were you thinking about when you were lost out there?" She waved a hand toward the river.

Helt swallowed the last bite of his sandwich and picked up the half Elena had given him. His plan to slow down hadn't worked. "I was thinking how strong you are." I was thinking about how I wish I had known you before this happened. "I was thinking about how lonesome it is when there's no one to listen when you want to think out loud," Helt said. He rummaged in the sack and found the half-sours. They were good with ham sandwiches. With the cider, not so much.

"You want to tell me secrets," Elena said. "Do you think we're safe here?"

"Safe? Possibly," Helt said. "But I want to think out loud and I think no one's listening." He checked his interface to see if he could call up the locator system here. He couldn't. There was too much rock between here and the transmitter receiver at Petra station.

"Heh. Yes, this is a dead zone. That's why I brought you here. We can talk."

"Our interfaces are listening," Elena said. "But that's no problem. You can tell me anything. I keep secrets. And after all, there's no danger that what I learn might incriminate you in something like, you know, murder or whatever. You were in a diner, with cameras. You're safe."

"Ouch," Helt said.

"Beyond ridiculous, isn't it?" Her eyes were shining, but if those were tears he saw, she blinked them away. "Ridiculous, but all too true," Elena said. "So tell me what you don't want to tell the people you work with. They don't listen?" She rolled an olive between her fingers and popped it into her mouth.

"Oh, I ramble," Helt said. "I bounce ideas off them all the time. They bounce them back. But what I say is always censored. Filtered. Has to be. Because it's work, and I want to keep on working with them, and some of the things I think about might come back to haunt me."

He stopped short. It was all too possible he wouldn't be working with the SysSu crew much longer. He'd be trying to hack out a place of refuge on Earth, one that was worth sharing with Elena. He censored that train of thought, the sun-bleached, exhausted colors that went with it, the desperation and the dust. "Is anyone honest? Really honest? We say we are. We pay lip service to honesty, but to stay sane when we work, when we love, we don't go around blurting out every truth about what we see and feel."

"Events like this murder, realities that frighten or hurt. Do you think they bring out more honesty, or more lies?" Elena asked.

"Both," Helt said. "You want me to tell you, honestly, what I'm thinking right now, but how do I do that? There's too much, too many tangents.

I'm here, with you, and in my mind I'm shadowing Doughan whether he wants me to or not, because I just found out that he and David II went out looking for something last night—and Doughan left his interface at home, so his location wouldn't show to me. Now I'm wondering if Mena is at home in bed when her interface says she is. And I still don't know for sure if Doughan is looking for sabotage. I think he is, but if there are reasons for him to do that, I don't know them. I should."

Elena licked her fingers, slowly. She closed the package of olives and put them away, very carefully, her eyes on her work and not on him. "I hope you find them," Elena said.

"You thought about your answer," Helt said. "You didn't say you knew I would. Would find the facts." That she accepted, would accept, whatever he found humbled him. "I don't know if I'll discover anything that gets you out of this mess, and it scares me. I'm scared. I'm scared of my own blind spots. I'm scared of failure. Does it show that much?"

"Yes," Elena said. "It does." She tugged a corner of the bedroll up to cover her lap and looked out at the sand, at the river.

Their cave had been in shadow when they entered it; it was darker now. Elena's eyes seemed immense, as gray and opaque as granite in this light. "Tell me what you're thinking," Helt said.

"I'm thinking you haven't told me enough," Elena said. "Tell me what it is you fear you won't discover."

"The identities of the murderer and the accomplice. Or accomplices, I should say. Ever." He was scared that she hated him and was hiding it from him, and he backed away from saying he was afraid he would find proof that she had killed a man. "What worries me is that I'm scared and I'm following trains of thought that may not be realistic. I want to know if you see the signs I saw that tell me Mena and Doughan are keeping secrets from me. Paranoia isn't one of my favorite mental states."

"If you want consensual validation, I may not be the right person to give it," Elena said. "I'm paranoid, too. But for what it's worth, I think there's something going on with Mena. I think she's walled herself off from me. She's not avoiding me; work goes on. But she's put up a barrier. I've never seen her so tense. I wouldn't know about Doughan. He's a stranger and he's not easy to read."

"He's not easy to read, ever. I'm getting the feeling he's convinced Ryan was a saboteur. How do I find out why Doughan believes that? Or knows that?

"I can't get my mind off what still needs to be done. I want to go find Doughan and David II and I want to stay here. For a long time. With you."

"With me," Elena said. "With a murder suspect. Here's a paranoid thought for you. The execs found me on that elevator and are using me as a scapegoat in the original sense of the word. If they don't find a murderer, they can send me away and everybody will feel safer."

Mena would not do that. Doughan and Archer wouldn't. It could not happen unless they had overwhelming reasons to protect a murderer.

If they were doing that, and the cover-up worked, the world could seem normal and feel safe for years, perhaps for their lifetimes. Maybe no one would ever know. But odds were, some file, some screen capture, some scrap of evidence would find them out. Perhaps years later. Perhaps after they were all dead. At that point, the deed would be dissected, rationalized, and probably forgiven for the greater good, as such deeds had forever been accepted in the past. The deception would be legitimized and become a tool to be used again, even here.

No. Not on my watch.

So that wild-assed theory had to be disproved. Helt had to know they weren't hiding stuff from him, even if it meant he had to practice some deception himself.

"I don't like that plan," Helt said. "It leaves a murderer loose. Not good. It wrecks your life. That's worse than not good. It's unthinkable. I'll leave with you. I said it and I meant it, but it's still unthinkable. I'm going to ask you something."

"What?" Elena said.

"To do something when we get back into range. I need to know who the execs are talking to, and where they are doing it. They said they would keep them on, and they've been doing that, but I think they're leaving them at home and meeting somewhere else to talk. So, once or twice, I'm going to ask you to verify if Mena is where her interface says she is."

"Is that all?" Elena asked.

"No," Helt said. "I want to talk with you a lot. I want to spend a lot of time with you. I want your help, your ideas. I want you to tell me when I'm ignoring things I shouldn't, or when I'm paying attention to things that don't help solve this murder, so we can both stay here."

"I see," Elena said. "Well, for starters, you'll be checking on Archer. Who's going to shadow Doughan for you?"

"Probably not Severo. He's so locked into chain of command that I just don't want to ask him."

"I don't know that many people in Navigation," Elena said.

"I'll find someone," Helt said.

Helt was in a power struggle with a person-in-charge on *Kybele.* He didn't like it. An alpha-male challenge was about the worst thing he could think of at this point, and Doughan seemed to be doing his best to set one up.

"Elena?" Helt asked. "Doughan's been asking me to call him out, even if he doesn't know it on a conscious level. Giving someone responsibility without authority is a sure way to drive that someone nuts. That's what Doughan's been doing, with this thing of not setting up clear guidelines for what Severo is supposed to do. Do you have any idea why? Why now? What purpose does it serve?"

"I don't know. I've never been around the man," Elena said. "Do you really think he's unaware of what he's doing?"

"No. So he has a reason for doing it. I just don't know what it is. I'm the IA. I'm supposed to be good at looking for the reasons for conflicts. I try to look for tilts and shifts in coalitions before they get dangerous. Sometimes I don't see them."

"So that's what those constructs are," Elena said. "The interacting spheres, the virtual world thing you live in so much of the time, where groups coalesce, and morph into different shapes, and divide, over and over."

"You've been scouting for traces of me that show in what I do," Helt said.

"Sure," Elena said. "And a bio search."

"So you know a lot of things about me." He hoped they weren't going to talk about the bachelor site Jerry knew about. Helt was not going there. Not.

"Schools you went to, countries you lived in. I've learned a lot of things about you. I know your birth name was Halvor, not Helt."

"The nickname stuck," Helt said.

"I know you got a C in botany. Why?"

Elena shifted close to his side and he lifted his arm so it fit behind her shoulders. Helt slid his arm beneath her jacket. His fingers explored the texture of the soft flannel that covered the warmth of her waist. His hand wanted to move to the mound of her breast, so near, and surely even more wonderful. Helt hugged her and decided to keep talking while he still had the ability to speak. The sensory input from his hand was occupying more than half of his mind and displacing everything else. Other methods of communication were going to take over soon, and leave him capable of grunts and moans, at best. "I thought plant sex was too weird. They do it in too many ways. I couldn't keep track of the names for all those parts."

"They're inventive, I'll grant you that," Elena said. "I thought of aquatic plants when I looked into your world, but those little globes in your construct are people. I pulled down some of the names. I looked for me. I'm not in there."

"No, you're not there. You have to cause trouble, or be a target for attention, positive or negative, for me to set vectors on your actions and put you in play in that game."

Helt leaned forward and explored the rucksack one-handed. He retrieved Mena's box and fished out a diamond of baklava.

"Your world thing looks like something alive, living and moving and growing," Elena said. "It isn't geographic. There are three . . . blobs, I guess you'd call them, where Petra and Stonehenge and Athens would be, but what you're doing isn't based on location, is it?"

"No." Muffled. Helt's mouth was full of honeyed nuts and buttered phyllo. He chewed and swallowed and tried again. "No. The connections don't develop from physical proximity. They grow from repulsions and attractions, from the acts of givers and takers and how people gather around one and avoid, or are pulled in by, the other."

"That looks good," Elena said. "What you're eating."

Helt leaned forward and retrieved the box. They munched through three or four pastries each. Helt drank the last of his cider.

"The shapes in my imperfect attempt to look at group interactions?" Helt said. "They cluster around successes and failures, more often than not. The model's predicted some areas of conflict. It didn't find the Seed Bankers. It didn't predict Cash Ryan's murder."

"And that scares you," Elena said.

"Yes. It does."

"I am reassured," Elena said. She lifted the beautiful oval of her face and looked up at him. She was so close, so apparently calm, so hard to read. "There's no way to say this that doesn't sound dramatic, but it's true. You hold my life in your hands. My future, at any rate. If you weren't frightened, I would be even more afraid than I am."

Helt wanted to curl up into a ball and die. He wanted to run away, run as far as he could, as fast as he could. He wanted to be strong for her, and he didn't feel strong. He felt stupid and he couldn't find any words to say that would make any sense at all. He couldn't tell her not to depend on him, and he didn't want to tell her not to trust him. He wouldn't lie to her, and he was about to lie *with* her under a burden of uncertainty that sat ill on his soul. She deserved more than that.

"I'll do what I can," he said.

"I'm sure you will, but not quite yet," Elena said. "You have powdered sugar on your chin."

Helt lifted his hand to check but Elena grabbed it. "Wait a minute," she said. She found a wet cloth in a bag in the rucksack and wiped her hands, and his hands. She folded the cloth to bring up a clean corner of it and wiped his chin.

Had he been four years old the last time someone had washed his face for him? Five? Whichever, it had been long before he was capable of growing the five o'clock stubble he felt on his jaw now. Helt nipped at one of Elena's fingers and then kissed it.

She pulled her hand away.

"We will make love." It was not a question, but Helt's unspoken concerns made it sound almost like one. "We don't have to." Not at all what he meant. "I mean, leaving the ship is my decision and you have no debts to pay because I made it." That he wanted to offer comfort, and perhaps, hopefully, a little time of unawareness of what she lived with every moment, what they both faced, there was no good way to say that, not one he could think of now or maybe ever. "I want—"

"So do I." She turned away from him, perhaps to hide a smile.

"Help me with this bedroll, would you?" Elena asked.

Somewhere in the process of opening the bedroll, of opening their clothes to the wind, of seeing Elena's perfect skin stained by the dull red light of sunset, somewhere, while he watched her kneel to stuff their discarded shirts and jeans into a corner of the bedroll so they would be warm if they ever decided to put them on again, Helt forgot to worry that first times can be clumsy. He forgot to worry about his endurance, his ability to wait.

He exulted in his nakedness, in the chill air that bathed every square centimeter of his skin. He dropped to his knees and pulled Elena close to make a single unbroken surface of warmth; thighs, bellies, chests pressed tight together, the length of him warmed by the skin of her belly but not warmed enough. Elena wrapped her arms around his back and clung to him as if she were drowning. His hands explored the smooth curves of her back while his mouth tasted hers. He kissed her throat, her shoulders. He cupped her breasts in his hands, traced the tight buttons of her nipples with his thumbs, and she leaned back, holding his waist to keep her balance, breaking the seal of warmth between them, to let him explore the little ridges of her brown nipples with his tongue.

He moved his hands to her hips. She shifted her pelvis, lifting it forward to blindly seek even more contact with his skin. He leaned back, away from her, and reached for a corner of the blanket. The cold slapped his skin where Elena had warmed it. They maneuvered themselves into the bedding and found each other's heat again.

After a timeless time, he was dazed and grateful, and amazed with himself and with her.

Not even the first time had felt like the first time.

When he looked up, the wash of moonlight on the sand beyond the cave, the irregular diamonds of light on the bedroll, on Elena's shoulder, were blue silver. The river's murmur was so loud here.

Helt was as comfortable as anyone alive ever needs to be, warm in the puffy bedroll, waking to the music of the river and the moonlight. He wondered if he should wake Elena. She slept so deeply, pillowed on his arm and perhaps even warmer than he was, with the dolphin's-back stone on one side of her and his bulk on the other. But she had been so exhausted. She needed a full night's sleep and then some. She'd sleep better in her own bed.

Helt shifted his arm. It was getting numb.

He yawned.

He reached for Elena beside him and she wasn't there. Helt lifted his head to look for her and icy air flowed into the gap at the edge of the bedroll. Elena was walking back toward the alcove from the river's edge. The moonlight had waned and the stars were bright in a black sky.

She had managed to get into her jacket and her jeans without waking him, but her feet were bare and she was hugging herself to keep warm. She climbed in beside him, shivering. Helt rolled on his side and fitted her against his belly, spoon fashion, clothes and all. The collar of her jacket made a nice pillow for his chin.

He noted, after a time, that his hand had slipped beneath the waistband of Elena's jeans and come to rest on the amazing softness of her stomach.

He thought about zippers.

He thought about the zipper on the bedroll, and the limitations of the space it enclosed.

It was time to do something about all that.

23
Code Talkers

The data construct centered on Cash Ryan's death hadn't changed much overnight, damn it. It was still a hollow sphere where various facts hung lonely out near the periphery. Elena's name glowed bright, closer to the center than any other because of that trip she'd made to Athens tower, and because of the affair she had had with Cash Ryan so long ago.

Elena was in her lab in Stonehenge by now.

Helt got out of his chair and started a pot of coffee. He felt good. A tiny flash of memory came floating by, the memory that Elena's sheets smelled vaguely, pleasantly, of sandalwood.

He went back to his displays. There would be other nights. There would be days when he wouldn't feel guilty about the time he'd spent with her when he should have been working on the Murder Mess.

The scent of freshly brewed coffee reached his nose. His first cup this morning had been a large mug that Elena had brought him.

She had padded into the bedroom carrying it in both hands. She wore a sarong thing around her hips that looked like white beaded buckskin. He sat up to watch her and couldn't decide if she looked like a figure on an Egyptian frieze or a dancer from one of the pueblos in the American Southwest, carrying her treasure of precious green sprouts, or in this case, coffee, with downcast eyes and tiny, toed-in steps. Elena sat on the edge of the bed and they sipped from the mug, one and then the other. "Yes, it's beaded buckskin," she told Helt when he reached out to touch it. "I brought it with me from the family place. It's repurposed, you might say."

"Pilar's?" he asked.

"No. My mom got on into ancestral crafts for a while and learned to work leather. The patterns are North American plains tribes, not Canadian northeast. But I like it. So you've looked up Pilar, have you?"

"I've listened to her music," Helt said.

"She was unique," Elena said.

Butter-soft leather studded with little nubs of cool, smooth glass beads, and warm skin beneath. Shortly after that, they shared a shower and then they went back to the bed.

Helt got his fresh coffee, took a deep breath, and shook his head to clear it.

He returned to a full-room surround of the news since yesterday morning. None of his sensors showed alarm. No one was chattering about Yves's sculpture, either. Some things stayed under the radar longer than might be expected.

His sensors said all was well, but his programs had missed a murder. They were designed to catch early frictions between departments, and they had, but from now on more was needed. Much more. He needed different parameters to mark stressors for the expert systems to highlight. The system knew to look at interface points between hardhats, nerds, and farmers; but he'd been looking at conflicts and not paying enough attention to the hybridization going on there. Bonds of shared purpose, of amicability, of mutual obligation were as important as conflict, and he wasn't observing the shapes, the possible outcomes. Damn. He would set some markers to observe the patterns in motion in his copious spare time, once this murder was solved.

He felt so alone. He wanted to be an eye in the center of the world, the focus point of a neural network, with tendrils of awareness that extended into every crevice of this spinning hollow rock, this world of his. He realized he thought of *Kybele* as a world now, world, not ship, and that startled him. This was home. He had wanted to come home for so long, and now that losing it was so very possible, he knew that his doubts, his reservations, his distance from the new world around him was gone forever, even if he went into exile.

His worldview program showed him flashes of sound and light in unexpected places, a visual of naked axons and dendrites writhing, blurred, seen through a translucent gel. An icon appeared that looked like a stylized pinecone on a staff, and where the heck did that come from? Mena? Dionysus, the god of insanity, he remembered, while the thyrsus darted from place to place, desperately striving to impose order on what it saw, heard, felt. And Helt, in the center, spun from view to view, gulping data from one place and the next because he felt, he knew something was happening behind his back, something that might be important, might take his world away from him, but the something was always gone before he turned to see it, hear it. Half blind. Half deaf.

Whoa. RESTORE. He'd cued the display with an unplanned jerk of hands and a vocalization. He must have.

His world returned to normal.

No, not normal. He had a murder to solve. NSS was spending a lot of time sorting out who *didn't* do it. Fine. That would leave only a few players standing at some point, but surely there was a better way. Hypothesize a motive for killing the man and test the hypothesis, sure. Come on, think.

"What did I just see?" Elena asked. She was in her lab in Stonehenge and he had called her with a twitch of them.

He started to wipe his face with his hand, but maybe Elena wouldn't see how sweaty he was. "Nervous fingers," Helt said.

"It looked like you were inside your own brain."

"I hope not. I miss you," Helt said.

"Soon." Elena smiled and vanished.

It was still early. SysSu was deserted unless someone was crashed in the bunk room. All the "Occupied" markers on the office feeds were dark. He didn't want to wake anyone up if they were home asleep, and even if he wanted to talk through his unease, safe candidates for that weren't available right now.

So, no hypothesis yet. With or without one, he had a to-do list.

The surveillance warrant authorization to spy on Yves had not gone to Severo yesterday. Damn. Helt pulled up the boilerplate, signed the warrant, and sent it over. NSS should have been keeping track of Yves and Susanna since early afternoon yesterday. The timeline showed that Severo hadn't tagged Yves for 24/7 monitoring until 1500 yesterday, two hours, more or less, after Helt had sent his request. So Severo had checked with Doughan before he gave the order. Okay. Doughan hadn't talked to Severo yet about Helt's priority in the investigation, maybe. It was just something Helt needed to work around.

Severo was at his desk in NSS headquarters now. Helt left him there, undisturbed.

The two remaining Seed Bankers in NSS had not been questioned this weekend. Doughan was going to set up meeting times, but he hadn't, yet. Records of Doughan's interface said he'd spent the night in his bachelor quarters in Athens and wasn't there now. Helt found Doughan in the

Navigation offices on Level Two, looking scrubbed and rested and ready for the week.

"About Bruguera and Ueda," Helt said. "If possible, could we set up a time for that?" Doughan's face didn't show surprise or hostility.

"Sure," he said. "1400."

"I'll be there."

The two Seed Bankers in SysSu, the ESL teacher and the day-care worker, hadn't been questioned this weekend, either. And there was one left in Biosystems, Andrea Doan. Mena's unhappy brewmaster had not yet told her story. That needed to be done today. Helt had a gut feeling that questioning Doan and the rest of them was going to be another example of finding out who hadn't murdered Ryan. But their innocence would narrow the pool of suspects by three, at least.

He found Mena, a shapeless snowman in a white coverall, in a seed vault under the Wilderness tower, in one of the frigid corridors set deep in *Kybele*'s rock. Rows and rows of drawers and lockers lined each side, strobe-lighted for now by helmet lights and soon to be dark again. Another shapeless snowman walked beside Mena. The second snowman had Elena inside it.

"Good morning, Helt," Mena said.

"Hi, Mena. Hey, Elena."

The snowman containing Elena waved a thick glove at the security camera. He wouldn't be able to be alone with her again for hours.

"Mena, do you think we could talk to Andrea Doan today? This morning?"

"I think so. Let me get these pumpkin seeds put away," Mena said. She opened a locker, the big lever on its door designed for manipulation by hands in thick gloves, and pulled out a steel box. The nitrogen-filled box with the seeds in it was marked with a drawing of a pumpkin, the words PUMPKIN, LONG ISLAND CHEESE, and a number. The number was in Biosystems records. The icon and the all-caps name were there in case humans lost the location files, Helt supposed. Like so much on *Kybele*, the vaults were designed with as few moving parts and as much redundancy as possible. Mena dropped the packet in the box. "I've been stalling on Andrea. How about eleven?" Mena asked.

"Sure," Helt said.

"I'll go up and talk to her myself. Human to human. I'll bring her to you. Eleven, in my barn, then, unless something changes."

"Sounds good," Helt said.

Elena closed the door of the locker.

"We wanted something else here, didn't we?" Mena asked.

"Lychee seeds," Elena said.

"Oh, right. For the new baby's family. I can't believe we haven't started growing lychees yet."

"And some local soil for me to vet before we seed the plot with it."

"Right. Always. Which vault are they in, Helt?"

Mena could ask her helmet and get the info, but it was as easy for Helt to do it. "413. Three vaults spinward to the next corridor, then turn left. Bye, you two," Helt said. He hoped they would pick a lychee stock with bright red shells, so the little boy could have fun throwing them.

Not every kid gets a tropical forest to play in, but the kids on *Kybele* would have their choice of several. Well, plantations, not tropical forests exactly. The tropical food habitats would stay wet and warm, even during the periods of near-arctic climate planned for Center from time to time. He would ask Mena someday if there was a useful liana, like, one that produced food or something. Swinging from vines was just such a cool thing to do.

Elena's lab was not that far from Mena's barn. Helt could stop by her lab before eleven or after the interview. Yes. Just to say hi. Yes.

On down the to-do list was nudging Severo or Doughan about NSS plans to shield the deportees as they left. Severo could be asked to spy on his boss and the other execs, but. But Helt wasn't going to do that, not yet. If what Helt could find turned paranoia into provable concern, then, yes. He decided to bother Severo anyway.

Severo was alone at his desk.

"You're early, Helt," Severo said.

"You've moved some more people off the SM hour list this weekend," Helt said. "Thank you."

"You're welcome," Severo said. "Dr. Maury's still on it."

"I talked to her again yesterday," Helt said. "The stuff about the stalking is new."

"Ryan stalked her and the midwife both, yeah." Severo leaned back in his chair and looked at the Helt on his screen. "So maybe the doc and the midwife got together and offed Ryan. I won't rule it out, Helt. Neither should you."

"I won't," Helt said. "But I think from her reaction that Elena didn't know it." The possibility that Susanna and Elena could have killed Ryan together seemed so unlikely to him that he wasn't even looking at how they might have done it if they'd wanted to. And he had just lied to Severo with a straight face. It was seriously time to look at what Helt Borresen was trying to hide from himself, if that's what he was doing. "And from what we know, Midwife Jambekar was at home with her boyfriend."

"Maybe Susanna sent him to do the job. Maybe that's why you added him to the surveillance list."

"Doughan said to," Helt said. "We'll hand you whatever information we get out of Doughan's two remaining Seed Bankers by this afternoon."

"You still have two Bankers under the SysSu umbrella and nobody's talked to them," Severo said. "You want me bring them in?

"I'll do it. You want to be there?"

"Sure."

"Nudge me to set up the meetings at least by tomorrow, okay?" Helt looked at the to-do list on his screen. Final passenger list, interviews, news of path slides, and on, and on. "In return, I'll nudge you, this morning, about how you plan to handle getting the Seed Bankers on board the shuttle."

"A little extra security, but that's all. Plainclothes, plus the usual honor guard stuff we do when anybody leaves."

A combination good-bye, thank-you, and welcome aboard ceremony, with videos to show the relatives, were traditional when contract workers left and new ones came up from Earth. This time the welcome aboard part would be missing.

"Groan," Helt said.

"Groan why?"

"Groan because the execs haven't come up with their lists of replacements for the Seed Bankers. I don't know when the execs plan to give out the news to the new colonists, either. But I know it has to be kept quiet."

Oh, fuck. Mena had said loud and clear that she was going to keep Susanna unless an actual criminal charge was filed against her. If that happened, one more colonist hopeful would be headed off-ship. And if there was a criminal charge against Elena, add Helt to the off-list.

That meant more last-minute juggling.

"You'd better remind them. Write it down on your to-do list," Severo said.

"I just did. Bye."

Helt picked up his coffee cup and took it to the waiting pot, but he didn't want more coffee, not really. He cradled the cup in his hands and went into the hall. His sense of frustration felt like a knot between his shoulders. He had lied to Severo about his certainty that Elena was innocent. He lied, and he had always wanted to think of himself as an honest man.

He sent a reminder to the execs.

Helt. Need final personnel assignments for the shuttle.

He made a circuit of the lobby and looked, in passing, out across the agora, where tendrils of morning fog were lifting from the flower pots and dewdrops were beginning to sparkle on the eaves of the Library. He had lied to the NSS chief because he wanted to hide something from him, and, by extension, from himself. So what was it Helt Borresen didn't want to look at?

That he'd been testing Elena, not just for facts about a murder, but for damage the suspicions had done to her. And hadn't found it. That he had, last night, and this morning, even inside his lair in SysSu this morning, known for the first time since his childhood what homecoming means.

He noticed he was in the hall, walking past the bunk room, which was empty, and into the lounge, holding a quarter cup of cold, useless coffee. The coffeepot was empty and unwashed, and there was a murder to solve to keep his home safe.

Who had murdered Cash Ryan? Not Elena, but he couldn't prove that. Not the Seed Bankers. Not Susanna. Any discomfort Cash Ryan was causing any of them would be over when he left the ship. He told himself to ignore them for now and look at what was happening around him.

He stood in front of a sink full of hot water and suds and the coffeepot was clean except for a stain beneath its rim. He scrubbed it.

Yves; he didn't really know Yves, but if the sculptor had found Ryan stalking his girl, he had the strength to kill Ryan and cart him up the elevator alone.

Fact. It doesn't make any sense that there's no record of the World Tree anywhere. Someone in SysSu could have trashed the records as they showed up; people would assume their chatter about it was still around unless they looked for it. Someone was hiding Yves.

Hypothesis. Yves Copani killed Cash Ryan.

Really? He didn't get to stay on *Kybele* but neither did Cash Ryan, and killing the guy didn't change the equation that left Susanna on board and Yves and Cash gone. Yves could have killed him somewhere on Earth, with less risk than doing it here.

Fact. Yves Copani ate dinner with Helt the night of the SM, and if he'd cooled and killed Ryan and hauled him up the elevator, he'd been really fast at doing it.

Helt rinsed the cleaned filter cup. He rinsed the coffeepot and rubbed his thumb across the shiny glass to hear it squeak. He settled it in the dish rack with exaggerated caution.

Hypothesis. Yves Copani killed Cash Ryan because he knew Ryan was stalking his girl. Okay, but that didn't explain why the World Tree was hidden. Archer could do that, maybe, but why would he? Helt began to wonder if Doughan had asked Archer to hide the sculpture; it was too improbable that no one on ship had blabbed about it somehow, somewhere. And Doughan's insistence that the Seed Bankers should be hounded fit the hypothesis that Doughan was hiding Yves.

Doughan's indifference that Elena was the prime suspect was weird, too. Doughan knew that Elena was, by far, the best person to head Biosystems if something happened to Mena. Mena, as far as Helt knew, wasn't looking at the next-in-lines to replace Elena, and that reaction of Mena's about keeping Susanna on board? Given Doughan's role as spokesman for the execs for the next three years, he should be a lot more bothered by it.

The theory that 90 percent of human behavior is herd-oriented and the rest is wolf fit everything Helt knew. The wolf was in charge at the moment. Helt's neck hairs were standing up.

Murder cannot be tolerated. If *Kybele* was to survive, no must mean no. If Doughan and the execs were hiding a murder, for any reason at all, they were dangerous to her survival and they had to be removed.

It was a no-brainer. It was the right thing to do. Helt had to do it. If the leader is unfit, if the leader is protecting a murderer, the challenge has to be made. But it was unlikely the murderer was Yves, so Helt was back to square one. Or sphere one, where Elena's bubble circled closer to Cash Ryan's than anyone else's. Doughan was protecting Elena? Because Mena wanted him to?

The wolf was in charge, for good or ill, and in that model, the imperative to challenge the pack leader led to stability. It had to be done, but the wolf pup in Helt was whimpering.

Helt wanted the security of Doughan in charge, Mena in her vineyards, and Archer grumbling away in the office down the hall. A place for everything and everything in its place, including Helt Borresen, the little boy who still wanted home and family. The grown-up Helt who had wanted to come home, too, but had given up that dream and replaced it with the dream of having it all happen here, somehow, someday. The Helt who always thought of himself as a man of principle, had always thought there were lines in his brain that knew right from wrong.

Helt rubbed his neck.

If Doughan learned of Helt's suspicions, Helt might not be able to get the information he needed. Therefore, everything he did had to look like business as usual. Make that, everything he did that might get back to Doughan.

He was back in his chair, the cold coffee replaced by a half cup hot from his own pot. He had no memory of seeing anything in the hall he'd walked through to get here.

It was time to talk to David II, the chief among Doughan's successors. Unless David II was out somewhere on a project, he was just below Athens. There would be time to get there and still make it to Stonehenge well before eleven. It was time to stop worrying about Doughan, one way or another.

David II was at his desk. "May I come down?" Helt asked. "Now, if possible."

That could have been an instant of irritation on David II's face, but it lasted only an instant, replaced by a look of interested anticipation. "Of course."

"This should only take a few minutes," Helt said. "I'll be right there." And he asked himself, on the elevator, why he wasted words in polite disclaimers. Some of Doughan's time was unaccounted for. David II might know where he'd been. And once Helt knew that, he would know what to do next. Right.

Hardhat Athens was a different space from Level One. Its agora didn't provide a view of buildings meant to be admired. In fact, buildings couldn't be seen. The elevator opened on a garden, vertical and lush, trees and vines, some of the foliage browned by autumn. An array of chrysanthemums, vivid in their pots near the elevator, were probably destined for display on the Athens agora above. Behind and above them, bright berries of holly prepped themselves for the winter season. Helt stepped onto the rough multicolored aggregate in front of the elevator. "David II's office, please," Helt said, and some of the pebbles lighted themselves to lead him across the aggregate and down a wide path through the maze.

David II's office was, like Mena's, remarkably unassuming, a portable construction just beyond the gate in a broad industrial hangar. Bare lights illuminated crawlers, sweepers, and, as usual, things Helt didn't recognize. Today, there was a boxy, spiky apparatus on a pallet, waiting to be loaded and shipped somewhere to do something.

"Come in," David II said. David II worked standing. His workstation was chest high and had a treadmill beneath it. There were a lot of objects fastened to the walls and there was very little space for anyone else to stand.

"This is sensitive," Helt said.

David II walked past the workstation and opened a door, and then another one, and led Helt through an oval door. Today Helt recognized it, for the first time, as what it had always been. It was a decommissioned airlock, and he realized that David II's private office was a repurposed artifact from *Kybele*'s earlier years.

In the larger room, chairs surrounded a folding table equipped with workstations. David II motioned to one and sat down at another. "Sensitive. Yes. Otherwise, you would have continued our conversation from a distance."

"Has Severo asked you for an alibi on Wednesday evening?"

"No," David II said. "I've located some traces of myself, very boring ones, during the time in question. I'll send them up to NSS now, if you like."

Meaning, "Showing videos to you now will waste time that I don't have."

"That will save time," Helt said. "Yours and mine. Mena, Doughan, and Archer were asked, Thursday morning, to keep their interfaces live 24/7. But I have very little information about their whereabouts on Wednesday evening. I'll find some, I'm sure. As a matter of record, their whereabouts will have to be verified."

David II was quick at processing. Helt had offered cross-checking Doughan's whereabouts as something procedural, routine, but he hadn't made a procedural, routine request. David II's expression remained neutral, calm.

"They've been lax in providing documentation," David II said.

"They are busy people."

"Yes." David II smiled. Sure, there may have been some resentment about the task, and it hadn't been their idea, but still. They were busy people. They were execs. David II had dealt with execs all his life, and he was becoming one now. "I have very little social contact with the heads of Biosystems or SysSu. But as it happens, I saw Doughan, briefly, Wednesday evening. Let me look. He came into The Lab around . . ." David II consulted his records, the ones he would be sending up to NSS. "A little after 1600. I don't have the time to the minute."

"You mean The Lab that's a bar?" Helt asked.

"Yes. I was there with Simmons. One of the earthworks architects. We'll have to change that name, earthworks, someday." The statement was made in complete seriousness.

Helt didn't know Simmons. The earthworks people who modified Mena's croplands had their offices in Stonehenge now. Eight years ago, Helt had spent a few workdays wandering around here because of some dissatisfaction about what the earth movers were doing. He'd suggested the move, and now that they knew exactly what high winds did to seedlings, day by day, relationships between them and Mena and her farmers were just fine, thank you.

"Did you speak with Doughan?"

"He didn't look too sociable. He went straight to the bar and got a go-cup. On his way back, he stopped by our table and said hello. We invited him to join us. He said he'd had a rough day and was going home."

Helt entered DOUGHAN, WEDNESDAY 18, THE LAB. 1630. (BARTENDER? PURCHASE?) "That's helpful. That's *really* helpful." He wanted to ask where Doughan had gone yesterday, and last night. There had to be a way to get that information elsewhere, even if Doughan's interface didn't show it. He wanted to ask what David II thought of Doughan, truly thought of him. He wanted to keep the wealth of information that was David II available to him, and time was short. "Cash Ryan seems to have been a loner, perhaps pathologically so. You were at the psych autopsy. If we make the assumption that he was unstable, could he have done any real damage to the ship?"

"Unstable. Both that and psychopath are euphemisms for the term *madman*."

"Yes," Helt said.

"If it turns out to be so . . . No system can be made proof against attacks from madmen," David II said. "But a single madman would have difficulty killing this ship. We're big, and we're redundant. We have five reactors in reserve close to the skin. Access to them is not easy. We have section seals and drones to carry foam to breaches. We could lose considerable air reserves but we could make more, and quickly. There's a seed bank beneath each of the six towers. Even if the ship dies, it is likely some of them would survive."

"What about outside?" Helt asked. "He worked outside."

"We who live inside are protected from the airless void by four kilometers of nickel iron and we plan to add ice and a plasma shield."

"It is vulnerable? The plasma shield?" Helt asked.

"Not from outside, not at this time. We won't be printing the mesh for it until we're under way."

"Thank you," Helt said. He hustled back to SysSu.

Someday he was going to ask David II if David I had ever told him why Petra canyon was twice as deep as the original specs said it should be. Someday there would be time for that.

SysSu was a division whose job was to stay invisible as much as possible. To guard communications, but, whenever possible, to be discreet about it. Should solving a murder case be SysSu's job? Via backup for NSS, via the communications node that Helt was supposed to be, well, this time, yes. He had to do what the execs expected him to do, and a lot of other things at the same time.

He needed some help that couldn't come from NSS. The specs for all sorts of clever devices for spying on people were on file. Helt picked out a few and started the printers in SysSu's parts shop.

What he planned to do was something he had sworn he would never do. Unauthorized surveillance was forbidden by *Kybele*'s privacy regulations, her code of transparency, and it was just flat wrong. He was the Special Investigator. He had the authority to break rules. And it was still wrong.

This was and was not a Trolley Problem. He'd spy on the execs and he would be spying on a lot of other people, and always know that the name, the integrity, the honor of the man he'd just pushed in front of the trolley in order to save the people in the car was Helt Borresen.

After a blink or two, he became aware that Nadia's office was now occupied. He filled his pockets with spybots, picked up his coffee cup, and went over there.

Jerry and Nadia were at their usual workstations, close enough to touch each other but apparently oblivious to that and to the world around them. They looked comfortable in each other's physical space. Helt didn't pick up any signals of hurt feelings between them.

"Coffee's fresh, Helt," Jerry said.

Jerry's T-shirt this morning was a brown so dark it looked almost black. It must be new. His braid was wrapped in a complicated way that looked like he hadn't done the job himself. More evidence that the two of them were okay with each other. That was good.

Helt topped up his coffee, sat down, and investigated the clutter on the table for something he could push out of the way. One of the objects seemed to be a rubber chicken. Plucked. Helt moved it aside to make space for his coffee mug and decided not to ask.

"Help me think," Helt said.

"So we can get this murder solved in two hours and get back to our lives?" Nadia asked.

"Exactly," Helt said. "And so I can get up to Stonehenge this morning. Mena and I are questioning a Seed Banker."

"Okay," Jerry said. "Monday morning review." The room became a projection of Helt's Murder Mess. Helt didn't know when the name had officially changed from Murder Management, but what Jerry was showing was private to this room, and the name fit. The sphere, with its Oort cloud of facts at the periphery, was still too empty.

"Motive, method, and opportunity," Helt said.

"We have method," Jerry said.

The method had been messy. Cash Ryan had been chilled down and thrown into a tree. If someone had seen Ryan hit the tree and hauled him in for treatment, that artery could have been stitched back together. Maybe.

"Do we?" Helt asked. "What Calloway said was that Ryan bled to death from a cut artery in his chest. But the fall was sloppy thinking; the killers couldn't have been certain the fall would kill him. I wonder. If somebody saw him fall and cut him down, might he have survived?"

He'd ask Calloway.

Calloway was in the clinic lounge with Martin Kumar.

"I hate to disturb you, but," Helt said.

Calloway grunted. "But none of the hale and hearty citizens of *Kybele* happen to be here this morning. We're goofing off. I was just gonna call you."

"We really need to know when Cash Ryan died. A four-hour window is turning out to be too large to close."

"And you think I have the answer." Calloway leaned back in his chair and folded his arms across his chest. "Maybe I do. He was dead when he was thrown off the tower. The cause of death I saw at autopsy wasn't wrong, but it wasn't the whole story. Actually, Ryan probably died of v-fib. Ventricular fibrillation, for layman types like you." Calloway looked across the table. "And yes, Martin, I jumped to a conclusion. It's a bad thing to do."

The statement got Martin's attention. Helt's, too.

"If someone had seen the fall? Could you have saved him at that point?" Helt asked.

"I don't think so," Calloway said. "Thing is, the human heart is designed to work at thirty-seven degrees Celsius. It gets confused if you chill it down toward twenty-seven. Instead of a pump, you get a sack of wiggling individual muscle fibers that don't pump anything anywhere. At which point your blood pressure drops, your brain doesn't get oxygen, and it's game over. Five minutes of anoxia and you're brain-damaged even if someone puts you on life support. Except if you're chilled, your brain is sort of protected, so the window to get stuff back together is longer. A lot longer, hours, but that's if you have a good team to get you on a heart-lung machine early, like in that first five minutes, and keep your brain oxygenated while you warm up."

Helt called up the autopsy report again. "His chest cavity was at twenty-eight degrees Celsius at autopsy."

"He'd been hauled out of a tree, intubated, and breathed with ambient air and rehydrated with a couple of liters of room-temperature saline before Martin here pronounced him dead. Room temperature was about twenty degrees Celsius that evening. That didn't change his core temperature much. But he was flatlined when the EMTs put the 'trodes on him, no cardiac function at all except for what you get from chest compressions. He was flatlined for brain activity, too. He bled more into his chest than most corpses would, but that's because he was tilted head-down in that tree."

"Postmortem bleeding," Helt said.

"Yeah," Calloway said. "But he left his shift alive and warm that afternoon, and he could not have chilled that much on the ground after he died. The soil temp that night was around ten degrees Celsius. Lay on it naked for three hours without a heartbeat and you might get from thirty-seven to thirty-five, if you're skinny. To get as cold as he was, you're looking at a fast freeze. Thing is, there's no evidence of frostbite. He got really cold, really fast."

"Thanks, Calloway."

"You're welcome." The big man gave Helt a toast with his coffee cup.

"Really cold, really fast," Jerry said.

"Cold with an air supply," Helt said.

"Why air?" Nadia asked.

"I'm making the assumption that the murderer had a compelling reason to kill Ryan rather than send him away forever," Helt said. "If so, whatever information Ryan had could not be safely exported to Earth—in the killer's opinion. Or had to be obtained from Ryan before he left *Kybele*. And if someone was after information, they needed his personal data stash, which is missing, or they needed a private place. A private place with air in it, so they could both talk. Must have been cold air. Very cold air."

"Or a closed suit," Nadia said.

"Not a closed suit. It would have kept him warm," Helt said.

The three of them viewed *Kybele*'s hollow Center, its towers and fields and forests. "Not in Center," Helt said. "It wasn't cold enough that night. Going down." He vanished the floor of Center and they looked down into the maze of unroofed buildings of Level One, the three little villages, Athens, Petra, Stonehenge, the train tunnels that connected them. Beyond the villages there was little but solid rock as yet. The maze would be much more intricate as time passed. Habitats and shops and industries would be built at the peripheries of the towns and spread laterally from the equator line until lighter g and increasing awareness of spin made things uncomfortable.

"Walk-in coolers?" Jerry asked.

"Mark them," Helt said.

During the time with Calloway, Jerry, Nadia, and Martin had been as calm as cucumbers with one another. That was a story Helt didn't have time to sort out now, but he was grateful the tensions between the three of them had vanished somewhere.

That somewhere was not a place for him. Helt was a totally cisgender male and it made him feel archaic at times. He wondered how Elena felt about partners and sharing and jealousy. That family of hers, business or commune or whatever you wanted to call it, was hard to read from what they let the public see.

Jerry set little ice cubes on the locations of walk-in freezers and fridges. They were clustered near the centers of Athens and Petra, in restaurants and food stores. Some really big coolers were in the food prep areas of Stonehenge. A few walk-ins were in the industrial areas of Level Two, beneath Athens. They were all monitored. Time and date stamps showed no activity in them during the time window.

"Ryan got off shift at 1500," Nadia said. "He was showered and dressed in the clothes he died in when he left his coworkers. He went up the elevator to Level One and then on to Center, if he took himself up the elevator to the observation tower. But he didn't do that. He didn't get on the Athens elevator on Wednesday evening, and he wasn't in the stairwells." Nadia ran fast clips from the surveillance cameras that afternoon. "Not at any recorded time."

"So he died on Level Two," Jerry said.

"Or in Petra, or Stonehenge," Helt said. "But we'd have to figure time enough to get him somewhere and then chill him, and then add the transport time over to Athens tower so he could be hauled up during the SM hour."

"On the train," Nadia said.

There were no captures of anyone supporting an unconscious human and getting him on or off a train that night.

"I suppose a high-speed emergency vehicle could have carted him around," Jerry said, "but that would mean the records of it were erased and the train schedules would have been altered. A cross-check on energy use for that hour would show it—unless those records were altered, too."

"Any record can be altered," Helt said. "That's the framework of our reality, for better or worse." He ran the energy use/trip comparisons. The SM hour looked just fine.

"Helt?" Calloway's face appeared. "One of the effects of phenothiazines is they stomp on the shivering reflex."

"I did not know that," Helt said.

"So Ryan might have chilled faster than the models show. He wouldn't have fought the cold."

"Time frame?" Helt asked.

"It would still take a couple of hours," Calloway said.

"Thank you," Helt said. "I think."

Calloway vanished.

"Back to Level Two under Athens," Helt said. They scouted Level Two's industrial complex, in easy reach of Athens but well beyond its borders. It was full of big spaces; warehouses, vaults for metals and ores, materials labs, shops that printed anything and everything. Hardhat country. A lot of it was unheated.

Much of the rest of *Kybele*'s hide was untouched rock, pierced by the spiraling shuttle tunnel that led to the port by the elevator.

"The seed vaults are bored deep," Nadia said.

"Not the seed vaults," Jerry said.

"Not a high probability of that," Helt said. You didn't go into the vaults alone, and when you entered, indicators blinked in NSS and Biosystems and the Athens clinic until you came out again. Those indicators had been on during the SM hour, and a look at them said no one had been in the vaults then.

"What do we have on Level Two that's cold and signal-dark, as opposed to just cold?" Helt asked.

Jerry and Nadia hauled maps of communication-live areas into position. The industrial complex, the shuttle port, and Navigation's offices on Level Two were live. The new tunnels went live as soon as they were carved out, conduit and camera mounts following the tunnelworm borers, as necessary as air.

Helt sighed. There was more dark space in the Athens plaza than in any public space on Level Two. Industrial areas weren't expected to be private; by design, places for hanging out on Level One left more room for private conversations. Industrial areas were monitored; inside buildings and outside where the traffic was both pedestrian and robotic.

"What do we have on visual for Ryan's work crew Wednesday afternoon?" Helt asked.

Nadia sent him a capture of a woman and two men in civvies walking across the Nav lobby and entering the Athens elevator. After a moment, a text overlay showed up.

Severo: Zaida Krupin, Jinhai Han, Dayhi Tung. They said Ryan didn't ride up with them that afternoon. He was in the showers when they left.

"Ryan isn't with them and he doesn't show on any captures from the Nav lobby Wednesday afternoon. We've scanned for him in the morning shots but there's no definite ID. No facial captures," Nadia said.

Therefore, Ryan had been murdered in view of the Athens tower camera while it was blind. It was that simple, wasn't it? Except he hadn't died in the SM hour.

"We didn't get far with that," Helt said. "I have some theories about motive. I'd like to hear yours."

"I don't get the sense of it, so I'm no help," Jerry said. "What's a good reason to kill somebody who's going to be out of the picture anyway?"

"Heh," Helt said. "One possibility is that the event was a rage reaction and completely unplanned. I don't want to completely discount that. When we collect enough strands of information from people who knew Ryan and weave them together, we'll find someone he could have goaded into temporary insanity, whatever that is. But that net is not woven yet. The list of people who admit to even having a conversation with him is . . ."

"Sparse," Nadia said. "At the lower limits of probability."

STALKED BY RYAN:
SUSANNA JAMBEKAR, ELENA MAURY
WORKED WITH RYAN:
ZAIDA ARENT, JINHAI HAN, DAYHI TUNG
POSSIBLE ACQUAINTANCES:
ORIOL BRUGUERA, KELLY HALKETT, MASAKA UEDA
BOSSES:
DAVID LUO I, DAVID LUO II
OTHERS:
YVES COPANI?
ELENA MAURY
VENKAT RAGHAVA

Elena's name was a weighted presence among the list of people who admitted to knowing Ryan. Weighted because she had lived with him and weighted because of her ride down the elevator at 2006. Jerry or Nadia could have mentioned it. They didn't.

"Maybe we can add a little density to this, increase the numbers a little," Helt said. "Zaida Krupin, the woman in his work crew, introduced Ryan to a group of women, and that's where Susanna Jambekar thinks Ryan first saw her," Helt said. "Severo talked to Krupin, but maybe she knows something more. Could you find out about that, Jerry? I'll be questioning four Seed Bankers today. Make that five. I'll be talking to one of them this morning. At eleven."

Helt looked at the time counter on his screen. He had time for what he wanted to do next.

"Sure, I'll check out Zaida," Jerry said. "On the concept that Ryan had information no one else had, I don't know. I mean, there's no indication the guy was a genius, or in contact with the high and mighty."

"The only high and mighty person who admits knowing who he was is David I," Helt said. "If he had time-sensitive information about Ryan, he would have done something long before now. Or he would have told David II to do something."

Helt looked at updates in the David II section of Navigation's logs and found a call to David II from David I. It had come in the wee hours of Sunday morning. Helt played David I's calm words as a voiceover; the list of Ryan's work locations was not long, Svalbard, Kitimat. Nothing in Northern California, and Helt wondered how Ryan had financed staying close to Elena in those years.

". . . but of course at the time I believed he had spent more time at Svalbard and Kitimat than he had. He had nothing to do with building *Kybele*'s engines; they were pushed over from China station. He had physical access to them, but never alone, EVA was always in teams. We tested the control systems as we brought them online."

"Maintenance on the thrusters is always ongoing," David II said. "Any harm he might have tried to do would surely be nullified by now."

The engines at the North and South Poles were housed at the ends of long cylinders, access tunnels to get in and out of *Kybele*. The engines sat on two-tiered platforms, turntables, oriented so they were motionless relative to Earth for now and kept that way by constant thrust against the spin of the poles. The tier closer to the body of *Kybele* made a stable, zero-g landing site for incoming vessels. The cage of the plasma shield spindle originated there.

NORTH POLE ENGINE AND EXTERNAL SHUTTLE ACCESS TUNNEL

SOUTH POLE ENGINE AND EXTERNAL SHUTTLE ACCESS TUNNEL

David I was listing the locations where Ryan had worked on his first tour.

"We were a thousand strong, no more, in those years," David I said. "We worked remote as much as we could, driving the bots from where the Nav lobby is now, but usually one or two people were out on EVA."

SHUTTLEPORT OPERATIONS COMPLEX, INTERNAL AND EXTERNAL

"The sun was suspended in Center before I came up. We had power, and enough water had been cracked so you could breathe up there. Center's fused glass floor was covered with wet black sand. The rivers were filling Second Sea. We had air in Athens, but we were still living in bubbles in the space where the Athens agora is now."

ATHENS AGORA BUBBLE LIVING QUARTERS

"And those are the only places he was?" David II's voice asked.

"There weren't many other places to be," David I said. "Stonehenge had a few Level One caves, sealed, to use for test plots. Petra canyon wasn't roofed over. You've looked through the shift logs and you know who was where then, every day."

"I have," David II said. He attached Navigation logs from those years to the conversation. "But they cover only the hours when he was on shift. Thank you for helping me fill in the blanks, sir."

The rest was polite good-byes.

"David II has looked over those records but we haven't," Helt said. "At the psych autopsy, David I said he planned to work fast on this. He did. This list came in only hours later," Helt said. And shortly after that, Doughan had found something more important to do than set up interviews with Seed Bankers.

There it was. The Special Investigator had not been informed. Helt was out of the loop. David II hadn't mentioned this information; he probably thought Helt had reviewed it before they had talked. Or David II was up to something. Something that involved Doughan, or maybe something on his own. It was possible that David II was protecting David I from something Cash Ryan had learned, something he would have done as soon as he got back to Earth. Something about why Petra canyon was such a deep, impressively deep, gash. It just broke that way, was the standard story.

Helt cleared his throat, definitively. "So we still don't have a motive we can count on, and the guy died somewhere cold, sometime before the SM hour, and we know he stalked two women but that little fact about him didn't come to light until he was dead. That's what we have for four days' work," Helt said. "That's not enough. I can't stand this. I'm going walkabout."

Jerry and Nadia looked at him to see if he meant it.

"I need fresh air. I need chocolate." He could hope they would play along. He very deliberately took his interface out of his pocket and put it on the desk, out of sight beneath the rubber chicken. "Come with me?"

They did, and their interfaces didn't come with them. Jerry and Nadia flanked Helt, one on either side. Once outside, Helt aimed for Venkie's cart. It looked different this morning. Venkie had put walls of transparent siding under his awning, ready for winter.

Helt set a slow, ambling pace through the dead zones of the agora. The tables outside the cafés looked sad and abandoned. The air was too chilly now for morning coffee sippers.

The plan was to leave the tables outside until after the good-bye ceremonies for the last shuttle and then bring them in for winter. That day would be warm by design. But Elena and Helt would be going back to Earth, where weather is not scheduled by request, unless he found the real murderer in the next three days.

"And what else do you need besides chocolate?" Jerry asked.

"I need your help. I need you to help me disprove some paranoid suspicions of mine," Helt said. "If you think they're probable enough to be worth disproving, I'll be asking you to hide information, alter it, and perhaps do other things. And all I can offer you in return is that I'll take as much of the blame as is possible, if any comes your way. You'll be acting on my behalf, so some of the stuff that pushes the boundaries of legal comes under the Special Investigator umbrella. I hope."

Jerry looked highly amused. Nadia looked worried. As well she might.

"Pushes the boundaries of legal, eh? Keep talking, Helt," Jerry said. "Tell us what's really on your mind."

"I'm pretty sure Doughan spent a lot of time this weekend doing hands-on, real-time checks on anything Cash Ryan could have touched while he was here," Helt said. "He didn't put up a single flag that he was doing it."

"Was David II with him?" Nadia asked.

"I don't know," Helt said.

"Do you think they think Ryan tried to kill the ship?" Jerry asked.

"You got it. That's my paranoid suspicion," Helt said. "And leaving me out of the loop, which they did, leaves me in an awkward position. If I call them on it, and I will, I'm sure they have a cover story ready. I'm going to act like I believe them and I'll try to do it with a straight face."

"Do you think you can do that?" Nadia asked.

"I plan to try," Helt said.

"As paranoid suspicions go, yours is world class," Jerry said. "So we're not really going out to buy breakfast. We're heading for the closed suit lockers in Navigation, so we'll have enough oxygen to watch the world blow up."

"I'm not quite that paranoid," Helt said. "I think we're safe enough. If Ryan did anything potentially lethal and Doughan thought he couldn't abort the process with two men—"

"Meaning Doughan and David II," Nadia said.

"Right," Helt said. "If Doughan suspected kill-ship sabotage, he would call a high-alert inspection of every system on ship. He hasn't. But I want to know what he suspected and what he plans to do about it. So I need your help."

"On the quiet," Jerry said.

"On the quiet." Helt watched Nadia and Jerry make their assessments and read each other's intentions as best they could. Jerry looked thoughtful. Nadia looked like she was constructing a complicated theorem involving risk and gain. "What about Severo?" Nadia asked. "He might be in a better position to—"

"Severo's a careful, loyal, man," Helt said. "He follows chain of command, and some of the things I need require stepping outside that. I think I could convince him to spy on his boss, but convincing him I have good reason for doing it means I show him information I don't have. Yet."

"And you need us to get it," Jerry said.

"I do. I need you to help me keep some secrets. If you want to back away from this, I understand completely, and I'll play this alone as best I can."

"I'm okay with it," Jerry said. "Nadia?"

Nadia tossed her hair and took a deep breath. "I trust you," she said.

She must have done the extrapolations. She must have factored Helt's concerns about the ship, about the amount of leg work left to be done, about his assessment of the threat to the power structure of her world as she knew it, and added in other things that Helt didn't have time to think about. She was fast, and she read straws in the wind, and Helt admired her.

"Thank you," Helt said.

They had paused at the edge of the tables on the sunny side of the agora. "Tell us what's first, Helt." Nadia frowned. "I know it's sunny, but I'm getting cold out here."

They started walking again. "I need you to walk by and plant a handful of bots near Archer's and Doughan's quarters."

"Egad," Jerry said. "Tradecraft!"

"You'll think of a way to do it, or you'll get caught. We'll deal with that if it happens. I don't think you'll be too obvious there, but then there's Mena's offices in Stonehenge." Where Elena was in and out daily. He'd do it the next time he went up there. And plant some in Elena's lab, too. "No, never mind on that. I can cover it, and you two don't go up there that often."

"Littering is a misdemeanor at most," Nadia said.

"But we won't get caught at it," Jerry said.

"Mena's house as well. First, we set up a Huerfano system for information I don't want to go to the cloud." Or to the execs, but Helt didn't say that. "We'll run it parallel with real info that goes to NSS and Biosystems, but I plan to add some fake data to that if I need to. While we're in the offices, let's keep the chatter going, and the work. Stay honest for everything we can."

Venkie waited at his counter. In the shadow of the cart, the air was warmed by his ovens.

"Good morning," Jerry said.

"Good Monday morning to all of you. Seven?" Venkie asked. He had a sack open and his tongs at the ready.

"You know it," Jerry said.

"That would be a wise choice for caloric restraint. However, I should tell you that this morning I made the usual breakfast samosas, and others filled with roasted pears," Venkie said. "I think you will find them pleasant."

"I think, then, ten," Helt said. "Five standard, five pear."

Venkie slid the pastries, steaming, into the bag. "I see you are still not able to announce that the murder of Cash Ryan is now a matter of history."

"Not yet." Nadia's words were not emphasized. They were simply a matter-of-fact statement.

"You say that with such assurance that I am sure the ship, like this sack"—Venkie handed the sack to Nadia and offered her a little bow—"is in good hands."

Nadia smiled and returned the bow.

"What are you hearing?" Helt asked. He pressed his thumb to Venkie's screen and paid for this morning's treats.

"I am hearing of impatience to be on our way," Venkie said. "I am hearing of sorrow about that as well. I am not hearing people talk about Cash Ryan."

"But if you do," Helt said.

"I will listen carefully."

"Thank you," Helt said.

Halfway back across the agora, Helt said, "We can't spend the day walking back and forth to dead zones out here so we can talk. I'm going to be in Stonehenge and down on Level Two with Doughan today. If I call you for face-to-face, download the silences, okay?"

"RSA?" Jerry asked.

"Oldie but goodie," Helt said. "With a letter macro for an access key. I haven't made one up yet."

"Nidag," Nadia said. "N-I-D-A-G." She traced the letters in the air as she said them.

"Okay," Helt said. "Nine days. I can remember that." It was norsk, and it sounded sorta like Nidhogg, the serpent who gnaws at the roots of Yggdrasil. He supposed Nadia had read the bio of Helt Borresen at some point.

He shrugged and followed Nadia and Jerry through the atrium and into the group office. Nadia went to the microwave stand, divided the pastries into groups of three plus one of four, and put the four into a sack. Jerry chatted with someone in Navigation and then called Zaida Krupin, who had been on Ryan's work team and had introduced him to Susanna Jambekar.

"Noon?" Jerry said. "I'll meet you."

Nidhogg translated as "gnawer of corpses." Helt didn't like the concept of necrophagia at all, even for the purposes of divination. Odin woke the dead, that was spooky, but he didn't wake them to eat them. Only to question them. They cursed him and what they wanted most was to be at rest again.

"We need to review Venkie's Wednesday again," Helt said. "List everyone who bought food before he closed, and then collate that with the list of people who went down the elevator to Level Two that day, minus the people who came back up before the SM hour."

"I'll do that if you get out of here and let us work," Nadia said. "Or maybe you'd rather be late to the interview you set up with Mena."

The time and date alert on Helt's screen flashed red, courtesy of Jerry.

"I'm gone," Helt said. He pulled a handful of bots out of his pockets and laid them next to Nadia's screen.

"Wait!" Jerry said. "Don't forget your interface." Jerry rummaged for it under the rubber chicken and held it up.

"Or your jacket," Nadia said without looking up from her screen.

His jacket was in his office. Helt grabbed his interface, doubled back for his windbreaker, and hustled to get to the station before the next train left for Stonehenge.

24

Kicking the Anthill

Mena wasn't in her office yet. Helt palmed the bots to the lintels of her door and turned back to look at the world. The air was chilly and the morning mist was turning into real clouds. From where Helt stood, with a good view of the dark slash of Petra canyon, he couldn't see his private rock. A campground was going to be built anti-spinward of the little mesa someday. He'd seen the blueprints, the places where more shafts would be bored from Center to Level Two and fitted with elevators and staircases. He was glad they weren't here yet. He didn't need more ways into Center than he was dealing with already.

He saw *Kybele* through a lens of time, its population grown to that of a medium-sized city, its climates and crops moving through periods of tropical heat and wet, and then, as the ship slowed to approach its destination, testing crop strategies, technical strategies, to try out on the new world. And he wondered if he ever saw anything for itself, as it was and not as it would be, as it was and not as a construct made of its past and its future.

Two women emerged from the elevator, Andrea Doan taller than he expected, her shoulders rounded a little as she leaned down to listen to Mena beside her. Andrea wore a canvas smock thing over her jeans, a work jacket with many pockets. Her fists pushed two of them forward. The effect was that of a pregnancy, but she wasn't pregnant and hadn't applied for a pregnancy. Her black hair was slicked back tight, as it had been in her mug shot, and it was shiny in the mid-morning October light. Andrea Doan was not as plump now as she had been in the mug shot, and Helt realized it had been taken fifteen years ago, when she came aboard as a colonist. She looked strong and she looked like she didn't care much for men, or women, either.

He watched Andrea Doan move, her legs longer than Mena's and not quite matching Mena's stride. Move ahead, halt and wait; it made the woman look impatient with her companion.

Forget the bio, he told himself. Remember that you have never seen this woman before. But he knew that her family had been in Mexico for three generations after leaving Vietnam and that she was a brewmaster, and he knew that Mena's farmers were happy enough to see her transferred from time to time.

Mena looked up and then both women did. Mena offered Helt a quick smile. Andrea Doan didn't. Mena opened her office door and Helt followed the women in. A waft of fresh hay and manure came with them. Helt sneezed.

"Bless you," Mena said. "Coffee?"

"Of course," Helt said. "Thank you." Mena motioned for her two visitors to take chairs at a worktable. It held workstation screens, but there was no clutter for Helt to focus on, no rubber chickens or other oddities.

What social preambles are appropriate before you announce to someone that their current life has been destroyed because of a bank deposit? Helt wasn't sure. Mena brought him a mug of coffee and supplied Andrea Doan and herself with cups of tea.

"So you're Helt Borresen," Andrea Doan said. She dragged her cup to a convenient position and ignored Mena's courtesy in offering it. Her face was broad, with regular features that were pleasant enough. She had smooth skin, no sun damage despite her forty-plus years. Her narrow lips were pursed in a thin, tight line, as if to guard against saying what she really wanted to say.

"I am," Helt said. "And you are Andrea Doan, who is responsible for some of *Kybele*'s finest beer. Do you know what you're in for this morning?"

Andrea Doan's eyes flashed pure hatred. She's bitter, Mena had told him. But she's a good brewmaster.

"Mena says you think I know something about the man who was murdered."

"I'm the Incident Analyst for SysSu," Helt said. "I've been given the title of Special Investigator to determine who killed Cash Ryan. I asked Mena to bring you here. There are questions I will ask, but I'm not here to arrest you."

"You would have sent someone in uniform for that," Andrea said.

The idea was tempting. Helt didn't think he was going to learn anything here, or from any of the Seed Bankers. The timing of the discovery that they were aboard irritated him. In some ways, he wished Archer had waited a few days to mention them. The Seed Bankers on Earth had no terrorist history at all and disowned members who thought violence was a good idea within nanoseconds, and that didn't fit with what had happened to Cash Ryan.

"You worked in the brewery on Wednesday," Helt said. "After that, you show up on the security camera records at a grocery on Level Two Stonehenge, at 1600. You left the grocery and went on foot to your quarters. You went from there to a potluck harvest supper at 1818. The people who were there told NSS you left them at around 2100. You didn't have time to kill Cash Ryan that night and your neighbors can prove where you were. You aren't under suspicion of murder. There are other things we need to know."

"I don't know anything about this and I don't want to talk to you," Andrea said.

"Andrea, please," Mena said. "This is important."

"To you, perhaps." Andrea did not look at Mena. "Not to me."

"Please think of this as a citizen's duty." Mena's voice was one she seldom used, the "I will brook no nonsense" voice of the Biosystems Executive who meant precisely what she said.

Andrea Doan had obviously heard that voice before. "I see. I want legal counsel," Andrea said.

Helt found himself wanting to lean back in his chair to get away from her. He didn't do that. "Everything we've said and will say is being recorded. But if you think legal counsel is needed . . ."

"It's Obrecht." Mena's voice had returned to its usual gentle cadence. "You asked me to call him, and I did. He says he has represented you before. Will he be acceptable, Andrea?"

"Yes." Short, clipped, and resentful.

"Giliam, are you here?" Mena asked.

Giliam Obrecht's freckled face and his remarkably narrow nose appeared on the table screens. "I'm here. Andrea, this was short notice, but I'll give you the coaching I would have given you in private. Just talk to them. Answer their questions. I can ask to have things removed from this record if needed, but I doubt that will be necessary. Here's the history of our interactions in the past, for the record."

A sidebar appeared with the information that Andrea Doan had lodged a complaint against a noisy neighbor. Obrecht brought both parties to his office, a conversation ensued, and that had been the end of it.

Helt took a deep breath and moved his table screen so he could get a full view of the real, unrecorded Andrea Doan sitting at the table here. Maybe she wasn't completely antisocial. People invited her to dinner, at least.

"Cash Ryan was a contract worker who was going back to Earth," Helt said. "We think that two people, perhaps more, were involved in killing him. Of course we want to know who those people were, but the burning question is why they did it. And we don't know that."

Andrea hadn't touched her tea. Her disapproving look didn't change at all.

"Think about it." Helt leaned forward and tried for eye contact. Andrea didn't flinch from it, but her gaze was flat and hooded and hard to read. Helt wondered if she ever blinked, but then she did. "A man's going to leave *Kybele* and be out of the picture forever, but someone kills him. Did you know him?"

"No."

"What about him was worth killing? What was so important about him that just letting him leave wasn't an option? Have you heard anyone talking about him, anyone wondering why he died?"

"No," Andrea said.

"Not even gossip?" Helt asked.

"Just that a man was killed."

Helt moved away from her a little and settled himself more comfortably in his chair. "I've told you why you're here but I haven't told you why *I* am. We know about the money, Andrea. The Seed Banker money."

Mena put down her teacup. It made a sharp sound on the hard surface of the table. It didn't break. "Helt—what are you doing?"

"I'm asking questions, Mena. That's what I'm doing. Personally, I don't think the Seed Bankers had any reason to kill anyone, much less an outsider like Cash Ryan. We suspect he was a psychopath. We know he was a stalker. I am worried that he might have threatened to sabotage something on *Kybele* for some twisted reason or another, and I don't think I'm alone in that worry. So here's a question, Andrea Doan. Do you know if Cash Ryan approached anyone in your group? For any reason?"

Andrea Doan's eyes were wider now.

"These are the names of Seed Bankers we know are on board," Helt said. "We've talked to Kelly Halkett and Susanna Jambekar. We'll be talking to the rest of them today." He flashed the names up.

ORIOL BRUGUERA
ANDREA DOAN
KELLY HALKETT
SUSANNA JAMBEKAR
BENSON LUSENO
AKILA SHENOUDA
MASAKA UEDA

Andrea Doan gave no visible reaction, no acknowledgment, no denial.

"Here's what I think I know," Helt said. "The stated position of the Seed Bankers is that Earth needs to have an off-planet source of genetic material. *Kybele*'s been exporting some stocks to some of the seed banks and frozen zoos on Earth. Those places have been and will continue to be vulnerable to attack and sabotage. Some are lost and can't be restored."

"That's common knowledge," Andrea said.

"Therefore, *Kybele* should stay nearby and safe," Helt said, "and not go chasing off after a future that may not be viable. Am I right about that?"

The muscles in Andrea Doan's neck stood out like ropes. Her lips were sealed tight. She stared at Helt. She hadn't glanced at Mena since she sat down, and she didn't now.

"It's not an evil position to have," Helt said. "It's a sound argument. It is, however, not *Kybele*'s goal."

He let the silence in the room last for a time.

"Freedom of speech and freedom of opinion are important in this ship and I will protect your right to both as long as I am here," Helt said. He could close this and let her run now to spread the news, and he decided to do that. "I will also respect your right to say nothing at all if that's what you choose to do."

Those narrow lips opened at last. "That's what I choose," Andrea said.

"If I were in your position, I might feel the same way," Helt said. "However, if there's anything you want to tell me, now or at any time, I hope you will call me. Not because you like me. Not because you trust me. But because I'm in a position to take action on what's happened. And what hasn't."

Andrea Doan's look said it would be a cold day in hell before Helt heard from her about anything.

"What hasn't happened yet." Helt let the implication hang in the air, to plant the tiny hope that he might be able to change her fate.

"Am I free to go?" Andrea Doan asked.

Helt nodded. He stood when Andrea did, because that's what his mother had taught him, and watched the woman stalk out the door. Andrea didn't slam it behind her, although Helt was braced for the noise.

Mena's teacup was in front of her mouth, a shield to hide her lips. Helt had seen her do that before, sometimes to hide a smile. He didn't think she was hiding a smile right now.

"Well," Giliam Obrecht said.

"Do you think she'll come straight to your office?" Helt asked him.

"I will be remarkably surprised if she doesn't."

"So will I," Helt said. "But I'm hoping she'll contact some of the other Seed Bankers on the way."

Giliam Obrecht sighed. "You seem to have given Legal some new clients. Seven of them."

"I'm afraid so," Helt said. "You have the list, right?"

"I have it. Mena, why didn't you warn me?"

Mena put her cup down. "Because I didn't know any of this was going to happen," Mena said. "Have a good day, Giliam."

"I'll try."

Mena flicked the screens dark. "Talk to me, Helt," she said.

"Gladly." Helt held out his coffee mug. "May I have a little more coffee, please?"

She got up and came around the table to take his cup from his hand. "At least you say please." Her back, turned away from Helt, was rigidly straight. She brought the mug back steaming and sat down in a chair next to him. She looked at him as if he were a mold on a cluster of grapes, something to be destroyed if it threatened her crop.

"All the Seed Bankers have been under surveillance for days," Helt said. "They haven't been in dead zones at the same time; they have had no face-time together for Severo's people to listen in on. Even the two Seed Bankers in Biosystems, who might be expected to cross paths in the Library, haven't done that."

"So you kicked the anthill," Mena said.

"Mena, NSS is plowing through alibis for as many people as they can for the four hours we need to fill in. I want the Seed Bankers implicated or thrown out of the pile."

"They know, as of now, that they're on their way out," Mena said.

"Maybe not quite yet," Helt said. "It could be that Andrea went to

Giliam's office before she talked to them. But they'll know very soon, even if she did."

"Why aren't you worried about what they might do before they leave?" Mena asked.

"As I said, they are in sight and hearing of NSS day and night. I gambled that the risk would be small."

Mena looked at the wall, not at him. "You're rushing things because of Elena."

"Yes," he said, and he wondered how Mena felt about what they had been, Helt and Mena, what they could never be again. Whatever she was feeling didn't look like regret. It looked like anger mixed with fear. "Yes, in part, that's true. But, like you and Archer and Doughan, I'm not fond of the idea of leaving a murderer loose on board."

Mena nodded.

"And you could, as you said, keep your midwife and Andrea, if you want to," Helt said. "Neither of them killed the guy."

"I said I wanted to keep Susanna. It was a bluff."

"To mess with Doughan's head?" Helt asked.

"You know me too well."

But that couldn't have been her only reason. Mena's outburst after Susanna's interview had been meant to be alarming, and it had been. It wasn't unplanned; couldn't have been. She was after something else, perhaps a reaction from Doughan but possibly one from Helt. He didn't know what she had on her mind when she gave them both her challenge, and her intent was no clearer to him now than it had been on Sunday.

"Your position of power is an odd one," Helt said. "Until the ports are sealed, you and the other execs have absolute authority about who stays on board. There is no legal recourse for anyone if you choose to send them away, so Andrea can yell and bang her heels on the floor all she wants. It won't change a thing."

"And poor Giliam will have to listen to it," Mena said.

"He's trained for that. Do you really want to keep Susanna?" Helt asked.

"Yes. I don't know. I wish I knew."

"Will you let me know when you do? The execs need to have their lists of new colonists ready. Biosystems and SysSu can pick two new colonists each, and Navigation gets three."

"I hadn't thought about that," Mena said. "Most of the people on the

Biosystems list were on leave from one institution or another, experts on sabbatical."

"You know some of them want to stay," Helt said.

"I haven't asked," Mena said. "Helt? Usually if there's someone truly special, someone who belongs here, I know it because I hear about it. Not this time. So I have to wonder why I didn't get the speeches, the pleas to keep Jane or John whoever as a colonist. Is it because Biosystems people have closed ranks against outsiders so soon? Are we acting like an elite? A cadre of the chosen; no newcomers wanted?"

"I think the whole ship is doing that," Helt said. "Closing ranks. We're all we have, and we'll work with it. That's a mind-set that has a heavy dose of reality in it."

"I didn't realize. Yes, that's my attitude, and I'm the boss. So people here think I don't want newcomers and I wouldn't listen. That scares me."

"Have you stopped listening?" Helt asked.

"Perhaps I have."

"What's wrong, Mena?"

She looked at the wall for an instant longer and sighed. "Whitetop."

"Huh?"

She stood and walked to the window. "Whitetop, hoary cress, *Cardaria draba*." Mena's words came fast, as if she was relieved to offer up a worry she could talk about. "It's Asian, a mustard, an invasive species if you're re-creating North American grassland, and that's what we did here. It's pretty, white flowers and soft leaves, and it's not good quadruped feed, and it takes over. It's in some of the meadows. A stray seed got in somehow, and thrived."

"You'll get rid of it," Helt said. He got up and stood beside her at the window. The view was clouded fields and distant trees. He saw nothing moving there.

"We will. It's just sometimes—Greenhouses are tricky, Helt. This is a very large greenhouse." She stared out at the curved world. "Do you have any idea how wrong things could go?"

A hollow ball coated with green slime was a worst-case scenario, a nightmare to imagine even for him. He didn't want to think about Mena's nightmares.

"When did you find it?" Helt asked.

"Some flowered this year," Mena said.

"You've associated your visiting profs with noxious weeds," Helt said.

"Some of them are North Americans, yes. It's unlikely they brought the seeds in. Quarantine is thorough. But they arrived when the weed did." She looked up at Helt and her face was a little softer, a little more relaxed. She tried a little smile. "I suppose I could look at the short-timers again. I will. I'll find colonists for us to keep before the shuttle docks."

"I know you will." Helt hesitated for a moment but Mena didn't reach out to touch him, or hug him. "Send the list when you can, okay?"

"Andrea Doan was on a harvest crew that gave themselves a potluck celebration dinner," Mena said. "She was included out of common courtesy. She would not have been there otherwise. She's hard to love. I feel sorry for her, actually."

Mena turned back to the window.

Elena was in her lab, where Helt wasn't going to go, but he remembered the bugs in his pocket and went downstairs. He pasted a few bots over the lab door. It was open. Elena heard him; he wasn't trying to keep quiet but he hadn't said anything.

"A minute," Elena said. She closed her screens and spun her chair to look at him.

"I don't want to bother you," Helt said.

She stood up and stretched. "Bother me," Elena said. She shrugged off her lab coat and grabbed a jacket from the rack. This one was a windbreaker, dark gold. "You have a little time before your next appointment."

Helt nodded. "So I came down to plant surveillance bots on your door. Your lab was bugged already, but these are all mine. Only special people get them." He touched her lip with a finger.

She looked him over and sighed. "I'm glad you included me in the elite. Let's get lunch, shall we?" She shooed Helt out the door and closed it behind her. "We can take the next train to Petra if we hurry."

They went up the stairs to Center at a jog-trot and made it into the seats before the door closed. Elena stretched her legs out in front of her and took a few deep breaths. They shared the passenger car with about six people, all in Biosystems coveralls, all of them absorbed in their interfaces.

"How was your morning?" Helt asked.

"Other than having someone bug my lab, it was good."

"You've kept your interface open and you've kept it with you. It's possible not everyone's done that."

She was watching his face. She nodded. "I slept in a little. I only put in an hour at the lab so far. That's not so good." She scooted back in her seat, propped her right ankle on her left knee and rubbed her calf muscle.

"Hurt?" Helt asked.

"A little. I broke my ankle when I was a kid and sometimes my calf cramps up."

"May I?" Helt covered her hand with his and she let him take over. He worked his fingers down the two long ropes of muscle below her knee and found the knot. He kneaded it, gently at first and then a little harder.

"That's it," Elena said. "Right there. Oh, ouch. Good ouch," Elena said.

He felt the knot soften.

"Should I stop?"

"For now."

Helt let his hand rest where it was. Elena's smile was a promise. Her eyes picked up the colors of her jacket, topaz gemstones incised with radial lines of dark gray, and Helt could hardly wait for the door to her house to close behind them.

"Distract me." Elena lifted his hand away. "Tell me what you should be doing somewhere right now instead of massaging my leg."

Helt sighed and reached for his interface. He checked to see if the surveillance camera showed Andrea Doan on her way to Athens. She was. Yves Copani was with his work crew. His crew was on camera; it was a safety regulation.

"I've seen your appointment schedule," Elena said. "Tell me what's not on it."

Test Yves to clear him or implicate him in the murder. Spend a couple of days sussing out Earthside Seed Banker connections and politics before we question four of ours this afternoon. Find out where Cash Ryan died.

"Cash's story about himself isn't on it. Not your fault. Jerry's looking for it; we all are." Elena's hand was beneath his on the armrest between them. He traced the ovals of her nails with a fingertip. They felt like smooth, warm pearls. He traced them again.

"You thought about that before you said it. It's something else. You have a suspect and you don't want to tell me about it," Elena said.

"Yes."

"You can keep that sort of secret. I don't mind. But you aren't smiling."

"There's something else, something wrong that won't be fixed by kicking the murderer off-ship. Something about governance and power. We carry an atavistic drive to exclude outsiders rather than embrace them. A need to feel safe from external threats, even when there aren't any. This tri-partite system of ours sounds good, a government based on the practicalities of getting us to destination. Food and clothing, that's Biosystems Shelter, and power to make stuff, that's Navigation. Keeping information flowing and available so the other two divisions can do their jobs, that's SysSu. The divisions need each other, so they'll play fair, is the idea. It's a good theory, but there's not much historic precedent to say it's going to work."

"As in none, not really," Elena said. "The Jesuit experiments in South America tried to do that, be fair as they saw fairness; they ruled with the counsel and consent of the governed. But they weren't as isolated as they needed to be to survive."

Helt was pleased that she knew of them. They had worked in an isolation that could no longer exist on Earth, and their intentions had been good ones, better than most, at least. "They had an invisible god to set limits when the Jesuits wanted them set. We don't."

"Helt, we have Buddhists and Muslims and Christians and Neo-pagans and adherents to religions I can't even pronounce on this ship."

"When we need to get married or birthed or buried, some of us have marked down a preferred ritual, yes. A small minority. But the colonist contract gives precedence to reason." Outside the window, the pillars for the Petra section seal passed by, a lethal guillotine waiting to wall out disaster. It meant they were close to the station.

"That's a religion, too," Elena said.

"I know. Sometimes I think a god construct, maybe one of the divisions here, has to personify that abstraction, Reason, has to be the honcho, the Dude of Dudes. We're built like that. We need hierarchy, whether we like to admit it not."

The train slowed for Petra station. A few people waited to get on for Athens. Helt followed Elena out of the warmth of the car, out into cold gray mist.

"It's going to rain," Helt said.

"So we're promised." Elena zipped up her windbreaker.

Helt thought they would get lunch at the canteen and started to go in.

It looked warm and crowded in there. Elena shook her head. "I made lunch for us at home."

"Before you went to Stonehenge."

"I admit to a sad lapse in my devotion to duty," Elena said.

"You guessed I would come and find you this morning."

"I hoped you would. But if you didn't, I figured we would have lunch for dinner."

Whirlpools of mist rose from the river. Helt couldn't see the houses on the opposite wall of the canyon.

"You're saying that when a creature is frightened, it looks for protection and calls it a god," Elena said. "An organism's response to threat has common pathways, whether the organism is a single rabbit or the group of humans walking around *Kybele* right now. Surely someone's factored that need in, here."

"The best scholars on Earth helped with the gaming of this place. But they were a committee. They weren't here. They aren't us."

Drops of water were forming on the lintel over Elena's door. A particularly large and cold one fell on Helt's nose as he stepped in. He brushed it away.

The warm air in the house carried hints of oregano and meat and other good things. He followed the odors of cooking, and Elena, into the kitchen. She lifted the lid from a slow cooker and stirred the steam.

"Pork and green chile stew," she said. "Quesadillas to go with."

Helt leaned over her shoulder to sniff the stew. It smelled wonderful. Elena's neck was handy, and it smelled good, too. He pulled the damp windbreaker away from her shoulders and kissed the nape of her neck.

"I think it could simmer a little longer," Helt said.

This time, he could see her skin, all of it. He could marvel at the strong line of her hip and thigh, a curve of perfection against the window's cloud-gray light. He could match the textures his fingers explored with the intent expression he saw on her face, wonder what she saw in his as her fingers traced the line of his jaw, the corner of his eyebrow.

They had all the time in the world. They had the sound of rain and a shadowed room. She gripped the back of his head and pulled him closer.

Unspoken questions asked with touch and movement, do you like this? This? Is this good? Is this better? No, wait. It will be better if we wait, but there's rhythm, demand, the mingling of sighs and gasps, and after a time he could not tell whose breath he heard.

We have all the time in the world.

He looked up, later, at her lifted knee, the triangle of her leg in silhouette against the backdrop of the right angle of the far corner of the room, and it was the most beautiful geometry he had ever seen.

Elena yawned and stretched and nudged him out of bed.

The green chile held plenty of heat to warm his throat and his belly, but it was deep rich heat and not at all painful. He ate too much of it. Contentment.

Elena served up flan when he was finished with his chile. It was perfect, trembling, tender. He scooped up the last spoonful of caramel from his empty bowl and noticed Elena was frowning at her interface and that it was damned late and he'd better get going.

"What is it?" Helt asked.

"You asked about Ryan's net stash."

"If we had his interface, no problem. If he'd left anything on his home screen, no problem. But he didn't. We have every name that thirty thousand people use on this ship. Seventy-two thousand names, more or less. We're trawling them. We'll find him. Jerry's pulled some lists and of course the likely files are encrypted. It won't be easy, but we'll find him."

"When someone's picking an alias, a common thing to do is keep the first initials. But Cash wouldn't do that. I went to the name he used for his poetry and tried initials up, initials down. Penny Dreadful, O, C above, Q, E, below. Cynric, of kingly lineage. Ryan means 'little king.' I think that one's good. Now, small coins that start with 'O.' "

"Øre," Helt said. "But he would have used the English 'O'; the funny norsk letter would have made the pool too small. The Swedes spell it o, r, e."

"Obol, octavo, ochavo," Elena said. "More letters, if he wanted more letters."

Helt leaned over the table and looked at the screen of her interface. Reading upside down, he saw,

ORE CYNRIC

"One more," Elena said.

Helt moved a little closer and braced his elbows on the table.

ODELL CHALMERS

"Odell, the rich, Chalmers, son of the lord," Elena said. "Cash, so words that refer to money, and perhaps when he was older he decided to give up the fantasy he was a changeling and admit he had a father. I'm just guessing here."

"I know," Helt said.

"Send it to Jerry?" Elena asked.

"Send it to Jerry," Helt said. She did. Helt keyed an access code for override to files with that user name. He watched the lists flash into place on the instant, locations, documents, histories, essays, maybe, cached by Odell Chalmers. Filed on the *Kybele* server and from an ISP near Kitimat. He kissed Elena in hopes that she wouldn't catch a glimpse of them. This was going to help. This was really, really going to help.

"It's here. Do you want to see?" Helt asked.

"No. I don't."

"You're wonderful," Helt said. "Maybe what we need is in here. Maybe this is almost over."

"I hope so. But you were right. I didn't want to look. I still don't," Elena said.

25

The Seed Banker Revolt

They began at the end of Ryan's decoded net stash, Nadia in SysSu with her other work pushed aside, Helt in the train on his way to Navigation offices. The end was the last entry made by Odell Chalmers, posted from *Kybele*'s skin at 1159 on the day he died. During his lunch break, from the crawler he'd been driving that day, he'd written:

AN UPPER HAND
BUOYED BY PALMED SECRETS
RISES TO POWER
AND MOVES YOURS

There was nothing else in that document. At breakfast, in his apartment, written and then deleted, SPIKED SAFE ON SHIFTING ICE.

That was in a poem whose first entry had been made eighteen years before, in Svalbard.

"Hoo, boy," Helt said.

"But it shows where he was, when," Nadia said.

Helt lifted time, date, location data out of the cache of Odell Chalmer's/Cash Ryan's entries and set them aside, a skeleton of fish bones. "If you overlay it on what David I found out about him, there's a match. No secret trips." Helt added a couple of fins to the fish. "No, a few that David I didn't report. Trips to Anchorage," Helt said.

"Anchorage? I'll look at those," Nadia said.

A few minutes later, she said, "It was overnights, no real break in the timeline. That was when he had a job at Kitimat."

Working back, again, from the end, Helt found a document stash of essays. Maybe they were essays. The entries were about coworkers who had no names, only initial letters or nicknames. T did this. Neckwart did that. The reports were flat, with actions reported in the same tone an anthropologist might use when observing apes. Just the facts, no attempt at analysis. Most had not been edited or viewed for years.

More poems, one begun in Vancouver, five years ago.

TO BREAK THE STAINGLASS
HEAR THE VIRGIN'S STACCATO SCREAM
SWEET
BUT THE ROUSED CORE SNARLTASTES ONLY UNPAINED LEAD
SEEKS RAZOREDGE FLOODSURGE
BLOOD AND SALT

Edited during the time Elena was on the Olympic Peninsula, on leave from *Kybele.*

Back again to recent entries. There weren't many. A sort of prose poem about the olive tree and the fountain outside Ryan's quarters.

RUSTLE OF SPEECH IN A LANGUAGE HE CAN'T UNDERSTAND, FOREVER CHANGING IN ERRANT BREEZES. SEMAPHORES OF LEAVES IN UNNATURAL LIGHT. HE WONDERS IF SOMEDAY HE'LL HEAR THE WORDS, SEE THE PATTERNS.

Helt ran Find for the word *I.* It wasn't there. Cash Ryan referred to himself in the third person only.

"Let me overlay this on what we have from his home unit," Helt said. There were time and date match-ups, but Cash had been careful. He'd kept the home unit neutral, for public view, a bland record that Jerry had said was "not quite there," because the rest of it was here, and it still wasn't enough, not the manifesto Helt wanted to find. "We need Jim Tulloch in on sorting out hidden messages in his poetry, if there are any."

"I saw the third person," Nadia said. "And I see that Ryan needed the stimulation of someone else's pain." She sent the folder to Jim Tulloch. "Ryan was ugly, Helt."

And Elena had made love to him. Something dark stirred that asked how she could have, what her blind spots were. Helt felt anger rise, a reaction to the bloodlust he sensed in Ryan's tortured lines; he knew he owned at least a trace of it himself. He wondered if it was something Elena had seen in Cash Ryan and saw now in Helt Borresen.

Stop it. She left him long ago and the man is dead.

AN UPPER HAND
BUOYED BY PALMED SECRETS
RISES TO POWER
AND MOVES YOURS

Created two weeks ago. Ominous, that when he knew he would be leaving *Kybele* for good, Cash Ryan felt himself to have wielded power of any sort. And on the topic of powerless people, Helt was on his way to a meeting with two people who had signed away their right to determine where they would spend the rest of their lives. He wasn't looking forward to it.

"Nadia? How many of the Seed Bankers are cleared for the SM hour? Andrea Doan was busy in Stonehenge; I posted that. Susanna was with Yves, we have camera on that. But the others?"

"Interesting, that," Jerry said. He was back in the SysSu office after talking to Zaida Krupin, and he frowned at the screen in front of him. "Severo hasn't put anyone on it, probably because the interviews are supposed to nail the alibis down."

"We need their alibis run through and posted about an hour ago," Helt said. "What about Zaida?"

The train slowed for Athens station.

"I got nothing new on Ryan's interactions with the crew, just that he was quiet. That Zaida tried to introduce him around when he was a newbie, once or twice, but then she just left him to his own devices. Said he was a pig. A skinny hog."

Duh. Helt tapped his fingers on his forehead, but the face palm he wanted to give himself was more like a giant punch to the ear. NIDAG. Jerry had threaded his real report into the spaces of the conversation he was having with Nadia, right now.

Reading the interstitial as the door opened at Athens station.

Jerry. Zaida on night shift 10/11, overtime favor for a friend. Saw Doughan call up a Tunnelworm +/−2230 and climb in. Was curious.

"Did she? Thanks, Jerry."

Helt searched the Tunnelworm logs. Doughan had ridden a worm, the fast transports that carried workers back and forth through the airless tunnels to the poles, on the night of October 11 and for three nights after. Each trip had been to the North Pole and had lasted about four hours.

It was okay if Doughan made unplanned inspections. He was the exec. Helt didn't know his schedule for such things, and he doubted Doughan posted one. It might be a coincidence that he'd gone to Cash Ryan's work locations three nights running. Uh-huh. Sure it was.

Helt looked for more trips. More trips at night. Only the scheduled trips that took the crews outside showed from then on, with the exception of the ride Severo took the morning after the murder.

The train Helt was on in the here and now stopped at the shuttleport.

There was no one in the lobby except Giliam. He looked small and vulnerable out there. He would make an easy target; tall pillars and shadowed alcoves surrounded the wide expanse, designed for rapid clearing of passengers and freight. Helt, very aware of the back of his neck, walked toward Giliam and tried not to look like he was checking every shadow for motion.

He couldn't see into the Customs office, and he wondered if it was empty or if an NSS officer was in there, maybe several of them, who just happened not to be visible at the moment. Giliam was facing Helt. The door to Doughan's office was behind him. Helt saw it begin to open and deliberately moved his eyes there and back. Giliam raised an eyebrow in acknowledgment.

Once Doughan was in full view, Helt nodded. Giliam turned and fell into step beside him. Their steps sent echoes to the high ceiling and back again.

"Right," Giliam said, sotto voce. "Let's play it by ear, shall we?"

"I expected to see two engineers," Helt said.

"Yes, well." They were three strides away from Doughan. "We're a few minutes early," Giliam said as Doughan stood aside to let them come through the door.

No, they weren't. Helt said nothing.

Doughan looked around the empty lobby and followed them in. The exec's relaxed, athletic stance seemed to be painted over a base of combat readiness. Helt looked for signs of fatigue and decided he found them, a slight pouching of the skin under Doughan's eyes, some rapid blinking, but maybe he only saw them because he was looking for them.

"Where are Ueda and Bruguera?" Doughan asked. He closed the office door. This time the projection that dwarfed his desk was a view of *Kybele* herself, an expanse of black stone peaks and valleys with a sharply curved horizon. Helt imagined the snowball *Kybele* would become once she picked up her load of ice, imagined the landscape as a clean white expanse on a black background, infinity spiked and salted with unwavering points of stars.

One of the struts of the plasma shield passed overhead, part of the immense spindle built around *Kybele.* It was only a massive girder in the sky now, tinted blue by reflected earthlight. Once activated, the structure would look inert until it encountered interstellar rubble. When it did, the tent it formed would incandesce with lethal energies. Helt tried to imagine the fireworks display when that happened, and couldn't.

"I asked them to wait for a few minutes," Giliam said. He walked to the group of chairs near Doughan's Huerfano. "They are in SysSu, where the most excellent Nadia Tay and Gerard Beauchene are doing their best to distract them. The engineers seemed somewhat anxious, and I must say I find their anxiety quite appropriate."

"What the . . ." Doughan began.

"Legal circumlocutions manufactured by me so that I can buy time for your suspects are not on my agenda," Giliam said. "They are *not* my clients, nor can they be. Helt asked me to review, closely, the Seed Banker affiliations of these people."

"And you have," Doughan said. On Earth below, beyond the sharp curve of *Kybele*'s horizon, clouds covered northern Europe. It was raining in London and dry in Spain. Helt looked for a tiny dot that could be the incoming shuttle, but he didn't see it.

"I accepted the Special Investigator's request, naturally, although that means I can't defend any of them if charges are made."

Doughan gave a slight, curt nod. "What did you find?"

"One of these people was a card-carrying Seed Banker for two years, twenty years ago, membership paid for by a parent. Four have attended lectures by Seed Banker speakers, think-tank presentations . . ."

"Who's the former member?" Doughan asked.

"Ueda, who's waiting upstairs."

"A card-carrying member," Doughan said.

"Who never attended a meeting and never corresponded with the organization or its members. California produce was the foundation of the family's wealth. Considerable wealth. Ueda's father bought him a two-year membership in a related organization based in Japan. Support for Seed Bankers is a family tradition. Ueda didn't follow it."

"I see. What about the other engineer who's scheduled to be here now?"

"Oriol Bruguera went to a Seed Banker lecture or two," Obrecht said. "His attendance may have been job related. He was working at Svalbard at the time."

"I'll ask him about that," Doughan said.

"The others? Their connections are as peripheral. The files are in NSS if you'd care to look at them," Giliam said.

So Helt's intuitive skepticism had been right, but his twinge of satisfaction about it vanished, replaced by an overwhelming feeling of dismay. Something had gone very, very wrong.

"So you don't think these seven people are a Seed Banker cell?" Doughan asked.

"Their histories demonstrate no more involvement than anyone who has an interest in *Kybele*'s unique political stance would have," Giliam said. "Exposure to the occasional lecture, glances at articles after headlines caught public interest."

"What about the money?"

"It isn't there," Giliam said.

His matter-of-fact delivery of that bombshell made Helt blink.

"It *what*?" Doughan asked.

Giliam had to be joking. Helt could find no indication of a joke, or psychosis, in Giliam's face. The legalist's expression was one of amused alertness. He stood on the balls of his feet, his hands together behind him, rocking back and forth, waiting for their reaction.

"It isn't there as far as the Seed Bankers know," Giliam repeated. "Oh, the money is quite real, and it's in their accounts. But it's hidden from the account records they can access."

They were all still standing. Doughan turned on his heel and walked toward his desk. "Helt, sit." Halfway there, he said, "You, too, Giliam."

Giliam didn't sit down. He followed Doughan.

Helt's worldview had just tilted, and he didn't like the feeling at all. Archer had given the Seed Banker list to Doughan after the first meeting of the execs, when suicide was still on the books. Helt had accepted the list at face value, had looked at biographies on Midwife Susanna and on Engineer Kelly Halkett, on Andrea this morning, but he hadn't studied the rest of the list.

Archer wouldn't have faked bank accounts. Someone else must have. Which meant SysSu had missed a hacker. But SysSu didn't miss hackers.

"I brought the information I have." Giliam handed over a Huerfano. Doughan looked at its little screen. "Helt linked me the copy he had of the bank statements of these individuals. In that list, each of the accounts received a single deposit of a half million Northern Coalition dollars in the past year. On different dates; the most recent six months ago. The deposits came from two different companies, one in Timor, one in Celebes."

"Archer said something about that. He says they're shell companies for the Seed Bankers," Doughan said.

"When I accessed these seven accounts yesterday, here on *Kybele*, as if I were the account holder, those deposits don't exist. Were never made."

"How'd you do that?" Helt asked.

"You asked me to look at Seed Banker accounts," Giliam said. "I'm a bank auditor for SysSu from time to time, Helt. I have access."

Helt wanted to grab something solid and hang on to it. He gripped the arm of the chair he was sitting in, but it didn't help much. "Archer said they had done nothing with the money. He found that strange." A cascade of possibilities ran through his mind, but he couldn't process this, couldn't fit it together. Archer Pelham was a careful man. Archer had looked for strange sources of money on an ongoing basis, he'd said, and found them, and brought these seven people to Doughan's attention. And Archer had been wrong.

Someone who didn't know Wesley Doughan might not have seen the hesitation, the *augenblick* required for Doughan to process the information and run through possible responses. Helt saw it. He was pretty sure Giliam saw it, too. He wondered what was showing on his own face.

"Helt, did you know this?" Doughan asked.

"I should have. I didn't." He had trusted Archer. Giliam knew the list came from Archer; Helt had told him so.

The next move belonged to Doughan. Helt hoped Doughan would do the right thing, get this into the open. It would be so easy to close ranks, to fall into the trap of hiding his fellow exec's slip-up from the public. But Giliam wasn't the public.

"Whatever Archer thought or knew—" Doughan said. "Oh, hell. Let's ask him."

Helt's sense of relief was physical and profound. A lot of back and shoulder muscles returned to more or less normal but his neck was still tight and it was going to hurt later.

Severo's voice spoke from Doughan's desk. "We have a situation."

Helt looked down at the red light blinking on his interface. Jerry's face came up. Giliam tapped his own interface. "We need you up here," Jerry said. His words came through while Severo kept talking.

"Eight people are in SysSu and they want to talk to Helt real bad," Severo said.

"Eight? Which eight?" Doughan asked.

"The Seed Bankers. And Susanna's boyfriend."

It could be that Cash Ryan had framed them all. He had some skills at manipulating data; he'd managed to doctor his work résumé.

"Bring them here," Doughan said.

"No!" Helt said. There was, there had to be, a connection between them and Cash Ryan, even if wasn't Seed Banker money. If he could get them focused on what the connection might be, if they could believe that all that was wanted from them was a solution to this murder, if. But the balance between trust and suspicion was going to be hellishly difficult to maintain. "Jerry, take them to the conference room upstairs."

"Here. This area is easier to secure," Doughan said.

Helt stood up. "If they get violent, you and Severo can shove them through the windows," Helt said. "I need the resources I have up there." Meaning, in this case, Jerry and Nadia. Meaning Archer down the hall. He went to the office door, opened it, and held it open.

Doughan looked up at him and didn't move. So the battle's lost, Helt figured.

"You gave me the job," Helt said. "Let me use the tools I have. Let's get this settled in the next two hours so we can get back to work. Sir."

Stonefaced, Doughan pushed himself out of his chair and walked past Helt without a word. Giliam caught up with him two steps past the office door.

Helt closed the door carefully. The muscles in his forearms were trembling.

The train enclosed them in the strange privacy common to the role of passenger. The three of them took one of the four-booths with a worktable, Doughan and Helt side by side, close enough to touch and completely isolated from each other, Giliam opposite, all of them elsewhere with minds and fingers busy. Helt called Archer, audio.

"What is it?" Archer was in his office, good.

"Bad. Look at this and tell me what happened." Helt sent the differences in account balances last Thursday side by side.

As the impact hit, Archer pushed back in his chair and gave the data a profoundly disapproving look. "Where did this come from?"

"Giliam," Helt said.

Giliam looked up from his own work at the sound of his name. Someone else's conversation. He pulled his screen closer to his nose and returned to his own pursuits.

"Where is he?" Archer asked.

"With me. We'll be in the conference room upstairs."

"Where's Doughan?"

"He's coming, too," Helt said. He switched to Jerry, audio. "The Seed Bankers all have alibis now?"

Jerry. All except Halkett and Benson Luseno. Text. Jerry had someone in the office with him.

"Okay," Helt said. If all of them had documented alibis the announcement of that might clear the air. But they didn't. Helt would have to sidestep that inconvenience.

He peered into usage and found Archer and Giliam in a rapid text exchange. Doughan and Severo, ditto.

Jerry. They got together in The Frontier before they came up here.

Helt. Thanks.

It was a five-minute ride and it was over.

The train told them to watch their step.

The stone paving of the agora was rain-washed, wet. The afternoon light was set for dark autumn gray. In a surely unintended consequence of its diffusion, thin silver frames outlined the edges of walls and windows and turned the buildings into an architect's blueprint with no depth, no solidity. Earthlight could never do this. Helt stepped carefully on the apparently liquid surface of the agora. It felt solid, not at all like a mirage. That was reassuring.

The air in SysSu hit his face like a warm slap. Doughan and Giliam on his heels, Helt led them upstairs.

Two NSS officers flanked the conference room door, probably stationed there by Severo. The feel of this discussion was not going to be casual.

Nadia had left three chairs vacant at the center of the horseshoe of people. Helt took the center one, facing the empty display stage, comforted, a little, by controls familiar to his fingers and the feeling of security that comes from home territory. He glanced at the empty gray windows at the far end of the room. It was awfully damned quiet in here.

Doughan on his right and Giliam on his left, and faces. On the right side, Doughan's side, Nadia got up from her chair next to Doughan's and went to the coffeepots. Next to Nadia's chair, Susanna Jambekar, in blue scrubs, huddled beneath a miner's jacket that probably belonged to Yves. He sat beside her, his body-builder arms bulging beneath the rolled-up sleeves of a work coverall. Yves didn't look cold. His hands were flat on the table in front of him, as immobile as the stone he loved to work, but he was watching every motion in the room.

Nadia and Jerry began the coffee ritual, each one carrying a coffeepot, one on each side of the room.

"Cream? Sugar?" Nadia asked Yves, and the silence broke into murmurs and mutterings.

Down the line to the left, Giliam, Jerry's empty chair, Andrea Doan, who sported a bright red slash of lipstick, Kelly Halkett in his work coveralls, Severo next to him.

Beyond Severo, the two soccer player engineers, Ueda and Bruguera, an unlikely contrast of genetic heritages from lines that went back to medieval Japan and Roman Gaul. Helt did a thumbnail assessment of them as athletes. Ueda looked like he'd be fast on his feet. He had a compact body, the sort that wants to get pudgy unless a person works hard to stay fit. Oriol Bruguera was called "Birdy" because of his name. He looked more like a hawk than an oriole, a thin, hungry hawk. Beside them, Benson Luseno, a Kenyan brought up in Liverpool, an ESL teacher with offices in the Library. His dolichocephalic head was shaved to a gloss and his hands were delicate, small and plump, like a child's. Akila Shenouda sat at his left, an archaeologist out of Egypt. She was young and had been here five years, a member of the most recent batch of colonists.

Helt took a deep breath. "This is a mess. It needs fixing. You want to talk to me; I want to talk to you. We have work to do and some misconceptions to explain." The expressions he saw ranged from expectant to openly angry. He saw outrage, wounded dignity, and varying degrees of fear. Akila seemed terrified. Helt glanced at her history; at age four she'd been injured in a water riot in Cairo. So many histories.

It was time for stagecraft. Helt had to look like he knew what he was doing, had to let every move, every modulation in his voice, reinforce the conviction that this meeting was going to stay calm and reasonable, that there would be time to say everything that needed to be said.

He knew at least the first move of the game he wanted to play.

"I assume you're here because I showed Andrea Doan a list of your names."

"She contacted us, yes," Kelly Halkett said.

"Yves?" Helt asked. "Your name was not on that list."

"I'm here with Susanna," Yves said.

Someone, any one of them, could have objected, or asked that Yves be excluded. Yves looked up and offered eye contact to anyone in the room who wanted it. Some met his gaze, others made little acknowledgment of his presence. No one objected. Maybe it was the muscle-to-fat ratio of Yves's arms that kept them quiet.

"From the morning after Cash Ryan's murder until about twenty minutes ago, we worked under the assumption that the people in this room belonged to a Seed Banker cell and had been funded to carry out a plan to keep *Kybele* from leaving orbit."

Helt couldn't watch all the reactions, but the cameras wouldn't have that problem. A lot of screen cap review would be going on later. What he did see were people whose initial shock was quickly replaced by a determination to look impassive. Doughan and Severo had worn those masks from the beginning. Giliam was busy with his screen and seemed oblivious to the room.

Helt felt like he was facing a jury.

"Here's what we saw Thursday morning. October the nineteenth." Helt distributed a summary of each person's bank account to the individual screens facing them; a slight nod to a privacy that did not exist. "Please note the deposits, and the dates of the deposits."

Yves leaned over to look at Susanna's screen. He looked at Susanna's face. He looked back at the balance. Oriol Bruguera whistled. Kelly Halkett frowned. The other reactions were mostly disbelief.

Doughan, silent at Helt's right hand, seemed content to let his presence say that this gathering was happening with the full consent of the execs on *Kybele*. Helt sensed no impatience in him; he was attentive, alert, neutral, and impressive.

Helt still didn't know if any of the people in the room had seen the inflated numbers go by; if the fake balances had been sent, however briefly, to personal screens.

"As a precaution, I asked Giliam to look at the deposits again," Helt said. "This is what he found. What we think you might have seen on Thursday, if you happened to check your account that day." Helt split-screened the individual balance sheets, without the Seed Banker deposits, side by side with the inflated numbers.

Jerry. Who's looked when? You want that?

Helt. Yes. Damn straight he wanted that. **Helt. Did it show on personal screens? Or just to SysSu that day?** If someone had slipped *him* a half million, would he have squawked about it to the bankers? It would be tempting just to wait it out for a while, see how long it took for the system to catch the error.

"So that's the money you were talking about," Andrea Doan said.

"Yes. Deposits from companies known to be fronts for the Seed Bankers, designed to draw attention to the nine of you."

"Is it real?" Kelly Halkett asked.

"It's real," Giliam said.

"Is it still there?" Halkett asked.

"It is," Helt said.

"Cash Ryan did this?" Susanna asked.

"Cash Ryan or his murderers. You've been under surveillance because of this information, all of you."

"Then I trust you'll stop doing that as of now," Kelly Halkett said.

Severo leaned forward and rested his forearms on the table as if protecting the space between them. He looked at Kelly Halkett. "I'm not sure turning off the surveillance would be a good idea. I tell you, I'd like to get some people off overtime. They say watching you guys is boring."

That brought a few polite smiles, but even polite smiles lifted the grim mood in here, a little.

"But the thing is, if none of you killed him, you're in danger from the people who did." Severo leaned back in his chair again.

Helt could have hugged him. The goal had been surveillance, not protection, but the danger was real enough. Severo was, in a way, doing his best to cover Helt's ass. And his own, and Doughan's, for that matter.

"We've questioned some of you, one at a time," Helt said. "We had planned to talk to each of you individually, but Jerry tells me you all showed up together."

"We wanted to know what was going on," Kelly Halkett said. "We wanted to find out why suspicion for this terrible crime was laid on us. You've told us. That was the question I was delegated to ask."

Helt. Kelly named spokesman at the Frontier?

Jerry. Yes. btw, Doan, Halkett, Luseno and Shenouda checked their bank balances Wednesday morning.

It was interesting that Halkett had been picked out for leadership in that quick meeting. Helt had found him to be taciturn, even slow to catch conversational cues. Revise that; his slowness was more likely the effect of careful thinking, and the group must have found something solid to cling to in him. Andrea Doan, sitting beside him, had her arms crossed over her chest. Her neck looked distended, like someone was choking her. She looked like she was going to have a stroke.

"We're looking for the source of those deposits." Alerts should have flared for the accountants in SysSu and for Archer. They hadn't. "All of you have my sincere apologies that we didn't find that out before today."

"This is an outrage," Andrea Doan said. Her voice was a guttural growl. Jerry shifted in his chair and looked at her. Andrea's eyes were on Helt. She made a sudden motion and Jerry caught her right fist. Helt felt, more than saw, Severo and Doughan decide not to go into attack mode. But he'd seen Severo glance down and plan his route under the table and across the empty center space to Andrea's chair. Yves had put his arm around the back of Susanna's chair. His right arm was in sight, palm curled, ready to become a fist.

"Easy, now." Kelly Halkett's Scots burr was thick in his voice. "Easy," as if she were a skittish horse.

Jerry put Andrea's hand on the table and patted it. She kept on staring knives at Helt but she stayed in her chair.

"Yes, it's an outrage," Helt said. "Again, you have my apologies. We made assumptions based on bad information. It was a mistake. We're correcting it as fast as we can. Our assumption is that the hacker wanted attention directed to you. The question is, why?"

"We're on a hit list?" Susanna asked.

"Or Cash Ryan knew he was in danger and wanted to point us out if something happened to him." Benson Luseno spoke public school English, baritone, carefully modulated. Pitch perfect. Thank you, Professor Luseno, and all the mysteries you've read.

"It's possible," Helt said. "Looking at what Cash Ryan did in the past three years—we know he stalked Susanna Jambekar and Elena Maury."

Not everyone in the room had known that, and their faces showed it.

Akila looked across the table and stared hard at Susanna's face, searching for something, but Helt couldn't sort out what it was she wanted to find there. Andrea closed her lips into a thin line that made her red lipstick vanish completely.

Helt. Nadia, look for e-mails Andrea/Odell Chalmers?

"One possibility is that he hacked your bank accounts in a way that would get you sent off this ship." Helt had just told all of them they were on the off-list, or had been. Now they weren't, as far as Helt was concerned. But Kelly Halkett's and Benson Luseno's actions on Wednesday evening were still not verified.

Assume innocence until someone's proved guilty. But someone is, and that someone could be in this room.

"Susanna and Dr. Maury were unaware they'd been stalked until we told them about it. We know that Dr. Halkett had very little contact with Cash Ryan. The rest of you? However brief, if you had interactions with him of any sort, let's put them on record." He'd start with Benson Luseno. Akila Shenouda after that.

Doughan tapped his interface and stood up. "Pardon me." The exec addressed the room at large. "Archer wants me. I'll be just down the hall."

To Jerry and Nadia. Helt??

Jerry. Doughan wants Archer, actually.

Helt wanted to talk to Archer himself, right now and not later. He wanted to see, up close and personal, Archer's reactions to the deposit records Helt had just sent him. Obviously, Doughan wanted to do that, too.

Doughan's departure put a different mix of energies into the room. The big boss was gone, and that lessened performance anxiety a little. Doughan's interface traced him to the door of Archer's office. He had gone where he said he would go. It was time for Helt to get back to work right here.

Helt. Okay. Akila-Ryan connections? Proximity captures?

Nadia. I'll get them.

"Professor Luseno?" Helt asked. "Far-fetched speculation is welcome."

Benson Luseno had seemed oblivious to Andrea's outburst, to Doughan's departure. He had been a quiet observer, but he seemed to be carrying on an interior monologue, as if rehearsing a speech.

"This morning's message from Dr. Doan certainly led to plenty of speculations by me," Benson Luseno said.

"Speculations about Cash Ryan, please, sir."

Benson Luseno took a quiet, deep breath from the diaphragm. "Cash Ryan came to my office only once. He appeared at one of my Tuesday office hours. Two and a half years ago, as best I can recall."

Heh. Well-modulated tones, volume just so, Benson Luseno stepped into the role of professorial authority.

"He brought a handwritten poem of his, on paper, and asked if I would critique it," Luseno said. "I post reviews now and again."

As self-promotion went, it was fairly inoffensive, but Helt didn't think he wanted to read them.

"I told him I attempted such an exercise—and critiquing poetry is only that—only on published works, because budding poets can be so easily discouraged."

Nadia. Akila works in Library, has an office there. Research for her dissertation on Chalcolithic metallurgy.

"But he persuaded you," Helt said.

"He seemed so earnest, so naive," Luseno said.

"And you read the poem."

"I told him I would look at it and he could return on the next Tuesday. You're going to ask me if I have a copy of the work. I don't. The poem was blank verse, at least, no attempt at rhyme or meter. It described the daily life of a cyborg. One who performed boring, repetitive work, day after day, with precision and a troubled conscience."

"Do you remember any of the lines?" Helt asked.

"No. I do not. I do remember I sensed a mingling of disgust and longing in it. It was quite disturbing."

The professor stopped.

"Disturbing," Helt said.

"The conceit was journal entries, one entry per year. Each year, different parts of the machinery of this cyborg were mutilated, quite graphically. The troubled conscience belonged to the cyborg as it sought ways to work around its disabilities."

"What did you tell him?" Helt asked.

"I handed it back to him when he returned and asked him if he was familiar with *My Last Duchess.* He looked at me with an utterly expressionless face and left the office."

"*My Last Duchess,*" Helt said.

"I find it odd, yes, that I chose an unfaithful woman as an example of a poem he might read," Luseno said. "There was no specific mention of gender in Ryan's poem."

Helt found it odd that Luseno mentioned the victim of founded or unfounded jealousy but not her death-dealing husband.

"Did it cross your mind he might have been dangerous? A threat to you or anyone else?"

"I've read a great deal of student poetry, sir. One becomes less and less alarmed by it over time." Said with the faintest trace of amused disdain. Luseno seemed to know it would be a closing line.

Helt nodded. "Thank you."

Nadia. Six Ryan-Shenouda delayed-proximity captures two years ago. None since.

Andrea/Odell Chalmers, messages, yes. Flirting.

Akila tensed when she realized it was her turn. Arched black eyebrows guarded sloe eyes; her eyes were her best feature. She had long black hair.

"Do you remember any contacts with Cash Ryan, Dr. Shenouda?" Helt asked her.

"Miss, please. I'm ABD—I'm trying to recall if I did," she said. "I don't think so."

"Could he have contacted you about your work?"

Akila Shenouda looked at him directly for the first time. "I correspond with most of the experts in Chalcolithic archaeology. That's five or six people on Earth. I get the occasional inquiry from a student, but no. My answer is no."

Nadia. Shenouda captures ready.

Helt. Thx. He glanced at them quickly.

Helt. Expand #6?

Nadia did. The last capture was outside the Library, same location as several others, 1817 on a spring evening two years ago. Akila, shadowed under the portico, reached for Officer Evans's hand. Officer Evans, Severo's second-in-command. They walked away together. Cash got up from a café table and went in the opposite direction. Helt decided not to show the footage.

"Thank you, Miss Shenouda." He looked toward the far end of the table, its empty seats with their backs to the darkening windows. He'd heard Susanna's story, Halkett's, Andrea's, and now, Luseno's and Dr. Shenouda's, if only in part. That left the football-playing engineers. A usage check showed him that Ueda and Bruguera had been texting each other nonstop, in here, while the others were talking. "Kelly Halkett told us that Drs. Ueda and Bruguera played football with Cash Ryan."

Oriol Bruguera looked at Halkett with surprise. Masaka Ueda shook his head. "That is not entirely accurate."

"Please tell us," Helt said.

"Birdy and I have been reviewing what we know of this man," Ueda said.

Jerry. You want text? Nothing else in there.

Helt. Gimme.

Helt caught a glimpse of it and then nodded to the engineers. Their messages to each other in the past few minutes were reviews of where and when they remembered being around Cash Ryan, and nothing more, from the quick read he gave them.

"Between us, we came up with this," Masaka said. "We were messing around the field one afternoon after work and Cash Ryan showed up and watched us for a while. We said hi, and he told us he had grown up in North America, and didn't know football, and wondered how hard it was to learn."

Birdy nodded agreement.

"So we said, well, it's not easy, but if you want to try . . ."

"But it didn't come to much," Oriol Bruguera said.

"He showed up a couple of times and then didn't," Ueda said. "He could have learned to move the ball around, I think."

"He was athletic enough?" Helt asked.

"Yeah, but you know how it is," Birdy said. He drew a rectangle in the air and his hands zigzagged an imaginary ball across an imaginary field in it. "You tap the ball around, you've done it all your life. Someone who's doing it for the first time, you have to be really patient, you know? You start talking about strategy and the need to study the field, know where your mates are likely to go, cooperation, passes."

"Maybe Birdy's chatter scared him off," Ueda said.

If Ryan's game had been to stay invisible by tending to the norm, a team sport would have helped. Jerry had mentioned that Ryan was a little too standard, that his presence in the records felt thin. Play a little in the intramurals, look like part of a team. If you have to learn human behavior by observation and you're bright, and that was Jim Tulloch's model of Ryan, you can mimic being normal really well. Up to a point.

"We told him to practice, every day, every day," Birdy said.

"And that was it?" Helt asked.

Birdy Bruguera nodded.

"That was it," Masaka Ueda said.

They had rejected him. It was too simple a theory, but there it was. So far, everyone here had rejected Cash Ryan in small ways. Elena's rejection had been a bigger blow than anyone here had given him, but Cash hadn't named her on the Seed Banker list. Helt *assumed* it was Cash's list. Perhaps he had other plans for Elena. Perhaps someone else had made the list. Helt couldn't rule that out. He'd hoped Archer would show up with an explanation of where and when it had been made, but he hadn't, yet.

Helt's eyes were tired. He rubbed them, because he wanted to, and because he wanted to look a little bit vulnerable, wanted to show some of his very real fatigue. Stagecraft.

"So," Helt said. "Andrea, we've heard from everyone here but you."

She shook her head. "I didn't know the man."

"But you did exchange a few e-mails with someone named Odell Chalmers."

He watched as she sorted through memories and set her jaw.

"Why is that important?" Her delivery of the question was dull and flat, an automatic challenge while she searched for a way to become the wounded party in this interchange.

"Odell Chalmers was a net name Cash Ryan used." Helt watched her realize that SysSu was now familiar with her skill with expletives. Her last e-mail to Odell Chalmers had included some inventive insults in English and in Spanish, and some truly twisted emoticons that didn't require translation.

Andrea's reaction could have been anything, embarrassment, defiance, a useless denial. What she did was shrug her shoulders and smile at Helt, the smile of a kid caught with her hand in the cookie jar. He liked her better, seeing that smile.

To give her credit, Andrea hadn't gone running straight to Giliam; she'd alerted the others on the accused list first. Find her a cause and she would divert her bitterness to defending the innocent. Helt would offer this newly made theory to Mena, and maybe Andrea's life would be a little easier for her—and for those around her.

Helt looked away and stared at the windows, not at any individual face. The agora was lighted for night now; gold lamplight against a dark sky. "All of you see it, don't you? The common thing in all these stories. Susanna and Elena and Andrea turned down Ryan's invitations for sex. Akila, camera captures show he didn't get close enough to you to even ask. You were well guarded. You can see the captures if you want."

"I—would like to see them," she said. Helt sent them to her screen.

"Birdy and Ueda didn't want to play ball with him, in a very real sense," Helt said. "Benson Luseno didn't recognize him as the next Byron. And Kelly Halkett approved a transfer request from a crew that didn't want to work with him. In one way or another, all of you rejected him."

"He wanted to ruin our lives because we hurt his tender feelings?" Kelly Halkett asked.

"Maybe," Helt said. "It's a theory. I'd prefer facts." Like facts about where Luseno had been on Wednesday night, and Kelly Halkett's location that evening. Unanswered questions were still hanging in the air. "You know, none of you need to feel special. We're building individual narratives for that single day on almost everyone on this ship. We have to, because this guy was so invisible to us. Information that's been recorded is what we have to work with, and by design, there are large areas of everyone's life that aren't captured. We're connecting dots about that." Luseno, Halkett, you aren't off the hook yet. And if Archer surprises me, none of you are.

To Jerry and Nadia. Helt. Can you herd them to The Lab? Give me a few minutes and I'll join you if I can.

A few minutes, for Helt wanted to see what was going on in Archer's office. Helt glanced over and watched a sotto voce interchange between Jerry and Severo.

"I'd like to stop here for now," Helt said.

Jerry lifted his head and looked at the group. "I figure NSS owes you a drink," Jerry said. "All of you. On Severo. It's happy hour at The Lab."

26
Cold Places

Archer's door was closed and Helt didn't hear Doughan's voice as he approached it. He heard a solo cello. His tap on the door was answered by Archer grumbling something undecipherable, which probably meant "Come in."

"The deposits were faked by someone in SysSu," Archer said.

His room was as dark as the agora its walls reproduced. His face was striped green and yellow by the pool of screen light. "The telltales were blinking when I came in here after the exec meeting that morning. Thursday. Large deposits that in each case I could trace back to the dates and depositors, as if the inflated balances had been there through months of routine deposits and withdrawals." He leaned forward to give his screen his under-the-eyebrow look. "It was well done, as if the system had fixed a glitch and was reporting it as clearly as it could. The companies that made the deposits are infiltrated by NCII, which is no surprise. "

Northern Coalition Intersystem Intelligence, Helt translated. It was tempting to build a conspiracy theory and it went like forces had shifted on Earth below. The Northern Coalition now wanted *Kybele* to stay home and was funding saboteurs to make that happen in a deniable way.

"I've checked in several ways," Archer said, meaning, he'd crawled through files to which very few people had access. "NCII had nothing to do with it. The fake deposits came from one of ours."

One of ours, Helt thought. One of ours, but I thought we'd scolded the mischievous long ago, and this was more than mischief. This was meant to hurt.

"It couldn't have been Ryan?"

"No." The cello, a recorded one, began a crescendo. Archer silenced it.

"How long was the play-money on view to the account holders?" Helt asked.

"Four hours," Archer said. "Four morning hours. I saw it, looked it over, and we went down to see Doughan. I didn't look again until Giliam got upset."

So some of the Seed Bankers had, in fact, seen the figures, and not said anything about them. As Helt thought he would have done himself—for a few hours.

"Where did you find the list of names you gave Doughan?" Helt asked.

"From the deposits." Archer looked up at Helt with a puzzled expression, as if he'd just noticed someone else was in the room.

"Not in Cash Ryan's records?"

"No."

"Not in the Odell Chalmers stash?"

"I haven't studied those documents at all," Archer said.

"Ryan couldn't have done it?"

"No. I thought he might have used right-to-forget protocols on some of the information, but they don't work and never did and aren't legal anyway. To fake his transcripts and such he used something so transparent it shouldn't have worked."

Archer sounded bemused, as if he were thinking out loud and no one was around to listen to him.

"It took me longer than it should have to sort out what he'd done. I was expecting sophistication. Ryan simply copied the documents to his own files, changed the numbers he wanted changed, reformatted them to match the styles of the websites they came from. And then he put up links to the original documents, but nobody bothered to follow them. They were legit links, but, after all, the info David I wanted was already right there in front of him." Archer sighed. "And I imagine David II simply followed his lead. Trust is a dangerous thing, Helt. Never trust it."

"Where's Doughan?" Helt asked.

Archer turned back to his screen and brought up a locator map. He pointed at Doughan's dot on it, in the SysSu building. In Archer's office. "Right here."

On Archer's desk, close to the visitor's chair, Doughan's interface stared blind at the ceiling.

He'd seen Archer like this before, lost in his work, in pursuit of something he was determined to find, Helt told himself, except that really wasn't so. He'd never seen Archer quite so detached from the room around him, so unaware of his actual physical space. "Doughan's right here." Right.

Helt would have to review whatever Archer found here tonight, and he knew it.

Please, not senility, don't let it be that, he pleaded to the forces of entropy. Maybe there's a way to march him to Calloway for some diagnostics and maybe Nadia could help get him there. It might be diet. It might be fatigue; it might be shame that he had done something remarkably stupid and should have known better.

One of ours. If he didn't find the culprit Helt would be forced to accept that it was Archer. Archer would do it . . . to protect the ship. To protect a friend. Archer wouldn't do it.

Helt wondered if Mena had taken on the job of making sure Archer got the occasional balanced meal; Archer had said she brought him *galaktobourekos*, but maybe she brought him other things as well. For tonight, it was unlikely Archer, or SysSu's records, would come to further harm. Copies of the Seed Banker stuff were in NSS records, and Helt was being a hovering old maid.

Helt reached down and picked up Doughan's interface. "I guess Doughan forgot this. I'll take it to him. Good hunting, Archer."

He left the old man there, facing a screen filled with strings of code.

Out in the damp dark, he zipped up his windbreaker and shoved his free hand in a pocket. Doughan might have gone to his office. He might have gone home. Both of those locations could be checked easily enough. Helt walked toward The Lab. Elena was in Stonehenge.

Helt. I'll be working late.

Elena. I missed some of it, but wow. Just wow. Audio?

"Sure," Helt said.

Elena was in her dark lab with her embryos, and all that her camera saw of her face was a doubled red dot, an indicator light reflected from the lenses of her infrared goggles.

"I'm working late, too" Elena said. "The path reports came in from Mass General."

"Any surprises?" Helt asked.

"Some news. Some important news. He had a small, deformed amygdala. I texted Jim. He was right about that."

The man really had been a psychopath. There were physical defects in his brain. It felt so cold, so useless, to have proof of it now.

"I ran methylation assays on his neural DNA. I was looking for elevations, like you see with intrauterine stress or PTSD syndromes, but he's remarkably free of them. As if he'd never been stressed by anything. It's a marker on how he saw the world. The lack of markers is also a mark."

The hums of quiet motors and a gentle, tidelike swishing sound filled her lab.

"Really, truly a psychopath?" Helt asked.

"Or really, truly, an unexpected death. I wonder if Jim ever talked to his mother." Elena was only a voice; she had moved away from the indicator light.

"He was trying. Could you ask him?" Helt stood outside the faux-oak door of the tavern called The Lab and stared at the black screen of his interface. There was information to be found inside; who had come with Jerry and Nadia, who had not, and why. But he couldn't sit in the warmth and nurse a brew and let the chatter fill in some of the blanks for him; Doughan had gone missing.

"Tonight?" Elena asked.

"It's not that late. If I finish up early"—yeah, right, his inner voice told him—"should I come up to Stonehenge?"

"I don't know," Elena said. She looked away. "Jim's calling. Check in now and again, okay?"

"Okay."

The group from SysSu had picked a big round table crowded with mugs and glasses, dotted with red glass lights and pitchers of beer and bowls of salted peanuts. Severo faced the door, as always. He was deep in conversation with Martin Kumar, who sat next to Nadia. Jerry was on her other side. Then Akila Shenouda beside Officer Evans; Ueda and Giliam next. They had their heads together about something. Brugera and Yves were diagramming football plays, four hands drawing air pictures over a barrage of Spanish and Italian that may have been mutually comprehensible to them, but perhaps not to Kelly Halkett. He sat between the two of them and watched the display with a pleased expression on his face.

Susanna wasn't there. Andrea Doan wasn't, either. Jerry looked up from his unfolded screen and gave a wave. Helt waved back and took one of the empty chairs between Giliam and Yves.

To Jerry. Helt. I'm going walkabout with Yves. Alibis on Luseno and Halkett yet?

Jerry. Not yet.

Helt. More Ryan info here?

Jerry. Go away and we'll get some. We're having fun.

Helt figured that meant Jerry and Nadia were building some bridges with this group and Helt was, as yet, too heavy to walk on them. Trust is a tender thing, and Helt didn't really deserve it, not with this group. It would take time to develop some, if it could ever be done. If he was here to do the work after the last shuttle left.

"And *that* was the win for Real Madrid," Oriol Bruguera said, in English.

"Well played," Kelly Halkett said. "You bring back the game as if you had watched it live." He shoved a glass in Helt's direction and lifted a pitcher. Helt waved it aside.

"Can't tonight," Helt said.

"I *did* watch it live," Oriol said.

"From your mother's lap?" Yves asked.

"From my dad's. I was two years old. I remember it like yesterday."

"And the next game?" Yves asked.

"I remember nothing about that one. *Nada.*"

Yves shook his head in sympathy. "I understand, brother."

Helt grabbed a handful of peanuts and put them in a pocket. He took more and began to munch them.

Kelly Halkett looked at his companions and then at Helt. "So you're still working tonight."

Helt swallowed his peanuts. "I am," Helt said.

"There was another thing this group of accused asked me to tell you before we came up to the big room. It's that we, any and all of us, want to help find these killers. What we might offer is unclear, but we're trainable."

Yves and Oriol added grave nods of assent.

"Thank you," Helt said. The statement had been the group's decision *after* they had been told they were singled out as Bad Guys. Even knowing that, they'd offered their support. Yeah, maybe they thought the offer would make them look more sympathetic to a hostile observer, but Helt didn't think this was a PR maneuver. It felt more like an expression of an ancient imperative. The tribe is threatened; we must protect it.

Doughan had told Helt he had a character flaw, that he would have sympathy for the devil himself. And here sat Kelly Halkett, whose whereabouts on the night of the murder were still unknown, saying he wanted to help with a criminal investigation that could possibly lead to charges against him. Doughan's comment had been close to the mark, but what Helt felt for Kelly Halkett was both sympathy and admiration. "You're still willing to say that, even though we stalked you due to a mistake we made?" Helt asked.

"My calculations say that you began corrective action to rectify your mistake with all due speed, Mr. Borresen. That implies you're knowledgeable about the structural limitations of the materials you work with."

"Meaning humans." Helt swallowed hard. He'd need to get some water before he left. "Myself among them. I accept the offer of help, with gratitude. For tonight, I'd like to borrow Yves."

Yves, a man he scarcely knew, a man he hadn't managed to find time to talk to since he'd asked him to take a portfolio to David II, a man whose partner had been grilled, and not pleasantly, by him and the execs. Yves, who could have killed Cash Ryan out of jealousy.

"Just Yves?" Oriol Bruguera asked.

"For tonight, yes." Oriol looked disappointed.

Yves narrowed his eyes and gave Helt a look-over. Assessing for structural damage, maybe. Assessing for vulnerable points where damage might be inflicted, by Yves, physically. The sculptor shrugged and pushed his beer mug aside. "Yeah, sure. Let's go."

"As soon as I get some water." Helt grabbed a clean mug and got up. He headed for the bar to beg water and stopped on his way past Severo. "Have you seen Doughan?"

"I thought he was with Archer."

"He's not there now. He left his interface in Archer's office. If you see him, tell him I have it."

"You might try his quarters. It's time for dinner, you know."

"I know," Helt said. "I'll see if he's home." On his way back to the table, drinking water while he walked, it was just so perfectly damned clear that Jerry and Nadia and Martin Kumar were a trio, and happy about it.

Helt put his empty glass down on a table. Yves was waiting at the door, and he looked impatient.

Yves beside him on the clean, rain-washed street. The night was programmed for cloudy skies.

"I owe Susanna a personal apology," Helt said. "I hoped she would be with you guys."

"Nah, she went home to sleep for a while. She has the night shift at the clinic."

"Then I shouldn't bother her."

"You bother her already," Yves said. "You knew she was with me when the murder happened. She knew that you knew that."

But there was still the possibility that Yves could have killed Ryan outside the SM hour and stashed the body to wait until there was a safe way to move it. There was still a possibility that Susanna might have helped him do it, or killed Ryan herself.

"Susanna says half the time she was wondering what had you so uncomfortable and the other half she wanted to choke you. Yeah, you have some explaining to do," Yves said.

"Maybe I could talk to her at the clinic," Helt said. The clinic would be quiet. Helt liked night shifts. The camaraderie was different, the pace slower. For most jobs, anyway.

"You didn't haul me out here to tell me that," Yves said.

"No. I'm looking for a cold place with air in it, between Navigation and the Athens elevator," Helt said. And to find out if Yves had anything to hide, and to find out if the Special Investigator could sort if Yves was faking the scenario. "So I came to the expert."

Yves muttered some words that might have been Italian, but he didn't deny his expertise. "You mean a place a hardhat might know that a farmer or a nerd wouldn't." They turned a corner. "This isn't the quickest way to the elevator."

"I thought I'd drop off Doughan's interface. He left it in SysSu."

Doughan's street was lined with four-story townhouses, vaguely reminiscent of medieval Europe, maybe Amsterdam, set back from the street with plenty of greenery to look at rather than a canal. Light showed behind the drapes on the ground floor at Doughan's address. Helt called the house unit; it should be live. The request went to Doughan's study, here, and to his office in Navigation below. There was no answer. Helt climbed the stone steps and knocked on the door. Wi-Vi showed no motion inside. Helt's records said no voice, no noise in there since this morning.

"No one's there," Yves said.

"Maybe he's in his office." Helt looked at the street camera view of Doughan's house on his interface. He waved to himself as he and Yves walked away, followed by invisible snail trails of position locator blips. We were here, Doughan. We are looking for you. And if I'm at risk from Yves, I'm as covered as I know how to be.

"Cold places with air," Yves said. They took the elevator down and got on the train for the shuttleport.

Helt sent him the scenario for Ryan's death, the chilling that caused uncontrolled spasms of Ryan's heart, and then death, and then, later, the push from the tower.

He sent himself into the history of Archer Pelham, skimmed past his early brilliance in IT circles and found some surprising barriers about personal information. Helt came in sideways on one of them and found Archer Pelham's mother's name, and in two clicks he was in Silicon Valley, briefly, and then in an overlay of the world's wealth. Archer was a black sheep billionaire, never mentioned in public, and worth three times that from his own early IT work. He could have popped the money in the Seed Banker accounts via his connections with the Northern Coalition. The amounts were trivial to someone with Archer's resources. But his qualifications to be here weren't based on his grandmother's money. They were his own, and Helt grieved for him.

"So that's how it was," Yves said. He meant the murder.

"We think so."

Yves looked out at the stone tunnel rushing by. Helt was looking for any reaction, any certainty, that would tell him whether or not Yves Copani had been involved in Ryan's murder. Yves seemed to be treating this request as a problem to be solved, nothing more.

The sculptor was wearing his work coveralls, good protection against a wide range of temperatures, but Cash Ryan had died in civvies. Helt might get cold tonight, but he wasn't planning to stay anywhere long.

Doughan wasn't in his office on Level Two. The shuttleport complex was empty except for the watching eyes of its cameras. Helt used Doughan's interface to call Severo.

"You don't look much like Doughan," Severo said. He was at home.

"Who's that?" Daria asked. Severo's daughter was sitting next to him, reading a book to her father. Bright primary colors from the screen painted both of their faces. Daria was wearing blue pajamas with feet under a pink tutu with sequins on it. She was a five-year-old ballerina tonight, and looked the part.

"It's Helt," Severo said.

"Oh."

"I'll leave Doughan's interface outside his office door," Helt said. "Is the book exciting?"

"It's not exciting. It's *soothing*," Daria said. "I'm reading him to *sleep*!"

"Does it work?" Helt asked.

"Every time," Severo said with an exaggerated yawn. He leaned back in his big chair and closed his eyes.

"One thing. Is anybody on duty in the shuttleport at night?" Helt asked.

"Nah," Severo said. "The officer on night duty watches the place unless a shuttle's incoming. Everything we could do for an emergency response is automated. Fire, flood, intruders, even, just push a button."

"Thank you. Good night," Helt said.

"Shhh!" Daria put her index finger on her lip and frowned at Helt. She looked down at the book in her lap.

". . . *Thyme flies*," Daria read. "Daddy, that's not spelled right."

"English spelling doesn't have good rules like Spanish," Severo said. There's T, I, M, E, time, and the owl in the story is confused. T, H, Y, M, E is a plant. There's some growing in the kitchen."

"There's some growing in the kitchen." Helt looked down to hide the tears in his eyes. He was back in his mother's lap, and the book was the same, and he'd questioned the same word in the same place and she had said exactly the same thing.

He'd had ten years with her before she changed, and all of them had been good.

Helt blew Daria a kiss and put Doughan's interface down in front of the Navigation office door, in plain sight of the cameras.

"The whole industrial park is full of cold places with air in them," Yves said. "It would take us two, three days to look at them all."

They walked to the center of the lobby. "We can narrow it some," Helt said. "I need a place where people won't stare when you walk by, because this whole thing began after a day shift. Whoever works near Nav offices would still have been there."

"Stick him in the airlock," Yves said. "Nobody goes in there unless there's a shuttle."

"I'm looking for a room-sized space. That one's too big."

"Too big for what?" Yves asked.

"Too big not to show on power use monitors if somebody cycled the airlock. There were no blips down here on Wednesday."

"You're thinking like a nerd. You need to think like an architect."

"Why?"

"If you design a structure, you have to design in places for somebody to be when they build it. You have to have access space to hide the machinery you don't want to look at and a way to get to it to fix it."

"Is there a way to get back to the elevator so the security cameras wouldn't see you? We don't show Cash Ryan anywhere after he got off shift on Wednesday. He worked out on the skin and then he changed into civvies and went somewhere and vanished."

Yves rocked back and forth on his heels, surveying walls and doorways and lintels. He tilted his head and looked up at the ceiling. "This place has too many eyes for that. You're saying he didn't get on the train," Yves said.

"Not from here." Helt's screen showed Yves the diagrams for the Nav lobby overlaid with dots to mark camera placements. Yves hadn't missed eyeing a single one when he looked up, but then, he would know where the cameras were supposed to be. "He got from the changing room to Athens tower, and got dead on the way, and no one saw him."

"Let's walk it through," Yves said.

Lights in the changing room woke when they entered. The glassy eyes of closed suits watched them enter, an array of shed human-shaped carapaces hooked to the wall, slumped like hanged men. At the far end of the room, an airlock led to the shuttle tunnel.

"You have a torch?" Yves asked.

"No."

"You'd better get one. You'd better get into a coverall, too." Yves went to a bin and rummaged. "Hate to lose you before you get my colonist status cleared. One-oh-five long, right?"

"Exactly," Helt said. He took off his windbreaker, pulled on the coverall, and stuffed the windbreaker between its front and his stomach. Yves found a headlamp on a shelf and handed it to him.

There was a trapdoor in the ceiling. Yves reached up and pulled an attic staircase down and stepped on it, jumping once to check that it was stable. "Come on up."

Think like an architect. The space above the ceiling held ducts and conduit and beams that crossed the floor, supports for the ceiling below. Helt stood up and his head didn't quite touch the raw rock above.

"There's headroom," he said.

"The architects didn't have to think about building costs. What this much height tells you is that one of them had changed a lightbulb in a hard spot somewhere. Once, anyway." Yves pulled the staircase back up and the world went dark.

Helt pulled on his headlamp and followed Yves, walking the girders. He felt like he was playing a sidewalk game, except in this one the object was to step on the cracks, not between them. "You could get lost up here."

"Sure." Yves moved with the grace of a circus acrobat. "If you don't have an interface with you. In that case, you find a trapdoor and look down."

"Have you worked up here before?"

"Nah. This was tunneled out four, five years after the core was hollowed. Long before my time."

"I wonder if Mena's thought about spiders in places like this," Helt said. It was bound to happen, sooner or later. For now, the place looked dust free, almost sterile. But he wasn't looking at the place in bright light.

"You scared of spiders?" Yves asked.

"No," Helt said. Step, judge the next secure footing, step.

Yves, four beams ahead because he moved faster, knelt and pushed a staircase open. His chin, lighted from below, looked carved out of rock. Behind the sculptor's crouched shoulders a wall rose, black stone that went up and vanished in the darkness.

"We're beside the train tunnel," Yves said. "Utility closet." Yves backed down the ladder and Helt followed him down past shelves of cleaning supplies and hand tools. On the floor, cleaner bots snoozed in corners. There were two doors; one marked Navigation and the other, Tunnel. Helt pushed the trapdoor closed and followed Yves out of the closet and into the dark.

The lines of track that ran toward Athens were silver traced on black. Yves turned and the tracks ahead jerked into view, disappeared, reappeared.

"I'm trying to figure a scenario where Ryan and his killers climbed up there and why they would do it," Helt said.

"You asked how to get from here to Athens and not show on a security camera," Yves said.

"So it can be done; you're proving that. I didn't ask you how probable it was."

"No, you didn't. There's a walkway out here. It's wider than it looks. Plenty of room on it for repair vehicles."

"What happens when the train comes?" Helt asked.

"You don't have to get your back against the wall, but you'll probably want to. Don't watch the headlight. Plays hell with your night vision."

"Right," Helt said.

"There may not be a train. We didn't call one."

"We could just go into the lobby and ride over," Helt said. He found the distance that would keep him from bumping into Yves and focused on Yves's left hand as it swung back and forth across the line of lighted track. The right-hand wall of the tunnel was farther away than his arm could reach.

"There's a cold place or two on the way, maybe." Yves set a brisk pace. Helt fell into the rhythm; Yves's stride was a long, swinging near-lope that covered ground quickly. Helt's hands were getting cold but he wanted his arms beside him for balance in the dark. "Back at The Lab, when you told Birdy you understood. His team lost the next game, right?"

"Yeah. It took Real Madrid five years to recover."

They walked on. Helt imagined Elena in her office, out of the dark lab where the embryos slept, in the warmth and the light and sitting at her desk; he imagined Susanna sleeping, warm. The chill in tonight's air would help wake her on her walk to the clinic. Archer would still be in his office, or maybe he'd gone home. Helt wanted to look at them all, look at them in the light from his little screen and watch them, listen to them, but here was dark and cold and the most important thing to see was Yves's hand swinging back and forth, and to know they were getting somewhere.

If Doughan picked up his interface and powered it off, Helt would hear a beep. If Doughan saw it and left it where it was and went on to wherever he was going tonight, surveillance cameras would tell Helt about it; they were keyed to alert him, their functions set for Doughan's face, stature, walk.

"I never think about temperature control in the trains," Helt said.

"Shirtsleeve weather to get to work year-round," Yves said. "Shirtsleeve weather in this coverall I'm wearing, too. You cold back there?"

"Cool enough," Helt said. "What's ambient in here?"

"About two degrees on Level Three but we'll be picking up some heat from the factories soon. Maybe three or four. Turn on your suit, Helt. The tab's on your left shirt pocket. "

"Oh." Helt did that, and in three, no, four steps his shins weren't cold anymore. He turned on his headlamp, too, and got a good look at the back of Yves's neck and not much else. He'd been seeing the pool of light from Yves's lamp and doing fine with that, so he turned his own light off again.

"Who killed Ryan? You know yet?" Yves asked.

"I wish I could say I know for sure. Knowing where he died could tell me a lot about that."

They walked on. The mineral-scented air was quiet and the grade was uphill; the train climbed from the Nav offices, actually on Level Three. David II's industrial kingdom was on the real Level Two but the differences weren't noticeable when you came back and forth on the train.

Helt was aware of the shapes of his kneecaps, the blades of his shins; the chill on his bare hands. This tunnel wasn't cold enough. Not nearly cold enough. A man could keep walking for hours in this. He wouldn't be comfortable in civvies, but his core temperature would stay okay as long as he was moving.

"See up there?" Yves's headlight vanished the track and jerked upward to shine on black nothing. Helt kept his pace and wished Yves would look back down again.

"See what?"

"The section seal."

"Divides the industrial park right under Athens from Navigation," Helt said. He'd never paid attention to it on his trips to Navigation offices and back. He'd never looked up from his work, safe in the shirtsleeve weather inside the train and always going from one task to another. "I know there is one, but I don't see it."

Yves nodded and the light swooped up and down. "Another five minutes and we'll be there."

"Don't nod," Helt said. "Makes me dizzy."

"Okay."

They walked on. Yves had never changed his pace, and Helt found the new normal of a view of a line of track and Yves's swinging hand comforting, in its way.

"Here," Yves said, and the bulk of the section seal was just ahead, its right-hand pillar marked with a groove of deeper black cut out of the rock, a vertical channel to guide the seal door down. There was a door in the tunnel wall beside it. Yves pulled on the handle, hard. Helt heard a swish of pneumatic seal moving over stone. Another door, and indicator lights in the darkness beyond glowed vivid green in the dark. Motion sensors turned on the lights and Helt winced in the sudden glare.

The space was taller than the tunnel, twice its height at least, and it was big enough to hold sweeper bots and some standing consoles and tool cabinets. Huge cables went up and up the darkness and vanished in the darkness overhead.

"This space is plenty big enough to hide somebody in," Yves said. He reached out and pushed on one of the cables. It didn't move at all. "I wouldn't have done some of these things the way they're done, but this is so damned primitive I love it. The seal drops if a simple mercury barometer sinks to a critical level even if no one tells it to. It drops if you push a button, or it comes down on remote if somebody signals in one of those drills Navigation likes to call."

"Doughan likes to call," Helt said.

"There's a motor to haul it back up, but look at this."

Yves put both hands on a long crank attached to a wheel. "Counterweights and pulleys. We have g, and that's the force that brings the seal down. And if we don't have g, there's something gone so wrong that it's likely we're all dead anyway. But one strong man could get his feet under these stirrups on the floor, here"—Yves pointed at them—"in micro-g, crank the seal down if he had to, and crank it back up again."

"It's beautiful," Helt said, because it was. "But I think it's too warm for what we need."

"Too warm. You're hard to please." Yves led the way around and past the cable display and through another pair of sealed doors that opened onto the Athens side of the seal.

"I need minus ten," Helt said.

"That's where we're headed."

They reached the doorway to the industrial park after a five-minute walk that seemed level. The courtyard around the Athens elevator on Level Two was too bright and too hot after the dark cold of the tunnel. The contrast brought back memories of ski lodges and fireplaces, the feel of windburn on Helt's face making itself known as he came in from the cold.

Beside the Athens elevator was a doorway marked EXIT. Just where it should be; there were stairways between one level and the next near every elevator. This one was lighted, and it went up to Level One and down into *Kybele*'s virgin rock. Down, with landings and turns. Helt stopped on one and looked for a camera. There wasn't one.

"What are you looking for?" Yves asked.

"No cameras," Helt said.

"This stairwell will be a dead end until it's time to dig out Level Three. No reason to come down here unless you're on maintenance duty, and you have lights and cloud access for that."

Helt called up a blueprint for the Athens elevator and got it. The signal was fine.

He followed Yves on down, and the air got colder again, and colder yet. Eight landings, four stories, two sets of footsteps ringing on metal stairs bolted into rock. The stairwell ended in a cul-de-sac and another door. Yves opened it.

They stepped into darkness again. Yves's headlamp strobed the walls of a vault. It was long and room-high and it looked like a corridor to nowhere.

Twenty paces, twenty meters more or less, and Yves stopped and held out a cautioning hand. Helt walked up beside him and looked down into a black hole. He turned his headlamp on. The vault opened on a shaft that went deeper yet, the true bottom of the elevator shaft, a place of massive cables and pulleys, its floor about three meters down. There was no safety rail. There was a ladder hooked to the wall of the shaft, on Yves's side of the vault.

"Think like an architect," Helt said. His interface measured an ambient temperature of minus eight. Close enough. His face felt the freeze. He rummaged in the pockets of the borrowed coverall for gloves. The soles of his shoes let some of the cold in. "This is where you get to the elevator for maintenance." There weren't any gloves.

"The cables get checked now and again. There's a schedule. Cold enough?" Yves asked. He unzipped the collar of his coverall and pulled a hoodie up, and let its facecover drop into place. His headlamp was bright enough that the translucent fabric didn't bother it. A hood seemed like a fine idea. Helt fumbled with the collar zipper on his coverall until he found its sweet spot. He pulled his own hood out of his collar.

"Close enough to the Athens elevator, and cold enough. I'll get the lab techs down here," Helt said. A stark and terrible place to die, a mausoleum of naked rock. Helt tucked his hands into his armpits. He looked at the walls, the floor, the ceiling, for scuff marks or slime or drops of blood, but if traces of anything were left on walls or floor, they were microscopic, for he saw nothing. Had they left Cash Ryan alive, in the dark? Had he waited with dread for the sleepy feeling, the calm, that people say they feel when they are dying of cold?

"If someone offed Ryan here, they would have to climb those four flights of stairs to carry him back to the elevator." Yves could haul someone up that far. Elena could, too. It might take her a little longer.

"Not really," Yves said. "Athens Level Three please," he asked his pocket. The cables began to move, too close to Helt for any sort of comfort. He had a wild image of catching a sleeve on one and getting hauled down and flattened under the pulleys below. He backed up a step and watched the bottom of the elevator coming down, a black square of functional, mindless bulk.

It slid past the open shaft, its inner doors smooth and polished and unfamiliar, because Helt had never seen them; they were always toggled to outer doors and this vault didn't have any. The elevator stopped precisely, its floor flush with the floor of the vault.

"Heh," Helt said. Someone had lured Ryan down here, or followed him down into the cold. Ryan had to have been wearing a coverall, unless he had no choice about it. Handcuffed, maybe, but the autopsy didn't show any abrasions around his wrists. His crew said he had left the changing room in civvies.

"Where we going?" Yves asked. He checked his interface. "Susanna's awake."

They were standing inside the elevator. Helt was in front of the button panel and he hadn't moved. "Oh. Sorry. Too much to think about. Level One." The elevator closed its doors and moved, silent and up.

"Yves?"

"What?"

"Thank you. Go see Susanna. Keep her company until she goes on shift. She'll want to know the gossip from The Lab."

"I could come back after that," Yves said.

Helt shook his head. "I think Cash Ryan died here. You nailed the cold place I was looking for, and I thank you. I want to walk a few things through."

"You're a worried man," Yves said. "Are you sure you'll be okay?"

"I'll be okay," Helt said.

Yves shrugged and stayed in the elevator as its doors closed.

Helt took the train back to Nav. On the way, he looked in on Elena, still in her lab. He didn't call her. Severo was in his quarters. Doughan was still offline. Helt still didn't know if Yves was a murderer, but he was almost certain he wasn't. He hadn't flinched when Helt told him the techs would be looking for DNA traces down in the vault. Yves could have shown him the wrong place; there could be, had to be, other hidey-holes in the growing warren under the civilized areas of *Kybele*. But using the vault seemed so handy.

27

Orbital Transfer

Doughan's interface was still lying on the floor in front of his office door. Helt unlocked the door, walked in, and lighted the panoramas.

"I've never been in here," Elena's voice said.

"Really?" Helt asked. He turned in a circle and showed her the projections of Earth below and the starscape that filled the rest of the room from floor to ceiling.

"Well done, but theatrical," Elena said.

"There's more." He touched a keypad on Doughan's desk. The panorama of Earth below parted in the middle as the doors behind the desk slid into the walls. Behind them, six workstations faced a projection wall. The blind eyes of their screens stared at an outsider's view of *Kybele*, spinning against a background of stars. "Mission Control for the big burns."

"I don't like this," Elena said. "I feel like someone's going to come in and chase us out of here."

"Maybe they will. Our location is live to NSS. I'm surprised the audio alarms haven't gone off yet. Good evening, Officer Evans."

"Good evening. What are you two doing in there?"

"Dr. Maury's in Stonehenge. I'm checking some files. A precaution." He thought about lying and telling Evans that Doughan was worried about something in here. The hell with that. The Special Investigator was investigating, was the real answer. "Would you watch our backs, please?"

"You got it," Evans said, and vanished. But she'd be watching, and listening. It was just as well.

"I could come down there," Elena said.

Helt went to one of the six empty workstations, entered a password, and scrolled through displays of equations and numbers. "No. Please no. Look over my shoulder and help me," he said. "There's just a thing or two I'd like to see . . ."

"And then you're done for tonight?" Elena asked.

"Yeah . . . Stay with me. Evans will keep us sequestered from the news feeds. You won't show up on the morning show."

"Don't tempt me," Evans said. "Helt, I want to thank you for the way you dealt with Akila."

That startled him. He didn't know what to say. "You're welcome, but what did I do?" Helt asked.

"The details about the stalking—I've seen the videos. It could have been embarrassing for her and you kept it private for her."

"Nothing would have been gained by showing it to everyone," Helt said.

"Even so, it was thoughtful. Dr. Maury?"

"Yes?" Elena said.

"I'm so sorry any of this happened."

"Thank you, Officer." Elena's voice was low and soft.

"I'll be here, but please go back to what you were doing. We all have work to do tonight," Evans said.

"Will do," Helt said. He was still surprised by Evans's reaction. "Elena, you here?"

"Sure. What am I looking at?" Elena asked.

"Most likely, you're watching me chasing wild geese. It's a hazard when you have too much speculation and not enough fact. Let's say Cash Ryan wanted to convince someone he was vital to the ship's well-being. Let's say he decided that because he wanted to stay near you."

"That's what you think, or what you know?" Elena asked.

"What I think."

"But he was stalking Susanna," Elena said.

"And Akila Shenouda, but not for long. Susanna was a distraction to help him stay away from you until the ship was under way. He wanted to be careful and cautious. He wanted time . . ."

Helt continued down the lists of checklists.

"Lots of time. The way he saw things, you would change your mind and love him again, because of course he was lovable. In his own eyes. He loved himself, so . . ."

"So I would come to my senses sooner or later."

"Exactly. So, to convince someone . . ."

"Someone who has access to this room," Elena said. Helt inhaled, sharply. She didn't say Doughan's name.

"That he was needed here, it's possible he would pick . . ." Helt stopped at an array of columns of figures. Pure hunch. Burn durations to give the delta vee needed to move *Kybele* out of Saturn orbit and push her outsystem, *North* at the top of one column and *South* at the top of the other.

Helt gave himself a thumbnail view of Elena. She was staring at the same list from her screen in her Stonehenge lab. "You're thinking way far ahead, Helt."

"Yeah. Far enough ahead that nobody looks at these files too often. There's a set for the propulsion array on each pole," Helt said.

"The numbers are slightly different, right and left, very slightly." Elena took a deep breath. "That's because *Kybele* spins clockwise. Gyroscope effect. Sometimes I forget the basics."

Helt changed to a different set of figures. "This set here"—Helt ran his index finger down the screen—"defines the power output needed to get that delta vee, this one describes where on the Saturn orbit we should be when we begin the push, and this one underneath it is the elapsed time for the burn to get that power." Flawless. There was nothing here. He thought about the time it would take to review every file in here. It couldn't be done in one night and he was no physicist.

Think simple. Think . . .

Cash Ryan had faked his résumé and he'd been skilled enough to get by with it. He could have messed with something in here, but there was no sane reason for it. It would accomplish nothing except to get his ass kicked off the ship. There was no reason to mess with anything in here unless he wanted to prove to Doughan that he could hack the arrays of data in this room.

Helt moved to the files histories, time and date data, entries; everything looked fine, and then, and then. October. October 11. He pulled up a deleted file and split-screened it with the Saturn burn. Same file, but. But the numbers were slightly different, very slightly.

"Heh." He used his interface to look for copies in SysSu.

The charts in SysSu archives right now matched the original values. The numbers were old; before *Kybele* even had an atmosphere the calculations for this burn had been done and reviewed by damned near everyone who had ever calculated an orbit. He checked the numbers against an Earthside file from the Northern Coalition archives. They matched.

Think simple. Look at the edit log. There. October 4, October 11, October 18. Last Wednesday, the Wednesday before, and the Wednesday before that. The bad numbers went up on October 11 and came down on October 11. They were checked again on October 18 but they hadn't been changed since then. The files in here would have showed the original values to anyone who looked and they matched the original values now, all the way back for twenty years. They would be reviewed again, many times, as new data came in when *Kybele* got closer to Saturn.

"Helt?" Elena asked.

"Sorry. I got lost there. Let me look . . ."

Come in to the time and date log as *phpmyadmin*. Go to the *Table* screen, and click the operations tab. There's an autoincrement field that shows time and date. Just delete what you don't want and put in what you do, if you're the phpmyadmin. It's primitive, it's simple, and no one will notice unless they look.

Look at the backup files again. Yup. There it was.

"Why Saturn?" Elena asked.

"Because the rings are flashy? Something we're all going to notice and talk about."

There was a chain of command for this room, these files. Doughan, David II, and Severo were the first three names on it, then a list of people in Navigation who had the skills to take over in case of unspeakable disasters. None of them had looked in here in October, yet, as far as the records showed. The SysSu duplicates didn't show that there had been any activity down here, either.

The phpmyadmin had deleted the flawed numbers and replaced them with the original file, and deleted the time and date marker that would show when it happened. The phpmyadmin for this room was Doughan.

Helt leaned back in his chair, locked his hands behind his head, and looked up at the ceiling. Heh. There was a trapdoor up there, fitted into the rectangular patterns of the ceiling but easy to find if you knew what you were looking for. A way to change the lights, repair conduit, add power cables. He went over and tugged the ring that would pull it down.

The trapdoor moved. It wasn't fastened from above, but why would it be? This room could only be entered through the locked doors he'd opened, entered by people the exec let in. The hatch up there wouldn't be locked. It was an emergency escape route of sorts.

"It's all fine," Helt said for Evans to hear. "The files I was worried about aren't contaminated. Time to lock up." He idled the system in the room, left it, and closed the doors behind Doughan's desk. Time to go.

Doughan's interface was still beside the door, still easily seen from anywhere in the lobby. It was ringing. Helt nudged it with his foot. He called

Evans while he walked across the lobby. "No, Doughan's not down here. I don't know where he is. I left his interface here for him, if he checks in with you and asks about it."

"Thanks," Evans said.

"I'm coming to SysSu," Elena said.

The train arrived that would take him back to Athens. Helt stepped in. The car was empty. "Exactly what I was about to suggest."

The Murder Mess revolved slowly in the Huerfano in Nadia's office. More names were exiled to the periphery of it now, Seed Bankers out in the Oort cloud, even Kelly Halkett and Benson Luseno. NSS had put them on the alibied list this evening, after the beer fest at The Lab ended.

It would be okay to enter what he'd learned down there in the Navigation archives. It would be okay to enter it here. This copy of the Murder Mess was safe; it existed only on the Huerfano, nowhere else. But still, Helt hesitated. Coward.

The debris on the tables had shifted. The rubber chicken was nowhere to be seen. Helt picked up the deflated soccer ball. There was something familiar about it. He held it up in both hands and looked at it from underneath.

Heh. The shapes of stitched leather were the same shape as the petals that enclosed *Kybele*'s sun. Hexagons that enclosed a sphere. He just hadn't looked at the petals, or their shadows, that way. The discovery made him feel better. He was slow sometimes, but maybe he'd see what was in front of him if he just kept working at it.

Helt mauled the flattened thing back into a ball and put it down where he'd found it.

He put the cold vault into play on the public and private versions of the Murder Mess as the location where Ryan died, watched a few Navigation names cluster near it, Navigation techs who kept the elevators running, watched the names hauled away and archived because they'd been verifiably elsewhere on October 18. Elena's name still orbited Ryan's death. Yves? He had a motive, and a way to get Ryan from Navigation to the vault. He had the physical strength to get a dead Ryan on and off the elevator. But he'd come to see Helt at the Frontier Wednesday night. The timing would have been very, very tight. And he wasn't on the SM announcement list, unless he'd asked someone about that particular hour. Being able to hide that part of the murder could have been just luck. Right.

Helt got up and walked out into the empty hall. He came back in and filled Nadia's office with the State of *Kybele*. Interaction bubbles floated through their ether, gently bobbing to absorb the signatures of industrial hardhats on their night-shift routines, a few farmers walking out to pinch the moisture in the soil with their fingers, in the fields beneath Stonehenge, some night owls in Petra awake and glued to media of one sort or another. He wondered when the Seed Bankers' experiences would show up in the interaction bubbles. For now, the world was quiet.

He wondered what Doughan's warped files and Archer's gaffe would do to the configuration that spun around Cash Ryan. And he didn't touch a thing. Not even in the Huerfano.

Archer was at home; his interface and the new local bugs agreed about that. Mena was in her house in Petra, and Doughan could be any damned where but he sure wasn't home. Evans sat at her desk in NSS. He sent her the location of the vault.

"So that's where you and Yves Copani were," she said. "I couldn't see you."

"There aren't any cameras in the dead-end part of that stairwell. It's the vault I'm interested in. No cameras in there, either. Could you get the forensic techs down there in the morning?"

"Sure. You think that's the place?"

"I think it's a good bet," Helt said. "Thank you, Officer Evans."

"Melody."

"Melody?"

"You can call me Melody. It's my first name."

"I will. Good night." She wouldn't be able to look at what was going on in this office unless she called again. She had the public version of the Murder Mess at hand, and plenty of blank spaces to fill from the day's NSS reports to keep her busy. Helt walked out on the agora and waited for Elena in the middle of it, in a dead zone. The agora was dry now underfoot. A few lights were on in the Library, but Giliam's office fronted an inside corridor and had no exterior window to show, even if he was working tonight.

Four people came out of the train, a trio that walked toward a residential side street, maybe after a dinner in Petra, and Elena behind them, her shoulders hunched and her hands deep in the pockets of her windbreaker. She stopped a few paces away from him.

"What is it?" she asked.

"I need you."

"I'm flattered, but can we go inside first? It's a little chilly out here."

"Oh." Helt didn't feel cold at all. "Sure. I mean, I need to talk."

Elena nodded and fell into step beside him.

"There's a lot to sort out. So much . . ."

The displays in the atrium tonight were rectangles of translucent primary colors. After Helt passed them he realized they were arranged, left to right, in spectrum order, as if white light had been divided into its component colors by a nonexistent prism on the agora. Red through violet.

Helt led the way into Nadia's office and reached for his interface. It was in an unfamiliar pocket. He was still wearing a Navigation coverall. That's why he hadn't noticed the chill outside. He laid his interface on a table and pointed at it. Elena laid hers beside it and they went into Helt's office.

"Really private?" Elena asked.

"Really private." Helt woke his screens. "If NSS checks in, Officer Melody Evans will hear us . . ." He located *Jesuits* and sent the train conversation he'd had with Elena to his interface, "having a conversation about governance."

"SysSu is bugged by NSS?" Elena, in the visitor's chair, kicked off her shoes and tucked her feet up beside her.

"Not on my watch," Helt said. "But there could be. Bugs. Jerry sweeps for them every day in there and he hasn't found any yet."

"I talked to Jim," Elena said.

"About Ryan's mother?"

Elena nodded. "How he managed to get to speak to her is a story for him to tell. Summary is that Ryan never called home after high school graduation except to ask for money and make blackmail threats if she didn't pay up."

Helt looked for the report in the Murder Mess. It had been filed five hours ago. His eyes went to it. It was lengthy.

"Don't read it now," Elena said. "It's not a feel-good story. Again, summary. His mom's not psychotic, but she was blackmail-able. Not anything criminal, but she did some stuff in her adolescence that she didn't want her husband, Cash's father, to know."

Helt vanished the file. "Okay. Sounds like more confirmation on Jim's theory. Thank you for dealing with this, Elena."

"I'm glad to help. You're hot on the trail of something and it's bothering you."

"It shows?"

"It does."

"Heh. I have information overload and I'm getting punchy. So here I am in this coverall because I didn't think to take it off, and I'm wondering why Cash Ryan went down a staircase toward someplace he knew had to be minus ten if he was in civvies."

"Because he was wearing a coverall and somebody took it off him later. The one you have on flatters you, by the way. It brings out the color of your eyes."

It was dark blue, Helt noticed. He had blue eyes. The color was recessive, more or less, and might someday be really rare. He looked down at his chest and saw a corner of his windbreaker, rolled and stuffed in front for quick storage before that trip down the stairs. "Does it? Time to get out of this. It's hot." He pulled the zipper down, retrieved his windbreaker, and climbed out of the coverall. "But a coverall keeps you warm."

Elena held out her arm. "Let me see it."

Helt handed it over and Elena turned it this way and that. "Here." She held out a section for show and tell. There was a little zipper in the lining and a wallet shaped lump beneath it. "The power pack's under the left armpit. That's a good place, not in the way much. And it wouldn't be easy to tell if it needs a battery change or whatever. Unless you check it."

Helt started to toss his windbreaker to the corner stand, but there was a bulge in the pocket. Peanuts. His hunger woke, sudden and strong. He grabbed the peanuts and began to munch.

"You haven't had dinner," Elena said.

Helt shook his head. "Have you?"

"I guess I forgot."

"There's stuff in the lounge. I'll go get us something."

Elena got up and slipped her shoes on. "I'll come with you. Can we talk in there? In the hall?"

"We can," Helt said.

But they didn't. Helt picked up a jar of food bars in the lounge. Elena looked around, found chilled water in a fridge, and retrieved a couple of bottles. Helt fished out a peanut butter and jelly bar and offered the jar to Elena. She picked lemon, and they walked back to the office, munching on the way.

Elena tucked herself into the visitor chair again and settled the coverall over her knees. "Here's my theory," she said. "Cash wanted to convince Doughan he was valuable to the ship. So he got into the Mission Control room somehow."

"Are you cold?" Helt asked.

"No. I like the smell of you on this." She stroked the sleeve of the coverall, and Helt wished his arm was in it. Or out of it. As soon as he had this nailed, oh, yes.

"He got in through the ceiling," Helt said. "And he sat down and changed a file, and then climbed back out. I learned how to do that tonight. You've been thinking about this."

"And little else. He knew the password . . ."

"He didn't have to know the password. You get in there from the Nav office. Once those doors are open, somebody lets you in because you're supposed to be there."

"He counted on a routine schedule for data checks," Elena said.

"It's a Huerfano down there, of sorts, but there's SysSu backup." Helt pulled up the Mission Control room files, and tugged Elena's chair over beside his so she could see what he was seeing.

"Thanks," she said.

Also, she was closer. He liked that.

"This will just look like strings of numbers . . . Heh."

"Tell me."

"Every Wednesday. The files are scanned for edits and revisions every Wednesday." Helt leaned back in his chair and crossed his arms. The food effect was hitting. He felt better, less cranky, stronger. "The files were changed and corrected on the eleventh. Wednesday. And nothing happened, no alerts, no flap, nothing until the eighteenth. What was . . ."

Nothing had happened for a week after that. It was baffling.

"Doughan," Elena said.

Helt reached for a water bottle and opened it. He took a deep, cold swallow. "What was Doughan thinking? I'm really fighting this, aren't I?" Helt asked. Doughan, and now Archer. He didn't know what he was going to do. He did not know.

"You were. You aren't now. Doughan did a fix on an altered file and didn't tell anybody about it." Elena sighed. "That means nothing, in the greater scheme of things."

"Doughan could have thought it was a joke, or a test. He could have thought someone was checking to see if he really did check the alerts every Wednesday."

"Or he could have thought it was a ploy by someone who really wanted his attention." Elena leaned forward and got the unopened water bottle from the desk.

"But he didn't know who."

"Fingerprints?"

"When you walk in there, the workstation that's closest is the center one. The commander's position. Doughan had already used the keyboard; that's how he found the glitch, so he'd messed up the fingerprints Cash left."

"That's where you sat down," Elena said.

"Right."

Elena drank some of her water and screwed the cap back on the bottle. "So Doughan saw what happened, and fixed it, and then he waited. He might have checked to see if someone who had access had pulled the stunt."

"Archer." There, Helt had said the other name he didn't want to say. Archer fumbling through half-light, so fragile now. Helt hadn't wanted to see it, and Archer was involved in this, at least in the Seed Banker misdirection, and that was bad. Very bad. "The first thought would be software. But I'll bet he didn't call Archer on it. The next move would be to see how long it would be before Archer got antsy, if Doughan thought Archer was yanking his chain for some reason. So he waited, for a little while, but not very long, because he wasn't thinking about Archer, he was thinking . . ."

"He was thinking about everyone who had any business in the control room," Elena said, "and if any of them could *really* be trusted, because they had to be trusted, but if they couldn't . . ."

"If they couldn't, then he didn't know who to look for," Helt said. "He had to wait for the culprit to contact *him*, and he had to reevaluate every security system on this ship. He had to walk in and out of that closed room and look at everything in it and wonder what else was compromised."

"It must have been hell for him," Elena said.

"It took a kind of self-control I can't even imagine. Steel nerves. And then Ryan called him."

Wednesday, October 18. The list of interface calls, every last one of them on *Kybele* that day, tagged for Cash Ryan/Wesley Doughan. The system had to find at least one, and didn't.

No matches.

Not going to be that easy.

October.

No matches.

"Let's be archaic," Elena said. "Ryan slipped a note under the door for Doughan to find."

"To find Wednesday morning when he came in."

"A week. Seven days. It's a symbolic interval," Elena said.

"And Doughan read it and went to the changing room, Wednesday morning, and could have grabbed him by the ear and called Severo to take him away. But he didn't." From the brief, nondescript records on Cash Ryan, could Doughan have suspected the guy was a nutcase? "Doughan would have looked over Ryan's record that morning, what there was of it. There's no evidence of IT expertise in it, or of training by any agency that uses tradecraft. But Ryan entered the ship's sanctum sanctorum and set off no alarms at all. Doughan wouldn't have alerted Severo or asked David II, because . . ."

"Because?" Elena asked.

"Because he wanted to know what else Ryan might have done."

Helt looked up and met Elena's gaze. She was staring at him and past him. "And wanted to question him in a place where no one was watching." She nodded, slowly.

"So Doughan told him to come to his office after he'd worked his shift."

Elena shook her head. "Close. But what he told him was to come to the Athens stairwell."

"Right. Because they aren't on camera in the Athens lobby, those two. That leaves the problem of Cash wearing civvies, or a coverall with a busted heat pack," Helt said.

"Doughan has a coverall rolled up under his arm," Elena said.

"So he didn't have to knock Cash out and carry him down the stairs. What about the food? The samosas? The drinks. Oops. There's something I haven't checked yet." He looked for the list of faces pulled from Venkie's camera that day. All day. Jerry or Nadia had run the list in alphabetical order. Doughan had been there, at lunch hour, Wednesday. Helt turned Doughan's name red for Elena to see. " 'Here, put on this coverall, and we'll have a snack and some booze, right here on the stairwell.' Elena, that doesn't make sense."

"So they ate in Doughan's office," Elena said.

"That seems most likely," Helt said. "But the cameras don't show them in the Nav lobby, either."

"They climbed up and over, like you did."

"Not at that hour. Not from the changing room. There's too many people around. Maybe from the control room. That's private enough." No way they'd had a nice social chat in the stairwell. They'd been in Doughan's office, damn it. It was the only place that made sense. But they weren't on video in the Nav lobby or on the train ride to Athens. Too many captures were missing and the SM had lasted only an hour. Something was terribly wrong.

"Elena," Helt said. He got up from his chair and walked in a circle.

"What's going on? What is it?"

"We have to go back to the tower. We have to see where you were."

"We won't see much. It's dark, Helt."

Elena's deer had run the night Cash Ryan crashed down into the trees. "I mean we have to go back through it. Something went terribly wrong Wednesday night. Something is wrong with the timeline. You were watching the deer. They're chipped. You track them. You said they moved Wednesday night, and you said they ran in the wind, and they don't like wind."

"Yes, but—"

"When? When did they run?" Helt sat down again.

Elena watched him. Her eyes didn't leave his face and she shifted a little in her chair to get farther away from him. "I . . . I showed you as much as I could. It didn't help."

"I'm sorry," Helt said. "I'm so sorry. I didn't mean to frighten you." It's here somewhere, he thought. Please, he thought. Please. He pulled her chair closer and pushed a keyboard under her hands. "Show me where they were Wednesday."

She brought up a terrain map of Center, then zoomed in on the area beneath Athens tower. He saw the creek, the meadow, the dark green of the trees that bordered it. The trees were overlaid with little dots.

"The dots are the deer herd?"

Elena nodded.

"You said the deer moved, that they'd been in the meadow and then went into the stand of ponderosa where the body came down." Helt said. "I see them."

"I told you the deer weren't where we saw them on Tuesday. They stayed in the area most of the day Wednesday, but not in the meadow. Under the trees. Usually they come out to graze when it gets dark, but they didn't, probably because of the wind. They had moved to the shelter of the ponderosa, but they moved again before I went up to the tower. They ran."

The dots that marked the positions of the deer erupted from the ponderosa and ran anti-spinward, toward Petra, slowed when they found the scrub oak thicket Elena had pointed out from the tower, moved close to one another again. One by one, they found places to rest.

"They ran. Something spooked them and they ran." Helt grabbed the keyboard. The wind, the evening wind. On Wednesday it had come up around 1700, was at max by 1800, gusty and strong enough to carry Cash Ryan's body half a k. It had died down to a breeze by the time Elena got up there. "When did they run?"

"Around 1900. A little before. I checked on them a couple of times Wednesday evening. I looked for them again while I was waiting for the train. I backed up the timeline to see if I could figure out why they had moved so far, so fast. I almost didn't notice when the train got there."

Helt found the entry.

1852.

"They spooked right here. Eighteen fifty-two," he said.

"Yes."

He clicked through codes and found the train records from Stonehenge Wednesday night, the departure times, the location of Elena's interface. "You were where you said you were. Your interface shows you at the Stonehenge station." He zoomed the time stamps from her herd records so they were huge on the screen. "Eighteen fifty-four Wednesday. That's when you accessed this. At the Stonehenge station. But that's not the thing. Not all of the thing. Elena, you found when Cash Ryan came down from the tower. That's what spooked the deer. I'll bet on it. And it wasn't during the outage. It was eight minutes before that."

She looked at the screen and at him, and past him, her eyes wide, focused on possibilities and then on his face. "And I wasn't there then."

FALL FROM ATHENS TOWER: 1852.

"You weren't there then."

Maybe it wasn't real to her yet. Maybe it wasn't real to him. There would be consequences when he did what he was about to do. Evans might see the clearance and put it together with the time of the SM hour. She might not. He wanted to enter the time of the fall and smattering of data they had gleaned this evening into the Huerfano, Doughan's actions, the suspicions surrounding Archer like a thick cloud, but that needed a cautious hand, some explanations, even for Jerry and Nadia to see. And he had searches to do, hours of searches.

Even so. Helt flicked a few keys and brought up the colors, black letters on deep glowing gold.

ALIBIED

He scrolled the list, names rolling by in alphabetical order.

LE, GUIREN, SYSSU
MAURY, ELENA, BIOSYSTEMS
MIRIN, AKUA, SYSSU

"Better?" he asked.

Elena looked up at the screen. Her eyes narrowed and her face looked grim, not happy. "It's real," she said.

"It's recorded, so it must be real." Helt leaned over the arm of his chair and kissed her. Her muscles were rigid with tension. That there was no doubt of her innocence hadn't come home to her yet.

It was a good kiss, but the chairs were in the way. He got to his feet and lifted her and held her close, so close. He stroked her hair. "It's real," he whispered. "It's real." In his arms, she began to relax a little. He expected sobs, and waited for them, but Elena didn't do that. He held her, but he couldn't stop thinking.

He would enter the data in the Huerfano and search the files and find when and where the camera records had been so carefully altered, because Cash Ryan had been hauled up that tower when the elevator camera was live, and that changed everything. "You're just like your father," his mother had said. He really was just like his father, but he was beginning to sort out that what his mother called cold and undemonstrative had been a mask over worry, or a way to distance himself. Helt wanted to bawl like a baby, to laugh until he cried, to share Elena's relief and the fatigue that would surely follow.

After a time, she leaned back in his arms and looked him over in that clinical way she had sometimes. "It's good. I'm good. Really I am. You want to keep working," she said.

"Yes."

"You wouldn't sleep even if you came to bed."

"I couldn't."

"Finish this in two hours so we can get back to our lives?" Elena asked.

She had heard Nadia say it, or Jerry, or Helt. She had spent so much time listening, hoping. If only he could let her, let everyone, get back to their lives. He wanted to tell her he regretted all the anxious hours she'd spent, the anger, the hurt, the stress. He wanted to lie to her and say, "Sure," but that would be so unfair.

"I won't be able to do that."

"I know," Elena said.

"I want you safe. Things could get dicey tonight, and I want you safe. I want you home safe. Someone from NSS is tailing you. Someone will follow you on the train. Someone will watch your house all night. Try to sleep, beloved. Please try."

"I'll try," Elena said. "I'll keep the interface on my pillow. I'll feel better if I know I can hear you."

"In that case, we should get it from Nadia's office," Helt said.

28

No There, There, Yet

Helt found it, a segment of time from the Athens elevator gone, deleted, vanished. It had been an easy fix; the camera's state was null unless something moved. Only a few ticks in the timeline replaced whatever had been removed. The marker was right there. The SM time, the real one, ran from 1850 through 2000.

What he felt was anger, bitter anger. His beloved SysSu was full of incompetent idiots, people who didn't look at what they did or why they did it, or the extension to the SM hour would have been spotted. SysSu and NSS had stayed inside the box of one hour and ten minutes, confined by that boundary like mice in a cage. And who the hell was he blaming for that?

Helt Borresen was the incompetent idiot he had in mind.

File it. Put it away. He would pay for it in the middle of the night, some night years from now when he should be worrying about something else.

We didn't really stay there, he reminded himself. We've been looking for anything from the end of Ryan's shift to the time he was found dead. It's just that we sort of drew a box around the sacred SM hour.

Helt walked himself down the hall to the lounge and back again, went to the public version of the Murder Mess and increased the time frame from sixty to seventy minutes. He watched, with satisfaction, as Elena Maury's name moved to its new location, way, way out in the Oort cloud.

He added the time of the fall and the place of death. The vault's location exerted its force on the construct. A lot of Stonehenge and Petra dwellers joined Elena out in the periphery, well beyond reasonable suspicion. They were not close enough to the elevator. They had position locators on file before or after 1850 and couldn't have made it from home to do the deed and get back again. A hell of a lot of other names from Athens went scooting, because an hour and ten minutes was the new, improved, critical time, and now all that was needed was to fill in who rode the elevator that night in that invisible space.

That's not that different from where we started, Helt realized. Except now it feels different. Really different. "Well, I'll be damned," Evans said.

"Yeah," Helt said. "There's some other stuff coming at you. Documentation on where Elena Maury was during the time of the fall."

He sent the data to the version of the Murder Management files that NSS saw, that the morning shift would see in here. There were a few minutes of satisfying silence.

"Congratulations! Congratulations to both of you! Does Dr. Maury know?" Evans asked.

"Yes," Helt said.

"Oh, that's wonderful! I was so worried about her."

"So was I," Helt said. He was grinning like an idiot, and glad no one could see him.

But he didn't know who had killed Cash Ryan, not yet.

The hack came from someone in SysSu. One of ours. There were two techs here that night, maybe more people than that. You couldn't run what they ran on remote; if they'd done the deed they'd done it here.

The access records said the techs left a trail that evening, like everyone else here and most of the population of *Kybele.* Not on a security camera in SysSu. SysSu had nothing so primitive. Interface use was constant on the premises. Chatter, appointment schedules, info searches, inside SysSu there was no way not to leave trails everywhere.

The techs had left trails Wednesday night. They were demonstrably in SysSu for an hour before the SM. The techs would have known if Archer was here, or maybe they wouldn't. Archer came and went whenever he wanted and stayed sequestered in his office for hours without coming out.

Oh, shit. Archer didn't have to be *here* that night. Archer had hardwired access to SysSu in his quarters. He was the exec. He'd built the network. An offsite location was a security precaution. He'd implied he was home eating *galaktoboureko*, and he probably had been.

Helt went to Archer's office. He unlocked the drawer where Archer had stashed Cash Ryan's home unit. He picked up the sack and hauled it back to Nadia's office. His fingerprints were going to be all over the thing and he could have cared less. Fingerprints, even Archer's, would say so much less than a record of tampering, if there was one. Helt dug the innards out of the machine and hooked up the transfer cables that would strip everything out for review.

Split screen of the data that came up and the records Jerry had made of it that night matched all the way down.

Archer hadn't tampered with it since it went in his drawer. Archer had messed with the Athens elevator timeline. But messing with timelines didn't mean he'd killed anyone. It meant he'd helped Doughan cover up a trip up the Athens elevator.

Wait a minute. More than one trip.

The Athens elevator camera should have had very little down time at shift change Wednesday evening, and it didn't. The captures were less frequent after that bulge, as expected. But they didn't show Wesley Doughan, and David II said Doughan had gone to the bar that evening.

DOUGHAN, WEDNESDAY 18, THE LAB, 1630

The elevator didn't show him going up or down at any time after noon. He could have taken the stairs. Cameras didn't show him on the staircase, either. Or the staircase camera record had been nipped away, too.

Right there. Two little blips, neat little excisions of a time segment from the lobby camera that watched the elevator exit stairs. Any captures that might have been recorded between sixteen twenty and sixteen thirty-seven replaced by blank nothing.

It was objective. Doughan's location was verifiable via David II. Therefore, Doughan's travel had been erased that evening.

Helt added Doughan's deleted stairwell trip and Archer's likely role in hiding it to the factors in the Huerfano Murder Mess. The two execs hovered near Cash Ryan, flimsy wraiths, soap bubbles. But no one else circled him that closely.

Archer and Doughan were not stupid men. If Doughan had done this thing, he'd been convinced that the danger was so great, the risk so near, that he needed a quick answer from Cash Ryan.

Archer had covered for him after the fact; put that aside.

Transparency had been violated. Charges needed to be filed immediately, arrests should be made; crime was crime and justice must be done. Put that aside because Doughan was still prowling somewhere. That meant he hadn't found out what Ryan had done yet and he believed, he was completely convinced, that it wasn't something trivial.

Done what, where?

Ryan wanted to live here, not die here. He did something that he could get to and undo if he got what he wanted. Therefore, inside? Something he could get to from inside? Had to be, because when the thrusters were on nobody was going out the locked seals.

Oh, shit. That meant he had six years of time, both of Ryan's tours, to dissect and a surface area of too much to examine. Too much squared, with too many crevices, corners, that could hold a control box. If Ryan planted something long ago, it would decrease the search area, a little. There had been less interior surface thirteen years ago, fewer places to be.

But the past three years was a better time to stash something away. An interface. It could be something that small, that simple. Ryan couldn't depend on an interface he'd left twelve, eleven, even ten years ago. The thing would need new batteries from time to time, and code had changed too much. The thing would have to be reprogrammed from the bottom up.

So a new interface, or something that looked like one. A simple, everyday thing; if someone found it, big deal. Yes, there were more places to hide things now, but Ryan would want to be able to get back to where he'd left his control box.

Triggered from inside, but he'd worked *outside*. Something outside controlled from inside. Cash Ryan wanted to live here, not die here. He would not put the interior of *Kybele* at risk; he wouldn't want to risk his own precious hide. But he wanted to offer a real threat to Doughan, something—a threat to the external systems. A crippling but not lethal threat, something that would take years, decades, a lifetime to repair, rebuild.

So he could tell Doughan how valuable he was. How he, Cash Ryan would protect the ship from dangerous saboteurs, like the fake Seed Bankers.

And then the future was his. Rewarded for finding and disabling the threat, he could live happily ever after, with Elena, except what that twisted mind might do to the concept of "happy" made Helt shudder. The man had blackmailed his own mother.

This office was too small, SysSu was too small. Helt wanted the relief of seeing an infinite horizon; he wanted to *Gå på ski i fjellet* and look out at distant peaks, at moonlight on snow. Because he couldn't do that, he walked out through the lobby to the agora.

The agora was deserted. The hut in the mountains was long ago, the securities of *mor* and *far* and childhood forever unreachable, and this was the future he wanted to live in. It was in danger, and Doughan hadn't showed up yet, damn him. Doughan wasn't coming across the agora toward SysSu.

Doughan's interface was still in Nav, on the floor. The IA's trail tonight was clearly marked, if Doughan would only look. The IA had set out all the bait he could think of. Invading Doughan's private space, his office, should have been enough to bring him out. What was he waiting for?

The spectrum display in the lobby was in reverse order now, violet to red. Nothing else had changed. Helt had to keep moving. Lobby to lounge, lounge to lobby, with stretches and bends, and his muscles felt better, but the designated Special Investigator was still building endangered castles in the air, structures built of wild associations, improbable coincidences, hopes and nightmares. The only thing to do was to see how high they got before they toppled.

So okay, Ryan had messed with something outside, something that was vulnerable. Helt didn't have a clue, not an engineer's clue, not a commander's clue about what it might be. He wished he could ask Doughan what he needed to be looking for.

Because he was a careful man, Helt had checked the heat pack in the Nav jumpsuit before he put it on again and took the elevator down to Level Two. By the time the projections of *Kybele*'s surface were glowing in the Mission Control room, he'd sorted out that Ryan would want to set up his sabotage near Nav, near the shuttle port, somewhere near the waistline exit, the drop tunnel, where departing craft fell through *Kybele* into the Big Black. New colonist former contract worker Ryan would want to keep working on Nav projects.

The drop tunnel was close to the changing room. The tunnel was the most direct route to the surface there was, four kilometers of nothing that went straight down and out. Shuttles loaded and unloaded passengers and freight, closed their airlocks, were towed around a nice gentle curve and then dropped nose down through the longest polished black stone tube ever imagined.

Helt wanted a close look at the surface near the drop tunnel.

The nearest outside cameras were mounted near the periphery of the hole. There were others on the spinning struts of the plasma shield that would travel by every seven minutes. Because traffic was still leaving from time to time, the frame was stationary for now, floating in place over *Kybele*'s black and barren surface. The nearest strut was tethered a kilometer away from the shuttle bay.

Doughan's command chair was beginning to feel comfortable. Helt trawled visuals of the surface near the drop tunnel, staring at one square meter of rock at a time, circling the perimeter. He didn't see anything in the first circuit, so he went a meter out and began again. Whatever was out there was probably black. It was probably black and hidden in a pit. Black night on black stone for three and a half minutes, blue earthlight on black stone for three and half minutes; the movie was boring and this wasn't the way to scan it anyway.

Shape recognition was faster. Straight lines, squares, rectangles, curves sized at, oh, one meter, generous, to five centimeters, wimpy, and that meant the program might tag some pebbles, but.

Find.

Black, blue, black, blue, the fast-forward made Mission Control look like the inside of a crazed lighting storm. Helt reached out to thumbnail the flickers to a corner of the screens so he could look at something else, *anything* else. He needed sharp vision and his eyes were getting tired.

"Do you have any idea what you're looking for?" Doughan asked.

Helt felt himself jump in a startle reaction he hoped didn't show. He had expected, planned, *hoped* for Wesley Doughan to show up, and still, he was surprised by the behavior of his own right hand. It hovered immobile, frozen in place, flickering blue, above the keyboard. Doughan rolled a chair back from the next station and calmly began to sit himself down. Helt forced his hand to move and clicked the search display down to a thumbnail. Officer Evans was live in NSS, listening in. He hoped.

Helt took a deep breath. He started to tell Doughan he had no idea, really, what he was looking for, but he didn't. He'd been looking for Doughan, because he figured he'd come here, sooner or later. He didn't say that, either. "Something small enough to haul out in a tool kit, drop—"

"Or throw," Doughan said.

"Along with a wrench or something."

"Tools are tethered. You take a wrench and a clamp. You clamp the something and release the tether on the clamp."

"Even better," Helt said. His terror didn't make his voice quaver, and he would forever be proud of that when he got old. If he got old. "You clamp the something and leave the clamp on it. Then you say, 'Oops. I forgot something,' and you go back and get the wrench. And leave the something behind. I figured I'd start looking close to the shuttleport."

"Why?" Doughan asked.

"So Ryan could trigger whatever's out there on the skin without much power, and without checking out a closed suit."

"That's the craziest fucking thing I've ever heard."

Doughan didn't use the f-word in situations of ordinary stress. That he had now didn't increase Helt's sense of personal safety.

"I wish I'd thought of it." Doughan rolled his chair closer to the workstation. It was quiet in here. Helt heard his own pulse hammering in his ears. He had enough adrenalin flowing that any trace of fatigue was completely washed away.

"So what do you think it could be?" Doughan asked.

"Probably not an explosive," Helt said. "That would do some damage, sure, but turning rock into rubble wouldn't hurt us much. And I don't know what's vulnerable this close."

An unfamiliar "Meep, meep" came from the thumbnail. It had stopped flickering.

No matches.

"What was your search perimeter?" Doughan asked.

"Half a k."

"You're looking in the wrong place. Let's try the drop tunnel."

Views of slick, curved black rock scrolled by, a starscape behind them. "Why?" Helt asked, but the cameras finished their sequence and he saw a ladder, a substantial one with big fat steps, carved into a channel in the wall. Cables and pulleys flanked it on the right, a line of dull charcoal track between them. Doughan started at the skin end of the tunnel and focused on the ladder. There were shadows behind every rung of it, plenty of potential hiding space.

The view froze. The line of shadow at the left side of the ladder was irregular, thicker at the back. Something was fastened behind it. Helt reached to zoom it. Doughan was quicker. About five centimeters of black rod, the thickness of Helt's thumb, was fastened behind the left side rail of the ladder, just below one of the steps. The rod's end hung about five meters up from the big black outside.

"Antenna," Doughan said.

Helt went to site archives. The cameras were set to capture images every three days. Motion sensors, sure, but they cycled every three days in addition to that. The last set of images had been taken yesterday. He clicked back; the rod was there on October 6. It wasn't there on October 3. Now you see it, now you don't.

"That recent," Doughan said. "It's a relief in some ways. That thing wasn't there to be missed for very long." Doughan pulled his hands away from his keyboard and spread his fingers wide, made fists, stretched out his hands again. "It's really tempting to send a camera bot up for a closer look. It's really tempting to do that right now. Let's not."

Helt hadn't realized he'd been holding his breath until he started to answer. He exhaled. "Okay."

"I don't want to jiggle the damned thing or set off a motion sensor, if it has one. Do you?" Doughan asked.

Helt shook his head. "I guess Ryan figured we wouldn't find it before the shuttle goes by on its way out."

"We might not have."

"Heh. We did. But he had to know that unless things worked out the way he wanted, he'd be on that shuttle. Or maybe he didn't care. Maybe he was so sure of himself that he had no doubt at all he'd be staying."

"I wish I knew what it was." Doughan frowned at the screen. "Okay, so there it is. The question is, what is it supposed to do?"

"It's supposed to mess up something."

"Helt. I have to know what it is. I'm going to send a bot down with a sensor to tell me whether it's live or not."

"Then you'll call the bomb squad?"

"Let me see if it's live first." Doughan picked up a driver console. Call it by any fancy name you wanted and what Doughan held in his hands would still give you an advantage in any video game you cared to play.

"How long is it going to take this bot to get there?" Helt asked. He watched Doughan play with the controller. Sure enough, even if you were *Kybele*'s Navigation exec, controllers seemed to work better if you stuck out your tongue a little.

"Two, three minutes," Doughan said.

Helt shut up and watched the bot descend the line of track beside the ladder. It had manipulators and cameras on flexible stalks. It had a hitch behind it for hauling a platform. It could bring supplies up and down in the unlikely event that a departing craft developed trouble on its way out.

Doughan probably didn't know about the extra minutes that had to have been added to the SM hour. He'd come here without an interface because his was outside the door until and if he'd picked it up.

On one level, Helt's fingers busied themselves with the network that kept communications live and found that interface access was no problem in the drop tunnel. If you were in a closed suit, you could call home. No problem. On a different level, he watched himself working beside Doughan, both of them determined to get *Kybele* out of danger before they dealt with anything else. Time had stopped in here. No past, no future, existed until this job was done.

It was precisely the mind-set he got from time to time, the one that had kept him from looking for the real length of the SM hour.

Helt leaned back in his chair and looked at the trapdoor in the ceiling.

"It's not live," Doughan said.

Helt was very glad to hear that.

"It's not leaking charged particles, either. Here's a view."

Helt watched the bot hold up a manipulator arm and shine a light on the little box. A camera stalk wavered back and forth, focused itself, and sent its images to Mission Control. The best close-up was a sharply focused view of a rectangular black box with a raised bar code on its otherwise flat surface. Helt asked a program to read it. "It's a microwave transmitter, printed in the industrial park, here, on October 1."

"Appearances can be deceiving. It could be filled with explosive. I can't think of a bomb that size that could do anything more than scar the pleasant symmetry of our exit tunnel." Doughan still held the controller.

"You don't want to call the bomb squad," Helt said.

"Not yet."

If the thing blew itself to shards it would be hard to prove, beyond a shadow of a doubt, that Cash Ryan had put it there. There probably weren't biologic traces on it, though, anyway. It had been placed by a mittened hand, or a bot.

Helt looked at the specs on the bot's camera stalks. "You could X-ray it."

"Good idea."

The radiogram showed circuit cards and wiring that matched a slice of transmitter programmed into the 3-D printer specs Helt pulled here from David II's territory. Helt sighed. "Okay, it's a microwave transmitter-receiver."

"Aimed at nothing," Doughan said.

Helt had spent days trying to tease sense out of an hour that had just turned into an hour and ten minutes and looked very different because of it. He'd scanned screen captures that didn't show Cash Ryan stalking women until he moved the time frame. There was nothing on the surface that could be damaged—now. Not yet.

There had to be a visual somewhere in Nav files.

"What are you looking for?" Doughan had his elbow on the desk and was using his fist as a prop for his chin.

Time stops when you're busy. Helt tried to remember that, and never did. "A cross-section of *Kybele* that shows the ice layer in place."

"There won't be one over the exit port. A dome goes over that. We don't want to have to plow out to launch the landers and we want to keep that ice around for a long, long time. All the way home, actually. We'll be running excess heat out beneath it, freezing and thawing that ice, all the way."

"So no ice there to damp down the signal." Helt filled Mission Control with a projection of *Kybele* en route, a dirty white ball with the tiny glass eye of the drop tunnel at her waist. The snowball nestled inside a spindle of struts, struts that supported a gossamer net made of coils of superconducting wire.

"No ice there, but enough ice on *Kybele* to insulate the surface from some of the heat we'll be making, because the surface has to stay cold," Helt said.

"To protect the superconducting coils," Doughan said. "Because if a point on the mesh heats up—not much, just a little, because a puny microwave transmitter's been hitting on it every time it goes by, it transitions out of the superconducting state."

" 'And vaporizes the coil with a satisfying burst of energy.' I read that somewhere once." Because he could, Helt blew up the shield, well, the projection of it, in a satisfying display of multicolored fire. For a very fast job, he thought it was pretty good. Doughan leaned back in his chair to watch it fade.

"Yeah," Doughan said. "That little toy could do that. That bastard took a long-term view, didn't he?"

Build the plasma shield and deploy it. Turn it off around Saturn and scoop up ice. Deploy it again when we're leaving Saturn. *Kybele* could not even *get* to Saturn without that shield in place.

"I still want some solid proof," Helt said. "I want to find what generates the signal he planned to use to turn the thing on."

"He could have sent it a wake-up call from his interface."

"That's instant ID," Helt said. "I think he wanted something a little harder to trace."

"Like a transmitter, a duplicate of that transmitter-receiver out on the skin. I still want to bring that one in," Doughan said.

"I know you do. But I want the complete picture," Helt said. "I want unmistakable physical evidence that connects this to Ryan. When we present this, I want the narrative complete. I want the controller that turns this thing on and I think I know where it is." Helt leaned back and stared at the trapdoor in the ceiling.

"Up there?" Doughan asked.

"Yeah," Helt said.

Doughan's interface was not at the door of Mission Control. This time, while Doughan was climbing into a coverall in the changing room, Helt found some gloves and put them on. The camera on his interface would serve to photograph the interface or controller or duplicate transmitter-receiver in situ. He didn't plan to touch it, and he didn't want traces of Helt on anything he might find nearby. He found a plastic-lined canvas sack and stowed it in a pocket. There might be other evidence around.

Elena was home, far out of range of anything that might blow up here, he hoped. Evans knew they had gone into Mission Control. If Doughan killed him tonight, he'd have to destroy Helt's interface to hide what he'd done, and Evans would be listening until that happened. If only one of them came back . . .

All hell would break loose.

He would die fighting if he could.

Helt pulled down the staircase, the one right here in the corner of the changing room. This was going to take some acting. He had to cover how hair-triggered he felt. He had to move with caution and stay alert, and hide his fears, if he could.

It was really dark up there.

"We'll have to put usage monitors on these trapdoors," Doughan said.

"I'm afraid you're right. Are there any big torches on that shelf over there? Work lights?"

Doughan rummaged. "Not tonight. They've probably all migrated down to the new tunnels."

"It shouldn't matter."

Nothing mattered but getting this done, not now. Helt climbed until his headlamp cleared the top of the stairs and gave the surrounding area a close look. To do this right, he would have to check one side of a ceiling beam along its entire length and then come back along the other. "This is going to be easier with two people," he said, and got out of the way so Doughan could join him.

"My money's on that it's close to the wall. Signal strength is going to count," Doughan said.

"Start with the wall closest to the tunnel, sure. If it's here at all, it's close to a trapdoor. This one, or a different one, or the one over Mission Control. You take the right side, I'll stay on the left." Ryan was about Helt's height; Helt stretched his arm up to gauge how high something should be to put it in easy reach. He looked hard at what was close by. No foreign object was in reach of the trapdoor they'd just come through. The two of them moved toward the wall and stepped from beam to beam, searching, centered in bobbling circles of light that moved farther and farther apart. The wall was bare, black, and unmarred.

When Helt had been up here with Yves, Yves had led him in pretty much a straight line next to the wall to get to the train access. Doughan's control room would be somewhere to the left, along the beam his feet were on right now. Mission Control was walled with rock on three sides; it was well protected from the Big Black outside and from the rest of the ship. He'd seen nothing so far but smooth black rock, monotonous, pristine beams, and ceiling viewed from the top side. He didn't know what the ceiling was made of. "Nothing so far," Helt said. "I'm moving over to the area above Mission Control. I'm wondering if it would suit Cash Ryan's sense of fun to plant his little secret right over your head."

"Why not?" Doughan said. "This whole exercise is surreal enough that you might be right."

Helt was trying not to fall off a beam, and the concentration helped his tension. A little. "I'm assuming I've found the right beam." Helt made a left turn, held out his arms, and walked heel-toe on it. "It feels like about the right distance to me."

"Scientific method," Doughan said. "Aren't there numbers or signs on top of these trapdoors?"

"Usually a person would be coming up a ladder from below, not wandering around up here to practice walking a tightrope."

"Just walk on the floor—I mean, the ceiling."

"I don't know if it will hold my weight."

"I can't see your light," Doughan said.

"I can't see the trapdoor." Helt blinked and saw what he was looking for, the access he wanted, nestled between two beams. "Gotcha." The trapdoor was a nice-sized box shape, easy to see once you saw it.

"The controller?" Doughan asked. His voice said he was closer than he had been, that he was coming over to join Helt.

"The trapdoor." Helt didn't see anything, no bumps or boxes, not on the beams or the sides of the trapdoor box. Keep a safe perimeter away from it, was the idea. He got his interface out of his pocket, thumbed on the camera, and looked for a likely place to stand while he examined the next side. He wanted to be more than an arm's length away from the trapdoor, maybe two arm's lengths, to get a good, detailed view. There was nothing on the next side, either. He went two beams farther to get a good look at side three. It was clean. He looked up at the wall.

There it was, a black, slim rectangle, not on the stairwell frame but up on the wall, deep in the corner where the walls met, higher than your line of sight would be if you were concentrating on keeping your balance up here. You had to look up to see it and if you were coming up a ladder from below, you'd probably be looking for conduit instead. The thing had a little stubby antenna sticking out of it. The antenna was aligned parallel to the drop tunnel.

Helt walked the beam beneath him toward it, not too close. The best place to get a good picture of it would be right next to the wall, looking along the wall and up into the corner. Okay. That wasn't too close to the thing. Really, it wasn't. He put his hand carefully on the solid stone of the wall, as solid and safe as anything could ever be on *Kybele*. He braced his shoulder against the wall and lifted his arm to use the viewfinder function on his interface. He brushed away the spider web that floated past his face.

There were no spiders here.

The laser caught him in the left eye, a direct, unprotected hit.

29

An Eye for Wisdom

Helt dived for the trapdoor because it was going to be a bitch getting down the stairs with one hand, and his left hand was permanently attached to the white fire and the hot wet he had to keep pressed tight behind his fingers.

He fell short of the trapdoor. He figured he'd lie here forever. He wished Doughan hadn't screamed like that. Helt's ears were still ringing.

You're not dead, he told himself.

Someone was grunting and breathing hard right next to Helt's ear.

"Don't move," Doughan growled.

No way was he planning on it.

It occurred to him that if Ryan had set something else to blow up when he tripped the trigger on that laser, then he and Doughan had been utter and complete idiots. Someone should check on that.

"I said lie still!" Doughan's voice barked.

Helt hadn't known he was moving.

"The only thing that blew up was you."

Doughan's voice sounded like it was at the end of a tunnel somewhere.

"Roll him on this," Elena said. "Tie him on."

Helt was belly down between two of the beams. The ceiling held his weight just fine. He wanted to see where Elena was but he couldn't, could *not*, open his eyes. Doughan grabbed him and rough-rolled him up onto a flat metal surface and Helt felt straps bite into his thighs. Someone had a hand in his armpit.

"Harness strap," Elena said. She shoved her hand behind his back and a what felt like a strap tightened across his chest. She snapped the ends of the strap to something behind his head.

She was supposed to be at home, Helt remembered. Stubborn woman. No way to get here from home that fast. She stayed close. She followed me. She cares. She really cares.

"You're a heavy son of a bitch for a skinny guy."

That was Severo's voice. Helt opened his right eye and watched Severo's hand reach for the end of the stretcher.

The stretcher tilted. Helt didn't like that at all. His right eye was closed again but light came through it anyway, too damned bright. He wasn't in the crawl space anymore. Other arms reached up to help, holding the stretcher steady. Six people, three on a side, eased the tied sausage named Helt onto the wheeled gurney at the foot of the trapdoor ladder in Mission Control.

"You should be glad I got a nap before we started this. I'm rested and fresh," Calloway said. "Probably my hands won't even shake. You can relax your hand now."

Calloway? Helt risked a quick look through his right eye. He got a view of a belly in a white cotton scrub shirt and looked up to see Calloway's chin from below. Round light overhead with a handle on it. He was in the clinic and someone had drugged him because he didn't remember the trip here.

That was nice. He didn't think he wanted to remember that trip, but then he almost did and that wasn't nice at all.

"You can relax your hand now," Calloway said again, or maybe for the first time.

The fuck I can, Helt told him, but he couldn't manage to say it out loud. Somebody had done something to his muscles and the white fire where his eye had been still burned his fingers but Calloway was lifting his hand away from his face and that was somehow not a problem.

"Catch him, Martin." Elena's voice was clipped.

Catch me? I'm right here. Catch who? Helt heard a few scuffling sounds behind his head and down somewhere, so he was still probably on a gurney and the noise was coming from the floor. Helt would have craned his neck to look but he wasn't going to open his eyes, no matter what Calloway wanted.

Helt hung from the World Tree on a harness so Doughan could make sure they could slide him down easy, but a branch was in his eye and he was bleeding, bleeding fire from his eye and he tried to close it, to block out the light that was black but it stabbed and shrieked; a thousand Norns were cutting threads that should never be cut, never.

He fought, but someone was holding him down, someone with at least eight strong arms. "Take him deeper," Calloway's voice said.

"What do I tell him, Martin?" Elena asked. She sounded so unhappy, so frightened.

"Tell him to look . . .

at . . .

you . . ."

"I'm right here," Elena said, from the mouth of the tunnel where Martin's voice had chased itself in circles like a falling leaf, but Martin wasn't hurt; he was going to be okay.

Helt opened his eyes and saw her, Elena, his only her, her face inches away. So he kissed her with his eyes, his perfect eyes, and brought her with him into the tunnel, the soft, warm tunnel.

"Nice place, this Deeper," Helt said.

TUESDAY 0533

"Catch him, Martin." Elena's voice was harsh. When she gave an order, she gave an order.

Catch me? I'm right here. Catch who? Helt heard a few scuffling sounds behind his head and down somewhere, so he was still probably on a gurney and the noise was coming from the floor. Helt would have craned his neck to look but he wasn't going to open his eyes, no matter what Calloway wanted.

The focus jerked and Helt looked down from inside the monitor in the clinic lobby, the one he'd watched when Elena and Calloway were doing the autopsy. Doughan lay flat on the floor. Martin had grabbed Doughan's ankles and was holding them up in the air, about the height of Martin's knees.

"Did I faint?" Doughan asked.

Martin nodded.

That was a recording, from a past he wouldn't mind forgetting. That was before, when Doughan came to the clinic, not now. An assault of camera views fractured into a kaleidoscope, a stodgy robot plow making black furrows in a farm under Center, a view from a spybot that showed Doughan pacing back and forth in the bedroom of his townhouse, naked and muttering, The Frontier full of empty tables with a soundtrack of dishes clattering, too loud, too loud.

Kybele's hide loomed in front of him, her black, pitted bulk growing by the minute. It was a view that had to be from the control room of the incoming shuttle but he wasn't there. He was flat on his back and no matter how hard he shut his eyes the cascade of images wouldn't stop. *Kybele* spun like a top and Helt reached out to try to grab her because she was going to spin him off and he would fall forever.

He tried to scream.

"Shh," Elena's voice said. Her head was on his chest, and she had her arms tight around him.

"It's your new eye. That's all. I'm here. Shh."

The views changed to scrolling columns of code, and somehow that was better. Someone's in Mission Control and they're playing the shuttle feeds, Helt decided. That's what I saw.

"Don't be afraid," Elena said.

The room was dark.

"It's just your eye. Rest."

He had been asleep but he was waking up now. Elena was beside him. He didn't want to wake her. It felt like early morning, really early morning. The curtains hanging on her bedroom window didn't look quite right.

Helt closed his eyes. Binocular vision was neat. He'd missed it when it wasn't there.

TUESDAY 1313

"Today? Today is Tuesday." Mena kissed him on the cheek. "Tuesday afternoon."

That's what it said in the upper left. Helt wondered where the time and date tag came from, but it wasn't particularly bothersome.

"Are you hungry yet?" Mena asked.

Helt tried to shake his head in a no, but there was a strap across his forehead and soft bars on either side of his head.

“A few more hours and that can come off.”

“How long did the surgery take?” Helt asked.

“Four hours,” Mena said.

Why had Archer blacked out the feeds about the World Tree? They were here, right here, stills and videos, arranged in order from the first gouge Yves’s chisel had made to the perfection that loomed in Petra now, posted by different people at different times, but Archer had walled them away.

TUESDAY 1528

“How is he?”

That was Martin Kumar’s voice.

“Better,” Elena said. “He hasn’t been as agitated. I think those image commands you told him to use helped.”

1529 TUESDAY, OCTOBER 14, 2209

Yeah, it was the same week he’d lost a couple of days of. I know how to turn off the lights, Helt remembered, so he did.

TUESDAY 2312

There was something he wanted to see in the Murder Mess Huerfano. He couldn’t see it from here unless Jerry let him in.

He typed the letters on the interface he didn’t have and wondered where it was, really.

Helt. Jerry?

“I am so fucking glad to see you, boss!” Audio. Helt was afraid he would wake Elena. She was asleep in the chair, curled up with her head on the arm of it. She didn’t stir.

Helt. Shhh. Elena’s asleep. Show me the Huerfano?

Jerry. Can’t. You’re on remote and your locks are too good on it.

Helt. State of Kybele, then.

“You don’t need Jerry for that,” Helt’s voice told Helt. That was confusing. Helt turned off the lights again.

WEDNESDAY 0014

Helt had it all in order, a fix that would serve, and he’d scanned a thousand sources to do it, pulled premises and positions from think tanks, documents, philosophies, rants. He could do that now. He could have done it before, in weeks. This new eye was more than an eye, so he'd done it in hours.

Some of the people who had thought about governance and power were hidebound, hobbled into service of old traditions, and some were bright spirits who had looked hard at traditions, new or old, and gone on to things that were new in their antiquity.

He had reviewed them all even though he was tired, so tired, because the structure of governance that was needed to hold *Kybele* together shouldn't topple; it was stable at its heart. What the execs had done could never be undone, but if Giliam could put the patch into formal words and charges, it might serve.

"A tripod is stable on uneven ground if you just adjust the legs," Helt said. He knew where he was and when it was but he wanted to hear Elena's voice. "When is it?"

"Wednesday morning, just after midnight," Elena said.

Helt yawned.

"I'm right here," Elena said.

WEDNESDAY 0630, Helt read in the left upper corner of the world.

Cool sheets over temperfoam beneath him, not the aluminum stretcher. Elena was looking down at him, calm and matter-of-fact, and her hand was on his left forearm.

His arm rested on a bedspread he knew very well, gold brocade on black, some of the gold threads a little shaggy because Mena was fond of the pattern and she said it got softer as it aged.

Mena's bedroom wasn't exactly the same as he remembered it.

Elena had moved a chair close to the bed; playback showed her getting up to look down at him, and on the other side of the bed IV stands and monitors stood near the headboard. Elena focused on something in the array of readouts. Helt viewed her from a spybot over the bedroom door. She stood silhouetted against the curtains, and as she bent her head to check a monitor, he watched himself lying on Mena's bed looking at nothing. That made him a little dizzy. A close-up view of the monitors showed him that his pulse and blood pressure were normal. That was nice.

Elena sat down again and rested her cheek on his arm. There were so many things to play with inside his head but he knew they were outside, in files and records and in every sensor on the ship.

"Is this love?" Helt asked. "Is this how it feels?"

Elena lifted her head. Her smile was *La Giaconda*'s. No, better than that. "I can't know, for you. I think it is, for me. But we have . . ."

"Time to find out."

Helt stroked her hair with his free hand and closed his eyes. All of them.

WEDNESDAY 1312

Jim Tulloch was in the chair, not Elena. Helt had slept, deep morning sleep, and then he'd called a startled Giliam and told him what was needed. Giliam was working his ass off and that was good. Helt had gone back to sleep again, apparently.

"You presented Elena and Calloway with quite a challenge," Jim said. "The structures of the eye were completely coagulated; no surprise there. Replacement was going to be tricky anyway because of the amount of optic nerve that was fried. They were going to give you a standard eye and let the microbots do what they could with quite a lot more splicing than is routine. But you heard Martin's voice and insisted, in a definitive fashion, that you wanted infrared, at least, and anything else he had been working on with Nadia and Jerry."

"I did?" Helt asked.

"And you insisted that they call Archer in so they could get his input, too. You don't want to review the audio right now."

"Yes, I do."

Helt damped his internal review function after he heard a word or two of what he'd said. Jim grinned.

"I signed up to be a test subject," Helt said.

"All of us are." Jim wasn't smiling. He looked as sad, as serious, as Helt had ever seen him look.

"Give me a second or two," Helt said.

WEDNESDAY 1205

"If his vision is as augmented as Martin says it will be, he's going to be a magnificent tool." Giliam Obrecht's interface had recorded this an hour ago; Jim Tulloch had been in Giliam's office.

"Tool? Helt's no tool. He might become a madman." Jim stretched his legs out to full length and looked at his socks. They were both blue. "No, he won't. He's an adaptive bastard. I think he'll manage to narrow the fields when he needs to. I mean, well beyond switching to normal vision at will; Martin says almost everyone masters that in a few hours. Martin's given him an amazing number of choices for selective inputs."

"He's given us an amazing amount of work to do. Every lawyer and three linguists on ship plus several others on Earth have been set specific tasks, to be completed by dawn tomorrow. Directed, Helt says, toward the goal of saving the ship's future. And he's been checking in with one or several of us about every half hour. I feel whipped into near-frenzy, and what's worse, I'm enjoying the feeling. Have you seen him yet?" Giliam asked.

"I'm going over there right now. The dragons say it's okay."

Giliam looked worried.

"It was a figure of speech, Giliam," Jim said. "I'm not having auditory hallucinations. Mena and Elena say it's okay."

WEDNESDAY 1314

"You called me an adaptive bastard," Helt said.

Jim grinned at him. "I did."

"Adaptive bastard that I am, this still takes some getting used to," Helt said.

"What does? Augmented vision? Data you can access by focusing on a virtual keyboard?"

"I won't run amok. I'm wiring in safeguards against that."

"In your head?"

"In the social contract," Helt said.

"How do you feel?"

"I don't feel pain. There's some sort of local in there, Elena says. Timed not to wear off until the eyelids and the white part, the sclera, until all that stuff is healed up. The new stuff can't feel pain . . ." Helt checked schemata of the "tissue" layers of his new retina and its attachments to his optic nerve. Not a pain fiber in there anywhere.

"How do you feel about who you are now? How have you changed, Helt?" Jim asked his questions very gently.

"You just won't take an easy answer, will you?" Helt asked, and got the grin he was looking for. "I'm not hurt like my mom was. What happened didn't scar my sense of empathy or my ability to feel emotions. I'm still me. And knowing that makes it easier to . . ."

The spybots on the house were still working. Via their inputs, Helt looked for Elena and found her in the kitchen with Mena. Mena sliced something on a board and Elena worked at the kitchen table, a cup of tea beside her. The mood in there was rich with comfort, the feeling of small talk about important things.

". . . to accept the risks of love. The changes . . ." Out on the surface, microchanges in temperature marked *Kybele*'s spin from light to dark and to light again. The eyes on her poles marked the path of the incoming shuttle, on schedule, moving as it should be. Vibrations in Level Three said that crews were boring out more living space. If he asked for audible range near the crew down there, he could hear laughter and small talk.

In Center, a swirl of afternoon breeze brought down a drift of rustling aspen leaves.

". . . I wish I could show you. I can't, Jim. You'll have to trust that I'm still me."

Jim looked him over with a calculating look that spoke of skills he'd honed over years and wars, through failures and successes with people in grief, in despair, in madness, and seemed satisfied with what he saw.

"I'll call my mom, once we're under way. We're strangers, but I think—I *know*—we'd like to get to know each other. There's enough distance now. And we're more alike than we were. Now."

Jim nodded. "Yeah. You're still you. How do I look in infrared?" Jim asked.

Helt looked. Seeing him that way was still a little weird.

"I'll tell you if you get Giliam's ass over here when I bring the execs in for a conference."

"When will that be?"

"Probably sooner than you think."

"I love you, man," Jim Tulloch said.

THURSDAY 0600

Elena was so beautiful this morning, too, sleeping on her side, turned away so he could truly appreciate the beauty of her shoulder beside him. There would be more mornings like this. It was something he *knew*, and the certainty of knowing it was the most solid thing in this spinning world.

It had taken him a minute or two to line up the flood of memory, nightmare, analysis, and other things he didn't want to think about for a while, to stack the files into chronologic order and ready them for this morning's work. Helt looked at the ceiling and the State of *Kybele,* much augmented, capable of analyzing so much more now, cleaner, thicker, richer, and still imperfect.

Giliam had his presentation ready. Giliam didn't think he did, but he did. Archer and Doughan were both still asleep, and so was Mena.

Elena had been beside him since Monday night, cleared of the suspicion of murder in the hours so long ago in SysSu, but he hadn't acknowledged her relief or her joy then, or the mix of emotions she must have felt. He hadn't offered her support or sympathy or celebration. On that crazy night, he had done nothing but send her away. He'd been obsessed with ways to get Doughan to stalk him. There had been no time for her needs then and he wasn't sure what he could do now, or ever, about it.

Elena rolled over, looked at his face, and laid her arm across his stomach. "Your eyelid is going to be a little scarred. It was the best I could do."

"With what was available," Helt said. He reached for her hand and stroked her fingers. Her nails were so smooth. "Who's been taking care of your lab?"

"Susanna and Andrea." She leaned closer to his face. "You can't really see the sensor array unless you're close to the pupil. It looks a little strange."

"Monday night? I want to say something about Monday night. I sent you away," Helt said. "I wasn't there for you when you were getting used to the idea that the murder suspicion nightmare was over. I'm sorry. I'm so sorry."

"You had other things to worry about. And anyway, I didn't leave."

"You went to NSS and hung with Evans."

"I like her a lot," Elena said.

"Let's finish this up in the next . . ."

"Two?" Elena asked.

"Three or four hours and get back to our lives. I'll tell the execs we'll meet here at 1300," Helt said.

"Are you ready for that?"

"And Giliam."

Elena looked at him as if he were a contaminated cell culture. "You're not ready for this," she said.

The social lie he was about to offer shriveled up and ran away.

"I know," Helt said. "And Jim. Jim has to be here."

"You won't rest," Elena said.

"No."

"We'll talk about this after breakfast."

Elena got up and padded across the room to get her buckskin sarong.

"In bed?" Helt asked.

"Dream on," Elena said.

30

Old Masters

Giliam got there early. Mena ushered him in and went back to the kitchen. She'd brought in chairs and side tables, and stacked pillows from her great room behind Helt's shoulders so he was sitting up quite comfortably, his work stuff on a breakfast tray over the precisely smoothed surface of the brocade bedspread.

"Rembrandt, I'd say, the family assembled at the bedside of the dying patriarch, except you look far too healthy for that," Giliam said.

Helt accepted the statement for the sympathy it probably hid.

Giliam had his hands clasped behind his back and he rocked back and forth on his feet, evaluating the setting. "You haven't given me much time to sort this out, not even enough to check statutes on some of your more esoteric points."

Helt looked at the room around him to see how it might look to an outsider.

The bed lay in front of tall windows that let in dark rainy-day October light diffused by folds of sheer curtains. Sprays of vivid autumn leaves in Attic vases stood on Mena's tables here and there. The comforter evoked a sort of practical grandeur, maybe. Giliam was right. It was sort of Old Masters in here. "Sit down, Giliam. Mena does a good job, doesn't she?"

Giliam nodded and sat down.

"I looked over the draft of the changes to the Articles of Governance," Helt said. "It's good work, Giliam. Thank you."

"I'm not happy with the word *Lawspeaker* but no other term really works," Giliam said. "It was a strange role to play even in its historic antecedents, counselor, reference source, *goad.* What you've designed is a sort of sensory apparatus to praise successes and point out dangers in the body politic. It's not an executive position. Whoever fills it has no authority to do anything but advise. No authority at all."

"Heh," Helt said. "That's all to the good, isn't it?"

"Well, yes, but you can be ignored!"

"But not silenced."

"There is that," Giliam said.

Giliam Obrecht looked profoundly uncomfortable. Maybe it was the bedroom setting. "I'd be in your office for this but Mena won't let me out of here yet," Helt said. "House arrest."

He'd had his breakfast in the kitchen and made it back to bed, barely, with wobbles, was the truth of it. He'd spent the rest of the morning laying out decision trees of fact and conjecture, constantly revised via rapid exchanges with Nadia and Jerry and Severo and the changing status of the Murder Mess, the Huerfano version, accessed here so it could be displayed for everyone in the room.

"There are some aspects of this I simply haven't had time to consider," Giliam said.

Helt heard Archer's voice in the great room, heard Mena asking him if he'd come into the kitchen and carry a tray for her.

"You're not alone," Helt said. "You'll do fine. Let's play it by ear, shall we?"

The word *ear* reminded him that the long ear outside Mena's courtyard was still listening. Helt disabled it. Details, details.

Doughan came into the bedroom without stopping by the kitchen and halted at the edge of the bed. "Let me see that eye." He leaned over, inches away, to look closely at it, and then nodded. "Amazing." He looked around for the chair with the best view of the door, and sat down in it while Archer put a tray on a table. Archer came to the bedside in his turn. He clasped Helt's right hand in both of his, gripped it tightly and gave him the stare.

"It's okay, Archer. I'm back online."

Archer retreated without a word, set up a folding screen on his table, and lost himself in it while Mena went about the business of coffee and tea. She glanced into the great room, put her coffeepot down, and went to the door. Doughan watched her bring her visitor in. She indicated a chair and Jim Tulloch picked it up and brought it into the room.

"You, too?" Doughan asked.

"I'm here to keep Giliam focused," Jim said. He looked at seat location possibilities, brought the chair he was holding around to the other side of the bed, and put it down next to Doughan.

"Okay," Helt said. "Okay, you've been following the NSS reports, all of you. The latest news is that there are no traces of Cash Ryan in the vault Yves and I explored Monday night."

"There's nothing on the swabs, no DNA," Mena said.

"Even so, a strong case can be made that Cash Ryan was a terrorist and a traitor. The evidence for that would be stronger if I hadn't fried half of it."

"You're three minutes wrong about that," Doughan said. "The case was damaged here and there but it has Cash Ryan all over it. He opened that transmitter case and wired the laser in all by himself."

"So it's verified. Cash Ryan was a Bad Guy who planned some serious destruction."

It wasn't news to Doughan, but it seemed to be to Jim Tulloch. Helt watched him scoot down in his chair a little, stretch out his legs, and scan the company. He'd told Helt once that he never blocked the door when he was working, left an exit for a patient to take if he wanted to panic and leave. He had done that here, in this room. He'd placed his chair so that anyone here could get to the great room and Mena's front door if they felt they had to run for it.

Giliam had his head down and was entering data at a frantic pace.

"If I'd known that, if any of us here had known that. But we didn't," Helt said. "I'm supposed to notice if someone is making ripples in the communal pond. I didn't see this coming. If I had, I could have alerted Jim. I didn't; a man died. Your response was to give me the job of investigating a suicide that turned out to be a murder."

Helt didn't know how this was going to sell. He had to do it anyway. "You gave me the job because you had other work to do, and you had to do it in a hurry. I didn't find a murderer. I still haven't. I found a chain of mishaps done in haste. I have enough . . ."

He stopped because he was afraid. He stopped because he couldn't be sure he was doing the right thing.

"I have enough solid evidence to charge Navigation's exec with manslaughter, at least, and SysSu's exec with evidence tampering, at least."

Helt didn't expect surprise, and he saw none. He didn't expect denial, and he saw no signs of that, either. What he did see were tiny indicators of something that looked like relief in Doughan's posture and in the slightly slower rhythm of Archer's constant keyboard entries. Mena, by contrast, seemed to be bracing herself for a fight.

"The rule of law is clear. Charges should be filed and Severo should march you off the ship. It's the honorable thing for me to do." He sent the Murder Mess to their screens as a timeline. This time it wasn't the public version. It was the Huerfano version, all neat and tidy now except for some foggy blurs where Helt had no idea what had happened. "I don't want to do it. Here's what I think I know, salted with plenty of pure speculation. The facts are highlighted. They are not thick on the ground."

The room went dead quiet. Helt waited them out.

"This really isn't enough to successfully prosecute," Giliam said.

Archer looked up.

"It would be, except he doesn't have some of it right," Archer said. "Let's at least be accurate about our crimes. Wesley? Mena?"

"Let us help you, IA," Doughan said.

Mena gave a terse nod.

Let us help you. Let's get it right. It was the reaction Helt had hoped for, but his hope was based on projections that could have been faulty. Helt cleared his throat, because there was a lump in it. "Tell me where I got it wrong, then," Helt said.

He cleared his throat again. "Cash Ryan had a serious jones to stay on board; an obsession reinforced by the fact that he'd managed to get a tour up here. He had pulled off a faked degree, a faked job history, and that gave him absolute confidence, proof, that it's easy to fool people, even if your tool kit includes only bravado and a few hacks that any idiot can pull from the cloud."

"Add his successes at undiscovered stalking," Jim Tulloch said.

"Susanna was a substitute for Elena," Helt said. "I'm not protecting Elena, Jim. She doesn't need it. She was part of his plan, sure. Ryan hadn't conquered her yet; but he had no doubt he could if he had enough time. Agree? Disagree?"

"Agree," Jim said.

"Ryan hacked Mission Control files on October 11." Helt looked at Doughan, who raised a quizzical eyebrow. "That evening, within hours, you replaced the bad data he'd entered and waited him out. He signaled you on October 18 and you made contact with him and told him to come to your office after hours."

"I told him to get in the same way he got in before, or else," Doughan said. "He opened that trapdoor and came down from the ceiling, on schedule, calm as you please. I'd never noticed that hatch before."

"Yves showed me an entire area of hidden territory we don't pay attention to," Helt said. "You offered Cash some spiked booze and one of Venkie's samosas."

Helt sorted some files. "I can't prove that." It was a blurred entry on the timeline. "One hundred and twenty-three people bought samosas that day. You knew, because you'd done your best to find out that Cash Ryan liked his scope-and-speed. So you added some doses to his food. And then you gave him a coverall—with a defective heat pack in it—and walked him downstairs, and left him there for a while." Helt was just guessing on the coverall.

"I wanted to chill him a little. He was still awake when I got back," Doughan said.

"He'd built up tolerance to scope-and-speed," Mena said. "Even so, with the alcohol on board and the hypothermia, I'm surprised he wasn't more suggestible."

Mena's words were deliberate and clear. Mena, Helt wanted to tell her, stay out of this. I haven't written a part for you in this scenario.

"I came back and he was huddled against the wall," Doughan said. "That was expected. I grabbed him and pulled him up. I punched him in the belly. I wanted the punch to be hard enough to let him know I meant business but I didn't want to knock him out. He doubled forward but he came back from that and hit me in the ribs."

Doughan, standing in Mena's great room waiting for Mena to come back after Susanna's interview, had held on to his back. Helt couldn't remember him breaking his pose of perfect fitness at any other time.

"That's when he went out on me, Helt. I never had time to ask him anything."

"The sudden exertion threw him into V-fib. You called me," Mena said. "When I got down there, you were doing CPR. But Ryan was dead, fixed and dilated pupils, brain dead unless we got him oxygenated in a very short time and probably even if we'd been able to do it. I didn't have a defibrillator; which would have done nothing until he was warmed anyway, but I wasn't thinking about that. I had no kit at all."

She had been staring at the curtained window. She looked at each of them quickly, and then focused on Helt's face. "It would have taken twenty minutes to get to the clinic, and that's all I could think about. We had hauled him on the elevator by the time I sorted that out. We were still doing CPR."

"Trying to keep him alive," Helt said.

Mena shook her head. "I'm the one who suggested taking him to the observation platform. To buy time to find out what Ryan had sabotaged, if anything, and to decide how to handle the fact he'd died before we knew what he'd done."

Oh, Mena. Helt wanted to hug her or shake her. Hug her and shake her and make this go away like a bad dream.

Archer folded his arms across his chest and glared at Mena. "This was not necessary," Archer said. "Your involvement in the rest of the series of events was, for the record, quite minimal. Compared to mine. I came with you, you know."

"It was *not* minimal. I was unprepared. A syringe of pellet oxygen would have bought time; I didn't think of it until hours later."

"You're a vet," Jim Tulloch said.

"And he was a human, not a drowned calf. I would have done much better with a drowned calf, and maybe if I'd been thinking that way Ryan would have lived, and had enough brain left to talk to us."

"Coulda, woulda, shoulda," Jim said. "All of us know how that review feels. You are among peers no less fallible than yourself."

"That does not excuse my behavior," Mena said.

"Nor absolve you of your responsibilities, doc," Jim said.

Mena lifted her coffee cup to hide her lips. That she was keeping them tightly closed showed anyway.

"You have to go on to the next patient. Even if it's you. I'm telling you things you already know because I know them, too. I know them too well," Jim said. "So, he was dead. There you were with a dead man on the elevator."

"At the door to the Athens agora," Archer said. "Hauling the body to the clinic for pronouncement and disposal was an option, one we dismissed perhaps too quickly. I had accessed Ryan's bio while we rode the elevator down, Mena and I. I found that Ryan was not expected to show up at work for a week. I knew Doughan's suspicions about him; he'd told us, briefly, about the attempted sabotage. The man had already demonstrated erratic behavior."

Erratic behavior. Helt thought that was nicely understated.

"He had been drunk and drugged; my look at his records said he was a loner. No one was expecting him at work the next morning and we needed time to think."

Archer's precise choice of words was so familiar, so typical, so unchanged, even in this. Erratic behavior, not bug-fuck nuts. Pronouncement and disposal, not get rid of. "In Center, the odds were that his body might not have been discovered for days," Helt said.

"That, plus any damage that might have ensued from the fall, would have helped tip the odds toward a presumption of suicide," Archer said. "It was reprehensible of us to think of that, but I did, later, briefly. That night, the goal was to buy time."

"Did you take Mena home?" Helt asked.

"Yes, to Petra," Archer said. "Then I went home myself and repaired certain . . . discrepancies . . . in the SM hour. Jerry and Nadia discovered the body shortly thereafter. I was . . . I was dismayed it was found so quickly."

"What about the Seed Banker money?" Helt asked.

"It was an ill-advised ploy to deflect some of the attention from Dr. Maury," Archer said.

"Done as a favor to me," Mena said. She held her knees between her linked hands and leaned forward to look at Archer's face.

"I beg to differ, Mena. You did *not* ask me for a favor. I saw your distress when Dr. Maury's ride down the elevator was discovered, and planned a distraction that was sure to be found erroneous in a short amount of time." Helt got the stare again.

"I'm sorry it took me so long, boss," Helt said.

"As well you should be. My hasty thought was that the error would be discovered in time to do no harm, because we expected Doughan to find the sabotage quickly. We would have quickly made public what we had done, admitted our crime, and offered abject apologies to the entire ship and to the Seed Bankers in particular. The money is theirs now, a partial payment for any distress I may have caused them."

"Did I miss the Seed Banker list in the records?" Helt asked. "Is it there somewhere? We've been through Ryan's files until I'm cross-eyed."

"Oh, no." Archer shook his head and his right hand, but not in the same rhythm. "I went through his coverall after we stripped it off him." There was a scrap of paper in one of his pockets," Archer said. "I kept it. A list of names."

Archer reached into his shirt pocket and pulled out a wrinkled sheet of fiber paper, smaller than Helt's palm. He handed it over. Helt took it. The seven names were carefully handwritten in black ink. All caps.

"I transferred his interface to my Huerfano. I went through it and there was nothing helpful. Doughan disposed of the physical object and the coverall later."

"I did." Doughan nodded. "They went into one of the reclamation chutes and they'll never come back."

"I went through the bios on those names rather hastily after that first meeting," Archer said. "I looked for connections to Cash Ryan. The Seed Banker exposures seemed a common thread, one worthy of investigation." Archer looked at Doughan from beneath his bushy white eyebrows. "Surprised you, didn't I?"

Doughan started to say something. He didn't. He took a deep breath. "Yes."

Helt's mouth was dry. He took a sip of lukewarm coffee. "Okay. So that's how it happened. We've made the apologies to the Seed Bankers, maybe not as you planned, Archer, but it's done." He'd run the scenarios, he had a plan, and he didn't, couldn't, know how this would play out. "The three of you killed a man, and tried to hide it, and that's done, too. Giliam, could I have a little more coffee?"

Giliam got up and poured all round.

"You made mistakes in haste and there are consequences," Helt said. "I will *not* discuss lapses of judgment with you; I've just lost an eye to one of my own."

The coffee was nice and hot, and medium roast, and exactly right. Helt took a sip of it and lifted his cup to Mena.

"I cannot imagine anyone born on Earth who would have a better chance at keeping our ecosphere alive. You're the best, Mena. That goes for you, Archer, and you, Doughan, as well. I've run projections of how things will be with your successors.

"David II is brilliant and his ability to do the job is not in question, but he has some identity issues to sort through," Helt said.

For an eyeblink of time, Helt's control slipped and he was watching a recording made when David II was young and on Earth, talking to his father on *Kybele.* David II observed that Petra canyon was twice as deep as the original specs said it should be. "It's so much better this way," David II said. "So much more like Nostos will be. It's how I wanted it."

David I smiled. "That was *me*, not you. *You* will grow up to be less impetuous, I hope."

Helt blinked the memories away. "I'm confident he will solve them, but he needs time. Jerry will be an excellent SysSu exec; as for Nadia, IA will fit her very well. They could take over for you and me, Archer, in a heartbeat. But for SysSu—Mena, Elena is not the optimal candidate for your position. I've scrutinized Biosystems personnel as best I can, and I think Martin Kumar is the best choice. But not now. He needs at least ten years on his own."

He watched Mena think about what she knew of Martin Kumar, watched Doughan wonder about how Navigation would change with David II in command, watched Archer try to hide that he was pleased; Helt had agreed with him on who went where.

"Let me offer a plan," Helt said. "We'll discuss lapses in transparency and accountability later. Doughan, you have six hours before the shuttle arrives."

"Six hours and fourteen minutes," Doughan said.

"That should be time enough for us to make some changes. You won't be leaving on it. You don't march off to Earth, any of you. You stay."

"You don't plan to try to hide what we've done," Archer said. "It would be almost impossible to do, and in any case, I won't have it."

"I wouldn't ask that of you, Archer. After the shuttle leaves, you'll all get your chances for acknowledgment and atonement. Doughan gets a charge of something like involuntary manslaughter; Giliam can come up with the right wording on that."

"Close enough," Giliam said.

"And you two, Mena, Archer, get charged with aiding and abetting, or whatever."

"Your lack of knowledge about the nomenclature of crime is shocking," Giliam said. "But yes, lesser charges. I'll need time to properly draft them. I can't possibly do that in six hours."

"I know. The legal process happens here, not on Earth," Helt said. "Charges will be brought after departure, well after departure. Giliam will have plenty of time to come up with the right wording for them.

"Cash Ryan can't be charged with treason or attempted sabotage now, but what he tried to do—I think that will be clearly stated. Shortly after that, whatever the outcome, Doughan will call for a vote of confidence that includes all three execs. You'll have your chance to get booted out of office then."

Helt wanted to lean back and close his eyes. They burned, and holding the data flow at bay was so hard. The tripod structure the execs personified was sound; it would stay that way as long as there was someone to stand outside it and keep it stable. He didn't want to be that someone. He'd have to be that someone, for a while, if they bought this.

"It's that simple?" Doughan asked.

"A great deal of effort went into that simplicity," Mena said.

"I'll send you the list of references he consulted if you would like to review them." Archer's voice was very mild, very gentle. He'd been watching Helt since the injury, that was obvious. Archer was back on his game, if indeed he'd ever been off it.

"Not really. Will it work, Helt?" Doughan asked.

All of them had been watching the frenzy of his research since he struggled back to consciousness with a new eye. Of course they had; they were concerned about their fates, and that of the ship. "It may. It may not. There's the minor matter of changing the Articles of Governance. Giliam has a document for you to look at. We need to begin using it now, today, by executive order.

"You can do that, Doughan, but the changes will need to be ratified at some point. At some point in the near future."

"A minor matter." Doughan slapped the arm of his chair. "Let's get this done so we can get back to our lives."

Doughan got to his feet. Archer was back in his files again. Jim Tulloch was staring at his sandals and wiggling his toes, and Giliam looked like he always did, a little exasperated and very picky about dotted i's and crossed t's. Mena looked tired and sad and wonderful.

"Wait," Helt said. "Please. There's one thing I would like to ask you."

"Go ahead," Doughan said.

"Why did you ask Archer to hide the World Tree?"

Doughan stretched out his back and kneaded his healing rib. "Because Elena showed it to Mena, and Mena showed it to me, and then I asked Archer to hide it for a while."

"You knew Yves Copani," Helt said. "You let him work in peace."

"No, I didn't know him. I still don't."

"He'll be staying," Helt said.

"That's part of the deal, isn't it?" Doughan said. "Anyone on board now who wants to stay, stays."

"Yes."

"Accepted," Doughan said, and Archer and Mena nodded an okay.

"Yves's tree. It's a special thing in a special place," Helt said. "He pushed the boundaries of responsible behavior when he put it there."

"No question," Doughan said.

The files that showed its creation were online now, had been for hours. *In memoriam.* Yves had carved those words in a dark place, and nothing else. Helt thought he knew, and knew he would never ask, about the dead miner who had wanted to stay here, so long ago, who had been determined to make the journey. It was possible the miner's ashes were part of the sand at the tree's roots. It made no difference; the myth was free to thrive if it was needed. Free to be discarded if it wasn't.

"But you let it happen. All three of you."

"It was an executive decision. For the good of the ship," Doughan said.

Some myths are worth keeping, worth re-creating. Perhaps Archer and Doughan and Mena understood that better than Helt did.

"Heh." Halvor Borresen, Lawspeaker for *Kybele*, the first of his name, leaned back in his chair and closed his eyes.

"It's time to get to work," Doughan said. "Are we okay? Everybody? Helt?"

"For now," Helt said.